ANDROMEDA GRAPHIKA

Robert Brace

This is a work of fiction. All of the characters, organizations, and events portrayed in this novel are either the products of the author's imagination or are used fictitiously.

Front jacket photograph: Maenad with palmate thyrsus, Miami © Robert Brace
Back jacket photograph: Bacchante in ball costume, Venice © Robert Brace
Front cover photograph: Andromeda awaiting Cetus, battlements of Óbidos © Robert Brace
Back cover photograph: The goddess Fortuna atop a globe supported by two Atlases, Dogana da Mar, Dorsoduro, Venice © Robert Brace

Cover design by the author.

First Edition: April 2022

Library of Congress Control Number: 2021923360

ISBN 978-1-7373192-3-8

Privately published, April 2022, New York.

www.RobertBraceAuthor.com

ANDROMEDA GRAPHIKA

— PART I —

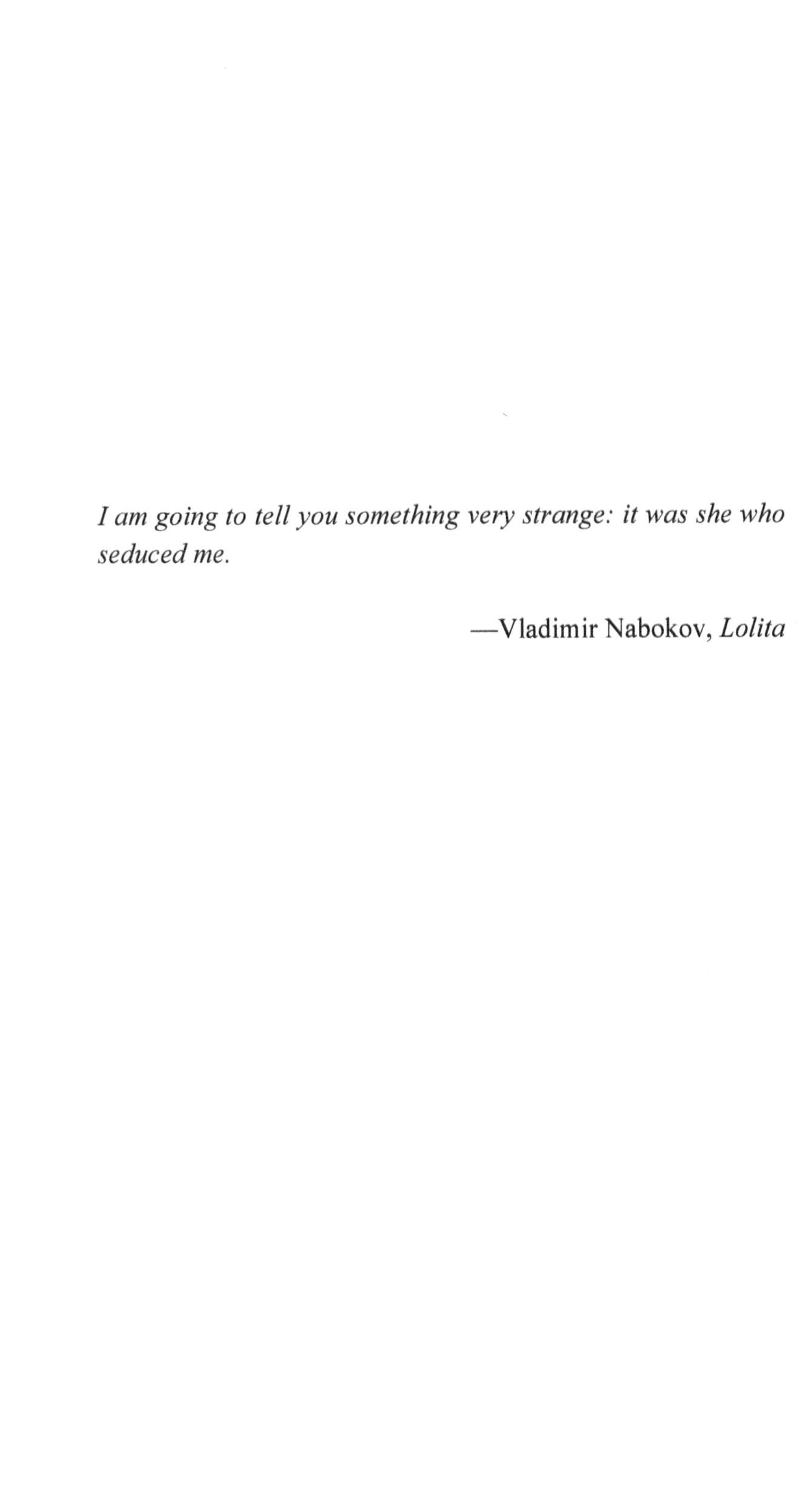

I am going to tell you something very strange: it was she who seduced me.

—Vladimir Nabokov, *Lolita*

I

[▸]

A GIRL STANDS BEFORE A MIRROR. There is a row of booths behind her, doors ajar: it is a public restroom, but the girl is alone. She wears embroidered jeans and a tie-dye top. Her feet are bare. She leans forward, hands on the sink, and studies her reflection. Her face is without expression.

Close up, she seems too young for what is surely to come—large unlined eyes and still with the pale pearl-like skin of a child. Her hair is dark brown, long and straight. Wide mouth, lips slightly parted. The girl stares at her image with a hooded look of cool wonderment, as if so far she has found life strange, but not yet sufficient to fully engage her.

She strips.

Her body is long and lean, slender-framed and small-breasted—awkward on the cusp of graceful: a body not quite grown into. She washes her face in the sink and dries it with a towel.

She throws her clothes into the trash.

There is a bag on the counter from which the girl extracts a small squared bottle of thick glass, an apothecary's bottle. It bears a hand-lettered label in Latin script: *Tinctura Belladonnae Foliorum*—the extract of belladonna leaves dissolved in diluted alcohol. The girl shakes the bottle, removes the stopper, and holds it aloft.

A single drop of golden belladonna, pendant.

She tilts her head back and positions the stopper above her right eye. She waits. She does not blink.

The belladonna refracts the image of the girl above whom it hangs. It elongates into teardrop shape before detaching from the stopper and falling, slow and now perfectly spherical, into her eye.

The girl blinks briefly, then carefully poisons her other eye. Now she may dress.

She returns the bottle to the bag. The clothes are packed in the precise order in which she must put them on. A small silver hairclip first: she is to wear her hair up from now on. Shoes next, high-heeled and secured with ankle straps. Then a short slim skirt the color and sheen of whose silken fabric changes with movement, varying from dusky ocher-hued browns to a deep dark moss. A long-sleeved blouse of green and gold in a chaotic pattern, shot through with slashes of metallic texture, cut low and loose. A leather belt, tan to match the shoes, very wide, ornately stamped and studded.

The girl applies makeup, heavy and elaborate around the eyes.

She stands back and inspects the result in the mirror. Her look is faraway now, disconnected and dreamlike, as the poison begins to work. Her neck is long and narrow, ending in an undulating landscape of collar bone and rib exposed by the low-buttoned blouse. The subtle curves of her breasts are visible if she leans forward, allowing the fabric to fall away. She puts on sunglasses, fashionably large-framed, a final touch. The effect is what the couturier had aimed for: glamour but reckless glamour; glamour that comes with a Newtonesque touch of expensive, indulgent, and dissolute abandonment.

She is a world removed from the simple girl of a moment ago.

She unscrews a tube of lipstick, applies it to herself and then, as a last act before leaving, scrawls a single word in large Greek letters on the mirror:

αμίτοιΔ

The girl leaves, throwing the lipstick into the trash on the way out.

SHE EXITS INTO A broad space, brightly lit. There is a scattering of leather armchairs, some occupied, but most of them are empty. Beige carpet; a bar to the left. The far wall is composed of floor-to-ceiling windows through which is visible a single slender aircraft. Sleek and alabaster-white, it is an object of sculptural purity. She has entered the departure lounge for the Air France Concorde.

The aircraft's nose is bowed. Like her, it demonstrates submission.

Her presence ripples across the room, a subtle wave of awareness spreading through the waiting passengers. Men in business suits glance up from their newspapers or laptops, and the uniformed stewardess behind the service desk stares unabashedly. There is an agitation in the air now, as if the woman were a nearby lightning strike, a sudden and unexpected violence that immediately trivializes all else.

She strides across the room to an armchair. She sits, composed and still and remote, either unaware of the attention or simply uncaring. She remains expressionless.

At the service desk, the agent picks up a microphone and makes the boarding call, firstly in French, then in English. There is no line, and the few passengers soon make their way onto the aircraft.

The girl stands. She is hesitant now, all but blinded by the poison. She walks long-legged toward the gate, offers her boarding pass, then disappears down the jetwa—

[II]

II

THE LAWYER EXAMINES THE WOMAN sitting in the adjoining room. She appears to meet his gaze but it is an illusion: the wall is composed of mirrored glass, and she can see nothing of him. He cannot tell if she is studying her reflection or simply staring ahead, lost in thought.

Beside him, the camera quietly whirs.

Light pours in through the windows on her left, revealing the topography of her face in vibrant shadowed relief. She is younger than he expected. Untanned; he had imagined skin turned to the color of old leather by the desert sun, but her face is no darker than his own, left pale by the New York winter. It is an intelligent face but reserved, too—the face of a woman whose interior reality will never be quite pinned down, as elusive as a quantum particle.

The lawyer can see why she was chosen.

He checks his watch and decides that he has kept her waiting long enough.

THE LAWYER ENTERS THE ROOM. The sofa is now vacant; the woman is on her feet and standing by the windows. She does not immediately turn, instead choosing to remain gazing out over the soaring pinnacles of the sky-reaching city. Then he realizes that it is not a choice; she has not heard him enter. For a brief interval before closing the door he is again an unseen voyeur, but the experience is more intimate without the glass separating them and he feels the fact of her physical presence in a sudden visceral rush. The lawyer is not an imaginative man but he cannot help wondering if this is a quality capable of being captured on film.

He closes the door.

"Miss Chamberlain, I'm sorry to have kept you waiting."

She turns but makes no reply. A brief impenetrable smile, and he suspects that she knows he is lying.

He crosses the room and offers his hand.

"I'm Tom Renzitti."

"Andromeda Chamberlain."

They shake hands. Firm grip, cool flesh. He had imagined coarse hands and broken fingernails, but hers are smooth and the nails neatly trimmed.

He realizes that he must get her back to the sofa, for the camera's sake.

"Let's sit down, shall we?"

He moves swiftly to the sole armchair, leaving her no choice but to resume her previous position, the place in which the camera will best capture her.

The room is called a conference room but there is no board table or high-backed swivel seats, just the low leather sofa and matching armchair surrounding a coffee table. Soft caramel-colored carpeting, discreet recessed lighting, a sideboard with small bottles of mineral water: a comfortable setting intended to encourage the sharing of confidences with counsel.

The lawyer has kept her waiting twenty minutes—a deliberate tactic designed to foster a loquacious nervousness without enduring to the point of inducing reticent hostility—something he routinely does when first meeting someone who is not his own client. He surveys the room as she takes her seat. The magazines lie upon the table untouched, still in the orderly, title-revealing cascade into which the staff place them at the beginning of each day. No coffee cup, although the receptionist would have offered. No cell phone or tablet device in evidence, fetishes to occupy anxious hands, replacements for the once-ubiquitous cigarette. For twenty minutes this woman has sat here alone, apparently content and without the need of distraction. Then he realizes that she is not even wearing a watch. All that time in the desert, Renzitti thinks: flat featureless land and high cloudless skies melting into a quavering, heat-shirred horizon. Time must have seemed endless in that desolate landscape, a commodity whose passage was too slow or too irrelevant to measure. He realizes that the delay tactic was a waste of time.

"Miss Chamberlain, thank you for coming."

He places his document case by the side of the chair. Renzitti has a few more standard warm-up remarks to make before getting down to business, but when looking up again he remains silent. Instead, he spends a moment examining this woman whose life he is about to change, and probably not for the better.

More angular than he expected. Finer-boned; he had imagined a husky flat-faced woman with broad wrists and blotched skin, someone who showed a lot of gum when she grinned, and who grinned too often. This woman retains the suggestion of a smile, sufficient for courtesy, no more. She wears a charcoal suit of fine wool, well cut to her slim figure. Black stockings and high-heeled shoes, unscuffed—he had half-expected work boots from the dig, covered in dust or something worse. Slender throat, a feature for which he is grateful. She has her hair up, neatly bundled in back, which serves to emphasize her face: alert intelligent eyes, subtly chiseled nose, smooth even features, a slightly skeptical expression—a face that would once have been termed *patrician*. But it is not her expression that has silenced him.

From the adjoining room she had been too far away, then when shaking hands she had been backlit by the glare behind her, but now that she is again seated, her face fully lit by bright winter light pouring in through plate glass windows fifty floors above Manhattan, the lawyer sees close up what he missed before: a scar, razor-thin, straight as a gun barrel, a swift emphatic slash stretching diagonally across her right cheek. There is no puckering of the surrounding skin, no distortion of her features, just the line itself, a long extended nick, as if from the tip of a rapier blade.

A dueling scar if on a man, in another time and place.

Makeup would have concealed it; he realizes that she elects not to do so.

She returns his gaze unblinkingly. This is what he feared most: a woman who could just walk away. The lawyer is not an outdoorsman—he once went two years without leaving the island of Manhattan—but right now he thinks of himself as a fly fisherman whose success depends entirely upon the precise but delicate placement of the next cast.

"I thought you would be more tanned," he admits.

"I've been back for some time now."

"Congratulations on the article."

"Thank you."

He briefly imagines her as she described herself that night, standing astonished and blood-soaked by the well, surrounded in a sea of moonlit white eyes.

"I expect you're wondering what this is about."

She nods in acknowledgment but makes no further reply. He shifts his weight forward.

"Miss Chamberlain, may I ask if your status is still freelance?"

"It is."

"And do you currently have an assignment?"

"No, I've taken a break since I got back."

Renzitti is well aware of this—like any good lawyer leading a potentially hostile witness, he does not ask questions to which he does not already know the answers. He sits back and continues.

"Then please let me reveal the purpose for which we requested this meeting. In short, Miss Chamberlain, we would like to offer you a story."

"We?" She raises a dubious eyebrow.

He sits back and allows himself a smile. "Forgive the imprecise pronoun. Naturally, I do not mean the firm itself. Rather, it is the client we represent who would be making the offer."

"A shy editor? That's a first."

This time he laughs. "Yes, it must seem a little strange, and I have to warn you that it will seem a good deal stranger before this meeting is over. For a start, apart from the obvious fact of being in the media, I'm afraid that I'm forbidden from revealing anything else about the nature of my client, including my client's identity."

"But a print publication, I presume?"

"Anything at all."

Now it is she who sits back. He had thought that this would be the point at which the woman would abruptly terminate the meeting, but when he examines her face for a reaction it is not a look of annoyance he finds, it is one of amusement.

"And what does your anonymous client want me to write about, Mr. Renzitti?"

In response, he opens the document case, extracts a broad manila envelope, and slides it wordlessly across the table. She undoes the clasp and withdraws the contents, a single eight-by-ten photograph. It is a portrait of a teenage girl, black and white, coarse-grained—perhaps a blow-up of a high school yearbook shot.

She studies the photograph. The girl is wearing a white shirt and dark blazer with a crest on the pocket, a private school uniform. Long straight hair, neatly cut but otherwise unadorned. Clear open face revealing none of the awkward self-absorption common in girls of that age. It is a photograph that other parents would have paused at when going through the yearbook, wondering about this interesting individual in their own child's class.

She looks up. Renzitti begins the explanation.

"Her name is Margot Vaughn. This picture is ten years old and it is the last known photograph of her. She lived in Miami. She came from an affluent family and apparently enjoyed a happy childhood, but ten years ago she abruptly disappeared without a trace. There was no violence, no evidence of mishap or wrongdoing; she simply left her home and never returned. Your assignment would be to find out what became of her."

"Isn't that something for a detective rather than a journalist?"

"The two have much in common: they're both investigators. But policemen do not investigate ten-year-old missing person cases in which there are no new leads, nor indeed any evidence of a crime having been committed in the first place. And of course they do not write articles about them."

"Who are the parents?"

"Nathan and Suzanne Vaughn. Nathan Vaughn runs an investment management firm. The mother is French and independently wealthy. Margot was their only child."

"Why me?"

"You have obvious qualifications, Miss Chamberlain. You are a journalist, you are available, and you are female—I think you will agree that this is a subject which would be most sympathetically handled by a woman."

"Editors normally offer assignments to people they know. Does your client know me, Mr. Renzitti?"

"I remind you that I am under an injunction against revealing any details about my client, Miss Chamberlain. However, I suppose I would not be giving anything away if I admit that it was the *New Yorker* piece that caught my client's attention. My client believes that this story should be more than just an account of what became of this young woman. It should also be the story of what made her do it. Why would a seemingly happy, well-adjusted child suddenly just walk away? On the face of it, it makes no sense. So too, when you think about it, does the incident at..."

"Manoukaram."

"Yes, Manoukaram. Yet it happened, and you explained it. Dozens of men hacked to death as they slept; you even made it seem logical."

Women weary of slaughter, themselves slaughtering. But the lawyer is mistaken: it was not logical; it was instinctive, animalistic.

She looks again at the photograph. She wonders if the lawyer is aware of the resemblance. Probably not, she decides—men miss such things.

"Okay," she says.

A pause of surprise.

"Okay?"

"Yes, okay. I'll take the assignment."

Renzitti is almost resentful—the fish has leaped from the water and bitten into the hook before he even baited it.

"But we haven't discussed the terms yet."

"I assume they would be industry standard."

"Then you assume incorrectly, Miss Chamberlain." He withdraws a folder from the document case, extracts a printed sheet, and passes it to her. "These are the terms that my client is offering."

She glances quickly through the sheet, then reads it a second time, more slowly now. At last she looks up, unamused.

"Absurd," she blankly states.

"Quite so."

"No legitimate publication would offer this much money."

"Miss Chamberlain, we are perfectly well aware that these amounts exceed the norm. Again I must plead the restrictions placed upon me for my inability to explain the reasons behind such unusual terms. All I can say is that they are, quite obviously, extremely generous. And they are in the contract."

"What if I can't complete the assignment? What if I never find the girl?"

"As stated, you will be paid the agreed sum."

"And expenses?"

"Again as stated: you charge whatever you wish to the credit card we will provide you. I am particularly instructed to emphasize that no expense should be spared, no matter how tangential it may seem to the purpose. All travel and accommodation arrangements will be handled directly by us: you tell us where and when; my office will organize the reservations and so on. And should you have any further out-of-pocket expenses we will happily reimburse them."

He can see that she is uncertain now, considering withdrawing her consent. How strange, he thinks, that the one feature that would have lured most people has repelled her. She returns her attention to the items in her lap, not to the terms sheet but to the photograph.

Do you know her? he longs to ask. *Is she you?*

He remains silent.

"Very well," she says quietly. "Do you have the contract?"

A woman who makes her own decisions, he thinks; a woman who does not need to consult others.

"I'll have an executed copy couriered to you this afternoon. But there are two more matters that we must discuss before we reach final agreement, Miss Chamberlain."

"Yes?"

"The first is the question of timing. The deadline for completion of the assignment is the second Monday in March. This, too, is something that I have been instructed to emphasize: there can be no extension of the deadline. The second Monday in March."

All assignments have deadlines but this one surprises her: the subject matter is not urgent; it is the sort of story that could be published anytime, as space and opportunity permit. She makes a brief mental calculation.

"Just seven weeks."

"Yes, it is. May I ask where you would begin your inquiries, Miss Chamberlain?"

"Miami," she says. "Her parents; the place from which she disappeared."

"Then you will not want to waste any time." The lawyer reaches into his jacket and removes an envelope, which he passes across the table.

She opens it: a first-class reservation for Miami, leaving tomorrow morning from Newark; a printout of an email from the Pelican Hotel in Miami Beach, detailing the booking of their penthouse suite; even an auto rental confirmation. All the reservations are in her name.

"You were confident," she says.

"Just prepared."

She returns the items to the envelope.

"You said there were two things."

"Yes, and before I reveal the second, please remember that I warned you this would get stranger before the meeting was over."

"I stand reminded."

He reaches into the document case and takes out a shallow box a foot square. He places it on the table without comment.

The top is labeled in upright black lettering, but she does not need to read it to recognize from where it must have come, for the box is of a particular shade of eggshell blue that has only one source.

"Tiffany's," she says.

"Indeed," the lawyer agrees.

He lifts the lid, revealing a circular metal collar sitting on a bed of black velvet. It is a hand span in diameter, three-quarters of an inch high, an eighth of an inch thick. She lifts it from the velvet liner. The metal is polished to a mirror shine.

She looks up at the lawyer.

"Am I expected to accept this?"

"No, you are expected to wear it. In fact, it is a condition of the contract."

"What?"

"For the duration of the assignment, you will be required to wear this item. Night and day. It may not be removed for any reason." He halts her developing protest with a raised hand. "Miss Chamberlain, believe me, we are well aware of how very peculiar this must sound. All I can tell you is that on completion of the assignment I expect that such oddities will be explained. I regret that I cannot offer you anything more than that right now."

He takes the collar from her grasp and opens it. It is hinged on one side and when open reveals a complex locking mechanism, concealed when the collar is closed. He picks up the key, a thin cylindrical device with multiple spiked protrusions, a key the like of which she has never seen before. He holds it up for her to see.

"As you can imagine, a lock opened by such a key is not susceptible to being picked. The collar is a one-off custom piece, so there are no duplicates. Furthermore, it is made of titanium. Grade Five alloy, to be precise, which is titanium with a little aluminum and vanadium mixed in, the same alloy used to fabricate the most critical components in aerospace applications. Titanium is much lighter than steel but many times stronger, and is a metal with highly unusual characteristics—it cannot be welded in air, for example; the atmosphere must first be purged with pure argon. What I'm getting at, Miss Chamberlain, is that once this collar goes on you must understand that it is not coming off except with this key, which we shall retain in the office safe."

They stare at each other for a long moment without speaking. Eventually the woman gets up and walks back to the windows, radiant with light. She removes her jacket and stands with it folded over her crossed arms, looking out over the city, leaning lightly against the frame. It takes the lawyer a moment to realize that she might be expecting him to attach the collar. He gathers it and walks over behind her.

The light captures the fine down along the nape of her neck. Her ears are complex, slightly translucent. The woman is as tall as he is but close up she seems frail, someone unsuited to the rigors of the real world.

She turns slightly, and he can tell that she is briefly surprised to find him standing behind her, but then her eyes fall to the collar. She stares at the thing for a long moment before turning back and raising her chin in silent invitation.

The lawyer reaches around nervously and snaps the collar into place.

III

ANDROMEDA TURNS OFF THE MAIN ROAD. So far, Miami has been all heat and noise, but the street she enters is a new world: empty of traffic and shaded by banyan trees whose branches meet in a cooling canopy high overhead. The houses are large and well separated, set back in big gardens with broad lawns. This is old Miami, she realizes, as it was before the coming of air-conditioning and mass tourism, a place where wealthy northerners built their mansions to wait out the winter by Biscayne Bay.

She drives slowly, checking street numbers. The top is down and she can hear the rumble of the engine, deep and irregular, unhappy at idle. The vehicle is a special model, according to the attendant at the airport, with twice the horsepower of a stock version. It had come with a text message on the navigation screen: *Miss Chamberlain, I took the liberty of reserving a vehicle with a limited-slip differential, and recommend that you do the same for the remainder of your assignment /TR*—a strange piece of advice that caused her to wonder less about limited-slip differentials than what sort of lawyer Renzitti was.

Andromeda finds the address. The property is surrounded by a high limestone wall, gray with age. There is an intercom by the entrance but the gates are already open: she is expected.

The grounds are expansive but ill-kempt. There are glossy-leaved magnolias and live oaks draped in Spanish moss, but between them what had once been lawn appears to be reverting to its native state.

Andromeda comes to a halt on a terracotta-tiled forecourt behind a dark Cadillac coupe. She shuts down the engine and the ensuing silence is abrupt, almost startling.

The house is a large two-story Italianate villa with a stone frieze and pilasters, but the stucco between them is weathered and crumbling. The windows are shuttered. If not for the open gate and other car Andromeda would have assumed that the house was unoccupied.

She goes to the front door and knocks. There is no answering sound from within, but Andromeda has the sense of being observed. She turns and sees standing fifty yards away a man, still as a statue, staring at her. Swarthy and Hispanic; he holds a machete in his left hand: he is the gardener and, considering the state of the grounds, not a very good one. He does not turn away but continues to stare. Andromeda's hand goes automatically to the scar, a gesture that she has not yet learned to control.

The front door opens. In this neighborhood she would have expected a maid to answer, but the man standing before her has the proprietorial air of an owner. He is in his fifties, but they have been well cared for years. Less than average height; a little overweight.

"Mr. Vaughn?"

"You must be Andromeda Chamberlain."

He offers his hand and forces a brief welcoming smile.

There are no lights on inside and once the door is closed the only illumination comes from shards of sunlight streaming through the slats, casting broad trapezoidal slashes across the room. Dust motes hang in the air. A clock ticks somewhere, emphasizing the silence. Tropical Gothic, Andromeda thinks of it—Miss Havisham would have felt at home here. She walks with care, her eyes not yet adjusted.

"Forgive the darkness," Vaughn says. "We've been forced to close the shutters."

"Is there a hurricane coming?"

"Photofrin."

"Photofrin?"

"A medical treatment." Vaughn comes to a halt and faces Andromeda. In the darkness she cannot make out his expression. "I'm afraid that my wife is very ill, Miss Chamberlain. She has Klatskin's tumor—cancer of the bile duct. There is a treatment: they inject her with Photofrin, a substance that reacts with light, then insert a red-light laser through her esophagus to the area of the tumor. Together with the Photofrin, the laser will kill the tumor, or at least they hope it will. Patients undergoing Photofrin treatment must avoid light for at least a month since that's how it works, hence the shutters."

"I'm very sorry, Mr. Vaughn. How long ago was she diagnosed?"

"Four weeks. She is in a clinic in Coral Gables at the moment."

"I hope she gets better soon."

"The physicians have made clear to us that the tumor is likely to have metastasized by now, and therefore there will be further cancers. After this procedure is complete she will undergo radiation treatment, which may kill them. There is always hope, of course, but the most likely outcome is not a cure, just a delay."

Vaughn turns and continues to lead Andromeda through the house. If discussing his wife's illness has upset him it is not reflected in his voice.

They walk through a small gallery floored in hardwood and devoid of furniture. The space is lit by a skylight. In the original design, it would have been a place meant to hang family portraits and the like, but now the two long walls are each occupied by a single large painting, eight feet high and ten feet wide. The one on the left depicts a gold bracelet lying on a metallic pink-red background; the one on the right shows a blue ribbon on silvery foil. They are obviously a pair, both of them richly hued and deeply glossy, acrylic perhaps, and massively oversized for the subject matter, exuberant neo-pop celebrations of the trivial, wallowing in their own voluptuous vacuity. Andromeda stops a moment to admire them, and wonders who the artist was.

"We could have covered the skylight too, but my wife insists that this room never be darkened," Vaughn says. "She takes great pleasure in these paintings."

He leads her to a shaded terrace in the back. There are a table and chairs. On the table is a tray with a pitcher of iced tea and two glasses. There is also a brown manila envelope, like the one the lawyer gave her the previous day, but this one is thick with whatever is inside. Beyond the terrace is a pool, but it is empty of anything other than dead leaves.

They sit. Vaughn fills the glasses and passes one to Andromeda.

"Thank you for agreeing to see me, Mr. Vaughn. I know that this can't be a pleasant topic for you."

"I'm more than happy to help anyone who might find out what happened to Margot." But the response is dutiful and rote, without real meaning.

"Do you mind if I take notes?"

"Not at all, but I should mention from the start that this package is for you." He gently pushes the envelope across the table. "It contains copies of every relevant document I could think of, including the investigative reports."

Andromeda interprets this to mean that he would prefer her just to listen for now. She thanks him and takes the envelope, leaving the notebook in her bag.

"Can you tell me Margot's full name?"

"Just Margot Vaughn. She had no middle name."

Andromeda notes the use of the past tense. Ten years is a long time.

"When exactly did she disappear?"

"April twenty-fifth, 2003."

"No brothers or sisters?"

"No, there were just the three of us. I myself was an only child, and all of Suzanne's relatives live in France, so there weren't even aunts or uncles or cousins."

"Please tell me the circumstances of her disappearance."

He puts down his glass, sits back, and smiles without humor.

"She ran away from home, Miss Chamberlain. *Disappearance* is a gloss applied to disguise an unpleasant reality, a word parents use to conceal their own failures."

"How old was she?"

"Fifteen."

"A troubling age for many girls."

"Yes, but not for Margot—at least not superficially. There were no disagreements about boyfriends or late nights or school grades, nothing like that. She did well at school, and pretty much kept to herself outside of it."

"Shy?"

"No, but she was a loner. A reserved girl, even as a young child. Strange really; she was nothing at all like me or her mother."

The universal misconception of parents, Andromeda thinks: the notion that their offspring should turn out to be like them, when the weight of human history teaches exactly the opposite: that each succeeding generation reaps a crop of entirely new individuals, as singular as if they had appeared spontaneously. He nods toward the envelope.

"There's a photograph of her inside."

Andromeda undoes the clasp. The first thing she withdraws is a copy of Margot's birth certificate. Next are copies of her social security card and a learner's permit. Then she finds the photograph, a glossy eight-by-ten, but unlike the lawyer's picture this one is in color and carefully lit, the work of a professional studio.

"It was taken two months before she left," Vaughn says.

Several thoughts crowd upon Andromeda as she studies this second image of Margot Vaughn. The most immediate is that Margot was more than just pleasingly attractive; she was strikingly beautiful: large clear eyes, generous mouth, skin the texture of tautly drawn silk. But it is the expression that distinguishes her: aloof, as if she had not wanted to give herself away to the camera, lips slightly parted in what might have been puzzlement or perhaps mild impatience with the photographer, eyes limpid and wistful, a little solemn. It is a beguiling face, the sort of beauty that has a physical effect upon the beholder, a face that might leave a man, for a moment at least, literally breathless.

A hazardous face for a fifteen-year-old girl to have, Andromeda thinks. Perhaps even burdensome.

She now better understands her father's description of his daughter. Margot would have been compelled to solitude, if not by disposition then by circumstance. Other girls would not have welcomed her company, obliterating as it would have their own first tentative steps into womanhood. And boys must have found that face intimidating to the point of unapproachable.

Andromeda thinks that in any case the girl in this photograph showed little desire for companionship. There is a cool detachment to her, not haughtiness but a simple and unassuming self-containedness: the absence of the need for other people.

Andromeda wonders if she is projecting her own adolescence onto Margot.

"Did she have friends?"

"A few. Not many, none close."

She looks again at the photograph. Margot was more than just content with her own company, Andromeda thinks; she found other people dull.

"She had recently gotten her learner's permit and wanted to buy one of those little Italian motor scooters," Vaughn says. "She had an investment account, to which we contributed dollar-for-dollar whatever she saved, but with the condition that she was not allowed to make any withdrawals, so to buy the scooter she had to earn the money. She did occasional odd jobs, waitressing and the like. My wife suggested modeling for clothing catalogs over the summer vacation—it's a big business down here—but to get the work you need a portfolio. Suzanne arranged for a professional photographer to put it together, and this is one of the shots."

"What did she do when she wasn't at school?"

"Read, did her homework, played music. Margot liked the beach, liked all water in fact. If a storm came through she would race over there after school, even if it was still raining, because the surf would be higher. She wasn't particularly athletic but she was very physical. I remember one morning I came down early—before six, not even sunrise—and found her out on the lawn doing handstands. I asked her why. She said *there's dew*, as if that explained everything."

Which of course it does, Andromeda thinks. She finds herself taking a quiet liking to this strange girl that it is her task to find.

She returns the photograph to the envelope.

"Please tell me what happened when Margot disappeared."

"My wife and I were both away. I was in Bermuda on business. Suzanne was in France, visiting relatives. The plan was for her to join me in Bermuda after the business was over, and we would have a short vacation before returning home together. It was the first time we had both been away without a babysitter for Margot."

"What was the business in Bermuda?"

"A conference; there's an investment advisors' conference there every year."

"Investment advisors?"

"Fund management. I run a hedge fund, Vizcayne Capital Advisors."

"Is it successful?"

He opens his hands in a gesture inviting her to take in her surroundings. She nods: no one but the wealthy could afford such a place—overgrown garden and crumbling stucco notwithstanding.

"My wife called home every day. When she kept getting the answering machine she became worried. Eventually she called some friends. They checked the house; no one was home. Suzanne took a plane back to Miami. She found Margot's note on the dining table."

"What did it say?"

"That she was leaving and we were not to worry."

"No explanation?"

"She said only that it was time for her to move on. Nothing else, just time to move on, as if we were people she had been renting a room from for all these years. She also asked us not to try to find her."

"Did she have money?"

"She cleaned out her investment account before leaving."

"How much was in it?"

"There's a copy of the last statement among those documents. It was a substantial sum—Margot saved her money, and she was a pretty sharp stock-picker."

"What happened after you discovered that she was gone?"

"I flew straight home, of course. We called the police. They came and investigated, but when it became clear that there was no crime involved they showed little enthusiasm. To them, she was just another teenage runaway. In the end we hired a private investigator. He was competent and thorough—I found him through my lawyers, who had worked with him before. He interviewed her friends and teachers, the neighbors, even the clerks at the Greyhound bus station. He monitored her credit cards and cell phone number. Somehow he obtained passenger manifests for the flights out of Miami that day. He got regular reports from the credit rating agencies, hoping for a hit on her Social Security number. But for all that he found no trace of her, not a thing. Soon the days turned into weeks, and then into months. He explained that it was time to call a halt to the investigation. There was nothing further he could do, he said, and he could no longer in good conscience accept our money."

"And you never heard anything more of her?"

"Not a thing."

"Is it possible for me to talk to your wife?"

"I'm afraid not." He puts down his glass. "I have told her nothing of your visit, and she is not in a state to relive what was no doubt the worst day of her life."

"May I see a picture of her?"

"Of my wife?"

"Yes."

The request surprises Vaughn, the first of Andromeda's that he has not anticipated. She is not sure herself why she asked.

"Yes, certainly. Please come with me."

He leads her back through the darkened house into what Andromeda assumes is a study, but the curtains are of tulle and the books are in French—it is his wife's room. There is a fireplace and facing it a low sofa. The mantle above the fireplace is lined with framed photographs. Vaughn takes one and passes it to Andromeda.

"My wife Suzanne," he says.

Andromeda studies it in silence. She can see where Margot got her good looks: her mother is an attractive woman, although the sharp beauty of the daughter is here softened and rounded into a less challenging handsomeness.

"I'm afraid that she doesn't look much like that anymore," Vaughn says.

Andromeda replaces the frame on the mantle and looks at the other photographs. All of them are of Suzanne or Margot, either singly or together. The last includes Nathan Vaughn. It is a large photograph of all three, not a posed shot but nevertheless well composed by chance. It is a street scene, Mediterranean, judging by the architecture in the background. A sunny day and street stalls. Nathan Vaughn is on the right, looking away. Suzanne Vaughn is in shorts and a sleeveless top, the only one looking directly at the camera. She is laughing—probably it is she who asked someone to take their photograph, and whoever is behind the camera said something to amuse her. But most striking is Margot, behind the other two. She is dressed in a summery lemon-colored slip dress and ankle-tied espadrilles, caught in profile while studying something on a street seller's cart, one hand reaching down toward the merchandise, the other absently sweeping hair behind an ear. Fine graceful fingers, long slender legs. A little younger than in the school photograph, but Margot already has the look of someone much older. This sense of precocity is helped by her height, taller than both her parents. She has an expression of mild delight at whatever she has discovered on the cart and is obviously unaware that she is being photographed.

The face of a happy, well-adjusted girl. No hint of the sullen demeanor of a teenage runaway.

"Positano," Vaughn says. "It was the last vacation the three of us took together, late summer on the Amalfi coast, just before Margot went back to school."

Andromeda hands back the photograph.

"Your wife looks like a very nice person, Mr. Vaughn. I hope that she gets better soon."

He replaces the frame on the mantle but makes no response. She thanks him again for having made time to see her.

Vaughn shows her to the door. "I hope you'll let me know right away if you find any trace of her," he says, but there is no conviction in his voice.

Andromeda returns to her car. She must not be harsh, she thinks—he is a man who, already battered by Margot's disappearance and a downturn in his fortunes, has been dealt the cruelest of blows: condemned to watch his wife slowly die. A bruised man, not someone to be taken at face value. Yet her quick, analytical mind has not missed the fact that during the entire interview Vaughn only ever referred to Margot by name, and never once as *my daughter*.

IV

ANDROMEDA DRIVES SWIFTLY along the causeway, flowing through occasional slower traffic. Her hair billows in the breeze. Ahead lie the cruise ships moored along Government Cut, bloated blocks of floating steel, slightly oppressive. On the left are islands and canals; on the right Biscayne Bay stretches away to the south, a broad turquoise expanse dotted with boats and sails on a more human scale. How preferable the feel of a yacht heeling in the wind, she thinks, to the manufactured pleasures aboard those cruise ships. A helicopter buzzes nearby, briefly matching her for course and speed. In the distance rise the office towers of downtown Miami, fortresses of refrigerated air sealed against the humid onslaught from without.

After the Vaughn house, the open air feels like a prison release—she starts to understand why Margot might have felt an urge to leave. Was it sudden, she wonders, something done on a whim, or was her flight more carefully planned?

Andromeda arrives at South Beach and cruises down Ocean Drive, Art Deco buildings on one side and palm-studded beachfront on the other. She spots the Pelican and U-turns into the valet slot.

The hotel is South Beach swank, a little boutique of a building entered firstly via the terrace restaurant and then through the hotel bar, an arrangement designed to ensure that patrons and guests get a good look at each other. Andromeda finally arrives in the lobby, a small space that is empty apart from a front desk the size of a shoeshine stand. This is presided over by a slender six-foot black woman in stilettos and micromini, and sporting a magnificent burst of black hair, as broad as her shoulders, surging forth like some lush tropical flower in bloom.

"Second floor," the woman says without greeting. "Turn right when you get out of the elevator."

"Do I get a key?"

"You mean you're a guest?"

"Checking in."

The woman laughs an apology. "Sorry, my mistake." She pushes a registration card and pen toward Andromeda. "Please fill this out."

"What's on the second floor?"

"Ford Models. I assumed you were here for them since you don't have any luggage."

"The bellhop's bringing it from my car; at least I hope he is." Andromeda senses the woman's sudden awkwardness—a moment that she is starting to recognize instinctively—and looks up from the registration card. "And as you can see," she says, "I'm not exactly model material."

They look at each other for a long moment before the other woman extends an arm across the small space separating them, as if to run a finger along the scar, but she stops halfway. "Actually, you'd make a killing. May I photograph you?"

"Now?"

"Yes." The woman reaches under the counter and emerges with a camera, a real camera that uses real film, obviously professional equipment. "I'm a photographer by trade," she explains. "Mostly I photograph fashion for the agencies. I refuse to do weddings or corporate events, which is what photographers usually do to earn a steady income, hence this job. But one of the benefits of working here is the occasional interesting guest." She pats her camera and grins a brilliant smile. "Grist for my Hasselblad."

"But I've been traveling all day," Andromeda says. "I'm a mess."

The woman ignores her objection and begins making adjustments to the camera, talking while she works. "That's the thing about photography," she says. "It allows you to capture things that are fleeting, things that would otherwise be lost forever, like the way you look right now after traveling all day." She looks up. "Opportunities like this are why I became a photographer."

Andromeda decides that to refuse now would appear small-minded; she agrees to be photographed.

The woman continues fine-tuning the camera. Andromeda does her best to bring order to her wind-blown hair, but then without warning the woman suddenly starts shooting. Andromeda had expected her to first put the camera to her eye, but with this apparatus the image is apparently viewed from above. She steps back, startled, her hand moving of its own accord to cover the scar. But then she realizes that this is what the woman had intended, to catch with the first photo not a formal pose but a frank reaction.

The session continues, proceeding in a whir of motor-driven frames.

"Undo your buttons," the woman says, without pause from shooting.

Andromeda undoes the top button.

"All of them."

Andromeda stops. Her instinctive reaction is to refuse, but there is an unexpected rightness to this impromptu little encounter, something too tenuous to articulate but nevertheless clearly felt and so, with the particular pleasure of an unanticipated desire impulsively indulged, Andromeda begins to unbutton.

This photographer is a good judge of character, she thinks, or rather out-of-character—other girls had been show-offs when Andromeda was growing up, not herself. She wonders if Margot Vaughn had grown up the same way.

One side of the shirt slips from her shoulder. Andromeda finds that she is less uncomfortable undressing in a hotel lobby than relieved that she put on good underwear this morning. The woman's soft patter of instructions gradually reduces to silence as Andromeda allows herself to respond more intuitively, submitting to the camera without restraint, and soon the only sound is the motor drive relentlessly rolling the film forward.

But then that mechanical whirr is joined by another sound: the approaching squeal of luggage wheels. The photographer looks up and Andromeda turns. Behind her, the bellhop has come to a halt and is slowly turning crimson while studying his shoes.

Andromeda turns back and this time when the women's eyes meet they fall into laughter. The receptionist puts down her camera and scribbles on a card while Andromeda buttons up, thinking that this is an unexpectedly effective way of putting the Vaughn house behind her. The woman hands her the card.

"My name's Clare," she says. "I'll develop the photographs this afternoon and leave prints of the good ones in your room. My number's on the back. Call me anytime."

They shake hands, and Andromeda wonders if she is being offered friendship or something else.

THE PENTHOUSE SUITE IS EQUIPPED with a wolf-skin rug, copper-sheathed walls, and a fish tank embedded between the bedroom and living room, so as to be visible from both. The bed is like the fish tank, playfully circular. It is the sort of place where rock stars might stay in order to party in style—Renzitti, or Renzitti's client, has a flair for the theatrical.

Andromeda goes out onto the terrace. There is a hot tub here to continue the partying alfresco, but the real luxury is the view: the Atlantic, here miraculously transformed from the bleak steel gray of the Northeast into a warm and inviting aquamarine. Andromeda still has the feel of the Vaughn house upon her, but the remedy is before her eyes. She goes back inside to change into a swimsuit.

V

ANDROMEDA LIES FACE DOWN, the sun on her back. Tendrils of warmth seep through her pores and slide along nerve threads before penetrating deep into bone—a defrosting from the northern winter. Her eyes are closed and she is drifting in a semiconscious dreamscape of sound: rhythmic waves washing along the shoreline; the rustle of palm leaves, almost violent if listened to carefully enough; occasional snatches of Salsa or Merengue when the breeze brings them her way.

The man watching her sweats in his suit. He wishes that he had remembered to bring binoculars. He is sitting on a bench in Lummus Park, facing the sea, a position he took once Andromeda selected her beach chair—close enough to watch, too far away for her to notice. He is pleased with her choice: the chair is away from the occupied ones nearer the shoreline—it seems that she prefers privacy over proximity to the water. He has waited patiently while the attendant set it up, and allowed Andromeda time to settle in. He watched her undress and apply suntan lotion, struggling to cover her back. Now she is apparently asleep.

He gets up, folds his jacket over his arm, and begins the long walk down to spoil her solitude.

ANDROMEDA CAN HEAR PEOPLE when they pass nearby, the sound of sand impacting under their weight. Light and fast if children, slower and heavier for adults. Then she hears another set, deeper than the others, approaching her directly. The footsteps come to a halt and she opens her eyes. It takes a moment for her vision to adjust before making out the figure standing before her.

He is a black man, probably athletic in youth but now with the thickening bulk that marks the passage of a big man into middle age. He wears wraparound sunglasses that conceal his eyes but she can tell that he is looking down at her. He is dressed in a suit with necktie and leather shoes, jacket off and neatly folded over an arm. Large shaven head, parade-ground shiny, and topped by a jaunty straw Trilby.

He squats on his haunches, head now level with hers. His face is composed and serious, a handyman calmly surveying a job before getting down to work. They regard each other for a moment in silence, but then Andromeda realizes that he is looking not at her face but the Tiffany collar. It must have caught his eye, she thinks, and he probably assumed that any woman wearing jewelry to a beach would likely bring cash too, and if not cash then at least he could take the collar.

Under other circumstances Andromeda would have sat up to face this potential threat, or might simply have stood, picked up her bag, and walked away, but—encouraged by the example of other women she had noticed on the beach and perhaps predisposed to an uncharacteristic exhibitionism from her recent hotel lobby photo shoot—Andromeda had removed her bikini top before settling herself on the chaise, and in her current state she has no intention of sitting up in front of this stranger.

She wonders if he removed the jacket due to the heat, or is using it to conceal a weapon.

"The collar's locked and it doesn't come off," she explains. "And it's not precious metal anyway."

This declaration is met by a look of bemusement from the stranger.

"You think I'm here to mug you?" he asks. "In wingtips?"

"Maybe you're a book that doesn't wish to be judged by its cover."

He ignores the remark and grabs Andromeda's bag from beside the chaise, too fast for her to snatch it back. He begins sorting through it with a deliberate care that no thief would use, extracting items one by one and examining them with a curious care: sunglasses; a water bottle; T-shirt; suntan lotion; bikini top; her notebook; a pen; a paperback that she purchased for the flight down and planned on finishing at the beach. The bag is soon empty.

He picks up the paperback and shakes it to find anything hidden between the pages. When nothing emerges he turns it over and studies the cover.

"The butler did it," he says, and casts the book aside.

He picks up her notebook and flips through it single-handed, surprisingly dexterous for a big man with large fingers, but there is little in it for him to find—Andromeda pulled it from her shelf fresh for the trip, and the single entry so far is a hurried description of the two paintings in the Vaughn residence, made after leaving the house so that she could look them up later. He spends a moment in study before tossing it with the rest of her things.

"No ID," he remarks.

"No."

"No phone either."

"No."

"Most people don't go far without their phones."

"Most people talk too much."

"Name?"

"Rhonda Greenway."

"What were you doing at the Vaughn house?"

"Appraising the art," Andromeda replies, an assertion that she hopes the entries in her notebook will make more plausible.

"Appraising the art?"

"Mr. Vaughn is thinking of selling his art collection. I was sent to evaluate the pieces."

"Who sent you?" he asks.

"Sotheby's."

"Sotheby's?"

"The auction house."

"Ah, the auction house. And?"

"And what?"

"And what are they worth? What did you appraise them at, Appraiser Lady?"

"Perhaps two hundred and fifty thousand."

"Two hundred and fifty thousand, huh?"

"Each."

"And where are you from?"

"New York City."

"When did you get down here?"

"This morning."

"How?"

"I flew."

"Well, at least that much is true."

He pulls a small piece of paper from his shirt pocket and holds it up for her to see. Andromeda recognizes it: her boarding pass.

"I found this in your car," he says. "Not a good idea to leave the roof down on a convertible, Appraiser Lady." He turns the boarding pass around and reads it. "According to this, Rhonda Greenway, your name is actually Andromeda Chamberlain."

He stands, returns the boarding pass to his pocket, and pulls out a phone. He begins tapping at the screen with his thumb.

"By the way, the artworks belong to *Mrs.* Vaughn," he says distractedly, without looking up. "*Mr.* Vaughn couldn't sell them, even if he wanted to. And as to their value, either of the two big Koons' would easily fetch a million on its own—which of course anyone sent by Sotheby's would already know. So whatever you're doing in Miami, Miss Andromeda Chamberlain, it certainly isn't appraising art." He holds up the phone and, before Andromeda realizes what he is doing, takes her photograph. The man stands and spends a moment studying the screen.

"Not bad," he says, but it is not clear if he means her or the image. He puts away the phone and again contemplates Andromeda. "Sun's hotter than you think down here," he says. "Don't get burned."

He turns and trudges away, his pace unhurried, no doubt aware that any alarm she might choose to raise would unlikely be taken seriously, given that technically he neither touched her nor took anything, apart from the photograph. But the approach had nevertheless been threatening, meant to intimidate. She watches him walk a hundred yards along the beach, Trilby bobbing above the big bare expanse of black skull, shiny with sweat. When he turns to take the path back up to Lummus Park, she can see that he is laughing.

VI

ANDROMEDA DINES THAT evening at one of the restaurant's terrace tables. The incident on the beach has not intimidated her; it has achieved the opposite: she feels elated at this unexpected but irrefutable evidence that there is something more to the story than a simple teenage runaway. She could have ordered room service but feels like being surrounded by other people tonight, and the jostling street theater of Ocean Drive will be her evening's entertainment.

A homeless man approaches. She noticed him earlier, going the other way—apparently Ocean Drive is his entertainment of an evening, too. But the first time it had been with the shuffling gait and downcast eyes of the hopeless; now he walks with purpose and scans the faces in the crowd eagerly.

His eyes fall on Andromeda, and he momentarily freezes. Then he approaches her directly.

Andromeda fights the urge to flee.

He comes to a halt on the other side of the table. He is wild-haired and unshaven, smelling of booze and body odor, and stares at her with eyes from which any trace of rationality has long since disappeared.

He begins patting his pockets. He mutters something hoarsely and keeps repeating it, as if it is important, something that he has to get right. "The lady with the scar," he is saying to himself.

Andromeda's hand moves to her fork, not much of a weapon but the best weapon available. The man finds what he is looking for and with grubby fingers lays the thing cautiously on the far edge of the table, as if to make an offering. Then he abruptly turns and disappears back into the crowd, apparently as afraid of Andromeda as she was of him.

Andromeda stares at the object on the other side of the table: a plain square envelope with a clear plastic window. She reaches across and picks it up. Inside is a CD. She pulls out the disc and examines it but there is no title, nor anything else apart from the manufacturer's minuscule lettering around the center hole, which she strains to read. It is not a CD but a DVD. There is no hint as to the content.

Andromeda realizes that the evening's entertainment is not yet done. She returns the disc to its envelope and calls for the check.

HOUSEKEEPING HAS COME and gone in her absence. The penthouse has been tidied and the ice bucket on top of the bar is full. The lighting has been turned low, and most illumination now comes from a score or so of votive candles that dot various horizontal surfaces in the room.

On the coffee table she finds a large stiff envelope. Inside are a dozen photographs, eight-by-ten black-and-white glossies still smelling of Dektol, all of them pictures of herself. The first is the first, a shot of unrehearsed reaction, her hand slightly blurred as it reaches toward her face, a look of consternation bordering on dismay, an uncomfortable photograph to look at. The others are well shot but less interesting as Andromeda became more at ease. In one her hand is mussing her hair and she looks pouty enough for a men's magazine. The last one turns out to be as good as the first: one thumb tucked into a pocket, the other hooked under the titanium collar, chin high, bare shoulder thrust forward toward the viewer—a challenging pose. In the background the bellhop has rounded the corner into the lobby, still oblivious, and the shot carries with it the subtle suggestion of an impending collision.

Andromeda replaces the photographs in the envelope. She agrees that Clare's talent would be wasted on weddings.

There is a knock at the door. It is room service with the pitcher of Mojito that Andromeda ordered on the way up from the restaurant—something with which to keep cool while watching whatever is on the DVD. The bellhop is not quite able to disguise his curiosity—she suspects that he has been chatting to his colleague from the day shift, and is wondering about this guest who undresses in the lobby and orders Mojitos by the jugful. She tips him and he leaves.

Andromeda shuts down the air conditioning and opens the terrace doors, allowing the night to flood into the room. A little street noise wafts up from below, mostly music. The air is heavy and humid and laden with ozone, smelling of warm salt and tropical decay—an evening on the verge of a thunderstorm.

In the bedroom she finds that the bed has been turned down, and there is a present on the pillow. It is not a room service chocolate. It is an envelope identical to the one in the living room, but this time there is only a single photograph inside. Clare, naked. The photograph is full length, capturing those long legs to advantage, and lit from the side, revealing the contours of her body in deep chiaroscuro. A beautiful body, beautifully photographed. There is a note on the back: *I would love to do another shoot with you—let me know if you're interested. Clare.*

Andromeda wonders whether this is merely a clever technique for finding fresh models, or if 'something else' had been the correct answer after all. Maybe Clare had taken the Pelican job to have ready access to the photogenic camera fodder from the resident modeling agency but, perhaps finding the professionals unwilling to pose for free, had hit upon this recruiting tactic instead. The photograph serves a dual purpose: it is intended as evidence of Clare's skill, but also as a warning about the nature of the proposed new shoot.

Andromeda has been photographed enough for one day. She returns to the front door, puts out the 'Do Not Disturb' sign, engages the dead bolt, and slides the chain across for added security. She returns to the living room and leaves Clare's photograph with her own on the sideboard before retrieving the disc and loading it into the player. A moment to figure out the unfamiliar controls, but soon the big flatscreen lights up into life.

Andromeda pours a Mojito, sits back on the sofa, and waits for the show to begin.

THE VIDEO OPENS with a shot of a woman holding a cocktail glass. It is filmed from the side and close up—full lips in full gloss, but her eyes are out of frame. The shot is subtly backlit, almost a silhouette. Through the reddish-brown liquid of the drink a maraschino cherry is visible, stem attached, sitting in the base—a Manhattan cocktail, Andromeda thinks.

The woman plucks the cherry from the glass by the tip of the stem. She tilts her head back, opens her mouth, and lowers the fruit. The video momentarily freezes as her lips close upon it, and a title appears:

Cherry Shotz!
America's Premier Adult Entertainment
Visit www.CherryShotz.com

More of Clare's work, Andromeda wonders, although that would not explain the mode of delivery. But as soon as the first scene begins she realizes that this film has nothing to do with the photographer. She finds the pause button and freezes the frame.

Andromeda sits forward and studies the scene on the wall-mounted screen for a long time. It is Margot Vaughn, and she is staring at her reflection in the mirror of a public restroom.

VII

BY THE TIME ANDROMEDA REACHES the counter the woman behind it has already guessed her identity. She began where travel professionals usually do: with the luggage, her eyes briefly dipping down to Andromeda's wheeled bag and registering the bright red priority tag. Clothes next: well-cut dress in lightweight fabric and high-heeled sandals—the clothes of someone arriving from a warm climate. Then lastly the collar, an item that she mistakes for expensive jewelry. Her computer system has alerted her to the latest arrivals and she assumes that this must be the first-class passenger from Miami for whom they prepared the Mercedes.

It is not until Andromeda comes to a halt at the counter that the woman notices the scar, the one thing that does not fit. The usual awkward pause, but Andromeda is learning to fill these gaps by now.

"My name is Andromeda Chamberlain. I think you have a reservation for me."

"Yes, we do." The woman reaches to the rack behind her and pulls out an envelope with Andromeda's name on it. The lawyer's people are efficient, she thinks: the person who answered her call that morning had emailed her flight details ten minutes later—first class, despite Andromeda's request for coach—and now she is in Los Angeles, following up on the best lead she gleaned from last night's film with Margot Vaughn. The movie, if it could be called a movie, had no opening titles and no closing credits—it simply ended with the final scene. But there had been some legal boilerplate proclaiming that the production complied with '18 USC 2257' and '28 CFR 75.' A little research revealed these to be Article 18 Section 2257 of the United States Code—federal law—and Article 28 Section 75 of the Code of Federal Regulations—the Justice Department rules for implementing that law. They required that producers of adult videos maintain records establishing that the participants were over the age of eighteen at the time of production. The film hardly fitted the genre—it fits no genre that Andromeda knows of—but given the content the producers had obviously felt the need to legally indemnify themselves.

The woman begins filling in the paperwork. Beside the rental agreement is a key with a bright three-pointed star on the fob.

"What other cars do you have?" Andromeda asks.

"Other cars?"

"Yes."

"You don't want the Mercedes?"

"No."

The woman reluctantly pulls out a laminated card with pictures of the various vehicles available and turns it around for Andromeda to see. She begins discussing the more expensive models at the bottom, but Andromeda points to the picture in the upper left, their cheapest car.

"What's that?"

"A compact hybrid," the woman replies, in a tone suggesting that serious people do not drive such vehicles in L.A.

"I'll take one," Andromeda says.

It is a small rebellion and probably pointless—neither Renzitti nor his client is likely to be aware of the change—but it pleases Andromeda just the same.

HALFWAY UP THE SANTA MONICA Mountains, Andromeda begins to understand the rental clerk's reluctance: the little car struggles to maintain freeway speed, and the buffeting from the big SUVs blasting by on her left threatens to blow the thing off the road. Eventually the vehicle tops Sepulveda Pass and Andromeda breathes a little easier as she begins the descent into the Valley.

The film specified as the custodian of records one Lester Klimp, with an address on the intriguingly named Firmament Avenue in Van Nuys, CA—right in the heart of the San Fernando Valley, the capital of America's pornography industry.

LESTER KLIMP'S OFFICE is located in a squat office block built in a style that Andromeda thinks of as post-Industrial Thoughtless, an anonymous lump of pre-stressed concrete out of place in a real city but right at home in suburban sprawl with poor zoning laws—the sort of building that silently oppresses its inhabitants with the unremitting evidence that they were not worth the cost of a genuine architect. No starry firmament here; just dull office space.

Andromeda enters the building and takes an elevator up to Lester Klimp's third-floor office, wondering how many women had made this same journey, heading to a place where the last remnants of their California dream collided with hard reality. But the suite turns out not to be the production offices Andromeda had expected; Lester Klimp is a lawyer.

The woman behind the reception desk looks up as she enters.

"May I help you?"

"I'd like to speak to Mr. Klimp."

"I'm sorry, he's not in. Do you have an appointment?"

"No, I don't. When are you expecting him back?"

"He's not in at all today. Can I ask what it's in reference to?"

"I'd like to see the records of a production for which he is the custodian."

"Are you with law enforcement?"

"No."

"Do you have a court order?"

"No."

"Then I'm sorry, but they're not public records. Is there anything in particular you wanted to know?"

"I'm trying to locate someone who appeared in a film. A girl, or a woman I should say."

"Have you tried the producer?"

"The film ended without any credits and so I don't know who produced it. The only thing I have is Lester Klimp's name as the custodian of records. There was a website, but all it had were videos for sale."

"What was the website?"

"Cherry Shotz-dot-com."

The woman breaks into a smile. "That's Cherry Falco. Have you tried him?"

"He runs Cherry Shotz?"

"He owns it."

"Would he have access to the records?"

"Honey, Cherry Falco has access to everything. I can give you a number for him if you like." The woman begins rummaging through a drawer, although there is a computer screen in front of her. She continues chatting away, apparently grateful for the unexpected company. "Cherry's a big shot in the business. His real name's Cherubim Falco, if you can believe it, but don't ever call him that. I don't think he's forgiven his mother for saddling him with such a ridiculous name—and plural, too. Probably why he ended up in porn." She finds the number and writes it on a slip of paper, which she passes to Andromeda. "Just tell him Cherise sent you."

"You know him?"

"I worked with him years ago. It's not my real name, but it's the one he'll remember me by."

VIII

ANDROMEDA WINDS SLOWLY along Mulholland Drive, checking house numbers. The road is narrow two-lane blacktop. It follows the ridge line, sometimes dipping and sometimes climbing, never straight for long. The windows are down and the sunroof open. Here, high up in the Hollywood Hills above the rest of Los Angeles, the air feels cooler and fresher, smelling of eucalyptus leaves and money.

There is little traffic; Andromeda thinks it must be the last place in Los Angeles where driving is relaxed. She locates the address and turns in.

Cherry Falco's residence has a short curving driveway ending in a small brick-paved court. Andromeda parks and gets out of the car. The place is surrounded by trees, turning it into a shaded bower. The garden is no better tended than that at the Vaughn house, but here feels more natural than neglectful. The air is fragrant with the profusion of plants, a floral perfume that might have been cloying but for the astringent camphor of the laurels. There are climbing roses and purple columbines and a flower with pale pink bell-shaped blossoms that Andromeda cannot identify. Cicadas sing from the trees. A rippling breeze allows waves of dappled light to cascade through the foliage.

She feels like a small girl having stumbled into a delightful little dell, a private enclave in which if left alone she could explore as she wished, hidden from the quotidian cares of the world. There is even a small fountain babbling in the corner, something with which to slake a thirst or make a mud pie. She immediately takes a liking to the place and secretly christens it *chez* Cherubim.

The house is a long, low flat-roofed structure built in the calm Mid-Century Modern style. An abundance of glass outside reveals open spaces within—an architecture that celebrates the two great gifts of southern California: light and air. The few sections of wall not made of glass are mostly covered in ivy. This is Andromeda's idea of a dream home—a comfortable but unpretentious residence amid a voluptuous abundance of plants: a place that welcomes its surroundings instead of trying to exclude them.

Only one thing mars the picture: an awkward sports car interrupting the space like an igneous intrusion. The license plate reads CHERRY♥—apparently in California the hopelessly solipsistic can include heart symbols on their vanity plates. The paintwork is a deeply lustrous dark metallic red—cherry red. Fat tires and four hulking tail pipes. There are two chromed nameplates on the rear deck, *de Tomaso* and *Pantera*, although which is the brand and which is the model is unclear. Italian sports cars are usually graceful in design, but the one before her now looks like it was drawn up by a hormonal teenager—something that reminds Andromeda this is not a little girl's place but a little boy's, and the time has come to call on Cherry Falco.

THE FRONT DOOR IS answered by an Oriental woman wearing a Chinese-style black silk suit, high-heeled gold sandals, and a look of amused curiosity. She leans languidly on the door frame, a hand raised high above her, and smiles at Andromeda.

"My name is Xi-Qi," she announces. "I'm the butler, among other things."

Andromeda resists the urge to ask, *Gardener, too?* and instead introduces herself. The woman nods in response; Andromeda is expected.

"Please come with me."

She leads Andromeda across a foyer and down some shallow steps into a wide sunken area flooded with light coming through plate glass windows on the far side. Most rooms are not walled off but separated by smaller details: a few plants between the bar and the lounge; a floating fireplace delineates the billiards room; a mezzanine holds a baby grand.

They take stairs down to the next level, larger than the first, and Andromeda realizes that she has underestimated the size of *chez* Cherubim. The modest bungalow she had imagined from above was just a glimpse, the island tip of Falco's massive sea-mount, rising from the swirling depths of Hollywood.

Xi-Qi the butler leads Andromeda onto the terrace, a broad deck cantilevered out from the hillside so that it seems to float over the city below. There is a pool, long enough to swim laps but there are no lane markings on the bright blue glazing.

Three people occupy the terrace. On the far side of the pool, situated so as to be best displayed, are two women with identical blond bobs, wearing nothing but sequined bikini bottoms. One reclines on a sun chair, supine, breasts pointing skyward like a space shot, apparently asleep. The other is standing, applying suntan oil to a chest equally immune to gravity.

Sitting on a sun chair on the landward side of the pool, placed to take advantage of the view, natural and enhanced, is the third occupant of the terrace, presumably Cherry Falco. Xi-Qi gestures for Andromeda to go on alone and retires back into the house.

Andromeda continues across the terrace. It might be winter in New York, but Los Angeles lives in eternal spring—the air seems saturated with light, and Andromeda wishes that she had brought her sunglasses from the car. On the far side, the recumbent remains asleep but the other woman pauses from applying oil and raises her Ray-Bans to better take in the new arrival.

Andromeda comes to a halt before Cherry Falco. He smiles in welcome but makes no effort to rise.

"You must be Andromeda Chamberlain," he says. "Great stage name."

"It's my real name."

"No kidding?" Falco seems delighted by this. He spends a moment unapologetically inspecting Andromeda, a man used to frankly evaluating female flesh.

Andromeda does some evaluating of her own. Falco is a little older than she had imagined from the phone call—mid-fifties, she guesses—but a combination of trim figure and full mane of wavy hair makes him appear younger. He wears a mustache of a type that would once have been fashionable at Studio 54. Swim trunks and deck shoes. Unbuttoned Hawaiian shirt revealing a gold chain to match the pinky ring. Deeply tanned; a man who spends a lot of time on this terrace.

On the table beside him are a cell phone, a cocktail shaker, two glasses, an ice bucket, a bottle of tequila, several limes, a professional-grade video camera, and a shallow dish of salt.

No books or magazines; Cherry Falco is not a man for the written word.

"Thank you for taking my call," Andromeda says. "I didn't realize that it was your private number."

She had expected a secretary or receptionist with whom she could make an appointment, and had been surprised when Falco himself answered the phone. He had brushed aside her request to schedule a meeting and told her to just come on over. Andromeda had reminded herself that business was conducted more casually on the West Coast and agreed to do so, used to adapting herself to local customs, even in lands as foreign as southern California.

"And the office would have been fine," she adds. "It's very kind of you to invite me to your home."

"Not at all." His eyes finally return to her face. He smiles openly, and she thinks how strange that a man whose business is the female form should be the one person to have shown no reaction to her scar. "The truth is that I don't go into the office that much," he says. "No point, these days. All you need is a cell phone and a laptop. Besides," he says, opening his arms, "I like to be out among the beauties of nature."

Andromeda follows his gaze. The beauties of nature are now both awake.

"Pixela and Plasticina," Falco says. "Pixela is the one with the bottle, I think."

The probable Pixela remains standing but now has one knee on the chaise, supporting herself as she applies suntan oil to Plasticina, slithering but still prone.

"A matched pair?" Andromeda asks.

"They perform as twins."

"They have amazing breasts."

"The best that money can buy. Kleinmann over in Westwood did them. I can give you his number if you like. He'll give you a discount if you mention my name."

This strange offer gives Andromeda pause. On the phone, she had not had the opportunity to explain what she wanted before Falco interrupted to invite her over, and now she realizes that he might have mistaken the purpose of her call. He has assumed that she was requesting a job interview.

A lot of things suddenly fall into place. The receptionist's helpfulness is explained: she probably gets a commission for every successful referral. And Falco had naturally invited Andromeda to his house: it would not be the sort of job interview that could be comfortably conducted in an office. The presence of the camera now made sense: no doubt Andromeda was expected to disrobe, and Falco would film her. Pixela and Plasticina were probably there to make her feel more comfortable, or perhaps she was expected to join them in an impromptu audition.

"I'm trying to locate someone," Andromeda says.

Falco's smile fades. "Locate someone?"

"A woman. She was in one of your films. The records are kept at a lawyer's office in the Valley, and the person I spoke to there said that you could grant me access."

"You mean you don't want to be in pictures?"

"No."

"No?"

"No."

"How can you not want to be in pictures? Everyone wants to be in pictures."

"Not me."

At first, Falco seems offended but then bursts into unexpected laughter.

"Well, if you change your mind you have my number," he says. "Now why don't you sit down and tell me about this woman you're trying to find."

Andromeda sits and for the first time notices the blinking light on the video camera. Falco is not intending to film her, she realizes; he is already doing so. Probably the camera had been configured to pick up her movement as she walked out onto the terrace—perhaps Xi-Qi had remained inside so as not to confuse the focusing mechanism with multiple targets. It has been filming her ever since. And if Falco had felt the need for a self-focusing camera it probably meant that the planned audition with Pixela and Plasticina had been intended to conclude with himself as participant-in-chief.

She sees Falco sense her recognition, and their eyes meet. Now it is Andromeda who bursts into laughter. Falco returns it with a satyr-like grin.

"For the record, I could hook you up with a top director. Quality high-concept glamour shot on thirty-five millimeter; no more obscene than a Botticelli." He raises a hand to halt her response. "Don't say no; just say that you'll think about it."

"Okay, I'll think about it."

"Excellent." He slaps his hands together and stands. "Now let's have a drink, and you can tell me your story."

Falco rubs a wedge of lime around a cocktail glass then dips it into the salt, twisting the stem to coat the rim. Deft and precise—Andromeda can tell that Cherry Falco is no stranger to mid-morning cocktails. He repeats the maneuver on the second glass then fills them from the cocktail shaker. He offers one to Andromeda and takes the other for himself before resuming his seat.

"To opportunity," Falco says.

Andromeda takes a sip and puts down the glass. "As I said, I'm trying to find a woman who was in one of your films, Mr. Falco."

"Cherry, please. What's her name?"

"Margot Vaughn."

"I don't recall it. Does she use a different screen name? Most people do."

"Not that I'm aware of."

"What do you want with her? Are you a relative?"

"I'm a writer. I want to write about her."

Falco pauses to consider this. On the other side of the pool, Pixela and Plasticina are writhing like lubricated eels, apparently still under the impression that the show will go on.

"Why do you want to write about her?"

Now it is Andromeda's turn to pause.

"I guess the simple answer is that I was offered the assignment. But I'm freelance; I could have turned it down if it didn't interest me. The truth is that I'm curious myself, although I'm not sure why."

Andromeda thinks that this is not a very satisfactory answer, but Falco seems pleased with the response and she can tell that he has decided to help her.

"Did her name appear in the credits?" he asks.

"There were no credits."

"No credits? What was it called?"

"There was no title either. There was nothing; it just began and ended. The only things other than the movie were the Cherry Shotz logo at the beginning, and some legal boilerplate about records."

"Section Seventy-five compliance," he says. "Every adult production has it. But they usually have a title, too, even if the title isn't very imaginative. Do you have any idea how many movies we make? Hundreds of them. Without a title, it will be difficult to find the records."

"I can describe the plot."

"Plot? We're not talking *African Queen* versus *Apocalypse Now* here—the plots are not exactly memorable."

"This one was very memorable. It began in an Air France departure lounge for the Concorde. It was the start of a journey, a real one."

"Concordes haven't flown in years."

"Since May seventeenth, 2003. Right after Margot Vaughn disappeared."

"So she ran away from home and ended up in adult movies?"

"No, I don't think so. Concorde flights ended not long after she left home, and the timing is too tight. She didn't run away from home and end up in the movie; I think she ran away from home in order to appear in it."

"Don't be so sure. People get desperate fast."

"She had plenty of money. Enough to last a year at least."

Falco pauses in concentration.

"What happened next?"

"She arrives in Paris. There is a car waiting for her at the airport, a big old limousine, a pre-World War Two car where the chauffeur sits up front, out in the open, and the passengers are in a separate compartment in the rear."

Falco nods his head. "Like an old Rolls-Royce," he says.

"Like an old Rolls-Royce, but actually a Hispano-Suiza—I was able to freeze the frame and read the radiator badge."

"And they went to a castle or something?"

"Yes, a château somewhere out in the French countryside. The Loire Valley perhaps."

"And there were other people there, in costumes. Like a costume party?"

"It was a ritual of some kind, I think. It was centered on Margot. It seemed that they were taking her back in time. She wore modern clothes on the Concorde, but in the car she was dressed in a big voluminous green gown and tight velvet jacket with a top hat and veil: a Victorian riding habit. Very elaborate." It was the presence of a riding crop that had suggested the equestrian aspect to Andromeda. The crop had been used to effect, but not on horseflesh. "At the château the regression in time continued: firstly, those high-waisted dresses from the Napoleonic era; then heavily embroidered Grand Siècle gowns with whalebone corsets and giant pompadour wigs; finally, classic Roman clothing."

Falco nods as she recounts the story.

"Was there an extreme close-up, shot in super-slo-mo: a drop of liquid falling into a girl's eye?"

"Belladonna," Sabrina confirms. "So you remember it?"

"I do. It was a bust."

"A bust?"

"I never made a penny on it."

"I suppose that it must have been very expensive to produce."

"For sure, but it wasn't me that produced it."

"It's not a Cherry Shotz production?"

"Most of my movies are not Cherry Shotz productions. Let me explain how the business works." He pauses to sip the drink before continuing, perhaps to order his thoughts. "The days of big studios are as far gone in the Valley as they are in Hollywood. When you see a film from Universal or Paramount or Twentieth Century Fox, it's not really the studio that made the movie; usually, they're just distributing it. The movie itself was made by a smaller organization, sometimes an outfit incorporated only for that specific film. They gather the financing themselves, often from sources outside Hollywood, although the studios will put in something to ensure that they get a seat at the table. Same with Cherry Shotz. We produce content, but mostly we just distribute. The filmmakers can't be bothered with that part, they just want to make their movie and have the professionals look after the business end of it. It's like authors and publishers. Authors write but publishers distribute. The mainstays of our business are the production studios we have under contract—usually just an individual director with a small staff—and they produce the content."

"And that's what happened with this movie?"

"No, that one was a little different. It just came in over the transom: the video arrived from France with an invitation to distribute it. I never met the director. I never even spoke with him—the nine-hour time difference makes it awkward, and we usually handle European stuff via email. In the end, we agreed to distribute the film here in the U.S. The paperwork was exchanged and we paid for the rights. It's unusual but it happens now and again, especially with the Europeans. The film was really too art-house for us. I figured it was some new director imagining that he was an auteur, but I thought he was worth taking a chance on because the guy obviously knew his stuff professionally. The production values were first-rate—that poison-falling-into-the-eye scene was not just dramatically effective, it would also have been technically very difficult to pull off. Plus, they'd done their homework on the contractual and compliance aspects, but as it turned out I never heard from them again."

"Remember the director's name?"

"No, but my office will have it."

"Then you'll give me access to the records?"

"I will," he said. "I'm a sucker for a pretty face."

The remark stops her short. No one has characterized her face since she returned from Africa, but Andromeda is certain the one word that no longer applies to it is *pretty*.

"I'll call my people and have them make photocopies," Falco continues. "You can pick them up from the office this afternoon."

"That's very kind of you."

"Sure you won't change your mind about making a movie?"

"I'm sure."

He smiles in easygoing acceptance. "Then I only have one more thing to ask: will you let me know how it goes? Maybe send me a copy of that article you're writing when it's published?"

"I'd be happy to."

The meeting concludes, and Falco stands to escort her out. Across the pool, Pixela and Plasticina are too preoccupied to be aware of Andromeda's departure.

IX

ANDROMEDA WALKS BY the garden back to her car. The terrace has spectacular views, but this is where she would retreat to if *chez* Cherubim were hers. Through the hedge she notices something discordant, something not part of the garden, something man-made.

It is metal, painted a strange pink-hued beige. She moves closer, disbelieving her instinctive guess, but then sees the confirming badge: it is a car, a small hybrid like her own. There had been a small hybrid like her own behind her as she came up the Hollywood Hills, the same odd color as this one. The driver had patiently held back, not pressing her despite the slow progress as she checked house numbers. At the time she had been grateful.

The car is close on the other side of the hedge, pulled onto the shoulder, the only way to safely park along this section of Mulholland Drive.

Andromeda circles back through the garden, keeping low, so as to approach the car from a three-quarter angle: too far back to be seen from inside, not far enough behind to be picked up in the rear-view mirror.

Through the hedge she can make out two men inside, both seated in front, both dressed in dark suits. The driver is drumming his fingers on the steering wheel in time with some music that she cannot hear. His shirt cuff shows above the suit sleeve. Large hands, big knuckles. The passenger holds a camera with a long lens resting on the dash, the sort of camera meant for taking photographs at a distance: a camera meant for surveillance.

So they were following her—the driver she had thought unusually tolerant with her pace along Mulholland Drive had probably been pleased that she was driving slowly. Now they are waiting for her to come back out.

Their car is probably an airport rental like hers—it is neither a color nor a car that many men would willingly choose to buy—and is no doubt as underpowered as her own. She wishes now that she had kept the Mercedes, something with which on the freeway she might simply outrun her pursuers.

Andromeda tries to think of another potential exit, but *chez* Cherubim is built on the side of a precipice. She retreats into the garden and returns to the front door. This time it is answered by Falco himself.

"I'll agree to be in one of your movies," she says, "but I have two conditions."

"What are they?"

"Firstly, I appear only as an extra. A clothed extra."

"We don't pay people to keep their clothes on."

"You won't be paying me—I'll do it for free. But only as an extra."

"A new face for free is quite an offer," Falco admits. "But I've got to tell you, if you imagine that you can keep your clothes on in one of my movies—even *gratis*—then you have seriously misunderstood the nature of the product."

She is forced to admit that expecting to remain fully clothed in an adult film is probably not realistic. A rapid negotiation follows. She concedes that her clothing will have to come off, but insists on wearing a wig and sunglasses throughout, and with makeup heavy enough to eliminate the possibility of anyone she knows happening to recognize her. In return, Falco agrees that her role will be limited to that of an extra, on the condition that she submits to one solo scene, the minimum the director is likely to accept. "Something natural and tasteful," Falco assures her, "like taking a swim."

The reference reminds her that on the beach twenty-four hours ago Andromeda had been all but naked in front of a thousand strangers' eyes—not a great leap from that to stripping in front of a camera crew on a closed set, she reasons. At least one consideration that would cause most young women to balk at the idea of appearing in such a movie—how to explain if her parents found out—is not something relevant in her case. And she realizes that she is not entirely immune to the compliment of desire, even so generalized and vicarious a desire as expressed in film.

"I won't do anything salacious or overt," Andromeda warns.

"What'll be asked of you will be less than what's asked of a mainstream actress: there'll be none of those nude scenes with pretended passion and fake lovemaking, scenes that succeed only in making all the participants, on both sides of the camera, look ridiculous. Instead, you'll be doing what is really just a high-style fashion shoot, very opulent and very glamorous. I can show you some examples right now if you want, and you can see for yourself."

"That won't be necessary."

Falco slaps his hands together in delight. "Then it's agreed."

"Not quite."

"Not quite?"

"I said there were two conditions," Andromeda reminds him. "The first was the nature of the role. We haven't discussed the second one yet."

"Which is?"

"Your car. I'd like to borrow it for the day."

"The Pantera?"

"The Pantera."

"What for?"

"For a taste of the fast life I'll soon be living."

"Extras don't drive de Tomasos."

"If I like it, then maybe I won't be just an extra anymore." She can tell that this last remark has hit a soft spot, but Falco is not yet ready to agree. He spends a long moment looking at her, as if to judge whether she is reliable enough to be entrusted with his car.

"Do you have any tattoos?" he asks, and Andromeda realizes that it is not her reliability he is trying to judge.

"No."

"Birthmarks, scars, stuff like that?"

"No birthmarks. One scar."

"Where?"

"You're looking at it."

The response momentarily silences him, and he stares at the slash across her face as if he had not noticed it before. He steps forward to inspect her more closely, taking his time, regarding her as an art critic might a piece about whose provenance he harbors doubts, but nevertheless is a work he appreciates, forgery or not.

"I'll get the keys," he says.

Falco returns to the house.

Andromeda examines the Pantera. The cockpit is sunk low into the body and the rear end, bulky because it contains the engine, makes it unlikely that anyone would be able to identify the driver from behind. But Andromeda wants to be sure, so she retrieves her sunglasses from the rental and a scarf from her luggage in the trunk. She is tying the scarf under her chin when Falco returns from the house.

"Very Audrey Hepburn," he says.

"Anything special I should know about the car?"

"Can you handle a stick?"

"Of course. Does it have a limited-slip differential?"

The question makes him laugh. "You are full of surprises, Andromeda Chamberlain. I have no idea if it has a limited-slip differential or not. In fact, I have no idea what a limited-slip differential is." He hands her the keys. "Take care of it."

She offers the keys to her rental in return. "Use mine if you need to go somewhere." He accepts them, but from his disdainful expression she can tell that it is not a vehicle Cherry Falco would risk being seen in. “I’ll bring the Pantera back by tonight.”

“You can keep it,” he says. “That is, you can keep it if you decide that you want to be more than just an extra. I’ll give it to you as a signing bonus.”

She realizes that, despite the smile accompanying the offer, he is entirely serious.

X

ANDROMEDA EDGES cautiously out of the driveway, unused to the heavy clutch. She stops to check for traffic. Her pursuers remain parked on the shoulder, but she can make out nothing inside. Andromeda pulls onto the road, careful to do so smoothly, not wanting any awkwardness to give away her unfamiliarity with the car.

The vehicle feels too low and too wide. She concentrates on driving, settling on third gear as high enough for any speed likely to be attained on this road. The car is loud and every touch of the gas pedal induces a deep metallic rasp. There is no other traffic. Andromeda comes to a stop sign. She uses the pause to take her eyes from the road and check the mirrors, but there is no vehicle behind her.

She pulls across and takes a last glance in the mirror before the next curve. A beige car comes into view, rounding the corner and yet to hit the stop sign. A glimpse only, but Andromeda can tell that it is the car that was following her.

The time for sedate driving has passed. Andromeda presses the gas pedal and the car bucks under the sudden application of torque. The tires emit a brief squeal, soon followed by the rising *basso profundo* of the engine. Her plan is to turn down a side street and disappear before the people behind her realize that she has left the main road. She comes to an intersection. She slows but not enough: as she takes the turn the outside wheels briefly leave the asphalt, but the chassis handles the transition, and Andromeda imagines that somewhere deep in its mechanical bowels a limited-slip differential is doing something obscure but clever.

She continues down the winding side street, slipping more easily between gears now that she has become accustomed to the transmission. The road loops back and begins heading up again—like most streets running off Mulholland Drive it is not a through road but just an access route to houses built along the spurs off the main ridge and which turns back before hitting the ravines. That suits Andromeda: by the time she returns to Mulholland her followers will be long past, and she can head the other way before they realize that they have lost her.

She arrives back at Mulholland Drive. Her pursuers are parked fifty yards away, pulled over to the side of the road, patiently awaiting her return.

They had been too far behind to have seen her turn down the side street: she realizes that they must have known where she went by sound alone—up here in the hills the Pantera's engine can probably be heard for miles. A quick check of their navigation system would have revealed that she had no way to go but back up. All they had to do was wait.

Andromeda turns back onto Mulholland, heading for Cahuenga Pass and the Hollywood Freeway. The road begins to descend. The car behind keeps closer now, any pretense of not following her discarded. The freeway comes into view, a concrete serpent winding down from the Hollywood Hills into the Los Angeles basin. Andromeda drives slowly until she comes to the on-ramp, then she hits the gas pedal.

This time she allows the engine to wind out. By the time she hits the freeway the car behind has just turned at the bottom of the ramp. She will put as much distance as possible between herself and her pursuers before coming to traffic, so that when inevitably everything slows down again there will be many vehicles separating them, sufficient for her to get lost in the surface streets before they can exit to follow.

The car tops the ramp with a rising howl, and then there is a wide expanse of open freeway before her, inviting speed. Andromeda tunnels her vision to the vehicle's trajectory, ignoring slower lane traffic and concentrating on the gearshifts. She dares not take her eyes from the road to look in the mirror but knows that her pursuers must be well behind by now. The induction noise from the headers behind her blots out all other sound.

For a few minutes the fast lane is clear, but as the freeway comes back in among the surface streets the roadway is suddenly full of vehicles. Andromeda comes off the gas and the exhaust emits a series of sharp crackling backfires, as if expressing indignation at this sudden slowing. She glances in the mirror. There is a scattering of cars behind, slowing like her, and in the far distance is the little hybrid, struggling to catch up.

Andromeda moves across lanes and takes the nearest exit, Sunset Boulevard. She comes to a light and uses the pause to study the mirror, but the car is low and the traffic heavy; she cannot see if her followers took the same exit. Soon she comes to the curves by the Whisky A Go Go, and in the reflected arc of vehicles behind her Andromeda spots them, a dozen vehicles away.

She comes to another light, stopping on the front row. Pedestrians stare at the de Tomaso as they cross in front of her. One man whistles, but whether at the vehicle or the driver is not clear.

There are well-tended lawns here; the grit of Hollywood is behind her. The sky is a crystalline blue, and the road ahead is broad and straight, flanked by towering royal palms in orderly rows, like a gateway to paradise.

Andromeda has a vision. It is not the first time—small epiphanies, she thinks of them, when she thinks of them at all. It hovers for a moment on the horizon, mirage-like, something just beyond reach. She struggles to understand what it is that she is seeing and squints unconsciously. The whistler stops and gazes in the same direction but, seeing nothing, moves on. The vision slowly takes form: ahead in the distance, a palatial pink building rising above the palms. It is both real and unreal. It quavers for a moment on the edge of her consciousness, like something half-remembered from a previous life, before finally resolving itself. It is the Beverly Hills Hotel, a place that Andromeda has never before seen except on the cover of *Hotel California*. By the time the light turns green, she has a plan.

She continues down Sunset Boulevard. At the hotel's sign she turns and takes the turnoff through their lush gardens up to the main building. Her pursuers follow. She proceeds slowly, allowing them to close in, and when she arrives at the hotel's entrance they are right behind her, too close to ignore the instruction on the sign by the front steps: *Valet parking only*.

The doorman approaches as Andromeda comes to a halt. He opens the door and offers a hand to help her from the car. By the time Andromeda has extracted herself a valet is at her side, tearing off a ticket stub. The hybrid has come to a halt a few vehicle lengths behind, and a second valet is already by the driver's door.

Andromeda ignores them and walks up the steps. She takes a last glance back before entering the hotel. The valet has done what she had hoped he would: he has pulled the Pantera just forty feet forward, so as to leave it on display among the handful of other cars of similar price and provenance parked by the main entrance. Automobiles are to Angelinos as heraldic blazons are to medieval knights, public declarations of position, and an establishment like the Beverly Hills Hotel could be counted on to leave a car like hers by the entrance, a silent but visible assertion of rank.

Meanwhile, the compact hybrid, being plebian, will no doubt be whisked away to some distant lot.

THE WAITER BY the pool is pleased with the new arrival—the presence of a pretty young thing encourages custom, and his income will increase accordingly. He assumes that she is an actress but familiarity has made him immune to their charms; he no longer tries to identify them. This one comes with distant bodyguards, two thick men trying but failing to remain inconspicuous among the sleek moneyed guests of the Pink Palace. The presence of bodyguards is not unusual at the hotel, but then the waiter notices that one of the two men is subtly photographing the woman, and he wonders whether they are part of her entourage after all.

"Good afternoon. Would you like the lunch menu?"

"Just a Bellini, please."

The waiter smiles—the pretty young things are rarely willing to eat in public—and goes to fetch the drink.

ANDROMEDA TAKES IN her surroundings, relying on her sunglasses to shield the fact that her gaze falls briefly upon her followers. They have taken a table by the pool, well away from her booth under the awning. Somewhere between plain and ugly; she does not recognize either of them.

Most tables are occupied. The people at the one nearest her are engaged in some sort of negotiation, a movie deal perhaps, but for all she knows it could be a leveraged buy-out. She can feel the gaze of other people upon her, and not just her followers—the pool area of the Beverly Hills Hotel is a place where people come to see and be seen. She feels safe here: it is a watering hole on the savannah, a spot where the animals gather to cautiously check each other out, and at which for a short while at least the lions refrain from eating the gazelles.

She abruptly stands and makes her way back toward the lobby. One of the men is immediately on his feet and following her while the other fumbles for money to leave on the table. Andromeda walks directly through the lobby out to the front entrance. She has her ticket stub ready but does not need it: the valet recognizes her.

"Leaving already, ma'am?"

"Yes."

He grabs the keys and races to the Pantera, opening the door for her. Andromeda gets in and starts the engine, loud enough to shake nearby palm trees. As she leaves the last thing she sees in the mirror are her two followers, standing in frustration at the curbside while their valet makes his way out to whichever distant backlot has their car.

XI

ANDROMEDA EXAMINES THE photocopy of what was purportedly Margot Vaughn's proof of age: a French driver's license—a *permis de conduire*. Her *date de naissance* is correct for day and month, but earlier by three years, sufficient to have made her eighteen when the movie was filmed. She cannot tell whether the counterfeit was part of the original license or a change made in the photocopying.

The *domicile* is listed as an address in the Sixth, something that at first Andromeda thinks invented, too—no waif on the run could afford Sixth Arrondissement rents—until recalling that this particular waif had made her way to Paris on a Concorde and been met by a chauffeur-driven limousine. She opens her notebook and transcribes the address.

4-bis place St-Sulpice
Paris 6

There is only one other document. Cherry's instructions to his office had not been quite as generous as he had led Andromeda to believe, and the envelope that had been left for her at the front desk contained only the photocopy of Margot's driver's license and this second sheet, with the name and address of the production company, nothing else. It seems that Cherry Falco was willing to help Andromeda only to the extent that it did not compromise the privacy of the other participants, or more likely his own business dealings—not even to the title of the film, which remains unknown to her.

The production company is Réalisations Argus, S.A. with an office out in Saint-Denis, somewhere Andromeda has never been but knows to be on the city fringes, where the Paris of the tourist disappears, and the Paris of the disaffected tire-burning immigrant takes over. At least this second address is likely to be genuine, since it would have been in the business contract.

Andromeda puts the papers aside and looks out over the ocean. Yesterday she had gazed across the Atlantic; today it is the Pacific. The sun is beginning to sink behind the marine layer lying offshore, waiting like a malevolent fog ready to engulf Los Angeles. She is sitting on a bench in Venice Beach. The Venice Beach bodybuilders are nearby, and she hopes that their public narcissism would obligate them to rescue a lady in distress, should her followers somehow track her down here.

After losing them at the Pink Palace, Andromeda had immediately returned the Pantera—too fast for them to get back there first, should they have been clever enough to think of it—and then, on the assumption that her followers would have recorded the little hybrid's license plate, she had gone to a branch of the rental agency and exchanged vehicles.

Falco was disappointed to learn that she was not keeping his car, especially as he had already coined a stage name for her: *Andromeda Galaxy!* The exclamation point would be part of her name, he explained—the sort of touch she thinks might be expected from someone with a heart symbol on his car's license plate. Meanwhile, he had called Michael Zapp—a former fashion photographer turned producer of what Cherry termed *glam-porn*—to see what opportunities were available. Zapp had rented a Caribbean villa for April, and he was happy to include Andromeda in the filming he planned to do there. "Very high-concept," Cherry assured her. "Basically a set of dream sequences, a sort of tropical *Decameron*." Andromeda accepted, being a woman of her word. Her current deadline would have passed, and at least the Caribbean warmth would be welcome after the New York winter.

Andromeda looks back down at the papers in her hand. It was not worth the effort to get these documents unfollowed, she thinks, certainly not worth her rash agreement to appear in one of Falco's films. Andromeda wonders about her own upcoming proof-of-age requirements, and considers the wisdom of using fake documents, too—perhaps she would be Andromeda Galaxy! after all.

She removes her sunglasses and reverts to the *permis de conduire*. The photograph is shot in the standard driver's license style—head and shoulders only, blank background, expressionless gaze into the camera—but even in this photograph Margot possesses the singular quality that drew Andromeda to accept the assignment. She gazes at the image, as if by staring at it long enough she might discern the source—not superficial looks, but rather a feature of character somehow conveyed externally, even in something as prosaic as a driver's license photograph. It is the quality of someone who could strip in a public bathroom and poison herself with grace, or retain a detached poise while having her voluminous Victorian dress hitched up in the back of a Hispano-Suiza. A singularity called *presence*, Andromeda decides. It is an inadequate word—although she knows of none better—because the term only describes; it does not explain. She supposes that the explanation must lie in Paris, but first she has another stop to make.

XII

BILL LEATHERWAITE REGARDS the woman on the other side of his desk with curiosity. She has accepted his invitation to sit, undoing her scarf while settling herself with an unconscious grace, and her long fingers seem otherworldly in their strange slow beauty, like creatures on a coral reef gently probing the depths. Beneath the scarf she wears a plain metal band. She sits with her back straight and her knees together, a posture that might be interpreted as prim—although Leatherwaite thinks that this is unlikely, given that the woman has invited him to watch what she said on the telephone was a vaguely pornographic video. She seemed almost surprised when he agreed to do so, but how many retired college professors filling out lonely days with research work at the Getty could have resisted such a peculiar call? Besides, she sounded intelligent and interesting—two qualities that he finds unusual enough in isolation, rare in combination. Certainly, her presence fills the room now and, septuagenarian or not, he finds it a little difficult to breathe.

"Thank you for agreeing to see me, Dr. Leatherwaite."

"Bill, please."

"Bill, then. And please call me Andromeda."

"Andromeda it is."

He wonders if she is disappointed. The Getty comprises two museums. The first is a spectacular complex of travertine and glass perched high above Los Angeles in the Santa Monica Mountains—technically the Getty Center, a much visited and photographed landmark, and it was probably there that she had anticipated being directed when first placing a call to the Getty's general number. But Leatherwaite is a classicist, and the Getty's antiquities are housed in a second museum located down on the PCH, the Getty Villa, the place to which the woman's inquiry was eventually forwarded. Much less dramatic than its modernist cousin, although not without a certain charm to the discerning eye, for it is built in the form of an ancient Roman country villa. But today the Getty Villa is blanketed in fog from the marine layer, and the place feels gloomy, vaguely sepulchral.

"There's a small theater downstairs where we normally show a visitors' orientation video," he says. "It has the necessary equipment and so I asked the staff to close it for our use. May I see the disc?"

She pulls it from her bag and passes it across the desk. He studies it for a moment, although she has already told him that there are no markings to indicate the contents.

"What was it that suggested a classical context? Do you have an academic background?"

"No, it's just an impression I have. My academic training never went beyond a general course they offered in college, Introductory Classics."

Clear and without apology, he thinks: she is self-assured, but not self-possessed. "I used to teach a course of the same name at UCLA," he says.

"I suppose that it must have been tiresome, teaching the Classics to people who can't read Latin or Greek."

"Actually, I rather enjoyed those classes. Don't say I said so, but the truth is that sometimes the translations are better than the originals."

"You are a heretic, professor."

"But it's true. Take Marlowe's 'Amores,' for example. *Thou ring that shalt my faire girles finger binde, Wherein is seene the givers loving minde*. So much more rapturous than Ovid's original. Latin is a language at home with jurisprudence and liturgy, but I find that it is not quite comfortable in love."

She laughs, and it is genuine laughter, an unbridled sound completely unlike the clipped and mirthless tittering he is used to: the noises people make when they have been brought up on a diet of television sitcoms; the noises people make when they have learned to laugh on cue. Nor does she possess that affected adenoidal twang, presumably acquired from the same source, that is so common now. He finds himself completely happy in this woman's company; he had forgotten that such interesting women exist. Leatherwaite is a peaceful man, but he feels a sudden surge of intense ill will for whoever gave her that scar.

"I'll get us some coffee if you like, then we can take it and watch the video."

In response, Andromeda pulls a bottle of wine from her bag and holds it aloft. "I brought this along to thank you."

The Getty makes its research resources available free of charge, and technically Leatherwaite is not allowed to take any form of gratuity, but he will make an exception for this woman. He accepts the bottle and begins to make the appropriate remarks, but stops when he glances at the label. He puts on a pair of spectacles to inspect it more closely.

"Mouton-Rothschild, 'ninety-three," he says. He looks up at Andromeda. "I take it that the nature of the label is not accidental."

"They drink it in the movie. And, yes, no doubt the choice was deliberate."

Mouton-Rothschild put a different painting on their label for each vintage, and in 1993 it had been a Balthus sketch of a young girl, naked. This left Europeans untroubled, but some American merchants had refused to stock the wine, and in a form of censorship by economic coercion, Mouton had been forced to relabel many of the bottles destined to cross the Atlantic that year. Balthus-labeled bottles were now collectors' items.

Leatherwaite removes his spectacles. “I’ll go fetch us some glasses.”

XIII

BY THE TIME THE film is finished their glasses are empty. A long silence follows, and Andromeda wonders if Leatherwaite is mesmerized by it, or merely embarrassed. He finally turns to face her.

"I've seen it before," he announces. Then, responding to her look of surprise, "No, I don't mean the actual film. But the scenes—I've seen them before."

"Where?"

"On the walls of Pompeii."

He excuses himself and briefly leaves the room, soon returning with a large book. He takes it to a table and after a minute of leafing through the pages comes to a halt.

"I knew it was there." He looks up from the book. "That scene with the kid."

It is one of the strangest scenes in an already strange movie. Margot is led through the woods by another girl, a pretty young redhead with pale skin. They are barefoot and wear loose linen robes, nightgowns perhaps. They come upon a baby goat—a kid. The animal is timid and shivering but apparently tame, and cautiously approaches. The redhead kneels, bares one of her small breasts, and proceeds to suckle the kid.

Margot watches, but as always retains an air of detachment, observer rather than participant, even when herself at the center of attention. There is an extended close-up of the animal's long pink tongue licking eagerly, and Andromeda wondered if they had to daub the girl's flesh in something to tempt it.

Andromeda joins Leatherwaite at the table and he slides the book between them, open at a full plate photograph depicting three figures, the middle one of which is a young female suckling a baby goat.

"This is from the so-called Villa dei Misteri—the Villa of the Mysteries—just outside Pompeii. Have you been there?"

"No."

"The frescoes were preserved by Vesuvius. There is a room with a series of them depicting one of the ancient Mysteries, probably Dionysian rather than Eleusinian, although scholarship remains divided as to their precise nature. Certainly an initiation rite of some kind." He points to the figure on the left, a satyr sitting next to the suckling female, playing pan pipes. "Remember the music that accompanied the scene?"

"Pipes."

"That's suggestive, but there's another panel that clinches it, I think."

He flips through several more plates until stopping at a large one rendered in a blaze of golds and purples against a background of cinnabar red. Andromeda sees right away what he must mean.

"She's being whipped."

"Presumably this corresponds to the scene in the back of the car," Leatherwaite says, "but that by itself is not conclusive. After all, flagellation is common in many rites and is regularly practiced in religious observances around the world—from the banks of the Ganges to the Passion plays of Oberammergau. But see who is doing the flogging."

Andromeda looks. It is a winged female figure, bare-breasted and alighting on one foot as if having just stepped down from Olympus. She holds the whip raised, ready to strike.

"Who is she?"

"The wings indicate a divinity of some kind. A vengeful Fury perhaps, or Nike or Nemesis. Now, let's compare it to the video."

He uses the remote control to rewind, stopping at the scene in the Hispano-Suiza. In the film, Margot's tormentor is nominally a flight attendant, dressed not in Air France livery but the sky-blue uniform of Pan Am, complete with pill-box hat, circa 1966. But this flight attendant is dressed as no genuine airline hostess ever would be: stiletto-heeled shoes, too-short skirt, and beneath her tightly buttoned jacket she wears no shirt.

"See it yet?"

Andromeda shakes her head—she does not know what she is meant to see.

"Above the left pocket."

And now she understands: the flight attendant's badge.

"Wings," she says.

"Indeed, wings—like the figure from Pompeii. And if you were to represent someone having descended from the heavens, who better than a flight attendant? But not just any flight attendant—note that she wears the uniform of Pan Am. A dead airline, an airline that ceased operations long ago. And if the airline is dead, but the hostess is here, then it follows that she must be divine, wouldn't you say?"

"Yes, I would." Andromeda sits back. "Tell me more about these rites."

"Well, as I said, probably Dionysian. Dionysus was the god of wine, among other things. Which reminds me." He stands and fetches the bottle, then refills their glasses. "The Mysteries themselves remain a mystery: the details of the ritual were closely guarded, and the penalty for disclosure was death. Nevertheless, there were leaks; there always are. We know that there was an intoxicating drink, *kykeon*, whose ingredients have been hotly debated but probably included a psychedelic drug derived from fungi, or perhaps a form of mint called *Salvia divinorum*—literally, wise divination. And the Dionysian rites had a significant sexual element. The Greek word *orgia*, from which we derive *orgy*, originally meant simply a gathering with the purpose of undergoing the rite—the derived meaning is an indication that these rites were sexual in nature. Clearly, there's an orgiastic element to the film, but it's somewhat stylized, even ritualized, not the wanton abandonment to physical pleasure that the word usually invokes."

"So it's an orgy in the ancient sense?"

"It would seem so. The purpose is not pleasure but initiation—something serious rather than frivolous, indeed almost solemn. Note that throughout the film no one speaks; they rarely even smile. And you remember that the story began in a bathroom? At the commencement of the initiation rite, the candidate would typically undergo a process of purification. That's probably the meaning of the first scene. She bathes her face, symbolically washing away her previous self. She even throws away her old clothes, casting aside her childish past."

"And poisoning her eyes?"

"Belladonna dilates the pupil. In ancient Greece it was used by women for its cosmetic effect, to make their eyes appear darker and more limpid. But there might be a second meaning. The enlarged pupil represents a wider opening of the eye—that is, she will be far-seeing from now on; her initiation is going to allow her to understand things that were previously closed to her—although in the strictly literal sense the belladonna would have actually blurred her vision."

"Hazardous for a girl traveling alone."

"Isolation is part of the initiation. A girl undergoing the Dionysian rites would first have been removed from her parents. We do not see this in the film, although I think we can assume that it has occurred."

"I know it for a fact."

"Very good. Next, the candidate undergoes some form of seclusion. Perhaps that's represented by the plane trip, a period that for practical purposes is entombment in an all but empty aircraft, on a journey that is taking her away from her past. I wonder how they managed to find a flight with so few passengers."

"The film was shot after that Concorde crashed in Paris. People stopped taking them, and they ended up shutting down the service. This would have been one of the last flights."

Leatherwaite nods, but something in the next plate has caught his attention.

"See the garland?" He points to a figure in the background, an attendant pouring water from a ewer into a basin. She wears a headdress of leaves.

"A laurel wreath?"

"Myrtle, more likely. Laurel was a symbol of victory or distinction, something given to the winner of an Olympic event, say. But myrtle is sacred to Venus; it is the emblem of love."

At the center of the scene is a priestess. She lifts a purple cloth from the top of a basket to reveal something to the initiate, something the viewer cannot see. Leatherwaite reads the accompanying text.

"According to this, speculation about the contents of the basket has included 'fruit, flowers, a phallus, or a snake.'" He looks up at Andromeda. "I think we know which one the filmmaker thought it must be."

He fast-forwards to the scene. Margot is brought into a room with a score or so of people seated in rows of upright chairs, as if an audience for a chamber recital. But the entertainment is not music, it is Margot. She is stripped. An attendant enters with a bowl and ewer. Leatherwaite hits the pause button but says nothing because the point is obvious: the attendant wears a wreath.

"Hit play again," Andromeda says.

The scene continues. The attendant pours not water but oil, and she uses it to coat Margot. The oil has been flecked with something shiny, and Margot's skin is turned into a glistening surface on which the candlelight reflects in sudden fractured bursts, an effect augmented by the filmmaker's choice of lens. Two more attendants come in, carrying a basket topped with a cloth.

"Purple," Andromeda comments, and Leatherwaite nods in acknowledgment.

A priestess enters and removes the cloth to reveal a snake, which she lifts from the basket and drapes over Margot. Margot sits and then reclines, allowing the snake to wind its exploratory way around her with more calm than Andromeda could have managed. The sound of its movement over her oiled body is captured clearly, as if to emphasize the onomatopoetic nature of the word *slither*. Some of the audience take photographs with small digital cameras, despite their Seventeenth-Century dress, one of the many anachronisms sprinkled throughout the film, as if to keep the viewer off balance.

The animal is big, a python perhaps. Morrison's Crawling King Snake, Andromeda thinks of it—*he's old, and his skin is cold.*

Leatherwaite presses the pause button again.

"Let's see what other scenes we can match up."

They continue through the plates, attempting to correlate them with the film. Sometimes the associations are clear, others less so, but there are sufficient to convince Andromeda that either the frescoes directly inspired the film, or both frescoes and film shared a common inspiration. Andromeda sits back and finishes the last of her wine.

"There were no credits," she says. "The film just ends; we don't even know what the title was."

"I think that maybe we do. Remember the beginning, where she scrawls out a word with lipstick?"

"I tried looking it up but couldn't find a translation."

"That's because it means nothing."

"Nothing?"

"Nothing as written. But where did she write it?"

"In the bathroom."

"But where in the bathroom?"

"On the mirror."

"Which means?"

It takes a moment for Andromeda to figure it out. "It means that it should be read backward."

"Exactly. In fact, there is a second clue, besides the mirror."

He retrieves a pad and pen, and writes out the characters.

αμίτοιΔ

"Note that the delta at the end is rendered in majuscule."

"Majuscule?"

"Upper case. But all the other characters are minuscule, that is, lower case. That's the second hint that we should read it in reverse." He writes out the transposed characters.

Διοτίμα

"Delta-iota-omicron-tau-iota-mu-alpha: Diotima."

"Which is what?"

"Not what, but whom. Diotima was a woman. There is only a single written record of her, in Plato's *Dialogues*, where she appears as a highly cultured and learned person. She is the sole female character in all of the *Dialogues*. The absence of corroborating historical references has led most scholars to conclude that she is fictional, but if that were true then she would be the only fictional character to appear in the *Dialogues*. All the others—Socrates, Anaxagoras, Alcibiades, and so on—were real people. Yet a woman so distinguished would unlikely have remained unremarked in that time."

"So what do you think?"

"I think Diotima was a real woman, but Diotima was not her real name—that was something the ever-polite Plato did to disguise her true identity."

"Which is?"

"Aspasia, consort of Pericles, and by common consent the most beautiful and gifted woman of the Golden Age. She was a *hetaera*: that is, a woman who rejected marriage—and the social seclusion that marriage meant at the time—for a life of freedom in movement and thought. The *hetaerae* were essentially courtesans; Aristophanes even suggested that Aspasia ran a luxurious brothel, and that it was an argument with Megara about one of the girls that precipitated the Peloponnesian War—but Aristophanes was the political enemy of Pericles, and he cannot be trusted. Certainly, Aspasia ran a school of philosophy and rhetoric, and many girls of good family came to her classes, then men, even powerful men—and eventually the most powerful of all: Pericles. You must remember that Pericles was the greatest man of Greece's greatest age, the aloof aristocrat who championed democracy, a philosopher-warrior, a living embodiment of the ideal of stoic restraint. The only time in his life that he ever lost his head was when he met Aspasia."

"So if Diotima is Aspasia, the title signifies what? Freedom for women?"

"Yes, but more than that, I would guess. Probably enlightenment in the general sense: as freedom from religious superstition, from political tyranny, from social repression."

"I like that explanation better than this book."

"What do you mean?"

Andromeda points at the description at the bottom of the last plate. "According to this the initiate, now transformed, is preparing for marriage." She looks up. "That seems unlikely."

"Why?"

"In the frescoes maybe. But in the film?"

"The initiate is being inducted into the grown-up world. Suitable preparation for a young woman about to enter marriage, surely?"

"Then the film would constitute the mother of all bachelorette parties."

"I think you're missing something. Technically, the initiate has remained a virgin."

Andromeda's immediate instinct is to contradict him, but as she thinks through the film in search of a counterexample Andromeda realizes that he is right: despite having been for two hours at the center of a pornographic movie, Margot's virtue has remained intact.

She looks again at the last plate. There is no doubt that this final panel corresponds to the ending of the movie. It shows the girl after the initiation is complete, sitting calmly while brushing her hair, something almost exactly replicated in the movie's final scene, right down to the little Eros holding a mirror to help her, represented in the film by a dubious dwarf. In the mirror, Margot looks not at herself but the camera, as if challenging the viewer to understand what has just taken place, and it is that unflinching gaze, reserved and enigmatic, that the camera holds for the extended final shot, several minutes in length.

Andromeda realizes that the film has come full circle, ending as it began: with Margot's reflection in a mirror.

XIV

THE BLACKENED SHELL of the building sits smoldering, still surrounded by the *pompiers* who have just extinguished it. Some of them are winding hoses or putting away gear, but most are standing and staring contemplatively at the building. Greasy water oozes across the sidewalk and into the gutter. One of the firefighters flicks the stub of his cigarette into it.

Andromeda realizes that she will not be calling on Réalisations Argus after all.

Beyond the *pompiers* and television crews and *Police Interdicte* tape, a multicolored crowd has assembled—last vestiges of a lost empire, remnants that became stuck to the imperial flypaper of metropolitan France. They are animated, as if the burning of a building was an opportunity for an impromptu *fête*, and already some of the film crews have turned their cameras toward them, sensing the beginning of another story. Then Andromeda sees among the crowd the familiar back of a shiny black skull, a head taller than everyone else, and made taller still by that same jaunty Trilby. He is staring at the building along with everyone else.

Andromeda's first instinct is to turn and leave while still unobserved, but on second thought she remains where she is, too lost amid the throng to be readily identifiable, and keeps an eye on Trilby Top while considering how best to proceed given this unexpected turn of events.

The implication is clear enough—they set fire to the offices to destroy the records—but there is something exaggerated in this smoking shell of a building, something unnecessarily theatrical. If all they had wanted to do was prevent her accessing *Diotima*'s production records then it would have been sufficient to have organized a break-in of the office. The fact of any missing paperwork would probably have gone unnoticed amid the theft of computers and video equipment and the like, and in a high-crime district like Saint-Denis such an incident would have been too routine to excite much interest from the authorities. Burning down a building is something else altogether, an act whose purpose is more than just the simple destruction of evidence, and something sure to invite a vigorous investigation from the *gendarmerie*.

The stakes have been raised, Andromeda realizes. Trilby Top's approach to her on the beach had been the opening gambit, and then having her followed in Los Angeles was their first countermove. This building has been burned down not only to destroy records, but also to deliver a message: *There are no limits to what we will do to stop your investigation*, they are saying—*you have been warned.*

She decides that in this crowd Trilby Top is not a threat, he is an opportunity, someone to be used, a potential source of valuable information. She makes her way through the onlookers and comes to a halt at his side.

He wears wraparound sunglasses and continues to gaze ahead, apparently unaware of her presence, but then he is the first to speak.

"Are you following me, Appraiser Lady?"

"The other way around, surely?"

"I was here first."

"How could you know that, if you weren't following me?"

"My, but you're contrary today."

"Please give my regards to your associates in L.A. I hope they're not still waiting for the valet to bring their car around."

"My associates in L.A.? I don't have associates, in L.A. or anywhere else. I work alone."

"Thuggery is such a lonely profession."

She hopes the comment might cause him to reveal something about himself in denial, but he just laughs.

"Last time we met, Appraiser Lady, I warned you about getting burned. And yet here you now are, surrounded by firefighters."

"I think they would probably take more interest in you than in me. Or at least those *gendarmes* over there would."

"*Policiers*. Only tourists say *gendarmes*."

"Whether *policiers* or *gendarmes*, either way I'm sure they would like to talk to you."

"How do you figure that?"

"You smell of lighter fluid."

He laughs again. "Must be my aftershave."

"No, it's lighter fluid."

"Well, that just can't be, Appraiser Lady." He turns his whole body to face her now and steps up close. "You see, I use matches." He pulls a matchbook from his pocket, holds it up so that she can see for herself, then drops it into her shoulder bag. "Why don't you keep 'em."

He turns and walks away, as casually as he did on Miami Beach.

Andromeda takes out the matchbook. The cover bears the name of the Caffè Florian on the Piazza San Marco, an address that makes her think Trilby Top might not have been lying after all—since flying out of LAX there would have been insufficient time for anyone following her to make a side trip to Venice.

She opens the flap. A single match is missing.

THE ADDRESS ON THE PLACE Saint-Sulpice is a world away from the grit of Saint-Denis, a handsome apartment building five stories high, heavy stone cladding at street level but elegant wrought-iron balconies on the upper floors, probably dating from the period when Baron Haussmann was transforming Paris from a medieval city of crowded alleyways into the grand capital of today. An ancient wooden door with a very modern lock bars access to what is probably a central courtyard. No mailboxes. There is an intercom, but not to individual apartments as she had hoped. Instead, it has just a single button, marked *Gardienne*. Andromeda does not bother trying it: no French concierge is going to reveal anything about her residents to a nosey foreigner. There is nothing to be found here, she realizes—she has wasted her time.

Andromeda returns across the river to the Ritz, a hotel she chose because it is a place used to accommodating people who for one reason or another need unusual levels of protection, even heads of state, and the security is accordingly tight. She pours champagne and a bath, then consumes one while reclining in the other to contemplate her next move. The fact that they—whoever *they* are—had felt the need to burn down a building to prevent her accessing the records of Réalisations Argus tells her that she is looking in the right place, but the bottom line is that both Paris addresses have drawn blanks. She is disappointed, and tries to think of another lead to follow.

It is not until she has emerged from the bath, still pink from the long immersion and leaning on the balcony rail while gazing over the comings and goings in the place Vendôme, that Andromeda realizes she does have another lead after all—not in Cherry Falco's documents, but in the DVD itself. The location is the clue: the château that was the setting for the movie. Perhaps it is a hotel that was taken over for filming, or more likely it operates as a venue available for corporate events and the like. In either case, there would be a record.

It takes just twenty minutes of searching on her laptop to find it: Château Valaire, located midway between Orléans and Tours on the Beuvron, a tributary of the Loire, 200 kilometers southwest of Paris.

Andromeda calls the concierge and asks him to arrange a rental car for her first thing in the morning. He asks her what *marque* she would prefer.

"The *marque* doesn't matter," she says, "as long as it's fast and has a limited-slip differential."

ANDROMEDA EMERGES FROM the hotel the next morning and lowers her sunglasses against the bright winter sunshine pouring over the rooftops across the square.

Today she will be asking questions, and her career in journalism thus far has taught her that the better dressed the questioner, the better the answers received. She has assumed the part of a fashionable *Parisienne*: Chanel suit, vaguely nautical; YSL scarf, equally vague; but very purposeful Louboutins whose red soles she hopes will convey a resolute determination to get at the truth.

The doorman greets her and tips his hat. He gestures toward the waiting car with an open hand.

It is a Ferrari, parked at the foot of the stairs and accompanied by the attendant who delivered it from the rental company. Andromeda realizes that the concierge has taken her at her word that she is indifferent to the *marque*, or perhaps he just wanted to be sure about the limited-slip differential. The paint scheme matches the soles of her shoes but Andromeda wonders how she will manage a clutch in high heels—she assumes that Ferraris do not come with automatic transmissions.

The attendant takes her through the paperwork, shows her the folder in the glove compartment containing the vehicle's documentation, including the *carte grise* that the police will demand should they pull her over, an event that he seems to think probable. He sets the navigation system for the best way out of Paris, then briefs Andromeda on the car's operation, which she is pleased to discover includes a Formula-One-style automated clutch with gear changes accomplished by pulling paddles behind the steering wheel, without need of a clutch pedal.

The attendant accepts his tip with thanks, ensures that Andromeda is comfortably seated with the mirrors correctly adjusted, and reminds her that *la limite de vitesse* in France is 130 KPH, and then only *sur l'autoroute*, something he has already explained twice. An hour later, doing approximately double that speed on an open section of the A10, Andromeda realizes that he was a good judge of character.

XV

CHÂTEAU VALAIRE SITS on a large walled estate with formal gardens immediately surrounding the château itself, but wooded beyond to maintain privacy. Andromeda has pulled off the road and parked by the front gates, which are closed and locked. Through the iron bars she can see little of the château itself, just the distant rooftop and chimneys protruding above the bare trees, but she immediately identifies one location from the film: the high circular turret in which Margot had undergone the strange psychedelic interlude that Leatherwaite identified as the *katabasis*, a going down out of oneself, the central and most secretive part of the Dionysian Mystery. This would have been too sacred to be openly depicted on the walls of Pompeii, but was apparently implied by the divination scene, which in the film had taken the form of catoptromancy—divination by observing reflections—in this case, the gently undulating images reflected in a bowl of mercury into which Margot had stared, and then seemed to merge, disappearing into the quicksilver like Alice through the looking glass.

The scene had been introduced with a long external establishing shot taken from where Andromeda now stands, recording a blood-red sun—made massive by the telephoto effect—sinking slowly behind the tower.

Andromeda walks from one side of the gates to the other, catching glimpses of the château through the leafless branches. What windows she can see are closed, despite the unseasonably warm weather, and there are no people in evidence nor any vehicles, confirming what the locked gates have already suggested: the château is currently unoccupied. But then a door opens in the little cottage to her left, a gatekeeper's lodge. A man emerges, elderly and slightly bent. The caretaker, Andromeda guesses, someone who in return for free accommodation keeps an eye on the property. He has spotted Andromeda at the gate, probably having been alerted to her arrival by the Ferrari's cacophonous engine. He blinks briefly in the sunshine, then begins shuffling over toward the gates. She assumes that he is only coming to tell her what she already knows—that the château is closed—but then she sees a broad grin of someone grateful for unexpected company. He doffs his cap as he approaches.

"*Je regrette, madame, c'est fermi.*" He opens his hands and shrugs his shoulders in Gallic acceptance, as if the fact of the property being closed was the act of an inexplicably changeable deity whose whims were beyond human comprehension.

"*Tant pis. C'est un château formidable.*"

"Ah, you are English?"

"American."

"Of course. You are too chic for the English." Andromeda laughs—he was obviously once a charmer. His eyes fall on the Ferrari. "You would like to see the château, yes?"

"Yes, I would."

"I can show you, if you wish."

"Thank you. You are very kind."

He withdraws a big iron key from his back pocket and begins unlocking.

"We will take *your* car," he states, and Andromeda realizes that it is not the prospect of her company that has attracted him after all.

They drive the short distance to the château. Andromeda is careful to rev the engine loudly before engaging gear, and then again prior to shutdown, ensuring that the old man gets his fill of wailing V-12. He smiles in silent appreciation.

She parks out front and they climb the steps to the entrance. In the bright light of day it all seems a little smaller than it had in the film, and less ominous than the anticipatory mounting of these same steps Margot had undergone on her arrival, filmed in the gathering dusk as if to emphasize her impending plunge into darkness.

They cross the portal and enter the main hall.

"The largest room," her guide explains. "When the château was built, the great country estates were expected to make the balls, you understand, and so there is need of a room of big space for the dancing."

"Is there ever dancing now?"

"Yes, at the *marriages*."

There had been dancing here in the film, too, but not the sort of dancing likely to take place at a wedding.

"Is that what the château is used for—weddings?"

"Yes, and for other things also too." But he does not elaborate, instead guiding her into the next room, the salon of the snake scene. They tour the first and second floors only, public rooms below and bedrooms above. The bathrooms are more generous than in most old houses and with fittings pleasingly old-fashioned. Andromeda recognizes the one used by Margot, still with the large freestanding tub in which she had stood as her attendant sponged her, and then the foot-wide showerhead under which the pair had finished the scene. Andromeda imagines that it must be like standing beneath a waterfall.

There is a third floor, and a basement where the kitchen is located, but the old man dismisses these as servants' quarters and doesn't offer to show them to her. Instead they go back outside and stroll around the grounds surrounding the château. During the circumnavigation Andromeda identifies two more locations from the film. The first is the hedge maze into which Margot had ventured, finding at its center the phallic herm that had come alive under her touch—identifiable with

Pompeii by the purple-colored cloth that had initially covered it in both the mural and the movie. The second is the site of the culminating scene: a twilight garden party. Andromeda takes off her shoes as they cross the lawn, a gesture that amuses the old man, but she enjoys the feel of grass under her feet.

"Have you worked here for a long time?" she asks.

"Since ten years."

"Do people ever use the property for location filming?"

"Ah yes, many beautiful women," he says, but when she questions him further it turns out that he means only that the château is a favorite for fashion shoots, convenient to Paris, close enough for the couturiers to bring their collections down by truck without the difficulty and expense of air freight.

"Do they ever make movies here?"

"Yes, one time," he answers. "Soon after I am arrived. Again, the many beautiful women. But I was not allowed; it was…no people…"

"A closed set?"

"Yes, a closed set. No people were allowed, except for the making of the film."

Andromeda is wondering how to frame her next question when he continues.

"But I did meet *Monsieur* Gidding."

"Who?"

"I am not sure how to say. *Le réalisateur*."

"The director?"

"Yes, the director. *Monsieur* Gidding. He came by to discuss the electricity, yes? He is to make the scene in the garden, but he did not want to use the generators they brought with them because they were too noisy. He wanted to use our electricity. I showed him the fuse box, and we shared an *eau de vie*."

The twilight garden party scene, Andromeda assumes.

"Do you know what his first name was?"

"Of course. Don't you?"

"What do you mean?"

"But, madame, he is *un homme célèbre*. Orlando Gidding—he is famous."

"Ten years ago I was a teenager. I didn't pay attention to such things."

"No, not then. I want to say he is famous now." The old man looks at her in disbelief. "Wait, I will show you."

He abruptly leaves her and goes back into the château, returning a minute later with a magazine in hand. He offers it to her, open at an article. They take a seat on a sunny bench.

It is a copy of *France Dimanche*, a French gossip magazine, several weeks old. The article's headline, rendered in a type size suitable for reporting the outbreak of war, reads *Dernière Infamie de Gidding!*—Gidding's latest scandal. Below it is a photograph of a man in a dinner suit descending a set of red-carpeted steps in front of a theater. On the sidewalk below, jostling with the waiting photographers, is a crowd. They are angry, fists raised and mouths open, shouting at the director. Some of them hold signs, but they are facing away from the photographer and Andromeda cannot read them. One woman thrusts out a crucifix, as if to ward off the Antichrist. The photograph is slightly askew; perhaps the person who took it was being manhandled by the mob.

There are many policemen, some wearing the distinctive high-domed helmets of the British constabulary. Most are facing the crowd and they look nervous; others are attempting to force an opening to the waiting limousine. Andromeda reads the caption: *Gidding à Londres, après le prévoir de Faust.*

Andromeda has heard of the film—although not yet released, the new *Faust* has already garnered sufficient controversy to be the subject of news articles. She picks her way through the text, which is brief in the way that gossip magazine articles usually are, to accommodate short attention spans. It ends on a note of Gallic pride:

> *Comme beaucoup d'exilés en provenance de pays anglo-saxon, de Oscar Wilde à Jim Morrison, Gidding se réfugie à Paris: il est un résident de longue date de St.*

> *Germain-des-Prés, et habite un appartement dans la place St-Sulpice exclusive.*

It takes a moment for Andromeda to translate:

> Like many exiles from English-speaking lands, from Oscar Wilde to Jim Morrison, Gidding takes refuge in Paris: he is a long-time resident of St. Germain-des-Prés, and lives in an apartment on the prestigious place St-Sulpice.

"And this is the man who shot the film here, ten years ago?"

"Yes, the same. He was not famous then, of course, but I do not forget him."

"What did you talk about?"

"I asked him what is the name of the film, but he said that it did not yet have a name. I asked him what it is about, and he said it is about zombies."

"Did you see any zombies?"

"No, I was not allowed on the set."

"You didn't look anyway? From the woods, perhaps?"

"No, they had security. There was a person at the gate. They told me he was to keep people out."

Andromeda understands: the old man would have liked to sneak a look but suspected that the guard was really there to ensure that he kept to his cottage. And the trees were in foliage, so he would have been unable to see anything through his windows.

She hands back the magazine.

"Did you ever see the film?"

"I looked for it, naturally, but I think that it must not have been completed." The old man shakes his head. "A great pity. I adore zombie movies."

XVI

ANDROMEDA RETURNS TO Paris at half the speed she left it, content to drive lazily in the slow lane while reviewing what she has learned.

They did not think of the château, or if so then not the château's gatekeeper. They had been ahead of her in Miami and Los Angeles and Saint-Denis, but had missed the most obvious clue of all—she had almost missed it herself. Andromeda feels a small surge of satisfaction in this minor victory. The puzzle is mostly solved now: a famous film director on the cusp of releasing a major new work once made a pornographic film starring an underage girl. Someone found out, and enlisted Andromeda to uncover the ultimate witness: the girl in question. If it becomes public he will be ruined, at least in reputation, probably also in his career—and on top of that, he will likely face criminal prosecution. Perhaps he will become like Polanski, permanently on the run, having to seek refuge in Switzerland or somewhere similar, a place where there are no extradition agreements for such things.

Andromeda wonders who her employer must be. She suspects an anglophone version of *France Dimanche*, some publication that specializes in sleaze, or perhaps one of the televised equivalents—

purveyors of what was once frankly termed trash but which in the modern media's endless pandering to the lowest common denominator had now become mainstream. If they had sent their own people the target would have been alerted, and so instead they enlisted a freelancer, one presumably too respectable to be digging up dirt. And they had hidden behind a lawyer for the simplest of reasons: to maintain their anonymity.

The plan did not work. The director found out and is now doing everything he can to thwart Andromeda: having her followed, employing a thug to frighten her off, even burning down a building in order to destroy the records linking him to the film.

That much is clear. What is not clear is what Andromeda will do about it.

She takes agreements seriously, but in this case the deal was misrepresented—there was never going to be an article, or at least not her article; the only intention was to find Margot quietly—and so Andromeda would have no compunction about breaking the agreement and simply refusing to do anything further. Had the director kept out of it then that is likely what she would have done, but she has been challenged, and were she to stop now it would appear that intimidation had worked. To report fearlessly is what had attracted Andromeda to journalism in the first place, and she had chosen to endure the uncertainties of a freelance career to ensure that no editorial oversight would ever compromise her. Any backing down—real or imagined—in the face of threats is abhorrent to her, but she finds the idea of being used by people who trade in muck equally repellent.

By the time she hits the Periphérique, Andromeda has made up her mind: she will continue as before, working on the article as if there were to be an article, and pursuing the original aim: to find out what became of Margot Vaughn. When the time came, she would decide for herself what to write, and how much she would tell Renzitti. In the meantime, if this Gidding person gets in her way again she will simply go around him.

It is not until she is on the exit ramp for the Boul. Mich. that Andromeda realizes there is still a piece of the puzzle missing: she does not know who it was that gave her the DVD in the first place.

XVII

ANDROMEDA PACKED NO swimsuit for the French winter, but she has underwear that could be mistaken for swimwear at a distance and decides to take advantage of the afternoon sun still pouring onto the southwest-facing wing of the Ritz. She takes a cushion and settles into a seat on the small balcony. The square below is a mix of traffic and pigeons and camera-wielding tourists. A bird atop Napoleon leaves his imperial perch and flies down to the adjacent balcony, seemingly for a closer look. The place Vendôme is like a heat sink, obstructing any breeze and gathering the warmth into almost summerlike concentration. Andromeda rests her feet on the rail and reclines in feline repose.

She presses the power button on her laptop, establishes the connection, and begins researching the man who made *Diotima*.

Orlando Gidding is thirty-eight years old. He is referred to by friends and enemies alike simply as "Gidding"; he does not respond to his first name. His father served as a diplomat in the State Department, and Gidding spent much of his youth abroad. His first film, made fresh after being expelled from the University of Grenoble's film school, *sans* degree, established his reputation as a trouble-maker.

The Fire Lotus was a love story set in Tibet. To film on location, Gidding needed permission from the Chinese authorities, who demanded first to see the script. Gidding wrote a special version just for them, shorn of the pervasive repression that formed the framework in the actual story. He received approval and was assigned a "cultural liaison officer" from the Interior Ministry. When the policeman was on the set they filmed the false script; when he was absent—something encouraged by an occasional purgative added to his tea—they reverted to the real movie.

During filming, Gidding was covertly introduced to a Buddhist monk named Tenzin Chodak. Tenzin revealed his intention to commit suicide by self-immolation as a protest against the Chinese occupation of his country. He asked if Gidding would film the act and pass it to the foreign press, thus bypassing Chinese censorship. At this point most directors would have balked, but Gidding went one better than the monk—he offered to write him into the script so that it would not just be part of a passing news cycle but sustained in a feature film, something that would never go away.

The monk agreed.

His suicide took place in the main square of Tibet's capital, Lhasa. The place was policed to prevent just such incidents, but Gidding arranged a snatch-and-run of a tourist's handbag, with the thief disappearing down a side alley. The beat cops, encouraged by a victim pointing and protesting loudly, had pursued.

Tenzin, saffron-robed, had serenely assumed the lotus position in the middle of the square. He meditated briefly, then doused himself with gasoline and lit a match. Gidding, alone, filmed the event with a videocam.

The ensuing commotion soon brought the police back to the square, then reinforcements. Gidding was arrested. He maintained that he had simply been taking a stroll after the day's shooting, and that his presence in the square had been nothing more than a coincidence. The fact that none of his actors or crew was present must have convinced the authorities and he was soon released—but they kept the video card.

Gidding had anticipated this. The card was a ruse. The video had been sent directly over his phone as he filmed it, away to some distant server that the Chinese authorities would have been unable to do anything about, even if when searching him they had been smart enough to figure out why, along with the phone, there was a USB cord in his pocket.

Six months later *The Fire Lotus* was released, and Gidding's position as the new *enfant terrible* of American cinema was established. The Chinese reaction was predictable—the movie was banned—but the fact that he had so artfully fooled them must have hit a nerve: an arrest warrant was issued, and were he ever again to step foot on Chinese soil it would likely mean many years in prison.

Less predictable had been the reaction back home. Gidding's ethics were questioned, and the consensus in Hollywood was that knowingly filming a man's suicide crossed an unwritten boundary—a criticism that would have been more convincing if those same studios, in their anxiety to reach a billion potential ticket buyers, did not self-censor their own scripts to suit the Chinese authorities. Gidding's response was a dismissive one-liner: *The only thing those people would ever kill themselves over would be missing a percentage point of gross.*

But Gidding had no tolerance for the studios or the rest of the Hollywood establishment, driving the point home by premiering *The Fire Lotus* at the Venice Film Festival and ignoring the two Oscar nominations the film received. He did not win anything in Venice but Tenzin Chodak did: a special award presented that year alone, for courage in the face of oppression, and which had been accepted by the Dalai Lama on behalf of the dead monk and the people of occupied Tibet.

Thereafter, Gidding premiered all his films in Venice.

Two more movies quickly followed, both uncontroversial but commercially successful, and then a fallow period. The article assumed that this was because Gidding, now financially secure, could afford to take a break, but Andromeda knows that it was not fallow at all: it was at this time he was making *Diotima*.

In one interview Andromeda finds a reference to the apartment in the place St-Sulpice. The address is not specified but Gidding refers to his apartment in Paris, on the Left Bank, originally his father's from a diplomatic posting, and where Gidding lived for several years when growing up. Asked why he kept it on, Gidding answered, *To stash my mistresses*. When reminded that he was not married, he replied, *No, but sometimes they are*.

It was a clever answer, Andromeda thinks, something that the French would not question. In reality, the apartment was where he stashed not his mistresses but his underage star of *Diotima*. She realizes that Gidding is good at deception, someone who plants plausible decoys to distract from the truth.

Gidding returned to his natural idiom—unrelenting character study—in his next work: *Madison Square Garden*, the first of his films that Andromeda has seen. The movie covers a twelve-hour period in the life of the fictional 'Seventies rock band 'Hedley Nell.' The opening twenty minutes are famously without real dialog, just snippets of preparation for the concert to come: the singer waking up amid a sea of groupies and shooing them from his room; the brooding guitar player, alone with his Les Paul, holding it with the tenderness of a lover—the only expression of affection in the entire film; a technician doing sound checks; roadies; cops; ticket sellers; concession operators; even the band's limousine driver, making sure that the liquor decanters in the back are topped up. Everything is slightly squalid and grimy, the colors luridly oversaturated, the photography itself grainy, as if the grit had gotten into the film stock. And all the time the pace of the film is subtly increasing, the scenes a little shorter, the cuts slightly quicker, mirroring the relentless hurtling forward of the music to come.

The concert starts, and suddenly everything else is trivialized. For half an hour Gidding let the music speak for itself, without distraction, and the result was to capture the urgent power of the great arena concerts of the era, and how they must have felt to someone in the front row. Then the aftermath: the band dining at a downtown nightclub as if holding court, surrounded by the famous and the fashionable, supplicants eager to bask in their reflected glow. Then the party moves back to the hotel—more booze, more drugs, trashing the rooms, and sex with the groupies filmed to the limits of an R-rating. Next, the come-down: a disagreement over a simple chord progression that quickly escalates, ending with the singer quitting the band. He storms from the room to the hallway and straight into a waiting shotgun, wielded by the father of one of the girls he had shooed from his room in the opening scene. The man pulls the trigger without hesitation.

When first watching *Madison Square Garden*, Andromeda had admired the movie but not particularly liked it. Now that she is aware of who made it she considers the film anew. As with *Diotima*, Gidding had apparently been inspired by classical modes, in this case, Greek tragedy: men full of hubris sowing the seeds of their own fall—if Sophocles were alive today, she thinks, he might have made *Madison Square* Garden himself. The singer's petulant reaction to having a groupie stolen by the drummer mimics Achilles' rage at Agamemnon over the same issue in the beginning of the *Iliad*. And the film clung closely to the Aristotelian unities: one action in one place at one time. Even the injunction against violence on stage had been observed: the ending had frozen with the buckshot still in mid-flight, shockwave and powder spray visible, inches before plowing into the singer's surprisingly unsurprised face.

This time, Venice gave Gidding the Golden Lion.

Finding details of Gidding's private life proves more difficult. He refuses to be photographed—unusual for any man, Andromeda thinks, let alone a presentable one: maybe he is familiar enough with his own medium to distrust it when turned upon himself. But Gidding can do nothing about the paparazzi, and the internet is littered with shots of him—usually with a woman close at hand, rarely the same one twice. A womanizer, she wonders, but then decides no: he does not flaunt his companions, as is usual for the type: he is just a man attracted to women, and who are attracted to him.

Gidding grants few interviews, although those that he does make for entertaining reading. He describes suburban life as *breeders huddled together like boobies upon a rock*, network television as *a laxative for the intellectually constipated*, and himself as a pariah: *to be born thinking is to be burdened with a condition that society does not understand and finds somewhat disturbing.* Volatile, she thinks, not a man made for constancy: he speaks as he films, in swift vibrant strokes. When asked about religion he variously describes himself as a heathen, a sun worshipper, and a Dylanist—this last replacing the Decalogue with Bob Dylan's seven rules of life, of which Gidding's preferred is Number One: *Never trust a cop in a raincoat.*

But for many people he is now a confirmed Satanist. *Faust* has been two years in the making and is not yet complete, but enough detail has emerged to make clear on whose side the director's sympathies lie. Stories of the film's production dominate the articles that Andromeda finds. At the time the project was announced Hollywood wanted in, and the studios had offered to finance what was to be a monumentally expensive undertaking. Gidding refused, and had instead leveraged his own modest fortune as much as his bankers would allow. When that ran out he had done what no one thought he would ever do: he had mortgaged the rights to all of his previous films—he was betting everything on *Faust.*

The project went badly from the start. Filming was to take place on the island of Rothermore, a rocky crag off the coast of Scotland where medieval monks had once built an abbey in the mistaken belief that the combination of steep cliffs and lack of safe landing ground would deter Norse raiders. The abbey was under the care of the National Trust of Scotland. At first, the authorities had agreed to filming but then, under pressure from religious groups protesting that the site would be desecrated by the making of such a movie, withdrew their permission. A legal battle ensued, during which it emerged that the National Trust did not own the property outright. Instead, they had been given use of it at a nominal rent by the descendants of a baron who, in return for his support of the Stuart Restoration, had been granted title to the island by Charles II. Thus, it was technically private property. Gidding made an offer that the family could not refuse, and entered into the three-year exclusive-use lease on the property. The National Trust was thrown out.

He had the location secure now but filming proved a logistical nightmare. There was no electricity; they had to bring in their own generators. The paths were too narrow and treacherous to transport many of the larger props; Gidding used helicopters to fly in furniture, trees, even live animals. Initially the crew had been accommodated on the mainland, but going back and forward by boat had proved too weather dependent and, after missing several days of filming, Gidding had relocated the entire crew to the abbey ruins, unheated and without adequate plumbing. They relied on boats for resupply, but during one extended winter storm the sea was too rough for more than a week. The fuel for the generators ran out, then the food. The one thing they had plenty of was water because their accommodations, rough enough to begin with, had flooded in the relentless storm.

Two of the crew developed pneumonia. The chief cameraman quit. But Gidding's real problem was with the lead actress, Rebecca Mallory, playing the role of Mephistopheles. Until *Faust*, Gidding had never used any real stars in his movies—*stardom is one percent talent and ninety-nine percent hype*, he once said—but in this case, Gidding felt that the role needed a powerful actress, and Rebecca Mallory was universally acknowledged as the most powerful actress of her time, lauded on both sides of the Atlantic for her vivid portrayals of diverse women, from Joan of Arc to Jacqueline Kennedy.

The trouble began from the start. Mallory was used to being deferred to, but Gidding was indifferent to her reputation and treated her as he did everyone else. When she insisted that she was playing Mephistopheles haughtily, Gidding calmly asked who had told her that braying like a donkey constituted haughtiness. The relationship deteriorated. Mallory, believing herself indispensable with the film half-shot and herself as the only household name in the cast, became increasingly obdurate. When she refused to finish the chapel scene without a change to the script Gidding fired her.

In the middle of the set, with Mallory still standing open-mouthed in disbelief, Gidding demanded a satellite phone. He had immediately called a nearby North Sea oil rig and offered them off-the-books cash to borrow their helicopter.

"Where do you want to go?" he was asked.

"To Paris."

GIDDING WAS FLOWN TO Paris. The spring fashion shows were being held and he attended three on the same day. During the third show, Givenchy's, Gidding found his new Mephistopheles.

Her name was Soline Djahidra, a twenty-three-year-old French woman of North African extraction. After the show, Gidding went backstage and sought her out. He introduced himself, explained that he needed a new actress for a movie he was in the middle of making and that there was a helicopter waiting. She had five minutes to ask any questions, he said, after which it must be a simple yes or no.

She asked no questions and said yes.

Soline Djahidra had never acted a day in her life, not even in school. Asked afterward how he had chosen her, Gidding said that she was the only woman he had seen on the runway that day whose entire character was not known to him within the first five seconds.

When he returned to Rothermore he found Mallory still there, apparently in the belief that the director would relent. She took one look at Soline Djahidra disembarking from the helicopter and realized that the end had come. Gidding paid the pilot to take her away with him.

The next day they began reshooting the film from the start.

Things improved, even the weather. Gidding's direction to Soline was little more than "be yourself"—by general agreement she fell into the role as if born for it. The crew sensed that the movie was beginning to come together and morale, miserable for the best part of a year, began to improve. But then tragedy struck.

They were filming outdoors, a scene in which Mephistopheles, as a demonstration of the power over nature she can offer the prevaricating Faust, provides him with a modern firearm with which to kill a wild boar. A gaffer and a soundman were standing a little apart from the others, on a ledge. When Faust shot the boar the ledge, perhaps loosened by the crack of the gunshot, gave way. The two men plunged five hundred feet to their deaths on the rocks below.

All eyes were glued to the space where a moment before the ledge had been, the only sound the bellowing of the wounded boar. Gidding had calmly turned back around and said, "Keep rolling."

A short pause of disbelief, then the cameraman had resumed filming, and the actors finished the scene.

Gidding achieved what he wanted that day: the scene had called for Faust's horrified reaction at the animal's agonized death throes—seeing in it a harbinger of his own ceaseless torments to come—and horror was what he got. But his crew never looked at him in the same way again.

Andromeda thinks about this for a long time. The general reaction was to confirm the opinion that had first been applied with *The Fire Lotus*: "Heartless Monster" one headline read; "Cold-blooded Megalomaniac" exclaimed another. Certainly Gidding was relentless in the pursuit of his work, and Andromeda had her own reasons for knowing just how determined he can be, but in the end she considers herself in no position to judge his actions that day.

The most recent articles concern what *France Dimanche* had labeled as Gidding's "latest outrage": the media preview in London. It was not a premiere because *Faust* was not yet complete. Instead, Gidding had previewed three rough-cut scenes to an eager press, ravenous like jackals for morsels from this already infamously cursed carcass. It was the third scene that caused the furor. Given that the movie was not yet released, the audience that night had been under an injunction against revealing details, but whatever it was caused the *Christian Science Monitor*'s critic to characterize the third scene as *a combination of obscenity and blasphemy hitherto unknown in the annals of cinema.*

Andromeda suspected a publicity stunt. Who but someone hoping for bad press would have invited a movie critic from the *Christian Science Monitor*? How did that crowd of protesters find out about the preview? And how did they know that there was anything to protest against to begin with?

Gidding, or Gidding's publicity people, had gotten what they wanted: the same story is repeated endlessly on dozens of websites. Most of the articles are identical word for word, the simple copy-and-pasting of someone else's work. But among these endless plagiarisms Andromeda finds a real article, something that somebody researched and wrote for themselves.

> *Last week in London, Orlando Gidding offered a glimpse of his upcoming movie* Faust *(full title:* The Tragical History of the Life and Death of Doctor Faustus, *alluding to the film's foundation in Marlowe rather than Goethe). It was not the entire movie on show, just a preview—a result of the competition rules at Cannes, which include the requirement that the film not have been premiered anywhere outside the country of origin. Gidding has already announced his intention to submit the film to Cannes, the first time he will premiere one of his works anywhere other than Venice. What is less clear is the film's country of origin: Gidding is an American who maintains his residence in France, the film was shot mostly in Scotland, but some of the interiors were executed at the Cinecittà studios in Rome. What is the country of origin? Perhaps Gidding decided to play it safe, and simply not show the film at all—certainly, the preview was little more than a trailer.*
>
> *Whatever the case, there is no doubt that at Cannes Gidding will be aiming for the Palme d'Or—the* ne plus ultra *of serious movie-making—an award that has validated the greatest films of the greatest American directors for the past fifty years: Scorsese's* Taxi Driver, *Coppola's* Apocalypse Now, *Lynch's* Wild at Heart, *and Tarantino's* Pulp Fiction.
>
> *The film might premiere in Cannes, but Venice need not feel snubbed—after the furor following the London preview, Gidding retreated to the city that has always succored him, reportedly renting a small island in the lagoon, no longer inhabited, where he set up a studio in the only remaining building, an abandoned palazzo, to*

> *finish the soundtrack and editing. Perhaps, after two years spent filming* Faust *amid the desolation of Scotland's Rothermore Island, an abandoned palazzo in Venice will seem like luxury. But any discomfort won't be for long: submissions to Cannes are traditionally due by the second Monday in March.*

Andromeda reads that last line twice, and suddenly realizes where her deadline must have come from; the fact that it matches the date for submissions to Cannes—even down to the expression "second Monday in March"—cannot be a coincidence. She goes to the Cannes Film Festival website and reads through the competition rules. Article Four states that once a film has been submitted it cannot be withdrawn—whoever her employer is wants the evidence in hand to reveal once Gidding's film is in competition, thereby cutting off the possibility of a graceful retreat.

Andromeda puts aside the computer and sits back. An official from the nearby Chancellerie has stepped out onto his balcony. He has a small espresso cup and saucer in hand. He studiously ignores Andromeda while pretending to gaze out over the square in quiet ministerial contemplation, but she can tell that he has noticed something is not quite right with her face. The sun is beginning to drop behind the buildings on the southwest corner of the square, and already the air is taking on the first fresh chill of evening, not an unpleasant feeling on naked flesh still warm, but soon she would have been forced inside anyway. She retreats into her room.

Andromeda lies on the bed and thinks through what she has learned. She is less sure of who her employer might be now. To dig away at scandal is one thing, but whoever is behind this wants to engineer the scandal for maximum effect, and cost is no object—to Andromeda it feels less a publication peddling sleaze than a person plotting revenge. Given his many enemies, figuring out who that individual is would be a monumental task. But at least the last article has made one thing clear: if she is to find Orlando Gidding she must go to Venice.

— PART II —

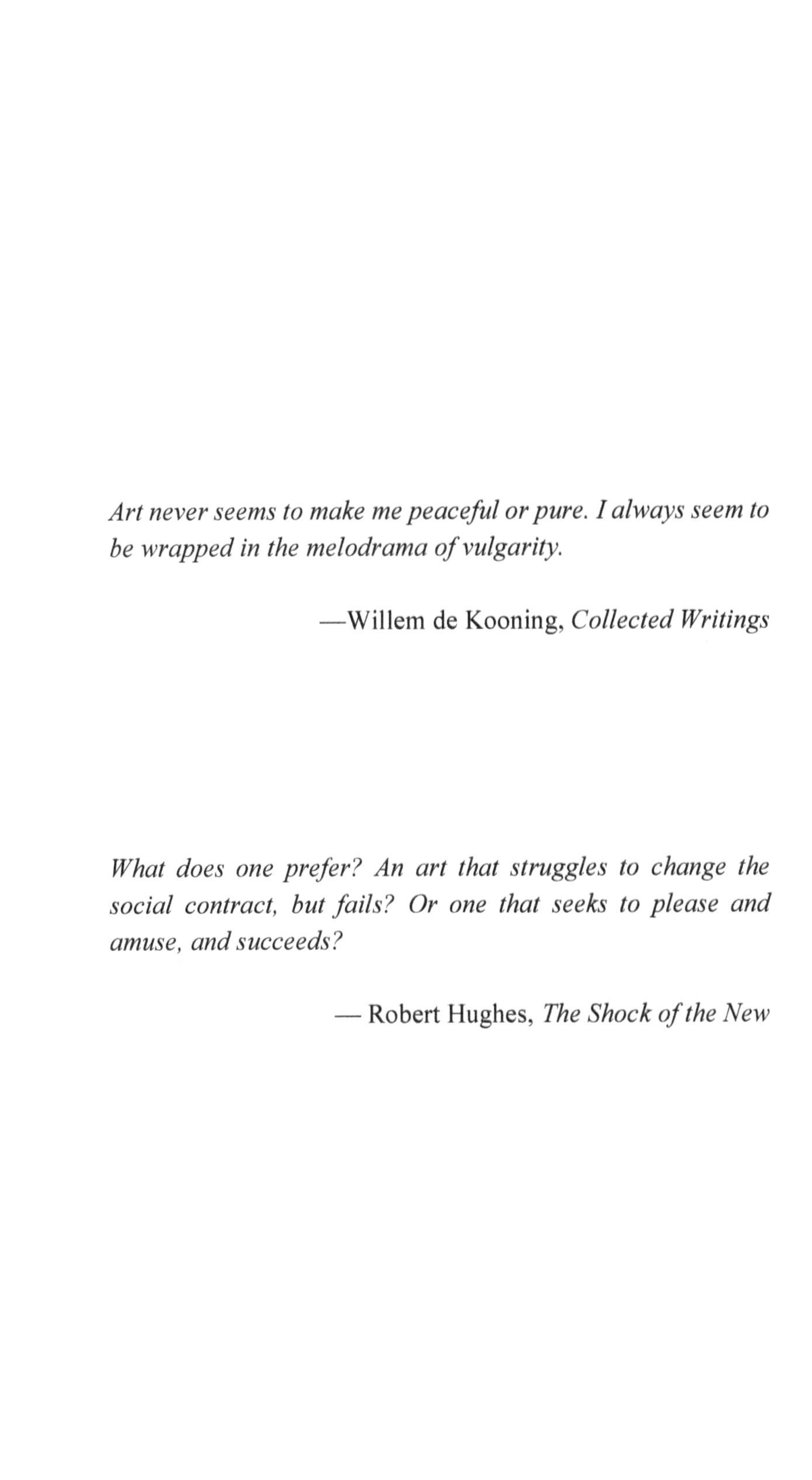

Art never seems to make me peaceful or pure. I always seem to be wrapped in the melodrama of vulgarity.

—Willem de Kooning, *Collected Writings*

What does one prefer? An art that struggles to change the social contract, but fails? Or one that seeks to please and amuse, and succeeds?

— Robert Hughes, *The Shock of the New*

XVIII

THE WAITER STEPS out onto the deck of the Hotel Bauer, walking briskly, although just a single table is occupied. He wears a white apron and holds a silver tray bearing a tapering stemmed glass glittering in the brilliant winter sunlight. He serves the lone customer on the terrace this afternoon, a slender woman leaning back with her legs crossed, the only person to have come outside despite the chill, and he cannot help inspecting her as he does so.

Double-breasted charcoal woolen suit whose short skirt reveals long black-stockinged legs. Black turtleneck, black knee-high boots. Soft leather gloves. Dark sunglasses. On her right cheek is a scar that the turned-up collar was probably meant to conceal. Too young to have earned her own way onto the Bauer's expensive canal-side terrace, but nor is there any hint of smug trust-fund entitlement—a millionaire's mistress, he concludes, waiting for her lover to arrive.

He retires, and Andromeda sips her prosecco while watching the traffic pass by on the Grand Canal. There are gondolas of course, including a *traghetto* making its slow passage across the canal from Dorsoduro, the passengers in dark overcoats standing with quiet dignity, as if for a funeral. The tourist gondolas are filled with loud people in colorful costumes, and Andromeda realizes that she has come to Venice during Carnival. There are more prosaic sights, too: chugging *vaporetti*, gray-painted Guardia di Finanza boats, a flat-bottomed barge full of fresh produce coming in from the mainland, and a garbage scow headed back the other way, returning the leftovers. A *vaporetto* pulls into Santa Maria della Salute, across the water from where she sits, and Andromeda wonders if the passengers realize how privileged they are to live in a city in which the buses are boats, or perhaps they secretly long for asphalt and exhaust fumes. Occasionally, a speedboat comes by, beautifully crafted like the one the hotel sent to pick her up from the airport an hour earlier, wood varnished so smoothly that it shines like satin, inboard motors rumbling deeply.

In Venice, even the boats are works of art.

As is the hotel, an elegant Venetian palazzo, crumbling plaster and exposed brick framing Fifteenth-century Moorish windows, a reminder that Venice once ruled half the Mediterranean.

Andromeda removes her glasses, allowing the sun to shine full upon her face. She breathes deeply, smelling brine and moss, lavender water that someone used when ironing the tablecloth, old stone, flowers somewhere. She feels comfortable on this terrace, in this city. It is like Manhattan in a way: another city-state lying off the coast of a continent, another place unlike anywhere else. She wonders if her attraction to such cities reflects a character flaw, as if unable to fit into the mainstream she is destined to live life on the margins—figuratively at least, although perhaps also on real islands, literal and littoral, somewhere physically out of other people's way. Like Hemingway in Cuba or Key West.

Andromeda pushes the thought aside; the prosecco tastes of promise and Venice urges forgetfulness. She is calm considering all that has happened; in the last week her life has been turned upside down, and the abruptness of the change has made it seem almost unreal, as if she were just an accidental player in a giant game of make-believe, something in which no one really gets hurt. Any reasonable person would have quit by now.

Andromeda will not quit, but she will take precautions. The first of these has been to notify Renzitti that there have been some odd developments and that from now on she will report in every twenty-four hours. He naturally wanted details but she was unwilling to give them, and certainly not to name the Gidding connection, since anything she told him would inevitably get back to his client and she has not yet decided how much she will reveal. But she has installed a GPS tracking application on her phone, and if she fails to report in Renzitti has agreed to use it to locate her whereabouts and alert the local authorities.

Clouds rise above Dorsoduro, great Tiepolo-like confections that do not so much obscure light as diffuse it, so that the city is suddenly bathed in a soft golden glow. The surface of the canal briefly turns into a shimmering copper-green, light that no art could capture, nor even a camera, light that is inseparable from movement. Andromeda watches it dance and then fade, a momentary fragment in time and space, immensely beautiful, something worth a thousand Titians.

She empties her glass and signals for the check.

THE LIBRERIA MARCIANA is not open to the public, and entrance normally requires a letter of introduction validating the research credentials of the bearer, but Renzitti's people have arranged an appointment for Andromeda. The attendant at the front door finds her name on the list. He directs Andromeda to the librarian's desk where she asks, "*Dove sono di carti della laguna?*"—her best guess at the Italian for, "Where can I find charts of the lagoon?"

Two hours later, in the courtyard of the old Zecca—glass-roofed and converted into a light-filled reading room—Andromeda sits at a large table with a dozen maps laid out in front of her. The most recent is from the last census, a simple way to determine if an island is abandoned. Two of the charts date from the early Nineteenth Century. One shows Napoleon's naval fortifications, built after he captured Venice and brought an end to the long history of the proud Republic. The second post-dates the Congress of Vienna, with the French now out and the Austrians now in.

Andromeda considers what she has discovered. Four locations potentially fit the description "a small island in the lagoon, no longer inhabited," on which Gidding could have used for his studio "the only remaining building, an abandoned palazzo." The first is Poveglia, a former *lazaretto*—a quarantine station for plague victims during the Black Death—where those who succumbed were thrown into pits by the hundred. It was later converted into a lunatic asylum where a particular doctor, who took pleasure in torturing his patients, eventually committed suicide by flinging himself from the tower. A suitable place to edit *Faust*, Andromeda thinks, and the building there is mostly intact. The island is listed as 75,000 square meters, which for comparison Andromeda calculates would be about the size of the Sheep Meadow in Central Park. She decides that it will be her upper limit for the definition of "small."

Isola di San Giorgio in Alga is her second guess, a former monastery and political prison, about a fifth the size of Poveglia. Next is a series of *ottagoni*, small islands fortified into the shape of an octagon and one of which, the privately-owned Ottagono Barberoni, seems a good possibility.

The first three candidates are located to the south of the city but the fourth and final is at the other end of the lagoon, past Burano and Torcello and far from tourist sights or boat traffic. Modern maps list it as Isola della Piselli—a bucolic "Island of Peas"—but on an old *Cinquecento*-era chart Andromeda finds it labeled as Isola Bisi. A little research reveals that *bìsi* means peas in the Venetian dialect, but *bisi*, without the accent, is the plural of the Venetian word *bisa*, snake. The depiction of a serpent on the chart leaves little doubt as to which meaning was originally intended. References to it are few, but Andromeda finds one item describing it as the former home of the

Dogandili family, an aristocratic clan listed in the Golden Book but nevertheless ousted from the city for unspecified crimes around the year 1500. They subsequently built a palazzo in exile on the Island of Snakes and apparently continued their debaucheries, now unchecked by Republican oversight or Inquisitorial interference. In 1572, the Senate—perhaps feeling the need for a robust housecleaning following the victory at Lepanto—had them all put to death "for the general good," and the island had been left to the snakes ever since.

Andromeda decides to leave it for last, although it is the only candidate with a genuine palazzo.

WHEN ANDROMEDA RETURNS to the Bauer she finds that an envelope has been pushed under her door. She sits at the secretaire by the window to inspect it. The envelope is addressed in an elegant script to *Signora* Andromeda Chamberlain. No address and no stamp—it was delivered by hand. The paper is of high quality, with the interior of the envelope marble-lined. Inside is a single stiff sheet of matching paper. It is in Italian and is apparently a ticket to a ball, a masked ball.

Andromeda puts the ticket back into the envelope and takes it downstairs to the concierge.

"I think there's been a mistake," she says, passing him the envelope. "I didn't purchase a ticket to this ball."

The concierge withdraws the sheet of paper, and as he reads his expression changes from puzzlement to understanding.

"There is no mistake, *Signora* Chamberlain. This is not a ticket but an invitation."

"I don't understand."

"This is not a ball to which one may buy a ticket. It is a private ball, by invitation only. You have been invited."

"But I don't know anyone here."

"The host is Mr. Jasper Slade, the well-known financier. Every year during *Carnevale* he hosts a ball, a favorite of *il bel mondo*." He pauses, thinking of a translation. "The international jet set, you understand? You are most fortunate, madam, for it is very exclusive."

"I've never met Jasper Slade."

He shrugs his shoulders, as if to say that the caprices of the international jet set were beyond understanding. He replaces the contents and returns the envelope to Andromeda.

"Perhaps it is not unheard of for an attractive young woman to receive such an invitation," he says.

Understanding dawns upon her. No doubt the financier likes to populate his party with single women, but they would need to be women who fit in, women who are affluent and worldly, the sort of women who would routinely stay at a place like the Bauer. She assumes that, for an appropriate consideration, the concierges of Venice's better hotels are enlisted to ensure that invitations are distributed to potential candidates.

The concierge reaches behind the counter, emerging with a card that he passes to Andromeda. It is for a business called Atelier della Luna dealing in *costumi teatrali*. "Should you require assistance with a costume and mask, we can recommend this establishment."

"Thank you," she says, accepting the card. "You've been very helpful."

Andromeda returns to her room. Between the financier's considerations and kickbacks from the costumers, she imagines that the concierge probably lives in a palazzo of his own.

Andromeda discovers that in her absence a book has been left on the nightstand, something that at first she mistakes for a Gideon's Bible, but which turns out to be a volume of Ezra Pound.

She picks it up and examines it, wondering how this book came to be in her room. A preface summarizes the poet's life: American born;

first published at 23; leader of the London expatriates at 25; scourge of capitalism at 33; Parisian Jazz Age exile at 36; Italian fascist at 39; imprisoned for treason at 61; declared insane at 62; released at 74; dead at 87. He had been taken underwing by Yeats, was a friend of Joyce, a mentor to Eliot, and a drinking companion of Hemingway, all the while writing and irascible. In 1933, *Time* magazine had described him as *a cat that walks by himself, tenaciously unhousebroken, and very unsafe for children*—here was a life! He was buried in Venice after having lived the last dozen years of his turbulent existence in the city—the only place left on the planet that he could tolerate, and could tolerate him. Andromeda realizes that the hotel must have supplied the book—probably it is the standard for their English-speaking guests; perhaps the French get Proust, the Germans Thomas Mann.

Andromeda tucks herself in with the volume, looking forward to the pleasure of a good book in a feather bed, but the jet lag finally catches up with her and she is asleep by Canto III.

XIX

THE MORNING IS CLOUDLESS and warm enough for Andromeda to have breakfast on the rooftop terrace. She checks the arts section of the *International Herald Tribune* in case by fortunate coincidence there is an article on the upcoming *Faust*, including details of where its director has isolated himself while editing it, but there is no such thing. She closes the paper and sits back with her coffee to consider the day.

The bulk of it will be spent on the water searching the islands of the lagoon; Andromeda will ask the concierge to arrange a boat. She had initially dismissed the invitation to the masked ball, but now reconsiders. If *il bel mondo* is in attendance, then someone there might be sufficiently acquainted with Gidding to know where he has holed up; perhaps the director himself has been invited, although from what she has read of him Gidding does not appear to be the ball-going type. The only cost would be a little time lost to arrange the costume. Andromeda takes the business card from her pocket and looks on the back where, like most business cards in serpentine Venice, there is a map, this one showing how to get to the Atelier della Luna from Saint Mark's square.

THE ATELIER DELLA LUNA is located on the second floor of a mustard-stuccoed building amid the maze of alleyways behind La Fenice. On arrival Andromeda is immediately taken in hand by the owner, an imperious madam who observes and instructs, and two young assistants, who obediently fetch and dress.

A multitude of costumes come and go; Andromeda is laced and tucked and fluffed, but her opinion is rarely sought. A process that she had assumed would take just a few minutes stretches to well over an hour. Finally, after several false starts—during which for a moment madam had appeared satisfied, only at the last minute to shake her head in discontent over some disqualifying unsuitability, visible only to her—the costume and accessories are decided upon; they will be delivered to the hotel.

When Andromeda eventually emerges from the atelier, it is into a startling new world. The sunshine of the morning has disappeared completely, replaced by a dense fog that has apparently rolled in off the Adriatic while she was inside. Andromeda can see no more than twenty feet.

She cautiously makes her way back to the hotel—a feat of navigation in the fog, even with a map. From her room she can see nothing of the water, although the hotel is right on the Grand Canal. Andromeda realizes that her plans for exploring the lagoon are on hold for now.

She sits and studies a street map, wondering what to do until the fog lifts. There are Saint Mark's and I Frari and the Accademia, but she does not feel like being indoors today, no matter what the weather.

Her eyes fall upon the volume of poetry lying on the bedside table, the envelope with the invitation to tonight's ball acting as a temporary bookmark.

Andromeda decides that she will pay a visit to San Michele and call on Mr. Pound.

IT IS A SIMPLE GRAVE, just a small stone plaque in the ground bearing the words *Ezra Pound*—not even dates, something befitting a man who had already said all he had to say over 87 long years and 120 long Cantos. San Michele is peaceful after the bustle of the city, the walls and cypresses suppressing all sound, even the bells and horns of the lagoon. Standing alone at the grave, she can hear the faint grind of fine gravel beneath her feet as her weight shifts.

Getting to the island had been surprisingly easy, despite the fog. The *vaporetto* to the Fondamenta Nuove had been only half full—on a day like today the tourists would instead crowd into the churches and galleries and *scuole*. The smaller *motoscafo* going across to Cimitero had been all but empty. Finding the grave had been more difficult, a maze of little pathways among tombs that after a while all looked alike, the fog turning the cemetery into a mysterious labyrinth.

There is a vase beside the plaque. Andromeda wishes that she had thought to bring flowers. An offering, although she is not sure to what—not the poetry in particular, and certainly not Pound's politics, but she would like to have made some little obeisance to a mind so ferociously independent that it had chosen insanity over submission. Perhaps it is sufficient that he is remembered.

Andromeda decides to read one of his poems instead. She opens the book at random and begins reciting in a whisper, just loud enough for Pound's ghost to take pleasure in the sound of someone reading his own verse. Then she hears the crunch of gravel away to her right. She is not alone.

The noise came from behind a small stand of cypresses, at the edge of visibility. It stopped abruptly, the furtive halt of a person freezing as soon as making the sound. Someone is watching her.

Andromeda immediately turns left and sets off at a brisk pace. She has no idea where she is going; she just wants to get away. Behind her she can hear the footsteps of whoever is following. Andromeda begins turning haphazardly, hoping to come upon the buildings at the cemetery's entrance, back with people and a *motoscafo* stop, or at least to recognize something. But in the diaphanous light everything looks the same: endless swirling mists pierced by veiled shadows that resolve themselves into gravestones or trees or tombs topped with wing-spread marble angels.

Andromeda realizes that if she can hear her pursuer, then her pursuer can hear her. That is how he is able to trail her in the fog, by following the sound. She passes a tomb, a large one meant not for individuals but entire families. The iron gate is open. Andromeda ducks in and immediately presses against the wall to the side, out of sight. She hears the approach of footsteps on the path outside. They go past, but then stop. Her pursuer is listening, wondering where she has gone. Then she hears the footsteps come back, slower now. Whoever is following her has noticed the open gate.

The footsteps come to a halt outside. Andromeda realizes what a foolish mistake it was to have allowed herself to become entrapped inside a tomb. She holds her breath. She waits for what seems a long time, but there is no further sound from outside. There is a sudden flash of bright white light: the person has taken a photograph. Then she hears the footsteps walking away. Andromeda slowly slides down to the floor, sitting while allowing her heart to resume its normal rhythm.

No one was pursuing her, she realizes. A tourist had simply been visiting graves, like her. He or she was no doubt as lost as Andromeda and had probably followed her in the hope of finding a way back to the entrance. And like most tourists in these digital times the person snapped away at everything, however trivial, including a fortuitously open tomb.

Much later, when Andromeda has recovered and found her way back to the *motoscafo* stop, she realizes that the book is missing. Andromeda thought she had thrust it into her bag while fleeing; in her anxiety to get away she had instead dropped it. If she could have retraced her steps to search she would have done so, but in the fog it would be impossible. Instead, she waits for the *motoscafo*. She looks around for a lone tourist, but all the other people are in groups. Whoever followed her is probably already on a boat back to Venice by now, unaware of the fright they had given to a girl all alone at the grave of Ezra Pound.

XX

A SLEEK MOTORBOAT, LYING low in the water, glides up to the landing. The vessel has been hand-crafted in the Cantiere Motonautico Serenella of Murano, and so is an inheritor of the Venetian Republic's naval traditions. The sides are of African mahogany, the interior is paneled in burled walnut. The fittings are made of chromed brass whose castings have remained unchanged for a century. It will outsurvive the man who owns it. It is varnished and polished and reflects the moonlight reflecting off the Grand Canal. At the stem is a small mast with a flag bearing the winged lion of Venice; at the stern another, larger, this one with the Italian tricolor.

The captain stands in the open cockpit forward, maneuvering the vessel without using the wheel, touching ahead or astern on the twin throttles connected to the two inboard diesels rumbling at idle behind him, and which if needed can send his boat up onto the plane and racing at thirty knots across the lagoon to the Lido. But not tonight; it is a short passage tonight, and he will be constrained by the speed limits on the canals.

He is wearing an officer's cap and uniform, for this is an important destination, and so his passengers will be important people. But when he has the boat safely alongside he looks up to find not the middle-aged and well-fed group of partygoers he had expected, but instead a lone woman, a young woman. She is obviously slender despite the many petticoats puffing out the lower half of her ball gown. Often the women who board his boat on their way to a ball have barely managed to stuff their ample flesh into their costumes, but not this one. When the Bauer's porter hands her down to the deck the weight of her body barely rocks his boat.

He wishes that he could have seen her by day. Then, as if having read his mind, she leans down close to him. The moonlight is full upon her face.

"Ca' d'Inverno," she says quietly.

She is not Venetian but she uses the Venetian term for a palace—*ca'*, a shortening of the word *casa*—used back in the days when the term *palazzo* was reserved for the residence of the doge alone. He knows the destination already—the Bauer people told him when they called to make the booking—but he is grateful for the opportunity to have seen that face more closely.

A remote face, in the way that genuine beauty always is; the real thing is never easily accessible. Wide mouth, clear uncertain eyes; he wonders what color they are in daylight. And that scar—perhaps she has been to the Ca' d'Inverno before.

The woman walks aft, confident despite the restrictions of Seventeenth-Century garments and the rocking motion of the boat. He waits until she has settled herself into the cabin, then with a practiced flick of the throttles he kicks the boat out away from the landing and gets underway.

As they cruise down the Grand Canal the captain turns the destination over in his mind. Palazzo d'Inverno: the Winter Palace. Or Palazzo d'Inferno, as people have come to call the place since Jasper Slade took it over. Slade was a cruel man, it was said. Jasper de Sade, according to one newspaper. But the captain is doubtful—people like to make up stories, and if all the rumors about the things that went on inside the Palazzo d'Inverno were true, then Slade would have had cloven hooves instead of feet.

XXI

ANDROMEDA'S BOAT ARRIVES at the palazzo, blackened tide marks at the waterline, moonlit stone above. There are lanterns on the landing, torches on either side of the entrance, candlelight within. No electricity; the palazzo is lit by flame alone. Other motorboats are lying off, coming to the landing one at a time to discharge their passengers. Soon it is their turn, and the captain pulls the boat gently alongside. An attendant wearing buckled shoes and a powdered wig bends to take the hand of the passenger as she alights. He escorts her down the landing and through to the lobby, where he takes her cape. She checks herself briefly in the lobby mirror, realizes that she has forgotten to put on her mask, and quickly does so before entering the ballroom and joining the other guests.

The ballroom is two stories tall, with a mezzanine around the upper level. At the far side is a marble staircase leading up and splitting into two before reaching the gallery. Hanging from the ceiling is a large crystal chandelier set with thin tapering candles, hundreds of them. The walls are paneled and painted in Rococo profusion; she has read up on the palace and knows that they were executed by the workshop of G.B. Tiepolo, some figures painted by the master himself.

She is not late but the room is already full of the bejeweled and bewigged. A small chamber ensemble plays in one corner. A juggler entertains in another. There is an air of anticipation: the murmur of an expectant theater crowd aware that the curtain will soon go up on the main event.

Faces turn to inspect the new arrival. They see a young woman in a dress of burnished bronze silk overlaid with golden lace, elegant but not overwrought, a tight bodice narrow at the waist and cut low, stiffly stayed. (She had to ask the Bauer to send someone up to help her put it on; then the two of them laughing as the maid, lying on the bed with her stockinged feet jammed into Andromeda's back, had pulled ever tighter on the lacing.) Three-quarter length sleeves finished in lace trim, from which emerge long narrow arms bereft of jewelry. No wig. Her hair is up, topped with a dainty tricorn hat sporting elegant ostrich plumes.

A waiter comes forward and she accepts a glass of champagne. At a regular ball she would have expected to be greeted by the host, but the aim of a masked ball is anonymity. Since it is a private palazzo whose artwork would not normally be accessible, she takes the opportunity to inspect the paneling. It is ornate, overpopulated by fat little *putti*, and ultimately forgettable.

A man joins her briefly, apparently also inspecting the panels, but when she turns in anticipation of a comment he playfully kisses her instead. Then a smile and a tilt of his glass in salute, and he is off, apparently in pursuit of further purloined kisses. She is left laughing with the *putti*.

There is a game; she is invited. Some form of blind man's bluff, and soon it is she who is blindfolded. It becomes apparent that the game is less a sport than an excuse for surreptitious fondling, but her stays remain secure long enough for her to successfully negotiate her turn. When another woman is at the center of attention she quietly slips away.

One of the salons on the side has food. She has drunk two glasses of champagne by now and decides that food would be a good idea. There are long tables around the sides with chefs and servers standing behind them in crisp white linens, the only people tonight not in Seventeenth-Century dress. They offer small plates of Venetian specialties that can be eaten while standing. She selects *sarde in saor*, preserved sardines—she has already been kissed and fondled without invitation; perhaps sardine breath will discourage further assaults upon her virtue.

She takes her glass and plate, and goes out onto the landing to eat. The motorboats are gone now, and the only sound besides the dull noise of the ball behind her is the gentle lapping of the water. The Rialto glows in the distance, moonlight on white marble. It is cold outside, but the cold is refreshing after the warmth within.

She eats her sardines.

She enjoys the moonlight on the canal, a little patch of lingering fog, the flickering of the torches.

Suddenly there is someone beside her. She turns, fearing being kissed or pinched while caught with a mouthful of food. But her companion is an elderly gentleman, an impish little man smiling a cunning smile. He is without a mask and wears evening dress instead of a costume. Andromeda is reminded of Houdon's *Voltaire*, the face drawn back at the sides, as if the result of an unsuccessful facelift, elongating the eyes and mouth, giving him a vaguely reptilian air.

"Madam, I observe that you have something no other woman here this evening possesses," he says.

"And what might that be?"

"A form so fine that it must remain unadorned with jewelry. I congratulate you."

She laughs and takes the last forkful of sardines. It is true, she realizes, the unadorned part. The other women are slathered with precious stones set in precious metal.

"I can't afford such things," Andromeda admits. "I'm not sure why I was invited."

"You do not know our host?"

"No, do you?"

"Yes. If you wish, I will tell you about him."

"Yes, please do."

She rests her empty plate on the rail. He pulls out a cigarette case—silver, engraved. Andromeda realizes that he has come outside to smoke, and politely waited for her to finish eating before doing so. He offers her one.

"No, thank you."

"You will not smoke?"

"No."

"Ah, but it is *Carnevale*, and these are special cigarettes. I encourage you to indulge yourself."

She looks down at the open case. The cigarettes are unusual: they are black, with long filters of gold.

"What are they?"

"Sobranie Black Russians: the Tolstoyan aristocracy of tobacco. Smoke one, and for an evening you will be Anna Karenina."

She laughs and takes one. The paper is stiff and thick and the cigarette feels surprisingly dense. He takes out a lighter and holds it open for her before lighting his own cigarette. She puffs, strikes a pose that she hopes is more Lauren Bacall than Lucille Ball, and tries not to cough.

"Are you familiar with the name Jasper Slade?" he asks.

"A financier, I think."

"Just so, he runs the Prometheus Portfolio—a well-known hedge fund, large and aggressive, viewed with distrust by many people, and some governments."

"Isn't he under some sort of legal cloud?"

"Very much so," the man tells her. "In fact—and at the risk of sounding overly dramatic—I must tell you that our host tonight is a fugitive from justice." He puts great emphasis on the last three words, mocking himself and much else besides. Andromeda finds herself taking a liking to this little old man, who clearly takes life and men's truths with a grain of salt.

"He's doing pretty well for someone on the lam," she says, glancing over her shoulder at the palazzo behind them.

"Indeed. But I understand that when he went on the lam, as you put it, he had the good sense to make sure that the money went on the lam with him."

"What did he do?"

"He was indicted for tax evasion. Plus, he was charged with some technical breaches of securities trading laws. But what really irritated the authorities was something else: he was accused of doing deals with the Iranians in violation of the sanctions. Slade apparently failed to understand that doing deals with the Iranians in violation of the sanctions is a privilege that the government reserved for itself."

"Do you think that any of it is true?"

"I think that some of it is true. He would not have exiled himself to Switzerland if it were not. Do you know that he has not set foot in the United States since he fled, more than thirty years ago?"

"They can't get him extradited?"

"The Swiss extradite poor criminals only."

"The Italians?"

"Perhaps once. But not now. You see, Jasper Slade has been pardoned."

Andromeda recalls it. There had been a great scandal at the time: an outgoing president had granted the pardon at the last minute, in the way that they do. By coincidence, he had just received a large donation for the new presidential library from the same source.

"Then he's no longer a fugitive?"

"Not exactly. You see, madam, presidential pardons apply only to federal crimes. However, the state of New York made it clear that the pardon means nothing to them: if Jasper Slade were ever to set foot on American soil, they would seek his immediate arrest and interstate extradition to face trial. So, as a practical matter, it is *status quo ante*: he is barred from returning to the United States." The old man flashes his cunning smile. "I suspect that the presidential pardon is the worst investment Jasper Slade ever made, don't you?"

She nods in agreement. He finishes his cigarette and turns to her.

"I hope that you will enjoy the rest of the evening, and not let our host's reputation alarm you. You are an American—think of it as getting some of those unpaid taxes back."

"I will. Thank you."

The old man makes a courteous little bow and retreats inside. Andromeda disposes of the remainder of her cigarette and finishes her champagne in thoughtful solitude, watching the passage of an occasional gondola along the canal, or sometimes other partygoers passing by on the *fondamenta* across the way.

The noise from the ball has become louder and more raucous while she has been outside. She pulls up hard on the top of her low-cut gown, guessing that the fondling is probably not done with for the evening, and goes back inside.

XXII

ANDROMEDA RETURNS to the ballroom. The juggler has been replaced by a troupe of acrobats around which a small crowd has gathered. The troupe is composed of two women and three men. All five are naked from the waist up. The men wear gymnastics pants with stirrups hooked under the soles of their feet. They look immensely strong, the muscles of their arms and chests and backs well defined, not with the awkward bulges of bodybuilders, but distinct and tautly drawn, like the flanks of a racehorse.

The two women are slender and petite. They wear boy-shorts of some thin lycra-like material. Like the men, they are well-toned. The troupe is obviously professional, and they perform a series of gymnastic demonstrations displaying strength and flexibility with seeming ease.

Andromeda joins the people watching them. One of the men goes to a small canvas bag in the corner and pats chalk powder onto his hands. He then lies supine upon the floor, forearms raised vertically, palms open. A girl takes a position astride him. She places her palms on top of his, then with a small jump lifts her feet from the floor and settles into a completely horizontal position inches above him, face down, legs straight out and toes pointed, supporting her entire weight on her arms alone, an impressive display of strength and balance. When she is settled, the man extends his arms until they are straight out, raised vertically, while the woman whose weight they support remains perfectly horizontal. Then she does what seems impossible: she rotates at the shoulders, her back and legs slowly rising from horizontal to vertical. The onlookers are impressed and clap appreciatively.

But it is not over. Vertical now, her face looking intently down into the face of the man supporting her, she begins to extend her arms. There are small gasps as several onlookers realize how difficult this must be. Andromeda can see the veins in her neck bulging with effort as, very slowly, careful to maintain balance, she performs a full handstand. When it is complete, the crowd claps more enthusiastically than ever. But there is more to come. The eyes of the performers have remained locked the entire time. The faintest of nods between them, then at the same instant they each suddenly release a hand, so that now she is performing a one-handed handstand, her weight supported entirely on his one arm. Every sinew and muscle in their arms and shoulders is visible, carved by the effort. Her chest is stretched flat, her rib cage protruding, her nipples small and hard, and Andromeda can see a bead of sweat drip from one of them down onto him.

Still, it has not ended. The man slowly raises his back until he is sitting up. Then he stands, the girl having maintained the single-handed handstand above him the entire time, something seemingly impossible.

Finally, it completes. The girl releases and flips over, landing lightly on her feet. The crowd claps and cheers, and Andromeda can see a smile pass between the performers. They bow to their audience. Then, as she straightens, the girl looks deliberately at Andromeda, her eyes narrowing, her face assuming a knowing smile, a look that is almost insolent in its familiarity. By the time her expression has fully registered in Andromeda's consciousness the girl has already looked away, and the troupe begins the next routine. Andromeda is left wondering if she imagined it.

She moves on, taking the grand staircase up to the mezzanine. A couple is flirting in the corner to the left. The man has the woman pinned with his arms on either side of her against the wall. She is wriggling, trying to escape, but is not putting any serious effort into it. He suggests something that makes her laugh out loud. Andromeda turns to the right to leave them alone, and enters the first salon leading off the gallery.

It is a large drawing room. Groups of people are scattered around, standing or lounging in sofas and chairs, drinking and talking. Waiters in wigs and breeches move about, keeping the guests supplied. One of them approaches her and offers more champagne, which she accepts. She surveys the room.

At a low coffee table surrounded by a long plush sofa and comfortably upholstered chairs a card game is underway. The stakes are high: all three women have surrendered clothing, and the one sitting in the middle of the sofa is already down to underwear. She apparently came prepared for the possibility of losing, for she is wearing beautiful undergarments, plus high-heeled shoes, and around her neck a long strand of pearls. Her underwear matches the pearls, not just in color but in sheen: the fabric is creamy and luminescent. The woman is dark-haired and very tanned, southern Italian perhaps, and the underwear looks good on her smooth brown skin.

The hand ends. There is laughing and clapping, and it is clear that La Perla will be further exposed. She grins widely, and her teeth are brilliant white. One of the men spies Andromeda. He stands and approaches. He gives off a faint air of unwholesomeness, something she finds common in European men, as if the rot of so much history had somehow entered their DNA. He puts an arm around her waist and with his mouth by her ear whisperingly invites her to join them. For fairness's sake, he explains, this can be accomplished at the initial cost of just her hat.

Andromeda smiles and declines the offer. The sardines are not working at all.

He returns to the game. Meanwhile, La Perla has discarded her top. She sits back smiling, casually twisting the pearls around a finger, her body elegant and inviting in the candlelight. Her breasts are round and full and as tanned as the rest of her—Andromeda imagines that she must spend much of her life cruising the Mediterranean, sunbathing topless. The two men sitting on either side of her are appreciative of what has been revealed, and they spend some moments in active admiration, much to her and the rest of the group's amusement, before the next hand is dealt.

Andromeda leaves the room and goes down the gallery to the adjoining salon.

There is gambling for more conventional stakes here: it has been set up as a casino. There are several tables, topped in green baize, two for blackjack, two for baccarat, one for chemin-de-fer, and a lone roulette wheel. The dealers are dressed in the same frock coats and breeches as the attendants elsewhere. A sign on an easel, in Italian above with an English translation beneath, reminds guests that all proceeds from tonight's ball will go to the Save Venice Foundation. The older guests, presumably the ones with the fattest wallets, have migrated to this room. It is nothing like a Las Vegas casino; the gambling here is quiet and decorous, an activity that accompanies rather than replaces conversation, both winning and losing being met with equal aplomb.

A cashier sits behind a small desk by the door. He invites Andromeda to inspect the chips, which he explains have been specially minted for the evening. She picks one up and is surprised by the weight. It is pure metal, gold, very ornate, and inlaid with the number 5 in what might be silver, or perhaps platinum. Others are inlaid with 10, 25, and 50. They are denominated in thousands of euros, the cashier explains—the minimum bet is 5,000 euros. She realizes that the Save Venice Foundation will likely do well out of the evening.

Andromeda thanks him and returns the chip, then goes to stand behind one of the baccarat tables, watching the play. Between hands, the man sitting in front of her takes the coaster from under his glass and writes a brief message on the back. He signals for a steward and quietly gives him instructions for delivery. The steward takes it around to the other baccarat table, where he leans down close by the ear of a woman, whispering while handing her the coaster. She reads it and smiles, then looks up and seeks out the man who wrote it. When she catches his eye she nods. She slips the coaster into her evening purse and with a quick word to her companion—a man so absorbed in the cards as to be unaware that she is being seduced under his nose—the woman excuses herself and leaves the room. The man in front of Andromeda soon follows.

Andromeda exits the gaming salon and continues her circumnavigation of the mezzanine. She passes by the front of the palace where French windows are set into a series of arches giving onto the Grand Canal. There is a narrow terrace outside, and on it the silhouette of a couple is visible, embraced. Perhaps the cornered girl and her pursuer have ended up there, or maybe that coaster had suggested the terrace for a rendezvous.

Andromeda continues to the far side. The wall here is pierced by a set of double doors, closed. There are voices on the other side. She tests the handle; the door opens a crack. It is much darker in this room, and she cannot see exactly what is happening. She slips inside, closing the door behind her.

It is a theater, of sorts. At the far end is a small stage with dark red velvet curtains hanging behind it. On either side are large freestanding candlesticks, whose dozen or so fat candles serve as the room's primary illumination. There is an audience, a score or more, dimly lit. At the back an opening leads to a second salon in which several small square-topped Arabian-style tents have been erected. The flap to the nearest one is open, and the interior is sumptuously outfitted with Oriental rugs, brocaded pillows, flowers in ornamental vases—a tent fit for a sultan.

The action taking place on stage is not a play but an auction. The article being auctioned is a woman, apparently a guest, still masked, smiling nervously.

In keeping with the Moorish theme suggested by the tents, the woman is flanked by two female attendants, tall and slender, shining black skin, Nubian perhaps. They are barefoot and bare-chested, wearing elaborate feathered headdresses and long skirts of white cloth like the fabric of the tents.

The auctioneer is at the side of the stage. He addresses the audience in a mixture of Italian and English, with an occasional phrase in French or German thrown in. It seems that technically what is being auctioned is a kiss. As with the casino, the proceeds will go to the Save Venice Foundation. The tents are provided for the winning bidder to take his prize in comfort and privacy.

The bidding begins, as with the gambling, at a minimum of 5,000 euros. The woman onstage is not especially attractive, but the bidding is spirited and she is encouraged by appreciative comments from the audience. Soon the bid has climbed to 20,000 euros, at which point a man in the back of the room not far from Andromeda is declared the winner. He stands and goes to the stage, where he offers his arm to the blushing prize. The audience claps loudly as he escorts her down past them and into a tent.

A new woman comes up and immediately has everyone's attention. She shows no discomfort at standing onstage in front of a room full of men, one hand casually on her hip and smiling with delight. The auctioneer is a fine judge of goods and urges the woman to "reveal herself for the benefit of Venice." With encouragement from the audience and the example of the Nubians beside her, she is soon undressing. This has the expected effect upon the bidding, and by the time the gavel comes down so too has all but her underwear, and the city is 45,000 euros richer.

The woman picks up her dress, but just drapes it over an arm and descends from the stage, not bothering to put on what will apparently be coming straight back off again.

Andromeda laughs—she had not realized that the evening was going to be quite so Stanley Kubrick.

Suddenly she finds herself joined by the Nubians, one on either side, escorting her toward the front of the room. She protests, but to no effect: either they do not understand her or have chosen not to. The auctioneer encourages the audience to encourage her, and by the time

Andromeda is brought onstage she realizes that to retreat now with dignity is no longer possible.

Andromeda submits to being auctioned.

She stands stiffly, facing the audience, hands clasped demurely in front of her in a posture of reluctant acceptance, one that Andromeda hopes will convey to potential purchasers that she would constitute a poor bargain. Yet her pose seems to have the opposite effect: the bidding is swift and active, and the auctioneer has trouble picking from the many raised hands which bid to next accept. As it progresses, Andromeda senses a subtle atmospheric shift in the room: it has changed from the good-humored banter of earlier into something more serious and competitive. Andromeda crosses her arms in disapproval, but this gesture serves only to redouble the bidding, and soon it is in six figures and soaring out of control. Even the auctioneer is taken aback, but he collects himself and allows it to continue. Eventually, it comes down to a battle between two men in the front row, an American and an Italian. It continues past 150,000 euros. Andromeda thinks it is ridiculous and wants it to stop, but it is too late and the bidding continues to spiral higher.

The American eventually bows out. The Italian, whose love of Venice must know no bounds, is declared the winner with a bid of 225,000 euros. He receives great applause, as if he had just conquered Everest or discovered penicillin. He turns to the audience and bows. The auctioneer thanks him on behalf of the city. At last, he turns and looks at Andromeda in silent appraisal, as if wondering exactly what it is that a quarter of a million dollars buys.

Andromeda descends from the stage and takes his arm. They walk to the back of the room, passing by the tent into which the previous woman had disappeared, and a gap in the flap of which reveals that she has elected to reward the winning bidder with more than just a kiss.

They enter an empty tent, and Andromeda is able to get a better look at the man who has purchased her. He wears a powdered wig tied off in the back with a black silk ribbon. His face is covered by a mask, also black, what the Venetians call a *bauta*, which has the section below the nose sharply angled away from the face, designed to allow eating and drinking while remaining masked, and a feature that gives the wearer a vaguely sinister air.

If he is to kiss her, she thinks, that mask will have to come off. She wonders what he will look like underneath.

He goes to a censer hanging from a tripod in the corner and lights it. The tent is soon filled with the odor of incense, pungent and aromatic. He asks if she would like a drink and she says that yes she would like champagne. He leaves to fetch it.

Andromeda inspects the interior of the tent. The frame is metal, supporting white cotton drapery whose edges have been trimmed with gold braid. The floor is piled with Persian carpets laid one on top of the other, providing a divan on which to recline. There are cushions and pillows of every size and shape: square, rectangular, triangular, cylindrical; sometimes covered in brocaded fabric, more often in soft silk. At the head of the bed thus formed is a chest on which sits a large vase filled with flowers, flowering reeds and branches several feet long, all carefully arranged to fan out over the interior, forming an enveloping canopy of flora above the bed.

There is a low table on one side and along the other a small cabinet. Andromeda opens one of the cabinet's doors and finds inside shelves lined with little crystal bottles in a variety of elegant designs, presumably Murano crystal. They are filled and labeled: frankincense, bergamot, Chanel No. 5. She opens the other door. There is a small Grecian urn inside—wide and shallow, something that Andromeda recalls from an art class long ago is called a *kylix*, intended for drinking wine while reclining. Black-figure; she cannot remember if black-figure antedates red-figure or the other way around, but in either case it would be worth a small fortune. She studies the exterior. It depicts a satyr and a nymph engaged in activities of the type museums place high up in the display case so that parents will be spared explaining the details to curious toddlers. He is pursuing her, rampant phallus leading the way. She rotates the kylix to see how the story turns out. The satyr catches the nymph, and in subsequent scenes proceeds to have his way with her in Attic variety. The bowl contains not wine but sexual paraphernalia, including little foil packets of lubricant that the nymph might have appreciated.

Andromeda takes the stopper from the frankincense, contemplating a dab of Biblical perfume, but it is too sharp to wear, and she settles instead for a little Number 5 on the wrists and behind the ears.

There is a small chryselephantine chest by the pillows, ivory inlaid with gold, the size of a jewelry box. She opens it. Inside there is a black velvet blindfold together with thick woven silk cords of the type once used to keep curtains back, but their presence here with the blindfold suggests another purpose. Andromeda closes the lid and replaces the box.

The man who purchased her returns. He carries a silver tray on which stands a bottle of champagne with a napkin wrapped around the neck, and two champagne flutes. He kneels by the low table, back to her, filling the glasses.

Andromeda arrays herself on the cushions. She will allow herself to be kissed of course, and perhaps a certain amount of exploration on his part as recompense for the outrageous price he has paid for her, thence relying on her tightly bound top and many protective petticoats to provide sufficient delaying action for an orderly retreat in the face of further assaults. She imagines allowing herself to be seduced, abandoning herself to nameless lovemaking with a nameless man. Masked sex, as anonymous as sex can be.

When he turns from the table it is not with a glass of champagne but with the napkin wadded up in his hand. He swiftly falls upon her, jamming it down over her face before she has time to react.

Andromeda struggles.

She claws ferociously at his face, but the *bauta* protects him. She summons all her strength to heave him from her, but finds that such strength as she possesses has already abandoned her—whatever was used to soak that cloth, intense and cloying, is disabling her with every breath. Chloroform, she supposes. And now she knows why he lit that censer: to disguise the smell. It is her last thought as she passes from consciousness.

XXIII

ANDROMEDA AWAKENS. She is disoriented, spinning. Her ears are full of white noise. She feels weightless, as if the laws of gravity have suddenly abandoned her and now—unrove from the world—she is spinning off into space, tumbling and tumbling away deep into the endless void, weightless matter spinning and falling through the vast dark emptiness.

The spinning slows and then stops. She is no longer falling. The white noise disappears, replaced by an echoing silence. All is quiet now, and still.

She is supine. Whatever she is lying on is flat, but too hard to be a bed. She has not yet opened her eyes but she can tell that she is bound, and there is a gag tied taut across her mouth. Her arms are stretched back over her head and secured with what feels like the smooth silk of the cords that she found in the tent. Her shoulders ache. The smell of whatever she was drugged with clings to her nostrils, unctuous and sweet. She feels cold and ill but realizes that with a gag she will likely drown on her own vomit if she were to be sick, and so she gives all her will to gaining control over the nausea.

Eventually it ebbs, and the smell of the anesthetic is slowly replaced by the odor of cool dank stone. Water drips somewhere, echoing—she is in a cellar perhaps, or a cistern. She opens her eyes.

There is a ceiling above her, vaulted, the ribs crossing and fading thirty feet overhead. The light is faint and unsteady, but she can see where water has seeped through the ceiling, cracking and pitting the plaster, exposing the brickwork behind. Wherever she is, it is an old room.

She turns her head to the right. The wall is a series of angled planes; the room is polygonal. There are no windows. She counts the sides. Six on this side, and so the room is twelve-sided: a dodecagon. Each side is embedded with a wall sconce impaled with candles—the room's only source of light. The space is not as large as the high ceiling suggests; it is as narrow as it is tall.

She turns her head to the left. The room is slightly different here: four of the six sections of wall end six or eight feet above the floor, and Andromeda has a sense that the open space beyond is occupied by several tiers of seats, a small theater in which the audience would look down into the space where she now lies. She cannot tell if any of the seats are occupied; the sconces on this side have been driven into the wooden pillars at the angles, and they are backed by reflectors of polished metal, intended to direct the light into the pit and so leaving the gallery behind in shadow.

But what holds her attention is not the space beyond the walls; it is the figure standing in front of them.

He is dressed in ball costume: black tricorn hat, frock coat and vest, breeches, and buckled shoes. His mask is of a traditional Venetian design called *Il Dottore della Peste*—the plague doctor—a mask with an exaggeratedly extended nose whose original purpose was to maintain distance between physician and patient in the time of pestilence, and whose long proboscis—half grotesque phallus, half beak of some curious but malevolent bird—retains a sinister air of ill portent.

It is not the man who drugged her. She does not know this man.

He is standing, one knee slightly bent, both hands casually resting on a walking stick in front of him, apparently content to study Andromeda as she studies him. The frock coat is plain black but the vest beneath is heavily brocaded with an abundance of metallic thread. The stick is polished ebony with a silver ferrule. She can see under the frock coat that he wears a dagger. The scabbard and hilt are jeweled and refract candlelight with the brilliance of genuine stones. This is not a tourist's rental costume.

Eventually, he speaks.

"Do you know what sort of room this is?"

Andromeda shakes her head.

"It is an anatomatoria," he says, "an anatomy room."

He has a Continental accent, but she cannot place the country. He brings the stick to his shoulder and begins to stroll casually around the perimeter of the room, slowly moving counterclockwise, talking conversationally as he walks.

"You have been brought to the Isola Bisi, the ancient seat of the Dogandili family after the family's head, Marc'Antonio Dogandili, was exiled from the city in the year 1522 for certain irregularities, one of which was an inordinate interest in anatomy. In those days the church frowned upon the dissection of corpses, you see. Boniface VIII had issued the papal bull *De Sepulturis*, specifically forbidding dissection and decreeing the punishment of excommunication upon anyone found guilty of its practice. But young Mark Antony, who inherited the title after the early—and some say suspicious—death of his father, was enamored of the new learning, and uncaring of the opinions of an irrelevancy in Rome. He persisted in the practice, and this was one of the reasons for his exile. Hence he had this room constructed in secret, the excavation attributed to the construction of a new family tomb, necessary now that members of the Dogandili clan could no longer be buried in Venice itself. The truth was known only to Moorish slaves brought in for the work, and who were sold off again when the task was complete. The entrance is concealed within the crypt, not a place with much passing foot traffic, but was nevertheless hidden in the paneling to ensure that it would remain undetected on those occasions when relatives were newly laid to rest."

From time to time he idly rolls the stick with his fingers as he walks, like a bandmaster twirling a baton. Andromeda twists her head to follow his progress, wanting to have something on which to focus to help quell the choking fear that is rising in her throat.

"As the years passed and the zeal of those who had ousted him waned, Dogandili would return to Venice, clandestinely at first, but later more openly as it became apparent that the authorities would tolerate his presence in the city, just not his residence. So it was that, despite his formal exile, Dogandili became part of the circle of Titian and Aretino and Sansovino, the fast set of their time. He was something of a d'Artagnan—which is to say, a fourth musketeer. This was at the height of the Renaissance, of course, and learning was in the air. Venice was at the center of this new learning: the stage had been set by the rise of the Academies, the encouragement of scholarship under men like Bembo and Bessarion, the many incunabula of Aldus Manutius, and fantastical works like the *Hypnerotomachia Poliphili*. Dogandili and his friends took a particular interest in the sciences, especially those sciences that might conceivably lead to profit. Thus they observed the stars in the hopes of finding the means of divination, and studied natural history to acquire the secrets of sorcery. Chemistry was common then: many people made alchemical experiments in the hopes of finding the philosopher's stone, or pharmaceutical experiments to achieve more immediate pleasures. The spur to anatomy was perhaps Titian himself—not yet the accomplished master whose services were sought by princes and kings but still a young man on the make, and far from flush: he needed models, and the dead demand no fee."

He completes the circumnavigation and comes to a halt at the place where he began. He faces Andromeda and opens his arms in a gesture of display.

"And so this anatomical theater was built. Material upon which to practice was acquired by various means. Aretino was a pornographer and blackmailer; he knew everyone's secrets and would have used them to encourage a certain looking the other way when it came to making these proscribed acquisitions. We can imagine them here as they might have been five hundred years ago, can we not? Dogandili with the knife poised above the body, Titian roving about with sketch paper in hand, the others looking on from the gallery with eager anticipation, all of them suffused with the thrill of the illicit and the diabolical."

He comes over and stands by Andromeda, looking down at her in renewed silence. The sharp point of the beak is inches above her breast. He is smiling slightly and his mouth looks wide and generous, an effect that is completely nullified by his eyes, which Andromeda can see through the holes in the mask, flat steel gray, eyes bereft of compassion or sentiment or pity.

"Sometimes they robbed graves," he continues. "Occasionally they worked on unclaimed bodies, corpses that had been more recently alive than the rather stale bodies of the buried dead, cadavers brought in secretly from the morgue. But sometimes even the freshest of bodies was not quite fresh enough. Young Mark Antony had acquired a taste for his ghoulish art, you see, and like any true artist he sought to push the boundaries. In short, he became a vivisectionist. He began to dissect the living."

Silence.

He runs a finger slowly across her scar.

His attention shifts to the side. Andromeda twists her head further to the left, to see what he is looking at. It is a small stainless-steel table, mounted on castors and with two shelves. The top one is covered in a white cloth that has been doubled over. He unfolds it to reveal a set of surgical instruments, neatly laid out. He removes a scalpel from the tray with his right hand, and with his left reaches out to the base of Andromeda's throat, which he grips with the gentle firmness of an experienced physician. Her entire focus now is on that other hand, the right one, the hand that holds the scalpel.

"He chose people who would not be much missed: prostitutes, criminals, the destitute. Orphans, too. Once he had them here there was no chance of escape. There is but one exit, and all the yelling in the world would never summon help: even were the sound to miraculously penetrate the earth, there would be none but the dead to hear."

He moves his left hand lower, across her breasts, working his fingers under the top of the dress.

"He stole people," he says, "much as I stole you. He stole them and brought them here and then cut them up alive."

He grips the top of the gown and pulls it up hard away from her chest, then uses the scalpel to cut the dress, slicing through the thick corset-like structure, drawing the blade firmly down between her breasts and further down, continuing to the bottom of the bodice, then working through the layers of skirt and petticoat with swift sure strokes, pulling the lacerated fabric aside as he goes. He is neither rough nor smooth, just business-like, working as calmly as a butcher trimming a carcass. Andromeda is conscious of his competence with this operation, the dexterous familiarity with which he wields the instrument. She thinks that this is not the first time he has used a knife to cut the dress from a woman's body.

When the last of the petticoats is cut through he pulls apart to two halves of the dress, allowing it to hang down, exposing her body, naked now apart from a small lace thong—the sole underwear she has worn tonight—and stockings. The Doctor turns to the gallery, and announces in a deep theatrical tone:

"Ladies and gentlemen, I give you Andromeda Chamberlain."

This declaration is met with polite applause. The gallery is occupied—through the shadows Andromeda can make out the faint movement of hands clapping. It seems that *Il Dottore* is intending to perform in front of an audience—but what sort of people can these be who would witness such a thing?

"Tonight's program will be in three acts," the Doctor announces. "Act One: Thesis."

He claps his hands. A door in the wall by the gallery opens, and two figures come in wheeling equipment. They are both female. Like the Doctor, they are dressed in ball costume. Both wear the half mask called a mezzo, but with elaborate plumes attached that rise high over their pompadour wigs.

One of them brings in a wheeled pole on top of which is mounted a wide, flat-screen monitor. She leaves it by the far wall and begins working with a piece of equipment mounted below the monitor at about head height. Soon the blank screen lights up with an image of the woman in extreme close-up, and Andromeda realizes that it is a camera she is manipulating. The woman moves to the side, adjusts the camera angle so that it points directly at Andromeda, then works the focus and zoom until the image, bright and clear despite the low light, completely fills the screen.

So whatever they are going to do with her, they have brought in a television set so that she can watch it herself. Now she sees what it is that she lies upon: a table, like a table in a hospital operating room.

Another monitor is wheeled in, and then another, each placed at equal intervals, the third one too far behind Andromeda for her to see it properly. The monitors are intended not for her but for the audience, set at various locations, allowing them to see whatever is to come from every angle.

When the equipment is in position the two attendants come back behind Andromeda. One of them takes a rubber tube from the table of surgical equipment and ties it around Andromeda's arm. The other removes a hypodermic syringe from an enamel pan, holds it up to the light, and squeezes the plunger until a small stream of fluid shoots from the end of the needle.

"We are injecting Miss Chamberlain with a pharmaceutical cocktail," the Doctor explains. "There is firstly a stimulant—in medical parlance methylenedioxy methamphetamine—but for simplicity we will refer to the drug under its street name: Ecstasy."

He wanders back from the gallery toward Andromeda, talking over his shoulder, still addressing the audience.

"The normal dosage is two milligrams per kilogram of body weight, which in this case would be less than a hundred milligrams, but given the circumstances I think that we will opt for a hundred and fifty. The drug will relax the subject, and will aid in her compliance with what is to come."

He turns to Andromeda and lowers his voice.

"You may feel brief nausea," he says, as if he were a real doctor, which from the professional commentary Andromeda realizes he might well be. "This will be quickly followed by a massive release of dopamine, and you will find yourself filled with an overwhelming sense of pleasure."

He stands and turns back to the audience.

"The second ingredient is Buspirone, which will for a time suppress the production of serotonin, the so-called 'rational' neurotransmitter. And then lastly there is a hallucinogen—LSD, to be exact, with which I'm sure everyone is familiar, if only by reputation." A little laughter from the gallery. "Two tabs' worth," he says with a smile. "Miss Chamberlain is in for quite a ride."

She is injected. Nothing for a minute, then it comes, a certain peacefulness at first, as if she has entered a state of profound beatitude that renders even the circumstances of her abduction more curious than terrifying, and which is soon accompanied by acutely heightened sensual awareness. Suddenly she is Alice, abducted into some mysterious and exotic Wonderland.

Andromeda loses track of time. Despite the coolness of the room she feels herself flush through with heat, as if a great wave of something warm and intense had washed across her body. Her breathing becomes fast and shallow. She looks at the Doctor looking at her, leaning on the wall below the gallery, legs crossed casually at the ankle, still twirling that ebony stick, watching the drug cocktail take hold.

He stands up straight, takes a few steps forward, and turns to the shadows in the gallery.

"Act Two," he announces. "Antithesis."

He again claps his hands. The nurses reappear. Both are naked now, except for their masks and wigs and high heels. Andromeda recognizes their bodies: they are the female acrobats from earlier in the evening. The taller and darker of the two carries a perfume bottle. She comes and stands by Andromeda. She is narrow-waisted but her shoulders are broad. Her legs are muscular. She is incongruously tanned, a Seventeenth-Century courtesan who spends time on the Lido, sunbathing by the Adriatic. Her skin is perfectly smooth and unblemished, with two exceptions. The first is a tiny smear of blood at the crook of her left elbow, where in the last few minutes she, too, has been injected, or has injected herself. The second is a small tattoo low down on her abdomen, something that would have been concealed earlier in the evening by the boy shorts. It depicts two concentric circles and their common center, the outer one horned on top and crossed below, something vaguely Hermetic or Rosicrucian.

Then she realizes that it is not a tattoo: the design is not inked; it has been burned into her flesh. Andromeda turns toward her companion. She looks for and finds the same symbol. Both of these women have been branded.

The first girl holds up the perfume bottle on the flat of her palm, so that Andromeda can inspect it. The bottle is exquisite, like the ones she had seen earlier in the tent. The colors are brilliant, unnaturally so, and she realizes that the LSD must be taking effect now, distorting things, blurring the lines between reality and fantasy.

The fluid inside the bottle is glowing gold and thick and unctuous. There is music, echoing from somewhere deep in the ground, although she cannot be sure if it is real or imagined. The girl opens the bottle and pours a stream of molten gold from it and it is searing hot and Andromeda realizes that now she is branded too, branded with a slash of molten gold across her body. The other girl is there and her hands are over her and suddenly Andromeda has been released and she floats now, high and higher as the hands try to hold her down but she is floating free and far below her the dead Earth revolves, massive and bloated and cratered and old dead Earth and dead soil. Flaming meteors rain down upon it. The Earth has been branded by the cosmos into a lumbering dead planet.

She orbits.

Beneath her, the planet rotates. The galaxy reverberates with the sound of stone grinding on stone.

She is immaculate. The curvature of the Earth is visible below. A cleft at Delphi appears, from which a figure emerges. A puzzle: she must identify the mask. Beautiful colors: it is Arlecchino—the Harlequin. He leaps, hoofed from cloven Earth and blushful Hippocrene, bearing images of time forgotten, vast and heavy and eyes of green glass. A satyr's eyes, and dark forest satyr breath. A Levantine wind comes blowing in from the east smelling of Arabia and the Bora comes down from the Alps and she is enveloped in the maelstrom, tumbling and tumbling away.

She awakens in an Elysian field. A rite will be performed and a mystery and a sacrifice. She is perfumed in preparation and a god comes to her and he says *When she is found* and she says *Who?*

It is the Bronze Age and it is the age of molten gold. Scaramouche smells the gold and he comes slinking in. The bird of prey watches him with close and knowing eyes. He suspects that the bird will devour him but he wants that gold and he wants and he wants. The history of humankind has been branded upon his dead eyes.

A rite will be performed and a mystery and a sacrifice. The rite is artful and requires a skeleton. Pierrot! Pierrot the acrobatic skeleton! He comes jangling in. He ruts the air and his old necrophiliac bones go clack. He performs the Twist. He is very good. He performs the Watusi. He rattles away in clattering skeletal a-go-go, and she wonders when who she is no longer young found.

A great wave of liquid gold has formed on the horizon. It builds higher and ever higher. It rushes forward irresistibly, engorged, swelling. It grows to the size of a skyscraper, an engulfing wave of liquid heavy metal, powerful, immense, unstoppable. The wave plows in. There is no possibility of escape. It surges over Venice, crushing everything before it, blasting the buildings to smithereens, sweeping away the city as if it were sand on a beach.

The tsunami retreats at last, dragging with it the entrails of the city. The devastation is complete. It is gone, all gone, nothing but desolate exhaustion in its wake.

It is the end of time forgotten, and it shimmers in a soft copper green.

All is golden, and light.

— PART III —

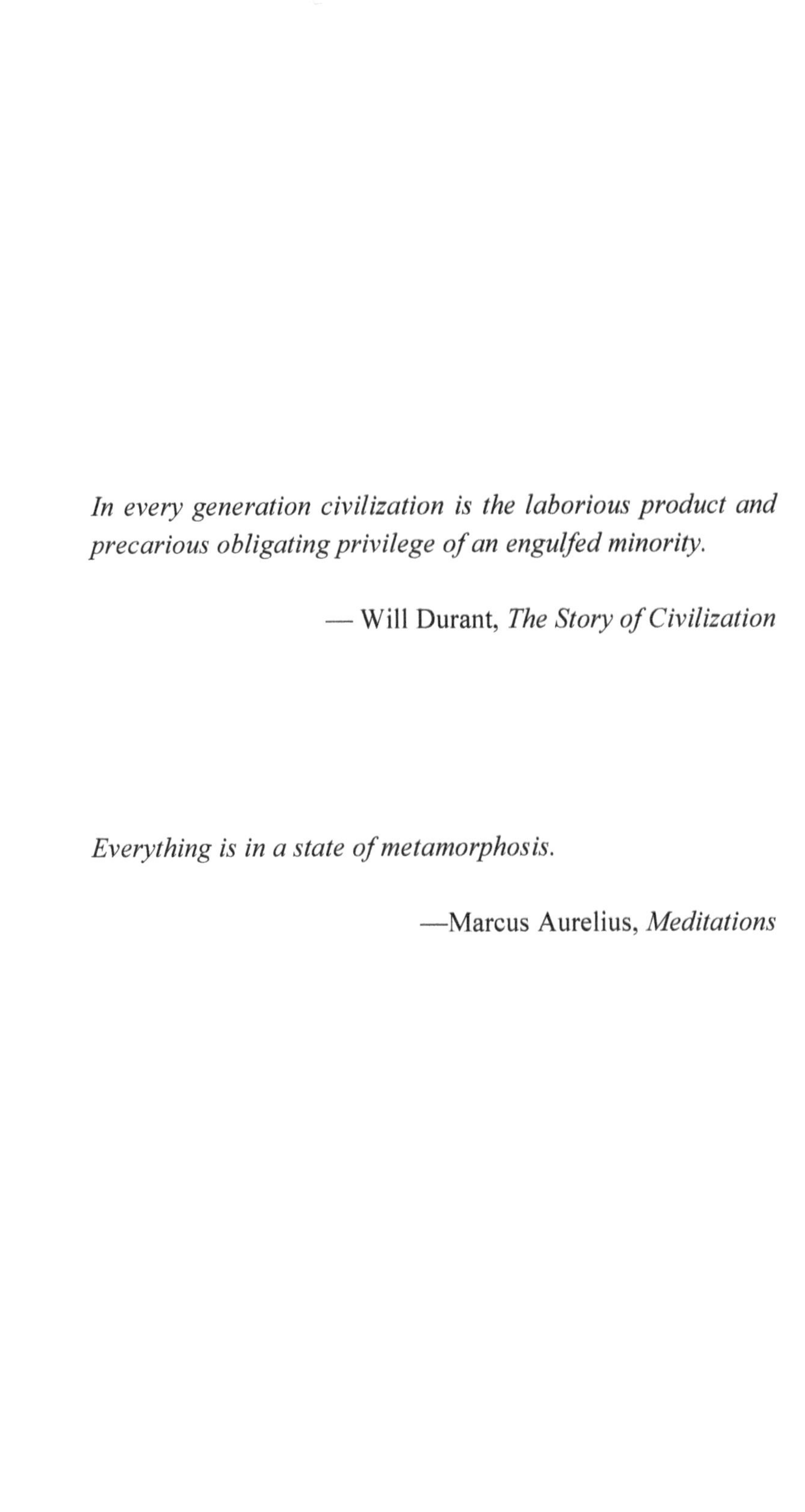

In every generation civilization is the laborious product and precarious obligating privilege of an engulfed minority.

— Will Durant, *The Story of Civilization*

Everything is in a state of metamorphosis.

—Marcus Aurelius, *Meditations*

XXIV

ANDROMEDA AWAKENS IN A darkened room. There is a small crack of daylight from somewhere. The bed is narrow, iron-framed, and uncomfortable—wherever she is, it is not the Bauer.

She gets out of the bed and goes to the window. There is no glass, just a pair of wooden shutters whose imperfect fit is the source of the light. She opens them, revealing a mass of brambles immediately below and beyond them a gray sky over the gray lagoon. On the horizon Venice is visible, the distant campanile rising like an exclamation point, proclaiming her queen of the Adriatic.

Andromeda is on the second floor of what is presumably the abandoned Dogandili palazzo. The windows have ornate pilaster frames and corbeled ledges; the external wall is rusticated with indentations sufficient to accommodate fingers: if she had to, she could climb down from here, and the brambles would cushion any fall. She looks back out over the water.

There is no sign of any boat traffic. Nothing moves on the lagoon, not even gulls. It is dawn on Ash Wednesday, the quietest morning of the year in Venice, and across the water the city lies silent and fallow, as if the excesses of Carnival have wrung all the life from it.

Andromeda turns around and inspects the room: plaster walls, mottled with mildew; floor of bare boards, swept but not well—she can feel the grit beneath her feet. The only furniture is the bed, chipped white enamel like a cast-off from an old hospital.

Whoever put her in it did not think to provide pajamas.

Andromeda removes from the shutters the wooden crossbar that had been used to keep them closed—not much of a weapon, but the best available. She goes to the door and cautiously tries the handle. It is unlocked, confirming what the window has already suggested: she is no longer a prisoner. She takes a sheet from the bed and, clutching it to her chest with one hand and crossbar raised ready in the other, begins investigating.

The remainder of the second floor shows no sign of habitation. Downstairs, she enters a large room with high ceilings that must once have been the main hall. The walls are freshly painted. Here the floor is polished, and at one end there are scrape marks where something heavy has been moved recently, but now the room, like the rest of the palazzo, is empty. The embers in the fireplaces on either side are still warm. In another room she finds more evidence of recent use: several broad tables, a modern stool on casters, a power strip with a surge protector, and a thicker cable leading outside. This is where Gidding worked, she realizes, but the equipment is gone now, and the palazzo is once again abandoned. In a small room used as a pantry she finds on the bench a brown paper bag with a croissant inside, and beside it a vacuum flask filled with hot coffee. Someone has left breakfast for her, and she realizes that she is hungry.

She puts aside the weapon, takes the breakfast, and follows the thick cable outside into what was once a garden. The generator that the cable would have been connected to is gone, but at the end of the terrace there is a portable toilet of the type used at outdoor events; she can see the name of the firm that rented it stenciled onto the side. A shower has been rigged under a tree, connected to a solar panel. She pulls the chain to test it, and warm water pours out.

On the far side of the garden is the tomb. Andromeda goes to the gate and is almost relieved to find it padlocked; she has no desire to reenter the anatomatoria.

On a bench by the shower is a small bag. Inside is a towel, some basic toiletries and, beneath them, clothes.

Andromeda sits and eats her breakfast, considering what she has discovered. She is evidently still on Isola Bisi, where Gidding had retreated to finish his movie. He has now abandoned the island, presumably to avoid any unpleasantness should she go to the authorities. She is not entirely sure what took place in the anatomatoria: she recalls Acts One and Two; her memories of the rest of the evening are clear and vivid, but too fantastical to be real.

Andromeda finishes the croissant and pours some coffee. The immediate problem is to get off the island, and she decides that after breakfast she will circumnavigate by the shore in search of a boat, or hail any vessel that might happen to pass by. She looks down at the coffee in her hand and is surprised to see on its surface small concentric circles, a strange series of ripples continuously radiating outward, reacting to some distant earth tremor too minor to be physically noticeable but enough to register upon the surface, as if the coffee were a finely-tuned detector of far away earthquakes, or nuclear treaty violations. But she realizes that the source is not seismic; it is her hand holding the coffee.

So this is fear, she thinks: not so much a conscious state of mind as an unconscious state of being, and apparently expressed externally in this fine but rapid, all but unfelt, shaking of her hand. Last night's theatricalities were meant to scare her, and they succeeded. Fear is to be faced down, of course—she drinks the rest of the coffee and puts the cup aside.

Andromeda showers and dresses. The clothes are not her own: safari shirt and cotton khaki trousers, sturdy flat shoes, as if whoever provided them knew that she would have the hard physical work of getting off the island ahead of her. She goes back through the palazzo and takes a path down through the brambles to the water, but when the landing comes into view she realizes that she will have no need of a boat.

Tied up by the landing is a flat-topped barge. On it is a car—a Hispano-Suiza. Standing next to it is a liveried chauffeur. He holds the rear door open in silent invitation.

Andromeda approaches. She steps onto the landing but not the barge. The chauffeur salutes in greeting. The car's wheels are chocked. Next to him is a roller bag that she recognizes as her own—they have apparently packed her things and checked her out of the hotel.

"Who are you?"

"My name is James, ma'am. I have instructions to take you to the airport." He reaches inside his jacket and emerges with an envelope, which he offers to Andromeda. To reach it she must step onto the barge.

Inside she finds no letter, just her passport and a printed airline confirmation in her name for a one-way flight back to New York, leaving Marco Polo at one o'clock.

"What time is it?"

James checks his watch, an anachronistically modern digital. "Nine-thirty, ma'am."

"Where's Gidding?"

"I'm told that Mr. Gidding left Venice early this morning."

"Going where?"

"I don't know, ma'am."

"Is he coming back?"

"I don't know that either"

"Where did this car come from?"

"Mr. Gidding provided it."

"How long have you worked for him?"

"I don't work for him—in fact, I've never met him. I'm just a driver with the chauffeur service that was given the assignment to take you to the airport. And if we're going to get there in time, ma'am, we really should leave now."

Andromeda sees no point in questioning him further. She settles into the back of the Hispano-Suiza and is almost disappointed to find no whip-wielding Pan Am stewardess awaiting her inside.

THE BARGE IS SLOW AND TAKES half an hour to arrive at the mainland, but it gives Andromeda time to think. Reviewing events as objectively as possible, she comes to the conclusion that the net sum of these many grotesqueries has been only to confirm her suspicion that tracking down Gidding is the key to finding out what became of Margot Vaughn. All that Gidding has achieved is to elevate his involvement with Margot from a side story to the main line of investigation. Gidding is foolish, she decides, like a puffed-up strong man running some petty state who, supreme in his own small world, imagines that he has the power to dictate events outside of it as well. There is no longer any question of her not following this thing through to the end, no matter who her employer might be. By the time they reach the mainland she has a plan.

After the ramp is lowered the chauffeur removes the chocks and cautiously drives off, maintaining a steady pace all the way to the airport. He drops her at the main terminal, but instead of heading to check-in Andromeda goes to the information desk and asks where the private jets leave from. She is told that they depart from general aviation, located in a nearby building separate from the main terminal.

Andromeda leaves the terminal and heads toward general aviation, wheeling her bag behind her. On the way across the lagoon she realized that Gidding would have good reason to leave Venice by private plane, something that was fast, in his control, and where he could take his equipment and precious reels of *Faust* without the compromises of commercial air travel.

There is just a single counter in general aviation. Andromeda asks the woman behind it if any private jets have left this morning. She expects a cautious response, but the woman immediately goes to her computer screen. "Only one flight so far today," she says. "A departure at 5:45 A.M. this morning."

"Can you tell me who was on it?"

"We're not allowed to."

"Can you tell me where it was heading?"

The woman returns her eyes to the screen. "Aberdeen, Scotland."

XXV

ANDROMEDA COMES TO A halt on a hill overlooking Burrenhead. It is still only afternoon but nightfall comes early during winter this far north, and the sea has already changed color from the slate gray of daytime into a lustrous dark graphite. Below her lies the town, little more than a village, a scattered semicircle of whitewashed stone houses surrounding a small harbor formed by the promontory from which the town derives its name. The port is filled with fishing vessels.

It was raining most of the way on the drive up from Edinburgh and Andromeda is thankful for having selected a Range Rover at the airport—a choice made because the vehicle is equipped with multiple limited-slip differentials—but now a late shaft of sunlight breaks through the cloud cover and briefly illuminates the town. Far across the water she can see the distant outline of Rothermore, shadowed and jagged, mired in mist.

Another island, she thinks—Gidding likes to conduct his affairs away from public scrutiny.

Aberdeen is the nearest airport but the only available commercial flight was to Edinburgh, necessitating the trek north across the great firths of Forth and Tay. She descends into Burrenhead and parks in the center of town. The center of the town comprises a general store, a post office, and the town's lone lodging, a pub called The Unrepentant Monk.

The proprietress of the Unrepentant Monk is a Mrs. Campbell, who immediately addresses Andromeda as "love." She assigns Andromeda the one room that has its own bathroom. When Andromeda goes back outside to collect her bag she finds that several people have gathered on the previously deserted sidewalk—the arrival of a stranger in Burrenhead is a spectator event.

BY THE TIME SHE EMERGES from her bath, it is completely dark. Andromeda dresses and goes downstairs. The pub is packed with more people than she would have thought lived in the village, but a small round table has been left unoccupied in the middle of the room, and beside it is a single chair.

Andromeda ignores them and goes to the bar, behind which Mrs. Campbell is serving.

"Fancy some tea, love?"

"I'd prefer a beer."

Mrs. Campbell laughs and pulls out a glass. "Are you hungry? I could do you some bangers."

"Bangers?"

"Sausages. Or there's some creamed haddock I could warm through." Andromeda shows no enthusiasm for either suggestion. Mrs. Campbell places the freshly drawn beer in front of her, overflowing foam sliding down the sides. "What about some nice toasted cheese sandwiches?"

"That sounds perfect."

She leaves to make the sandwiches. Andromeda raises her glass, turns to her neighbor and says, "Cheers," before downing a mouthful. Her neighbor smiles a toothless smile, taps his half-empty glass on the counter, and says cheers in return.

"Are you a fisherman?"

He nods in response. "Not much else in this town."

"I would have thought Rothermore Abbey would bring in good business."

"Aye, once. It's closed now."

"Why?"

"A man bought it. To make a movie."

"An American," his neighbor adds. "Begging your pardon, Miss."

A small crowd gathers around Andromeda, eager to join in the conversation. By the time the toasted cheese sandwiches arrive Andromeda has the gist of the story: Burrenhead is the nearest town to Rothermore and so had thrived during tourist season, taking sightseers out and back every day, providing sandwiches or feeding them in a little harborside seafood restaurant that is now closed. During the warmer months the limited accommodations at the Unrepentant Monk had been booked out weeks in advance, and many townsfolk put people up in their cottages. All that ended with the expulsion of the National Trust.

"Don't the film people provide business? They need food and transport, too."

"No, all their stuff is contracted out to the big oil rig service companies down in Aberdeen. They have no use for small folk like us. I don't think the Git even knows that we even exist."

"The Git?"

"Gidding, the man making the movie. Around here we call him Gidding the Git."

"Is he there now? On the island, I mean."

"No way we'd know, Miss. Lord of the bloody manor doesn't consult with us lowly peasants."

THE NEXT MORNING, Andromeda asks Mrs. Campbell if someone with a boat can take her over to Rothermore.

"Oh, not today, love," Mrs. Campbell tells her. "There's a storm coming in."

"Surely your fishermen have seen worse than this."

"It's not what it is now, it's what it's about to be. The whole fleet is in because of it."

"It would be quick," Andromeda says. "They could just drop me off and come straight back. Besides, there's a hundred pounds in it for whoever's willing to go."

The offer of a hundred pounds stops Mrs. Campbell short. She rubs her chin, as if the mention of money had made it itch. Her eyes no longer quite catch Andromeda's. Eventually she responds, quieter than before.

"Bert Naughton's usually pretty game. Let me trot over and see if he's up for it."

APPROACHING STORM OR NOT, it is afternoon by the time Bert Naughton's fishing boat is underway toward Rothermore Island. From the beery odor emanating from Naughton, Andromeda assumes that he had drunk until closing time the previous evening, believing that he was to have the following day off. The delay gave her time to purchase supplies from the general store—canned everything—to add to the backpack, binoculars, and telephoto-lensed camera she had already purchased at the airport duty-free. The wind has picked up since morning, now whistling loudly through the rigging, and the sea is rough with whitecaps. The deck bucks and jumps beneath her, and Andromeda finds that between the motion and the pungent combination of herring and diesel fumes she will be grateful to get back onto dry land.

Naughton is a laconic sailor, or perhaps just hungover, and responds to most of Andromeda's questions with grunts. She feels too seasick to press him. They hit fog as they near the island.

"Always fog here," Naughton says with disapproval. "The shoaling makes the cold water well up."

But Andromeda is pleased with the fog, for the one risk in her plan was that the boat would be spotted while approaching the island, and if they saw her land then she would be unable to observe the goings-on at Rothermore unnoticed, as she intended. Now they will be unaware of her presence, and she can decide if and when to approach Gidding.

Naughton turns on the radar and uses it to navigate inshore. The sea drops as they come under the lee of the unseen island. Ahead of them a small jetty suddenly appears through the fog, and then behind it the sheer rock face of Rothermore. Naughton brings the boat alongside for her to step ashore. "I'll be back when the weather permits," he says. "It can be treacherous out here, so take care."

Andromeda says that she will but Naughton looks unconvinced—she can tell that in his eyes she is just an unthinking American tourist with no understanding of the real world. He leaves with a wave, glad to be heading back home.

Andromeda watches him disappear then turns around. She can see no more than a dozen yards ahead. There is a single steep path leading up from the landing.

The light is already failing. If she is to find a good observation post before dark, she will need to get underway.

XXVI

ANDROMEDA BEGINS the long climb to Rothermore Abbey. She has hardly started when ahead of her a figure seems to briefly take form through a wind-blown gap in the fog, but the shroud of mist swiftly closes, and the figure disappears. She stops, wondering if she imagined it.

The figure was standing facing her, she thought, silhouetted by an ethereal glow from behind, two-legged but not quite human, the head monstrously enlarged. She thinks of Anubis, the jackal-headed deity of Egypt, but then dismisses the thought—no North African god could tolerate this Caledonian weather. Andromeda continues up the path.

Suddenly she is upon the figure, now just twenty feet away. She comes to a halt a second time. It is not a god with a jackal head but a man with a movie camera. His eye is to the viewfinder and so Andromeda cannot see his face clearly, but she sees enough to know that it is Orlando Gidding.

“Do you know who invented the movie camera?” he asks, without pause from filming her.

“No.”

“Two French brothers by the name of Lumière. The name means light, of course. Strange coincidence, isn’t it, that something whose fundamental purpose is the capture of light should have been invented by people named light?"

"Light is the fundamental purpose of motion pictures?"

"It is in my case." He looks out from behind the viewfinder. "Or, to be more precise, enlightenment."

"I take it that I am expected?"

"I arranged the boat."

"The housekeeper at the inn arranged the boat."

"No, all the good Mrs. Campbell did was to do as I asked her. I hope they didn't overdo the resentful locals act last night; I told them not to lay it on too thick." Another man might have smiled at this point, in sympathy or one-upmanship, but Gidding's expression remains neutral. She wonders if Naughton's last words to her—*it can be treacherous out here*—had been a deliberate double entendre. "The Picts are a fickle people," Gidding continues. "Close, but not averse to money. I like them; they can be bought."

Gidding's accent is stateless, the accent of a man who calls nowhere home. Atlantic Man, she thinks of him. He takes the camera down from his shoulder, holding it by a strap on the housing. It is a large professional-looking device, and Andromeda can see the canister indicating a camera that uses real film. She thinks that Clare would be pleased.

"You knew I was in Burrenhead all along?"

"Did you think the arrival of a mysterious woman driving an expensive vehicle would go unremarked in a remote Scottish fishing village?"

"How do they contact you?"

"I have a satellite phone. Or at least I had one, until the wind blew the antenna down. I'll have Kalki put it back up when the storm passes."

"Kalki?"

"He's my butler, who also serves as the maintenance man. And I have a housekeeper, who also cooks. Don't be alarmed when you meet them."

"Why should I be alarmed?"

“You’ll see. Let’s head up to the abbey.” He turns without waiting for a reply and begins trudging back up the path.

Andromeda remains where she is and pulls out her cell phone. It takes a moment for Gidding to realize that she is not following him, but by that time Andromeda has figured out that she has no signal.

“Cell phones don’t work out here,” Gidding says, “and of course there’s no landline. The only communication is via the satellite service, and that’s down. But it makes no difference: even if you could contact the mainland no boat would come for you now. I’m afraid that until the storm passes you have no option but to remain on the island. You’re welcome to stay here if you wish, but I think that you would be more comfortable in the abbey.”

Andromeda puts her phone away. The tracking application will not relay her position to Renzitti without a cell phone signal, and she realizes that she has entered a state rare in the Twenty-First Century: she is completely cut off from communication with the rest of the world.

Gidding turns and continues up the path. Andromeda has little choice but to follow him.

The glow that had first silhouetted Gidding came from a flaming torch, mounted on the rock face and giving off a sharp smell. Gidding stops and rubs the rusting iron sconce, little more than a ring. “Hammered into this rock over a thousand years ago by monks fearful of Norsemen and God,” Gidding says. “Everybody needs light. That’s why people pretend they’ll go to heaven.”

“Maybe the monks truly believed.”

“No one in the history of humankind has ever truly believed.”

“A difficult assertion to verify.”

“Show me this one true believer then.”

“What would you do?”

“Put him face-to-face with a wild boar and see how his faith holds up. We have them on the island.”

“True believers?”

“Wild boars. I brought them in for a scene in *Faust*. They’re vicious creatures—two hundred pounds of tusk and muscle. But, unlike men, they do not like light." He takes the torch from the sconce. "This will keep them away."

"It smells like asphalt."

"We use bitumen for fuel; difficult to get going, but once it's alight it doesn't blow out or get dowsed by the rain. The paths can be dangerous when wet, and in this fog a flashlight is useless." He looks up at the sky, although there is no sky to see. "We'd better head up before dark."

The ascent is a long one, zigzagging back and forth, rock face on one side and steep drop on the other. The path is mostly too narrow to walk side-by-side, so Gidding leads and Andromeda follows. Eventually they emerge above the fog, and for the first time Andromeda can see more than a few feet in front of her. They come to a halt at a small outcrop.

"Rothermore Abbey," Gidding says. Andromeda follows his gaze upward.

Only part of the abbey is visible, a dark soaring mass, sheer wet walls of rough-hewn stone looming high over them, topped with a tower and pierced with occasional windows too high to be accessible, but which are nevertheless barred by iron grates. The abbey is forbidding enough on its own, but the background of wind-whipped clouds racing behind lends the entire scene an ominous sense of Gothic dread.

"I don't know how to describe it," Andromeda says, "but I can see why you would want to film here."

"Depth," Gidding says, and she realizes that he has chosen the perfect word. "No digital recreation could ever capture that depth. Look at those clouds, endless slow explosions in slate green and gunmetal gray. And the vertiginous bulk of the abbey itself—trying to bluescreen that with special effects would be a waste of time. Movies made with CGI are just cartoons; I find them dull. True depth comes from reality. That's why I film on location instead of a sound stage, even though it's difficult and expensive. And, for what it's worth, I also think it's the reason that, say, Byron swam the Hellespont, despite being a cripple, or the Rolling Stones recorded at Nellcôte, despite the absence of a studio, or van Gogh found it necessary to make a gift of his own ear, despite the inconvenience of having to first remove it." He looks from the abbey to Andromeda. "Art feeds off depth, in all its forms."

"Are you intending to abduct me again?"

"You are already effectively abducted, I would say."

"Then what?"

"I was thinking that you might like to attend a world premiere."

"What do you mean?"

"My *Doctor Faustus*. No one has ever seen it. And I mean no one—no studio people, no editing technicians, no soundtrack coordinators, no one in the world but me. All I've released are a few rough cuts from some selected scenes, sufficient to give a flavor of what is to come but nothing more. The official world premiere will be in Cannes, but since you're now here I propose to show it to you first. If you wish you can take notes, ask questions—write an exclusive, if you're so inclined." He turns and faces her. "While you're here you will have complete freedom; the place is yours. You may go where you wish and do what you want. Everything on the island is at your disposal—except, of course, the ability to leave it."

"Will the storm last long?"

"A day or two, but it will take at least another day for the sea to sufficiently subside for a boat to take you back."

"Three days."

"Enough time."

Andromeda wonders for what.

XXVII

ANDROMEDA AND GIDDING ENTER the abbey through a heavy iron-bound wooden door, and as it closes behind them the sounds of the storm and sea are suddenly gone, replaced by a stark and unnerving silence.

They are in a large hall with a stone-flagged floor and bare stone walls. Andromeda walks to the middle of the room. Behind her, she can hear Gidding shutting down the camera. The air is cold and still and feels heavy with age. Andromeda's breath clouds in front of her. There is no furniture. The only illumination comes from torches mounted on the wall.

"Is there electricity?"

"Yes, we still have the generators, but when I was shooting *Faust* I used torches, and now I've grown used to them."

A man approaches from the far end of the hall. At first he is in shadow, and so all that Andromeda can see of him is an outline, towering and gaunt and slightly hunched in the way that very tall people often are, as if perpetually bending to fit under a doorway. But then he comes to a halt in the light, and Andromeda sees that he has a nose of silver.

Gidding comes beside her. "This is Kalki, my butler," he says. "Kalki was once a thief but not a very good one, which is how he lost his nose."

Kalki the butler-thief is grave of countenance but attempts a smile of welcome. He is a monster but a delicate monster, Andromeda sees, with well-formed hands and an economic precision of movement.

A fourth person joins them, a young woman who comes to a halt beside the butler. She is honey-toned and dark-haired with broad almond-shaped eyes, but much of the right side of her face is disfigured, the skin blotched and uneven from what must have been a bad burn.

"This is Leila," Gidding says. "About her I can tell you nothing; she understands well enough, but she does not speak."

Leila holds a small tray, and standing upon it is a long-stemmed liqueur glass figured as a tulip. The thimble-sized bowl is filled with a clear green liquid. She offers it to Andromeda.

"What is it?"

"Home-made," Gidding answers. "It'll warm you."

Andromeda accepts the glass, intending to sip, but then realizes that Leila expects the glass returned, so instead she empties it. The shot shoots straight through her, and Andromeda imagines that she can feel the fluid entering her nerve ends. She returns the glass and thanks Leila.

At a nod from Gidding both servants turn and leave.

"That was incredibly strong," Andromeda says when they have gone. "And very bitter."

"Leila infuses it."

"With what?"

"Herbs, wildflowers. I'm not sure exactly what. Leila is something of a witch, but she is also a very good cook—perhaps the two go together. And Kalki makes an excellent butler: even the most persistent of paparazzi think twice before intruding on my privacy with Kalki around."

"Do you know how she received that burn?"

"It's not a burn, at least not in the usual sense. When Leila was a young girl she liked to read books. Some men in her village disapproved of literate females. They walked up to her one day and threw acid in her face." Despite Gidding's warning, Andromeda feels a shiver go through her. "Their intention was to blind her—permanent darkness as a guaranty against any future reading—but like most deeply stupid people they were also incompetent: they missed her eyes."

"Where did you find her?"

"I found them both on the streets of Paris."

"Together?"

"No, separately. Kalki has been with me for many years; Leila somewhat less. Both of them are, quite obviously, outcasts. Kalki likes to be left alone with his thoughts, and Leila can now read as many books as she likes with impunity—she devours my library. A position that involves little interaction with the rest of the world suits them, and it suits me, too."

"You have an attraction for the disfigured," Andromeda says. "No wonder you came after me."

"An objective outsider might conclude that it is you who have come after me, but we can discuss that later. For now, I'll show you to your quarters."

Gidding leads her through to the next room, similarly proportioned to the first, with a passageway leading off one side and a large fireplace alight in the other. This room is furnished with modern rectilinear sofas and chairs, and Oriental rugs on the floor. The decoration is more ornate than the entrance hall, with carved wooden lintels and a frieze inscribed with Latin script.

"I call this the Griffin Room," Gidding says. He nods toward the fireplace, where a pair of large stone dragons supports the mantle. "It was the refectory when the monks lived here. The cooking would have been done in open pots suspended over that fire, and those creatures were meant to remind them that the Devil is always lurking, perhaps as a warning against gluttony. You can have the full tour tomorrow—it's easier to see everything in daylight."

He leads her across the refectory to a stone staircase, up to a passageway on the next floor, and then to her room. There is another fireplace, also alight, for which Andromeda is grateful. To the right is the bed, incongruously sleek and modern like the furniture downstairs. The desk in the center of the room is heavy and old-fashioned, with quill and inkwell, but beside it is a record turntable—technical and expensive looking, equipment for a genuine audiophile rather than a casual listener. An LP is playing jazz. To the left is a bathroom at the center of which is a large freestanding copper tub, brightly polished. Leila is beside it, pouring in scalding water from a metal bucket.

"There's no lock on the door," Andromeda says.

"It's a monastery. They didn't allow the monks to have locks on their doors."

"This room is too large to have been a monk's cell."

"True. In fact, it was originally the copy room. The monks made a precarious living by copying manuscripts. This room faces south and so gets the most light. That's why the windows are large, but we had to shutter them for the storm. The other side is a sheer cliff, and so it was the only place they felt safe building large external windows."

"Am I taking your room?"

"No. The reason it's furnished is that it was Faust's bedroom in the movie. I left all the sets in place, in case I needed to reshoot anything."

"Faust has a record player?"

"My Faust does, but the Miles Davis records were Mephistopheles' suggestion." Andromeda laughs and realizes that, despite the circumstances, she is looking forward to the film. "I usually dine formally," Gidding continues, "even when alone. Dinner will be at eight; we'll meet in the Griffin Room for a cocktail beforehand."

"As you can see, I am hardly prepared for dining formally."

"The costumes are still here too, and you're about Soline's size. Leila will find something suitable."

AFTER SHE HAS BEEN left alone Andromeda tests the bathwater: it is hot but bearable. She has just eased herself into it when she hears the door to her room open.

It is Leila, returning with arms full of towels and a small basket on top. She enters the bathroom without hesitation. Andromeda is too tired for embarrassment. Leila puts down the towels, lays out a robe on the bench, and then approaches the bath. She offers a bar of soap from the basket, which Andromeda accepts, then pours in bath oil from a small bottle. Andromeda expects something citrus or floral, but the oil has a scent that she cannot identify, vaguely oriental, something from a Batavian warehouse back when clipper ships fetched teak wood and spices from the East Indies. Leila kneels behind Andromeda's left shoulder, reaches around to gently take the soap, and then proceeds to scrub Andromeda's back. Andromeda leans forward to accommodate her. She can feel Leila's breath on her skin.

Eventually, the soap is returned. Andromeda thanks her and Leila smiles in response, the first time Andromeda has seen her do so. She picks up Andromeda's discarded clothes and goes to the bedroom. Andromeda again reclines in the tub. She can hear Leila continue to come and go in the other room.

Andromeda wonders if there will be any women in the film crew for her forthcoming pornographic debut; doubtful, but she would feel more comfortable if there were. She makes a mental note to order a wig—platinum blond, she thinks, something to focus attention away from the rest of her.

The water eventually cools and she stands to get out.

IN THE BEDROOM there is now a makeup console open on Faust's desk. It is a large one with a mirror on the underside of the lid and lights built-in on either side, a professional arrangement presumably intended for use in location filming. On the sofa an evening gown has been laid out, and on the floor beneath are shoes to match.

Andromeda sits at the makeup console. Leila joins her and with an inquiring gesture asks if she would like her hair up. She agrees and Leila sets to work with an enthusiastic competence that makes Andromeda suspect that she would prefer to be a lady's maid than a cook. Next comes makeup, and Andromeda submits with chin raised and eyes closed. When she opens them again the results are startlingly dramatic. Her eyelids are glittering gold, matching the dress. The lipstick is gold, too, although more subdued. Leila has applied more makeup than Andromeda would have used, perhaps used to doing so in order to disguise her own disfigurement, and assuming that Andromeda would want the same.

When it is time to dress Andromeda discovers that her own clothes are missing. Leila makes a scrubbing gesture with two closed fists: she has taken them to be laundered. It is a subtle reminder of Andromeda's status now: she is effectively a prisoner, Gidding's doll to be painted and dressed as he pleases. She wonders if any of his leading ladies felt the same way.

Leila goes to a brass-inlaid wooden box on the desk beside the console, which she opens in invitation to Andromeda. There is costume jewelry inside—more movie props. Leila bobs politely, her maid's duty done, and quits the room. Andromeda is left alone.

She retries her cellphone, but there is still no signal. She unplugs the turntable and uses the outlet to charge the phone instead.

Andromeda looks again at the clothing that has been selected for her. There is no underwear laid out with the dress. She tries the dresser but the drawers are empty. She tries the desk. There is no underwear, but she discovers several interesting things: more Miles Davis records, an art book of photographic nudes, a wooden box with a trident symbol emblazoned on the top, and a black velvet pouch with a straight-edge razor inside. Andromeda picks up the wooden box, no larger than a book but surprisingly heavy. It is locked. Beneath the symbol there is writing: Fabbrica d'Armi Pietro Beretta. She shakes the box and feels whatever is inside shift slightly, obviously hefty. If in a box marked

Beretta then presumably a pistol, she thinks, perhaps another prop left over from the movie.

Andromeda opens the razor expecting it to be a prop too, but when she brushes the pad of her thumb across the edge she realizes that it is the real thing, and very sharp. There is a spot of blood on the blade, dried to a dull rust color, and for the second time in the evening a shiver runs through her. Andromeda returns it to the pouch and closes the drawer.

She looks through the jewelry box. There is nothing that goes with the collar and so Andromeda selects earrings that will at least go with the dress. They are surprisingly heavy, and when she looks closer she finds hallmarks. Andromeda inspects some of the other pieces; they are not costume jewelry after all, they are the real thing. She selects a diamond-encrusted bracelet that best matches the earrings, then stands and removes her robe.

Andromeda puts on the dress and inspects the results in a mirror. Underwear would have been a waste of time: the dress could not have concealed it; the dress barely conceals her. There is a plunging back, and a plunging front, too. The material is layered silk, studded with thousands of tiny metal cylinders sewn into the fabric, but otherwise unlined and sheer. The two halves are joined at the sides not by seams but by clasps at the waist, so that walking reveals leg from hip to toe, and to lean forward safely is impossible. She hopes there will be no soup served tonight.

Lastly come the shoes—elaborate high-heeled evening sandals, suitably theatrical for a female Mephistopheles. Andromeda sits on the bed to do the straps and feels the mattress undulate beneath her. At first she thinks that it must be a water bed, but when she lifts the cover she finds something quite different. It takes her a moment to understand what she is looking at. The mattress is made of mercury, a pool of shimmering silver-colored liquid metal. She places a hand cautiously on the surface. It responds, but with unexpected resistance. She pushes harder and as her hand breaks the surface tension a little mercury flows over the sill and into a gutter on the side. She watches the globules race down the slope, separating and reforming on the way, resistant to all else but itself.

XXVIII

ANDROMEDA COMES TO A halt at the top of the stairs. Gidding is below in the Griffin Room, dressed in a dinner suit, sitting on the sofa. There are documents on the table in front of him but he is looking up, alerted to Andromeda's arrival by the clack of heel on stone.

"Leila chose well," he says.

"Leila chose too little. Please look away while I negotiate the stairs."

Gidding laughs and moves to the sideboard, on top of which sit an ice bucket and cocktail shaker.

"Is a Martini okay?"

"Yes. Dry, please."

Andromeda begins her descent. At each step the dress divides to accommodate hip and thigh.

"Did Soline Djahidra have to go down stairs in this dress?"

"No spoilers," Gidding says. "You'll see for yourself soon enough."

Gidding pours from the shaker. The glasses frost with the liquid. Andromeda reaches the base of the staircase. She is warm now but goes by the fire to watch the flames. Gidding joins her, offering a glass and raising his own in a silent toast.

She drinks, wary eyes over the rim on her host. He returns her gaze. The Martini is ice-cold and biting.

"This is very good," Andromeda says. "And I needed it."

"No vermouth. The great director Luis Buñuel said that to make a good Martini it is sufficient for light to pass through a bottle of vermouth on its way to the shaker."

"Are all directors obsessed with light?"

"Occupational hazard."

"I assume there's more to it than just getting the lighting right."

"Everything else is binary: it's either yes or no. Or fixed in some other way. Music has its fixed notes: twelve tones of the chromatic scale, endlessly repeated. And language has its fixed alphabet, twenty-six characters in prescribed combination and permutation. Only light is continuously variable, and so only light can express every subtlety, if you can just figure out how to capture it."

"So it is an obsession after all. As is mercury, apparently."

"Ah, so you've seen the bed."

"Am I expected to sleep on it?"

"Certainly, and you will no doubt sleep very well. The thing is surprisingly comfortable, and the metal is heated to just the right temperature. Mercury has a very high specific gravity, about two and a half times that of water, so lying on it is like floating in a warm sea, except that in this case the sea is much more supportive, and it would be impossible to drown."

"Isn't mercury poisonous?"

"Don't drink the bed."

She walks over to the sofa where Gidding had been sitting. What she thought were documents are actually photographs. The top few are face-down, perhaps placed that way as he went through them, but enough of one underneath is visible for her to identify the subject. It is herself, sitting back in sunlight on the balcony at the Ritz. She realizes that not all the photo-taking tourists in the place Vendôme had been tourists after all.

She would like to pick up the photographs and examine them but that would involve leaning over, so instead she looks back at Gidding. He offers no comment, apparently content to let the discovery speak for itself.

"I have no interest in you," she says. "I'm just trying to find Margot Vaughn."

"So I gather."

"Are you going to tell me where she is?"

"You're assuming that I know."

"Will you tell me what you do know?"

"Perhaps."

"When will you decide?"

"Three days from now."

"When the storm is over?"

"Yes."

"And in the meantime?"

"In the meantime, I will show you my new movie. And in return..."

"In return?"

"In return, you can tell me how you got that scar."

THE FIRST COURSE IS SOUP. It is served by the silver-nosed butler in a large barrel-vaulted space, now a dining room but according to Gidding originally the abbey's bakery and whose old oven, iron doors ajar, serves at a fireplace. Wooden wine crates line the end wall. Gidding retrieves a bottle from one of them with the comment, "Bordeaux tonight. We're having red-legged partridge. Kalki caught a brace of them this morning—these days he steals only from Mother Nature."

The table could have accommodated twelve but is set for just two, placed at either end. Andromeda keeps her back straight, and struggles to stop the spoon from spilling in the long journey from bowl to mouth.

"I got the scar in Africa last year," she says. "I was researching an article there."

"What about?"

"Archeology, at least initially. A few years ago an ancient trading post was unearthed in Mali, near the border with Niger. A petroleum exploration team discovered it while they were drilling through the desert to see if there was any oil underneath. Not much is known about the place, not even its name. The nearest town is Manoukaram, so it became known as the Manoukaram site. There is no river. Presumably there was once a wadi or an oasis, but eventually the Sahara spread and buried it in sand. The Sahara has been spreading for hundreds of years and has engulfed many settlements that were once on the margins, terminals for the caravan routes."

Kalki reenters the room carrying a domed silver tray matching his nose for the brilliance of its shine. He puts it on the sideboard and removes the top, revealing the two carcasses, roasted whole. He takes a carving knife and begins dismembering them with a grim efficiency that reminds Andromeda of the anatomatoria. She continues the story.

"Last year I got a call from an editor. She knew one of the researchers, a friend from the department back in the 'States that was sponsoring the dig. They had recently restarted following the summer break, and they found something, something interesting: a book. Actually, a scroll."

'What was interesting about it?"

"They expected it to be in Arabic but it turned out to be in Greek. Not demotic Greek but ancient Greek. No one in the team could read it and so they very carefully took a photograph of the first few lines, as much as they dared unscroll. They sent the image back to the University of Chicago and asked them to get someone to look at it."

Kalki brings the plates bearing the broken birds. He offers roasted vegetables from a salver, and places sauce bowls of thick gravy at each end of the table. Conversation is temporarily halted, and not resumed until the butler has refilled their glasses and left the room.

"What did they make of it?"

"Several people examined the image. The consensus was that it was an introduction to a play. Likely the play was being submitted to a competition, and the introduction was probably a speech the author intended to give before the performance, an appeal for a favorable response. The first thing the author says—the only thing in the fragment they had photographed—was to declare that he had fought at Marathon."

"Is that significant?"

"Aeschylus fought at Marathon."

"They thought it was Aeschylus?"

"They thought it was possible—how many survivors of the battle would have gone on to write plays? Aeschylus wrote many plays but few are complete, and mostly just fragments survive. None of the people who studied the image had ever before read that introduction, so if it was Aeschylus then that much at least was new."

"The discovery of a lost play by Aeschylus—I can see why you went."

"But there's more to it than that. It was not just the one scroll; there were dozens of them, still in situ. This was just the only one they had looked at."

"More Aeschylus?"

"No, something else. Remember that the site is assumed to have once been the southern terminal of an ancient caravan route."

"Yes?"

"A route that would have begun in the north."

"And?"

"Ancient Greek texts from the northern side of the Sahara?"

Gidding sits back glass in hand, puzzling over the clue. Andromeda takes the opportunity to stop talking and eat. The partridge is tough and chalky, not the bland meat of domesticated fowl but the vigorous flesh of an animal that has lived in the precarious wild—Hobbes's red in tooth and claw. She removes from her mouth what at first she assumes is a small piece of bone, but which turns out to be a little lead ball. Andromeda had imagined that the birds were snared; now she realizes that there must be a firearm somewhere on the island.

A look of understanding crosses Gidding's face. "Alexandria," he says.

"Exactly. The greatest library of the ancient world, the repository of human knowledge since the time of Aristotle."

"What happened to it?"

"Sometime during the slow decline of the Roman Empire it was burned to the ground and the collection destroyed. An incalculable loss. Historians have long speculated that some of it might have been saved, if only by looting, but little evidence for this has ever been uncovered."

"Until the scroll."

"Yes."

"What happened?"

"The team was told to do no more until specialists arrived. It would basically put the dig on hold, but it was vital that the scrolls be preserved."

"What did you do?"

"I got my shots, stocked up on anti-malarial drugs, and flew to Bamako, the capital of Mali. There's a ferry that runs down the Niger during the wet season, which was almost over. The ferry was carrying the supplies that would see the team through the digging season, so they asked if I could accompany them—unaccompanied supplies tended to disappear, and if they needed more they would have to fly the stuff in, which was expensive and would eat into their limited grant money.

"I agreed. It was eight hundred miles downriver from Koulikoro to Gao—five days and nights. I was the only white woman on board; in fact the only white person. There were as many goats and chickens as people. I slept on deck on top of the crates to be sure they stayed secure. I knew that getting sick would be a disaster so I brought along enough food to see me through—basically protein bars and those little plastic bags of drinking water that people use in West Africa. But when we came alongside on the second night the smell from the street stalls was too much, so I risked it. I survived, and for the rest of the trip I ate from the wharf vendors like everyone else. After five days we made Gao. Two of the team came down to meet me, and we loaded the supplies into their Land Rover and drove up to the dig. That was another two hundred miles, dirt track or no track at all—it took us eight hours to make Manoukaram.

"There were only five people currently in the team: three Americans, an Italian, and a Norwegian. Two of the Americans and the Norwegian were post-grad students. The other American, Professor Davidson, was the team leader. A private institute in Salerno was a co-sponsor of the expedition, and their Paolo Lucibello was the second-in-command. They also had a local guide who acted as interpreter and foreman. There were two villages nearby, sharing a single well located several miles away. Most of the physical digging was done by men hired from these villages.

"The next morning they showed me the site. There wasn't much to see: several open pits, the largest probably fifty feet square. They told me they had difficulty getting the men to work: they were keen when the job started, but as soon as they raised a sweat they just stopped. Nevertheless, the excavation had come down to mud-brick foundations, and it was while excavating these that they found the scrolls.

"There were a lot of locals around, all men. I noticed that they always split into two groups and the groups didn't get along. They showed up each morning even though the interpreter had explained that the dig was halted. I feared they might have been looking for things to take, and Davidson had come to the same conclusion: some gear had already gone missing. He moved the camp closer to the site so they could better maintain security, and had gone to a watch system after dark so that one person was always awake."

"Did it feel dangerous?"

"Yes, but the danger wasn't directed at us. The men from the two villages belonged to different tribes. We couldn't tell them apart but they could, and they despised each other. While there had been easy money from the dig they had put their quarrels aside, but when that stopped their enmity flared up. There was a lot of shouting, occasionally there were fights, more posing than actual fighting, but clearly there was bad blood between them.

"Soon I had pretty much everything I could get for the article before the reinforcements arrived, so I started to take a greater interest in the surroundings. I went out further into the desert. It was quite beautiful but not varied, and I didn't go far because fuel was at a premium.

"One day, I walked to the well. There were a dozen or so women there, very colorfully dressed. They were shy at first, but two of them had been to a missionary school and spoke some English. We talked. I asked them which village they were from, and it turned out they were from both: it seemed that the womenfolk got along fine; it was only the men who quarreled. Since it was the women who collected the water they saw each other regularly. Soon I learned that it was not only water-carrying the women did: they did everything: work the fields, raise the children, keep the house, husk the grain, cook the meals, tend the goats. What did the men do, I asked. Get drunk and make trouble was the answer. They only worked at the dig for the opportunity to steal, the women told me, and then only because they were paid.

"I was struck by how hard these women had it. I asked them how old they were. The two I was able to talk to directly seemed older than me, but it turned out one was eighteen and the other wasn't sure, but she thought she was twenty-two. A woman in her thirties was old, they told me, and few lived into their fifties.

"I started taking daily walks to the well. I wanted to bathe without wasting precious water that had been trucked into the camp, and since the village men never went to the well I could do so safely. The women thought I was an oddball for wanting to wash so regularly. It became a ritual: I would show up early each morning before it got too hot, they would watch me bathe, and then we would talk while I dried off. They asked me lots of questions about how I lived.

"You don't think of it in these days of media saturation, but there are still places in the world with no television and where people are illiterate: my life in Manhattan seemed unbelievable to them. They would make comments between themselves from time to time, and I would ask one of the English speakers what they were saying. Sometimes they wouldn't answer, but I got hints of how miserable their own lives were: not just the endless work—they were basically just slaves for the men—but also outright abuse.

"One day they asked me to come to the well that night. It was to be a full moon, and they had something special planned. I was wary but I basically trusted them, so I agreed. I took one of the Land Rovers out at moonrise. They were already at the well. I turned off the lights and got out. The women were in high spirits, and at first I thought they must have gotten into the men's liquor. They were dancing and singing. When I approached I realized they were naked. They offered me a bowl of whatever it was they were drinking and so I drank, too. It wasn't until I'd taken a mouthful that I realized it was blood. Then I saw the machetes. Most of them had one and they were holding them up as they danced and sang and stamped their feet. I looked closer at the women. It was hard to make out in the moonlight with their black skin, but I saw that they were covered in blood, in fact were drenching themselves in it, as if in ecstasy."

"A ritual sacrifice?"

"That's what I thought, too. A goat or two, I imagined, something that would constitute a feast in their meager lives. But then one of them calmed down sufficiently to tell me what had happened. It wasn't goats they had slaughtered, it was men.

"Apparently, they had had enough. The women from the two villages had been discussing it for some time, how much better their lives would be if the men didn't exist. They did nothing; they were only liabilities, people who made an already hard life even harder. Then a woman learned that the men from one village were planning to poison the well. The idea was for them not to use it, and allow the other village to poison themselves by drinking the water. But where will we get our water, the woman asked. The men hadn't thought of that, but it didn't deter them: they planned to go ahead and poison the well anyway. That was the final straw. The next day at the well she told the women from both villages what the men were planning. In the end, they decided to finish with them once and for all. From their point of view they had no choice: they could not survive without water, and nor could they flee—there was nowhere they could flee to, and they had no money anyway. They took the only way out: they decided to kill every male who was irredeemable, which pretty much meant every male over twelve years of age. They took a solemn oath between themselves, and that night encouraged the men to drink, something easy enough to do. When the moon rose they carried it out: between the two villages thirty-seven men were hacked to death as they slept."

"What happened next?"

"I returned to the camp. The Norwegian was on watch, and when he saw me get out of the vehicle the poor fellow was sick. I was covered in blood and some of it was my own: somehow in the melee around the well one of those waving machetes had cut my face, presumably just the tip. Amid all the hubbub I'd barely noticed.

"I roused the rest of the camp and tried to calmly explain what had happened, but when they understood that all the men had been butchered they were beyond calm. One of the post-grads kept shouting that they had to get me to a hospital, although I insisted that all I needed was a bit of basic first aid. The Norwegian was still sick; it seemed that he just couldn't take the sight of blood. Davidson panicked: he decided to immediately abandon the dig. I protested but there was no stopping him, and his panic infected the others, already spooked by my appearance. They piled into the Land Rovers without even breaking camp, just grabbing the bare essentials. I couldn't stay because there would be no vehicle, so I went with them. By sunrise we were in Gao, by evening we were in Bamako. They never returned.

"And you got medical treatment?"

"I made do with antibiotic cream and band-aids. That's why there's a scar, the wound was not sewn before healing."

"Which you don't regret?"

"No. I figured that it was less risky than a West African hospital."

"What happened to the village women?"

"Initially nothing, because no one knew. Apparently they buried the men the next day and then carried on as normal, tending their livestock and crops. No regrets, just the opposite; they were happy: for the first time in their lives no one was oppressing them. This went on for a week or so, but then word got out.

"The government labeled it terrorism. The army was sent in. The soldiers killed the old women immediately, and raped the young ones before killing them too. Then they looted the dig. Almost everything was left behind that night; the aim had been to just get away. After they'd taken what they wanted they poured gasoline over the rest and set fire to it, apparently in an attempt to conceal the fact of the looting. Of course they had no interest in the written word and so incinerated the scrolls along with everything else. Whatever was in them is lost forever now."

Gidding says nothing for a while, staring into the fire while Andromeda continues eating. She finishes her meal and sits back with the wine, contemplating her host/warden.

"So now I have answered your question: the scar was inflicted by a machete-wielding native on a frenzied moonlit night around a remote desert well."

"And you wrote about it?"

"About the events, yes."

"Including the fact that you yourself were wounded?"

"No."

"And that you bathed every morning before an audience of curious natives?"

"No, of course not."

"Or slept on the crates to keep them safe, or were lured ashore by the smell of street food?"

"It was a magazine piece. The article wasn't about me."

"Then I'm pleased to have heard the unabridged version," Gidding says. "That's the trouble with story-telling, don't you think: the medium itself gets in the way." He finishes his wine and stands. "Let's have coffee in the Griffin Room."

XXIX

KALKI SERVES A local sheep's milk cheese and then brings coffee. Gidding goes to the sideboard and uncorks a bottle of port.

"Fonseca Guimaraens 'ninety-three," he says.

"Not much for me. I've already had enough."

Gidding pours her a full glass. "My aim is to get you a little drunk tonight," he admits.

"Why?"

"Because now I will keep my side of the bargain." He brings the glasses to the table and sits. "I'm going to show you my *Faust*. But first, like Aeschylus, I intend to plead my case."

Andromeda tries the cheese, hard and full of flavor, while Gidding begins.

"Movie-making is a compromise," he says. "There's no avoiding it because making a film is a collaborative enterprise: there are actors, cameramen, sound recorders, film editors, and a thousand others. Collaboration necessitates compromise, but every time you compromise a little something gets lost, and the end result is always diminished by that gradual erosion of integrity. My aim in *Faust* was to minimize the compromise. I wanted it to be as singular as possible.

Above all, I wanted an honest work. Joyce once wrote that his only weapons were silence, exile, and cunning—without them one assumes that *Ulysses* would not have been possible. I used the same weapons.

"Firstly, silence. That was easy enough: I refused all interviews, although it annoyed the publicity people, and I didn't mix socially with the actors and crew.

"Secondly, exile. I chose Rothermore not only because it is a suitable location, but also because it's isolated and remote—not just for me but for the crew, too. I wanted them fully focused, without distraction.

"Thirdly, cunning. Well, yes, I've had to use a lot of that. Financing is always the difficult part: it never comes without conditions, and conditions mean compromise, and compromise kills art. So I funded it myself—fortunately, I have an excellent accountant. I mortgaged everything I own, and I did something that I've never done before: product placement. The clothing you're wearing tonight was supplied by the designer, and Cartier sent the jewelry—I must remember to send it back. At a contractually agreed point in the closing credits the words 'Miss Djahidra's clothing by such-and-such' and 'Jewelry by so-and-so' will appear—for a contractually agreed period of time and in contractually agreed-size lettering. But that was something I was happy to do: the fact that they're real makes for a better movie, I think.

"I like using real things, like this abbey: very little of the filming took place in sets; almost everything was shot on location here—no scenery, no decoration, no props. Using real things makes the actors better, too: they don't have to fake it as much. And I don't mean just in the obvious ways, like actors in front of a bluescreen having to pretend to interact with some computer-generated nonsense to be superimposed later. I mean in subtle ways, too. I realized early on that my Mephistopheles had to move well—it's how I was able to choose Soline without a screen test: she had complete physical control, calm grace with an underlying suggestion of hard athleticism. Having her wear real things helped bring out that quality, as if she were subconsciously aware of the swish of genuine silk, or the heft of real jewelry, and moved all the better because of it."

"Faust's clothing?"

"His, too. But my *Faust* isn't just about Faust, it's mostly about Mephistopheles."

"And for whom the first choice didn't work out."

Gidding takes a little time before responding. "Brando might have been difficult, but he *was* Kurtz, and so it was worth it for Coppola to stick with him. For me, Mallory was never Mephistopheles; she was miscast, and therefore the fault is mine. When I signed her I thought I needed an actress; it wasn't until later that I realized I had to have the real thing." Gidding stands and takes a torch from a wall sconce. "But why not come and see for yourself."

ANDROMEDA AND GIDDING descend deep into the abbey and the stone walls are soon replaced by bare rock, a subterranean passage hewn directly into the earth. They come to a heavy wooden door, but unlike the others this one has a lock. Gidding withdraws a large key and opens it, revealing a spiral stone staircase leading yet further down. They take it to the bottom where it ends at an iron gate with a dark space on the other side. Andromeda wonders if she is being led into a dungeon. Gidding unlocks the gate, and the hinges squeak as he opens it. He enters first and finds a switch. The flood of light reveals a broad room with rows of columns and a vaulted ceiling.

"The crypt," Gidding says. He extinguishes the torch by smothering it with a leather cloth. "I use it as the editing room, for two reasons. Firstly, it's cool and dry, which is good for the servers. I film mostly on film—nothing captures depth like celluloid—but then I copy over to digital for editing because it's more flexible. When the editing is complete on the digital copy I go back to the original film for the final cut. But digital editing requires heavy computing power, hence these servers." He nods toward a wall, where several computers stand in line. The floor around them is littered with electrical cables. "Another reason is that neither light nor sound penetrates down here. When the door is closed and the lights are off it is completely dark and completely soundproof—perfect for editing."

Perfect for imprisonment too, Andromeda thinks, but she keeps the thought to herself. The wall across from them is dotted with niches, and many appear occupied, like a catacomb. "Are those what I think they are?" she asks.

"If you think they're bones, then yes. This space is less a crypt than an ossuary. What little soil there is on the island was used for cultivation—too precious for proper burial, and so instead the bones of the monks were laid to rest in that wall."

"And we're going to watch your movie in here?"

"At least the audience will keep quiet."

"No doubt."

"If that bothers you, then I don't think you're going to like the seating arrangements." He leads her to the end of the crypt where sitting atop a stone plinth is a tomb, uncarved on the sides but with the figure of a monk reclining in beatific repose sculpted on the lid.

"Abbot Grellwyn," Gidding says, performing introductions. "He ran the place sometime in the Twelfth Century. No common ossuary for him: he wanted nothing but the best in the hereafter. The good abbot will be serving as our backrest tonight."

"We're going sit on a dead monk?"

"Mephistopheles would be pleased, don't you think?"

He leads her around to the other side of the sarcophagus. The stone plinth here has been laid with animal furs. A long bolster lies along the base of the tomb, and there is a scattering of cushions. Candles have been placed at either end and a tray on a low wooden stand sits in the middle, delineating the two seating areas. On the tray are a silver coffee pot and matching cups rendered in graceful Middle-Eastern design, etched with flowing arabesques. The candles are alight and steam rises from the coffee pot—Kalki must have preceded them to the crypt. On the floor is a hookah from which pungent blue swirl curls slowly skyward.

"In this theater," Gidding says, "you can smoke."

A screen is mounted on the end wall twenty feet in front of them, not much smaller than a screen in a regular cinema. The plinth and tomb form a natural seat facing it.

Gidding turns off the main lighting, leaving the sitting area illuminated by the soft glow from the candles. He goes to the projector, mounted on a frame behind the tomb, and begins threading the reel.

Andromeda sits. She removes her shoes. The crypt is the right temperature for servers but too cool for a barely dressed human being, and Andromeda draws the furs around her.

Gidding turns on the projector, and Andromeda hears the fan start. A faint square of light takes form on the screen, gradually brightening. Gidding returns with a remote control connected to the projector by wire.

"We'll have to wait a few minutes while the lamp warms."

Gidding pours coffee and offers a pipe from the hookah. Andromeda accepts it and draws cautiously, but the tobacco tastes sour and she puts the pipe aside.

"Let's begin," Gidding says. He pushes a button on the remote.

The first thing to hit Andromeda is not light but sound, loud music made more startling by the silence that proceeded it, and she imagines that the crypt's audio system could power a rock concert. Gidding leans across and says, "That should make the audience sit up. Led Zeppelin agreed to let me use it—I'm very fortunate: they almost never let anyone use their music."

The screen is initially black but then letters gradually appear, fading in like moonlight revealed by a passing cloud. It is the title *The Tragical History of Doctor Faustus*, but soon many of the letters redden and liquefy, running slowly down the screen, leaving only the word *Faust* intact. Then that fades too, and the music gradually transforms into the sound of a thunderstorm. There are no other opening credits—a good choice, Andromeda thinks, for Gidding has the viewer's full attention now, and she feels a faint thrill of anticipation as the movie begins.

A man struggles up a rainswept path. He pauses and looks up. The view he sees is the same view that Andromeda saw earlier in the day: the abbey, massive and bleak. The camera must have been shooting from the same spot they stopped at on the way up, and she realizes that the pause this afternoon had not been coincidental: Gidding wanted her to see this view for herself.

The man enters the abbey and discards his cloak. He is in his thirties, clean-shaven, long dark ringlets framing a serious, intelligent face.

"Faust is wet," he announces to the empty hall, apparently referring to himself in the third person. "Faust is wet, Faust is wet." He turns a cunning eye to the camera, and with a sly smile says, "Faust is wet, but he is not dampened." Then he winks.

Andromeda realizes that we are to be intimates, this Faust and the viewer. He is dressed in Sixteenth-Century garb: black coat over shirt and breeches, soft velvet hat, buckled shoes, but then he pulls out from under his coat a small notepad computer and holds it aloft with a flourish.

This strange device I have acquired wherein
I am assured that all the secrets of
Agrippa reside. Ha! Secret things and occult
knowings that the magus sought to shield from
the eyes of God and men will be to me all reveal'd.

Andromeda leans toward Gidding and whispers, although there is none but the dead abbot to disturb.

"Blank verse?'

"Only occasionally. Usually iambic pentameter; sometimes Alexandrines, as in that last line. But always intelligible—this is not to be a movie for English majors only."

Faust enters the library. He places the computer on the reading table—an Apple device with the brand's symbol prominently visible:

more product placement, Andromeda assumes. Faust opens the laptop cautiously, the way a man does an unfamiliar object. He presses a button. The screen lights up, and the usual Mac operating system theme sounds.

"Ah, magic," says Faust, who is obviously unfamiliar with computers. His look of anticipation soon turns into a scowl. "Password? What is this password? Faust knows of no password." He struggles to unlock the computer, but his efforts are futile and he becomes increasingly frustrated. At last he sits back in defeat.

"What would I not give to know this password," he declares.

A lightning strike hits the iron bars of the window, melting them. The blast blows Faust to the floor, and the flash momentarily blinds him. Mephistopheles appears on the mezzanine above, unseen by Faust. She is naked and bloodied and snarling. She is crouching on her haunches, fingertips on the floor, hair in wild disarray, a feral animal poised ready to spring. Her skin is inscribed with strange symbols. She scurries on all fours to the railing and looks down at Faust. Saliva hangs from her mouth. Her teeth look sharp. She growls a single low word, barely intelligible: *meat*.

Faust recovers himself and goes to the window, inspecting the misshapen remains of the iron bars.

"If I but had such power as could do this," he says.

Behind and still unseen by him Mephistopheles descends the stairs, a new woman. She is upright now. She wears the same dress that Andromeda is wearing and the same stiletto-heeled shoes. The markings on her flesh have vanished. Her hair is up and she is adorned with jewelry, having transformed from the demon of a moment ago into a sleek cosmopolitan creature, stylish and sophisticated.

She manages the stairs with more grace than Andromeda had in the same dress, careless of the quantity of flesh thus revealed, and glides over to the reading table on which cocktail gear has suddenly appeared. She pours herself a Martini and adds an olive with a playful plop. The sound makes Faust turn. He almost falls a second time.

"Who art thou?"

Mephistopheles looks up.

"You know who I am."

"I do not."

"I am your guest."

"I have no guest."

"You invited me.

"I invited no one."

"My dear Doctor Faustus, you most assuredly issued an invitation."

"Thou knowest my name?"

"Of course. We are old friends, you and I."

"I have never met thou before in my life."

"In another life, then."

"Depart at once."

"As you wish." But she makes no move to leave, and instead turns her attention to the computer, still open on the table. Faust takes a cautious step forward.

"What dost thou want?"

The question makes her look up. "What do *I* want?' She turns and comes toward him, a slow sensuous walk that nevertheless manages to be threatening. "My wants are simple and easily satisfied. This isn't about *me*, doctor, it's about *you*." Faust backs up to the window. Mephistopheles comes to a halt close in front of him, and places a long-fingered hand on his chest. He leans backward, his head out the window and hair blown by the storm. She leans forward, her lips inches from his. "The question we must ask ourselves, doctor, is what exactly is it that you want."

"I want for naught," he protests.

"I'm sure there's something I can give you."

"Faust desires nothing from thou."

"Yes, you do. Why don't I whisper what it is, and then you tell me if I'm right?" She puts her lips to his ear. "*Vade, triplex Jehovae!*"

"What?"

'You speak Latin."

"Away, threefold God? What dost thou mean?"

"It's what you want."

"The Holy Trinity to disappear? Such blasphemies are not the desire of Faust."

"No?" Mephistopheles stands back. "And here I was thinking that you wanted the password to that little old laptop over there."

For the first time Faust's face shows something other than fear. "*Vade triplex Jehovae!* is the password?"

"No spaces. Capitalize the first letter of each word, and don't forget the exclamation mark."

Faust rushes to the laptop and types in the password. It works, and he dances in delight. Mephistopheles smiles, and her eyes narrow.

For the remainder of the reel, Mephistopheles continues her recruitment of Faust. She will provide him with a feast, but insists that he must first dress for dinner. They go to his bedroom, where Faust finds a new dinner suit waiting, complete with shirt and studs and cuff links, patent leather shoes, and a blood-red cummerbund with a black pentagram embroidered at its center.

Faust tries casting some spells as he dresses, but for every incantation he finds on Agrippa's computer Mephistopheles goes one better. A charm to make audible the music of the spheres produces no discernable result, but at the snap of Mephistopheles' fingers a turntable appears, and she supplies the Miles Davis records. The doctor finds that he likes jazz. While she helps him with the bow tie he tries an alchemical recipe to transmute a cuff link into gold; Mephistopheles instead turns his mirror into quicksilver. At first he does not believe her, since the reflection is unchanged, but she urges him to poke a finger in it. He does so and finds that indeed the mirror has become a mercury waterfall, smooth as glass except where his finger interrupts the flow.

"I did the bed, too," Mephistopheles says. "Your chiropractor will thank me."

Faust goes to the bed, lifts the cover, and is astonished by what he finds. He soon loses interest in Agrippa's computer. When he is dressed they head downstairs, but before following her from the room Faust turns to the camera and confides to the viewer *sotto voce*:

It is my soul she contrives to capture
but Faust is no fool. With her I will amuse
myself and perhaps allow her to divert me
with an item or two of interest.

Faust turns to leave, but after a few steps he stops and looks back over his shoulder, again addressing the viewer. "I can stop any time I like, you know."

IN THE GRIFFIN ROOM, Mephistopheles mixes cocktails. Faust regards her with a combination of curiosity and suspicion.

"Thy name?"

"You may call me Mephistopheles."

"A dexterous appellation, yet art thou not sinister?"

"Sinister in every sense, but you may call me Mephistopheles just the same."

"What manner of creature art thou?"

"Demon."

"Which is?"

"A holy angel, in the humble service of my lord and master."

"Name thy lord, demon."

"My lord is Lucifer."

"Satan, the Prince of Darkness."

Mephistopheles sighs. "Really, I would have expected better from a scholar. The term *Lucifer* is of course derived from the Latin *lux*, meaning light—the very opposite of darkness, as it happens. Some, whom we will not now name, have sought to besmirch my master's reputation with puerile phrases such as 'Prince of Darkness'—it is an old political tactic: throw mud in the hope that some sticks. The truth is that my master is the morning star, Faustus; he is the bringer of light. He will be your redemption and your salvation." She fixes him with a cool gaze. "It would not do you well to speak ill of him."

"And art thou from Hell, holy angel of Lucifer?"

"Where else?"

"Speak of it."

"Of Hell?

"Yes, describe it for Faust."

She walks over and joins him, cocktails in hand.

"Hell is like an all-inclusive resort, but with better food and less tiresome guests."

She offers Faust a glass, which he accepts warily.

"What elixir be this?"

"A Martini."

"A magical potion?"

"Indeed—one sees things more clearly after consuming one."

He gazes into his glass. "Is that an eyeball at the bottom?"

"Cocktail olive."

He sips cautiously.

"Hast thou seen Paradise, demon?'

"There is no such thing."

"Of course there is."

'No."

"Then neither can there be a Hell."

"You've obviously never been to an all-inclusive resort." She takes a sip of her cocktail. "Why don't you tell me what this Paradise of yours is like, Doctor?"

"How would Faust know?"

"You're the one who claims that it exists."

"Very well. Paradise is a place where there are no longer any cares."

"What cares?"

"Money, for example."

"How very bourgeois." Mephistopheles snaps her fingers. Gold and silver coins rain down upon them. Faust is amazed, but

Mephistopheles merely holds a protective hand over her glass. Eventually, the shower stops. Mephistopheles casually skewers her olive with the long fingernail of a pinkie finger and then plucks the fruit from it with her teeth, still conspicuously sharp. "My master is adept at such things," she says.

"Producing money out of thin air?"

"We call it *investment banking*."

Faust stoops to pick up a sovereign, but as his fingers reach to grab the coin it disappears. He tries another and then another, but each time the same thing happens.

"The money just melts away,' he says.

"That, also, is investment banking." Mephistopheles waves a hand, breezily dismissing the subject. "Tell me, doctor, what other quotidian cares are absent from this purported Paradise of yours?"

"There is but one thing that truly matters: health."

"Health?"

"Certainly. *Mens sana in corpore sano*: a healthy mind in a healthy body."

"You're not a vegan or anything, are you?"

"No."

"Then why all this fuss with health? In my circles, a liver that is not enlarged is considered a sign of poor character."

"To live longer, of course."

"Oh, is that all? You don't need a Paradise for immortality, doctor. Where I come from it's quite *de rigueur*."

"So then how old art thou, demon?"

"As old as the wind."

"And how old is the wind?"

"It was born yesterday, and shall be born again tomorrow."

"Thou speakest in riddles."

"Everything is a riddle, to those who do not know."

"Know what, demon?"

"The secrets of the world. The true causes of things."

"Tell me these secrets, then."

"Ah, but such things are not free, doctor, and we have not agreed on a price." She finishes her cocktail and puts down the glass. "Come, let's eat. I'm famished."

She walks past him and out of frame. Faust turns to follow, but then remembers that he is being observed. He turns to the camera, slightly annoyed.

"I've already told you," he says, "I can stop anytime I like."

THERE IS A FEAST. The attendants are Moorish slave girls wearing harem pants and tops of silver chain. Some have musical instruments and they play strange tunes in Oriental quarter tones. Others dance before a food-laden table where Faust and Mephistopheles sit side-by-side. Mephistopheles has a large bone in hand and tears the flesh from it with those sharp teeth.

"Tell me more of these secrets," Faust says.

She answers between ravenous mouthfuls. "They're the sort of things that you were trying to conjure from that stupid computer, except ours work."

"Divination, then?"

"Of course."

"Can you resurrect the dead?"

"I dine with them regularly."

"Transmutation of the elements?"

"Tricky without a supercollider, but yes, transmutation, too. It's really just a matter of sufficient energy."

"Ascension to the celestial spheres?"

"Sure: golf on the moon; dune buggies on Mars."

"These are wondrous things," Faust says. Mephistopheles puts down the bone, now devoid of flesh.

"They are wondrous to you because you do not understand them. If you understood, such things would no longer be wondrous. They would simply be." She lifts her goblet and drains it.

"I long to understand."

"No doubt."

"Will you tell me more?"

"It's late, doctor. Thank you for the invitation. I've had a pleasant evening but I really must be going." She stands to leave. Faust stands too.

"But you'll be back tomorrow?"

"I regret that I'm otherwise engaged tomorrow."

"But I want to know more."

"Then know thyself, doctor."

"What?"

"Know thyself. Knowledge is not free, it comes with obligations. Before acquiring knowledge you must be ready for the responsibilities that accompany it."

'And then what?"

"And then... we'll see."

"How will I contact you?"

"You're the necromancer, doctor. Conjure something. Meanwhile, why don't you take a little opium, which I find is a wonderful *digestif.*" She nods toward a hookah that has appeared by his side. It is the same one that Andromeda smoked from earlier, and she suddenly realizes why the tobacco had tasted sour—it was not tobacco at all. The device puzzles Faust, but he soon works it out. He picks up a pipe and takes a few hesitant puffs.

"Will you join me?"

He turns back to Mephistopheles, and finds that she is gone.

FAUST RETURNS TO his bedroom, treading slowly, stupefied by the opium and left despondent by Mephistopheles' abrupt disappearance. "Mephistopheles!" he cries, "Mephistopheles!" but the only answer is silence.

Faust is forsaken. What if she never comes back?
The secrets she speaks of I have craved for years
And a fortune I have given away for this computer
that couldn't even conjure a candle, and yet she
turns my mirror to mercury with a snap of her fingers.
What power!

Faust goes to the mirror and begins to undress. He is undoing his bow tie when the quicksilver wavers, as when he placed his fingers in it earlier. He looks up, but nothing appears to interrupt the flow. When he looks down again he no longer sees his reflection. He brings the candle closer. The quicksilver now contains an image of a room, but not his bedroom. The room is in shadow except for a single narrow stage projecting fifty feet from a curtained entrance. The sole pieces of furniture are a chair placed on the floor at the end of the stage and beside it a slender stand supporting an ashtray. Whatever show is to come, it will be for an audience of one.

A figure enters. It is himself, still dressed in the dinner suit. He walks to the chair, sits in a relaxed posture with legs crossed at the knee, and lights a cigarette—a long black one with a distinctive gold filter of the type Andromeda had tried in Venice. Dramatic music begins.

A woman emerges from behind the curtains. It is Mephistopheles. She wears a stylish outfit but the cut is exaggerated, the sort of clothing seen in fashion shows but rarely worn in real life. She parades down the runway and stops at the end, directly in front of Faust but otherwise ignoring him, and poses first one way and then the other, as if being photographed. She then turns, goes back up the runway, and disappears behind the curtains.

A second later she reemerges, this time in a micro-mini, very high heels, and a completely new hair style, an impossibly quick change. Again she parades, again ignores Faust, again disappears behind the curtains. The next time she comes out with a fishnet top and hot pants. Then a maillot, then a bikini, finally underwear, sheer and brief.

When she disappears this time the music stops. The fashion show has ended. Faust stubs out his cigarette, stands, and leaves the room. The image in the quicksilver fades away, slowly replaced by Faust's own reflection. Then he finds in the reflection that he is no longer alone. He turns. On the bed behind him two of the Moorish dancers from earlier in the evening are lying in wait, naked, smiling shyly.

Faust laughs.

"A test, eh?" he cries out to the empty air. "You won't get me that easily, demon. You won't get me that easily!" He shoos the girls from his room.

XXX

THE REEL ENDS WITH THE tail of the film flapping against the casing. Gidding switches off the projector.

"That's it for tonight."

"Oh, but I want to see more."

"And so you shall, tomorrow night."

Andromeda sighs in disappointment. "I feel like Faust—unreasonably deprived."

"Then I wish all my audiences were you."

They leave the crypt. Andromeda feels flushed and light-headed and not at all like sleep. In the Griffin Room, Gidding gives her a candle, bids her goodnight, and watches her disappear up the stairs. In her room she receives a surprise: Faust's mirror is now there.

The fire is flickering brightly and she has no need of the candle. Andromeda inspects the mirror. It is full-length and fixed at a slight angle to ensure that the mercury slides down smoothly. At the base is a reservoir, and by lightly touching the frame she can feel the faint vibration of the pump that sends the mercury back to the top. She places a finger on the mirror and the quicksilver flows around, the ripples undulating outward as in the film.

Andromeda undoes her dress and allows it to fall to the floor.

She studies her reflection in quiet deliberation, much as in *Diotima* Margot had contemplated her own. The firelight sends her face into shadowed relief. Her right cheek is illuminated, but the scar is still invisible beneath the makeup. The flames reflect in the titanium collar, a nice Mephistophelean touch. Her breasts are small and firm like Soline Djahidra's, but pink-nippled rather than Soline's darker brown, matching her olive skin. Lean body. In this light it seems to be planar, a Cubist decomposition of broken surfaces intersecting at odd angles across tendon and bone—who would find that attractive, she wonders. Bag of bones, look at those ribs. Her arms are thin just below the shoulder, then expand in gently convex curves over what passes for bicep, thinning again at the elbow, the shape of a limb more suited to a praying mantis than a human being. For a moment Andromeda imagines herself as a predatory insect—those planar surfaces would be exoskeletal armor, her ribs a series of thoracic gills.

She wonders if Kafka was an opium smoker, too.

Narrow hips. Long slender legs, slightly awkward, as if having been stretched out of proportion to the body above.

Her flesh tingles as if caressed by some invisible hand. She wonders if it was really opium that she smoked earlier: opium is supposed to be a soporific, but in her case it has instead acted as a stimulant, heightening her perception and sharpening her senses to the point where she feels razor-sharp, a precision instrument all aquiver with possibility.

She feels hot with opium or whatever it was. She goes to the windows and opens the shutters. The great stone walls had muted the storm, but with the shutters open she is confronted with the tempest in full fury, a night untamed, brutish, violent. She grips the iron bars and presses hard against them, as if bound to the grate for a flogging. The windswept rain rakes across her body, strafing her flesh, and the wind whips wildly at her hair.

She undergoes flagellation by weather.

The cold eventually forces her back inside. She closes the shutters and goes into the bathroom, toweling dry and trying to comb the knots from her hair. Andromeda hoped that the rain would douse her strange nervous energy, but the wildness of the storm has only stoked it. She wonders if the mythical Andromeda had not secretly enjoyed being chained to a rock at the mercy of sea monsters. Perhaps she was annoyed when Perseus showed up.

She takes off her jewelry and returns it to the box. The book of nudes is on the desktop, although earlier she had returned it to the drawer. Someone left it out for her to find.

Andromeda takes the book from the desk and settles into a chair in front of the fire to warm up and dry off. She hooks a leg over the armrest, lies back in the cushions, and goes through the photographs. All women, none remotely insect-like. Then she comes to a photograph that she recognizes. It is the same one that Clare left of herself on Andromeda's pillow at the Pelican. The caption is *Self-Portrait*.

Andromeda looks at the front cover. *Nudes* by Clare Fontenelle. She checks the back flap of the dust cover, and there finds another photograph of Clare, now clothed. A brief biography states that she was born in New Orleans and now lives in Miami, but offers no other personal information. It lists the publications her work has appeared in, mostly well-known fashion journals, but also magazines as diverse as *Time* and *Playboy*.

She realizes that the presence of the book cannot be a coincidence: it is Gidding's way of admitting that he has had her followed since Miami.

Andromeda closes the book and goes to the bed. She presses a hand lightly against the liquid metal. It is unnaturally heavy, inertial. She cautiously lies down on her back and looks up to discover her own reflection. The ceiling is plated, the surface smoothly polished so that the image of herself is rendered softened, a glowing firelit gold contrasting to the chrome-like quicksilver and the band around her neck. The reflection seems oversized and rich and voluptuous, like the Koons' paintings. One leg bent, hair splayed across the pillow. The mercury carries her like a salted sea, like the Dead Sea. There is no comfort in this bed, and she knows that her dreams will be disturbed.

XXXI

ANDROMEDA AWAKENS LATE the next morning. Her first act after rising is to crack open a shutter and check the weather. The sky is low and leaden, and the wind is still high although no longer with the shrieking intensity of the previous evening. It is raining heavily, big drops that sweep in across her feet. The sea is a wild confusion of waves crashing against the rocks far below. No boat from Burrenhead would venture out in this weather.

She finds that again clothes have been laid out for her, again not her own. This time there is underwear, Italian, still in the original packaging. There are a shirt and a riding jacket and a pair of tight English breeches, plus three small ribbon-wrapped boxes, one with socks, the second a scarf, and the third a pair of soft leather gloves. On the floor stand knee-high riding boots, brand new. Everything is the correct size, even the gloves.

Andromeda dresses and goes downstairs. The Griffin Room is unoccupied but the sideboard has been laid with breakfast. There are two small chafing dishes of brightly polished copper, each with a little paraffin flame beneath. She opens the lids to inspect the contents: one has eggs, the other sausages. There is a loaf of bread on a wooden board, butter on ice, a bowl of marmalade, and next to the coffee pot an envelope with her name on it. Andromeda opens the envelope. There are two items inside: a note and a map. She reads the note first.

> *Good morning, Miss Chamberlain,*
>
> *I trust that you slept well. I regret that today I am occupied; perhaps you will take the opportunity to look around and see the abbey for yourself. In fact, I have arranged a little treasure hunt for you.*
>
> *There are five keys for you to find. Each of the keys unlocks something in the abbey, something that will bring you closer to your goal, and me to mine. I hope that you will enjoy the hunt, and look forward to seeing you again this evening at cocktails.*
>
> *Gidding*

Andromeda returns the note to its envelope and unfolds the map. It is a National Trust pamphlet, designed as a visitor's guide back when they ran the abbey. On this copy there is an addition made by hand, a large pentagram covering the floor plan, each point of which is numbered, presumably the sequence that she is expected to follow.

There is no fruit on the sideboard; Andromeda resigns herself to an English breakfast. At least the bread is fresh, the loaf still warm from the oven. She cuts a thick slice. There is a three-foot-long trident by the breadboard that at first Andromeda mistakes for a satanic prop left over from the movie, but she soon figures it out. She pins the bread to the prongs and toasts it over the fire.

After breakfast, she sits back with coffee and examines the map more closely. Counting the tower rooms, the abbey is built on seven separate levels, the steepness of the island having dictated a vertical arrangement. The floor plan is exploded, with a separate layout for each level. The principal rooms are numbered. There is a key on the side with the name of each room and explanatory notes.

The lowest level is the crypt, with which Andromeda is already familiar. A note warns that there is no disabled access.

Above that are the old grain stores and, on the landward side, a cistern. A note explains that Rothermore has no natural streams or springs, which is the reason the island was uninhabited before the monks came. Their only source of fresh water was rainfall—abundant enough on Rothermore—collected in gutters and then led by a series of conduits and drains into the cistern, hewn directly into rock.

The fifth point of the pentagram is on the cistern.

On the next level up is the bakery, where she dined the previous evening, plus the scullery and a buttery. An annotation explains that this last was a storage room not for dairy products but for casks of ale that the monks brewed themselves.

The fourth level is the first substantial floor. It includes the reception hall—which served as a gift shop under the National Trust—and the Griffin Room, here marked as the refectory.

The fifth level is the largest, and includes the cloister and the chapel, points one and three on the pentagram. Her bedroom is labeled as the copy and illumination room. The text tells her what Gidding had already explained: although most monasteries of the time supported themselves with primary produce, the dearth of cultivatable land on the island meant that the monks had to find supplementary income, hence the business of copying and illuminating manuscripts. The library is offset a little above the copy room, and the two are linked by the small staircase that Andromeda has already noticed in the passageway outside her room, convenient for the monks to take out and return the precious volumes from which they worked. The library is the fourth point on the pentagram.

The sixth and seventh levels are both in the tower. The higher of the two is the belfry, used not only to house the bells that tolled matins and vespers but also as a lookout post and alarm station, when should a longboat be sighted the ringing would summon the monks back behind the safety of the abbey walls. Not safe enough, however: the bells were looted during the Norse invasions, and a note indicates that the National Trust welcomes donations to a fund established to recast and install historians' best guess as to what the originals would have been like.

The belfry is at the tip of the remaining point on the pentagram, numbered two.

Andromeda sits back and considers this strange invitation. At least the riding habit is explained—she is to go on a hunt—but the idea that Gidding had suddenly transformed into a gracious host wishing to keep his guest entertained is not to be taken seriously. There is some ulterior motive, although Andromeda wonders less about the treasure hunt than what could be the nature of the activity that is keeping Gidding otherwise occupied.

ANDROMEDA BEGINS WITH the cloister, the first point on the pentagram. It is in the eastern wing. She climbs the staircase from the refectory as usual, but at the top turns right instead of left toward her room. The passageway is lined with flaming torches, and her new boots sound loudly on the flagstones. There are monk's cells giving onto the corridor either side, narrow and windowless—the ultimate reduction of Woolf's dictum to find a room of one's own.

The passageway turns left, with a glimmer of natural light at the other end. The rooms here are larger, originally comprising the abbot's quarters, and includes a room that the map identifies as the 'Chapter House.' Andromeda passes by them and emerges into the cloister.

It is a hundred feet square, all four sides lined with vaulted aisles. According to the guide, the cloister was used as a place to grow vegetables protected from weather and wildlife and marauding Danes. It still serves as a garden, but a garden unlike anything that the monks could have imagined. The ground is covered by a large geodesic dome constructed of hexagonal glass panels, each three feet wide, and the top of which rises to a height well above the surrounding structure. The storm has lost the intense fury of the previous evening and settled into a hard rain beating against the panels, but on the other side of the glass is a landscape that belongs to a climate thousands of miles removed from Rothermore's: it is a lush tropical rainforest.

Andromeda circumnavigates the dome, looking for a way in. On the far side is an entrance, but the rain is heavy and traversing the brief gap between aisle and dome leaves her dripping. She closes the door and leans back against it, looking up.

Several trees occupy the central area, smooth-trunked and heavily buttressed at the base, but spreading at the higher levels to form a canopy. Vines hang from the branches. Surrounding them is a profusion of plant life: smaller trees and shrubs and flowers, glistening green leaves and big bright petals in abundance. The air is warm and humid, perfumed by fruit and flowers. A steady mist falls from above, so faint as to be almost undetectable. She locates the source: narrow pipes with perforations to allow steam to escape: an industrial-sized humidifier.

The key is easy to find. There is a small clearing in the middle of the rainforest in which stands a black marble pedestal. Hanging directly above it, suspended on a long slender wire, is a sunlamp. The key is in a shallow bowl sitting atop the pedestal. Andromeda recognizes the bowl: that same *kylix* she had last studied while lying in cushioned comfort at Ca' d'Inverno, waiting for her purchaser/abductor to return with champagne.

Coiled around the bowl is a snake, not very big but big enough and with a brilliant skin of iridescent green and gold scales in a trapezoidal pattern. It is alert, and it is staring at Andromeda.

The presence of the snake is not an accident: the lamp was placed to ensure that the creature, cold-blooded and naturally seeking warmth, would remain with the key. Andromeda realizes that she is being tested. If she threw something at the snake to shoo it away the kylix would likely end up in pieces on the floor, and she would have destroyed something that could never be replaced. She rules out throwing anything at the snake.

Andromeda takes off her riding boots and fits one onto each arm, fingers pointed into the toes to ensure that they stay on. She approaches the pedestal. The snake responds by rising, ready to strike. Andromeda edges closer, arms extended, and makes a feint with the boots. The snake rears back but otherwise does not react. Andromeda moves closer. This time when she feints the snake strikes twice in rapid succession, two surprisingly hard thumps into the sole of the left boot. Then, venom sacs presumably exhausted, the snake does what Andromeda had hoped it would: it retreats.

It slithers down the pedestal and disappears into the undergrowth. Andromeda puts her boots back on quickly, in case the snake returns.

She examines the key. It is small and tarnished with age, a simple barrel-and-flange arrangement. There is fresh scoring on the barrel—a key not in regular use, but one that has been used recently. A key to manacles, she thinks, or to shackles.

Andromeda takes a walk around the interior of the dome. She finds no locks but did not expect to: whatever the key unlocks is old, not something to be found in here. She unfolds the map and checks her next destination: the bell tower.

THE BELL TOWER IS SITUATED AT the southeastern corner of the abbey. Stairs lead up, here made of wood instead of the usual stone. At the top Andromeda finds a trapdoor. She pushes it open and climbs into the belfry.

As with the cloister, the monks would have been astonished by what occupies the space now. It is a large sculptural rendering of the solar system, executed in brass and copper and silver, as gleaming as the chafing dishes of this morning. At the center is the sun, two feet in diameter, emanating rays. The planets are depicted, elaborately etched, and with what are presumably their alchemical symbols standing proud above their north poles. Andromeda finds that she recognizes one of them: the symbol for Mercury is the same as the sign branded onto the acrobats in Venice, except that it is missing the interior circle and dot. But then she finds that one, too: it is the symbol for the Sun. The brand had been a combination of the two: the Sun within Mercury. She wonders what it could mean.

Andromeda takes out her phone, hoping that at this highest point in the abbey, and indeed of all Rothermore, she might at last get a signal, but still there is nothing. It seems that Gidding was telling the truth about one thing at least: cellphones do not work on the island. She puts away the phone and resumes her examination of the strange astronomical sculpture.

Attached to a ring beyond the planets, on a plane tilted at an angle, are the twelve signs of the zodiac. The entire thing, fifteen feet in diameter, rests upon an intricate base of ratchets and pinions and gear wheels, all made of gleaming metals, wonderfully ornate and as complex as a watch mechanism. Andromeda walks around it, searching for a key. On the far side there is a crank with an ebony handle. She gives the crank a few turns and hears the sound of a spring winding. Beside the crank is a lever fit for railroad switches. She releases it, and the mechanism slowly begins to move.

It manages about an Earth year before winding down. She rewinds the spring all the way to the stop, and this time the model rotates for several Earth decades, a period that turns out to be just a single solar rotation for distant Saturn.

Andromeda searches the device systematically, carefully inspecting each item, and then explores then the rest of the room, but she finds no sign of any key.

She takes out the map to locate the third point on the pentagram.

THE CHAPEL IS THE largest interior space in the abbey, built in basilican style with a long vaulted nave flanked by columned aisles on either side. There are no pews, just spacious stone. At the far end are the only furnishings: an altar, and behind it a life-size crucifix mounted high on the wall. Andromeda walks down the length of the nave, leather-and-venom soles echoing in the still cold.

There are two items on the altar: a big brass-bound Bible, and beside it a chased silver reliquary.

Andromeda examines the reliquary first. She can tell that the construction is actually wood with the silver covering added as decoration, or perhaps as a hedge during uncertain times in which wealth needed to be portable. It has been beaten into a complicated pattern of interwoven winged beasts, presumably demons—behind every religion is a secret fascination with evil, Andromeda thinks, evidenced from something as simple as this box to ten thousand tiresome lines of Milton.

The reliquary is locked. Andromeda tries the key she found in the cloister and it fits. When she opens the lid a Jack-in-the-box jumps out and Andromeda steps back in surprise. The thing laughs aloud while bouncing on its spring for a few moments but eventually goes silent and still. It is a Punch-like character, bearing the usual obscene leer. Its clothing is patterned in brightly colored diamonds, the garb of Harlequin, and she wonders if the echo of Venice is a coincidence. In its right hand it holds a weapon, not the traditional club but instead a riding crop. There is a Pan Am flight attendant's badge pinned to its shirt.

Andromeda approaches. She unpins and inspects the badge. It appears to be genuine, bearing the tiny scratches of an object that has seen real use. She puts it aside and pries the riding crop from the doll's grasp. It is long and slender with a distinctive silver ferrule that Andromeda recalls from the scene in the back of the Hispano-Suiza. No tarnish; it has been freshly polished for her to find. She loops the strap over her wrist and tests it on her calf. The tip delivers a pleasingly loud thwack against the leather of her boots.

These are just morsels to whet the appetite, Andromeda realizes—Gidding's implied admission that he made *Diotima*.

She inspects the Bible. The pages are thick and stiff, parchment or vellum she supposes. The text is in Latin; if period-correct then presumably Jerome's Vulgate. It is open at Isaiah 14:12.

Quomodo cecidisti de caelo, Lucifer, qui mane oriebaris?

The opening *Q* occupies the entire left-hand page—the verso—a lavishly elaborated and illuminated capital filled with fantastical flora and fauna, including at the base a snake whose serpentine body forms the letter's tail, and whose coloring and pattern exactly match those of the snake she encountered in the cloister. The opposite page—the recto—is inscribed with the remainder of the verse in dense Gothic lettering. Andromeda ponders the passage. *Caelo* probably means sky—that is, Heaven—and *qui* is no doubt who, but she cannot decipher anything else.

Andromeda examines the rest of the chapel carefully but finds no key.

At the conclusion of the search she arrives where she began, by the altar. She comes to a halt and looks up at the crucifix. It is a realistic rendering, Christ hanging on nailed hands and feet, blood on his brow from the crown of thorns and the spear wounds in his side dripping vividly. A curiously miserable thing to represent a religion, Andromeda thinks, although perhaps not so puzzling: it is in the nature of religions to have a maudlin preoccupation with death. If she were religious she decides that she would be a Buddhist: how preferable those jolly jasmine-wreathed Buddhas to this gruesome thing.

She retains the whip, pockets the badge, and leaves the chapel.

ANDROMEDA ARRIVES AT the library, fourth of the five points on the pentagram. She has not been in this room before but is familiar with it from the opening reel of *Faust*.

In the middle of the room is the same reading table, but sitting on it now are two objects that were not in the film. The first is a key, but it is the second that immediately catches her attention: a flat brass apparatus, brightly polished, about a foot square, evidently an instrument of some kind. She picks up the device and studies the mechanism: a complex series of wheels and rings, some concentric, some eccentric. It is intricately engraved with Latin text, and for the second time in the same day Andromeda regrets not having learned that language. Several of the inner rings are etched with symbols that she recognizes: the same ones atop the planets in the bell tower. The outer ring is etched with zodiacal signs. Andromeda guesses that she is holding an astrolabe, an ancient device for measuring the heavens.

Overlaying the various moveable parts is a fixed circular framework. The horizontal diameter is marked on the left as *Ascendent Coeli*, on the right as *Descendent Coeli*. The vertical axis is tilted slightly, marked *Medium Coeli* at the top and *Imum Coeli* at the bottom. Each quadrant is divided into three segments, and each of these is numbered, one through twelve. They also are labeled, and Andromeda can guess the meaning of some of them: *vita* she knows is life, *lucrum* is presumably wealth, *uxor* is probably the root of *uxorious*, and so would indicate spouse. She realizes that this particular astrolabe is meant for more than just calculating the positions of heavenly bodies; it is also intended to divine astrological meaning from the arrangement. The twelve segments represent the so-called 'Houses' used in formulating horoscopes.

Andromeda suddenly realizes that she might have found a key in the chapel after all. Until now she has assumed that the keys would all be physical keys, but this second hint to look toward the heavens makes her realize that the Bible would not have been left open at Isaiah 14:12 by accident.

Andromeda goes to the bookshelves and scans the titles. The library is not especially large, several hundred works printed long after

Faust's time but with their dustcovers removed so as not to appear obviously anachronistic. Most of them are standard reference works: encyclopedias, dictionaries, a pharmacopeia, philately and numismatic catalogs. Many of them are in sets: there are all twenty-five volumes of the ninth edition of *Encyclopædia Britannica*, printed in 1889; a large collection of classical texts in Greek and Latin with accompanying lexicons; a hundred volumes of Voltaire's abundant correspondence; ten volumes of bound fascicles dated across decades of the late Nineteenth and early Twentieth Centuries, here titled *A New Dictionary on Historical Principles* and which, when she sees that it was published by the Clarendon Press, Andromeda realizes was destined to become the *Oxford English Dictionary*. She assumes that all these many sets were purchased primarily not for their use as reference works but simply as bulk fill for the shelves, although among them she eventually finds the single volume she is searching for: a Bible—in this case, a copy of the King James version.

She takes it to the table and looks up Isaiah 14:12. The verse left for her in the chapel translates as *How art thou fallen from Heaven, O Lucifer, sonne of the morning!*

The meaning of the first half is clear enough, but the last part is obscure: why would the Bible refer to Lucifer as the *sonne of the morning*? It echoes a similarly obscure line she had heard the previous evening in the movie: *My master is the morning star, Faustus, he is the bringer of light*. By now she knows that anything to do with light has special meaning for Gidding.

Andromeda returns to the bookshelves. She pulls out Volume VI of the nascent *O.E.D.* and takes it back to the reading table, where she looks up *Lucifer*. The dictionary specifies several senses of the word, but it is the first one that matters:

Lucifer

As proper name, and allusively. (With initial capital.)

1. The morning star; the planet Venus when she appears in the sky before sunrise

So there had been a key in the chapel after all—Isaiah 14:12—and now Andromeda understands what it has unlocked. She leaves the library and makes her way down the hall past the monks' quarters back to the southeastern corner of the abbey. At the base of the bell tower she takes a torch from the wall and begins the ascent.

On emerging through the trapdoor, the first thing she realizes is that the celestial model is not as she left it; instead, the arrangement has been returned to the original configuration.

She ducks under the zodiac and outer planets, coming to a halt at Venus. The globe is softball-sized and covered with etchings of the namesake goddess in naked repose. Andromeda taps it and the ringing sound confirms her guess: the sphere is hollow. She holds the base with one hand and, using the alchemical symbol as a handle, cautiously twists the top. It unscrews without resistance, the way something does that has been opened recently. Andromeda lifts the top. Inside she finds a driver's license. She recognizes it at once: Margot Vaughn's *permis de conduire*.

Andromeda replaces the top and moves to better light to read the *date de naissance*. The birth date is correct, something that she did not expect. If the date on the original license had been false then Gidding could always have claimed that Margot must have altered it, and therefore he had made *Diotima* under the legitimate belief that she was eighteen at the time. But the fact that the original is correct establishes that it was not the license that was falsified, but the photocopy. Andromeda is surprised that Gidding has allowed her to see this: proof that he knowingly broke the law, and falsified federally mandated records to cover it up.

Andromeda puts the driver's license in her pocket and feels there the key that she found in the library, almost forgotten. She pulls it out and inspects it. A modern key, little used. There is no writing on the fob but there is a symbol that in the library she had mistaken for a trident, but now sees is actually three upward-pointing arrows linked by circles at their base. It is a symbol that she has seen recently. She leaves the bell tower and heads back to her room.

ANDROMEDA HAD REPLACED the Beretta case in the drawer after first finding it, but now the box is back out on top of the desk, an obvious hint—Gidding must have been concerned that she would not recognize the Beretta trademark on the key fob. When Andromeda unlocks the case she finds inside not a pistol but a magnifying glass. The lens is six inches in diameter, thick, and deeply convex—the source of the heft. Underneath it is a photograph. It is of Margot Vaughn, sitting at an outdoor cafe.

The day is sunny but it must have been cold: Margot is wearing a big jacket and woolen scarf. There is an espresso cup on the table in front of her. She is sitting back and reading a newspaper, apparently unaware of being photographed. There are blurred items in the foreground: the edge of an umbrella, a waiter passing out of view—the photograph was taken at a distance by someone using a powerful zoom. Whoever took it had adjusted the f-stop and aperture to focus exclusively on Margot.

It is difficult to judge her age: she could be fifteen; she could be twenty-five.

Andromeda uses the magnifying glass to examine the photograph more closely. Most of it is blurred; only Margot is rendered in sufficiently sharp focus for the magnification to reveal hidden detail. Andromeda begins with the objects on the table. There is the espresso cup, but nothing is printed on it. She can make out a twist of lemon peel in the saucer. The remains of a half-eaten pastry sit on a plate.

Andromeda examines Margot's image. She is wearing sunglasses but they have been pushed back on top of her head, revealing her face. Taught skin and unlined eyes. Andromeda moves to the hand holding the newspaper—Margot's left hand—looking for a ring. There is none, but then Andromeda sees the newspaper's masthead: *Le Monde*. Below it is a photograph of a white-clad figure, otherwise unclear, but she can make out the accompanying headline: *Le Geste Qui Change L'Église*—the gesture that changes the church.

She considers this headline, and concludes that the only recent church-related event of sufficient importance for France's leading newspaper to have announced it at the top of their front page would have been the resignation of Pope Benedict XVI, an act that had taken place when Andromeda was in Venice, as far as she could tell while she was tied to an anatomical table deep within the bowels of Isola Bisi, as if the sinister nature of what occurred there had served to bring down the head of the Roman church.

Andromeda puts down the magnifying glass, having found what Gidding wanted her to find. He is not just admitting that he knew Margot Vaughn; he is saying that he knows where she is now.

ANDROMEDA ARRIVES AT THE final point on the pentagram, the cistern. It is full but water still pours in, rushing down from the drains above and emerging in a torrent from the conduit on the far side. The chamber echoes with the sound of it, a waterfall within a stone cavern. To Andromeda's left is a gutter that bears away the overflow, burbling in a low growl as if like her it wonders whether the storm will ever end.

There are no torches. Instead, the space is lit by what at first Andromeda mistakes for webs of tiny bulbs dangling from the vaulting, but which on closer inspections she discovers are clusters of living glowworms, hundreds or perhaps thousands of them spread across the ceiling, as if emulating the stars splayed across the heavens. The cumulative result is to bathe the cavern in a pale blue-green radiance, a ghostly effect aided by large underwater lights turning what would otherwise have been a black mass into a shifting depthless presence.

Despite the cold and noise it is a pleasant space, stone and water hidden away from the outside world, a private grotto brought to life with bioluminescence.

Andromeda searches for a key. There are no furnishings or fittings, just the narrow path that leads around three of the four sides, the conduit that introduces the water, the gutter that drains the excess, and the water itself. Andromeda searches quickly and then retraces her steps, looking more carefully now, but still she finds no key. Then she realizes why the water has been illuminated.

She stands at the edge and gazes downward. The water pouring in disturbs the surface, making it difficult to distinguish what lies beneath. She cannot see the bottom. Occasionally she catches what might be the glint of metal somewhere below, but then it disappears.

She kneels and tests the water with her fingers. It is icy cold.

Andromeda sighs; Gidding has saved the worst for last. She takes off her boots, then removes the rest of her clothing. She goes to the highest section of the path, the place from which she will gain the most leverage, takes a deep breath, and dives in.

The cold is electrifying, sending a shock coursing through her body. She ignores it and swims downward. The lights are self-contained units stuck to the sides, very bright, and they blind her as she swims past. The noise of the water splashing in from the conduit is muted now, replaced by a new sound, a deep rhythmic rumbling that seems to be coming from the very rock itself, vaguely musical, the beat heavy and tribal, as if beneath the Earth's crust molten magma was now singing to her, down where no one else could overhear.

An inconvenient time for an LSD flashback, she thinks.

Andromeda swims deeper. The music is replaced by pain as her ears begin to ache with pressure and cold; the need to breathe begins to overtake all else. She sees the bottom, not tiled like a pool but a layer of fine sediment dropped by rushing water having come to rest. In the middle of it, sitting atop a stone, is the key.

She swims to the stone and grabs the key. Her urgent need now is to get air, but Andromeda forces herself to secure the key in a fist first, knowing that to drop it into the silt would be to lose it forever. She twists her body, keeping low, so that her feet touch the bottom, then uses her legs to thrust off and upward. She kicks and strokes with her arms, fighting the urge to open the hand holding the key, but the top seems never to come. She must breathe but the lights are still above her, and she briefly wonders if in the intense cold she is undergoing some sort of disorientation—a side-effect of the pain in her ears perhaps—and is destined to drown in Gidding's cistern.

She breaks the surface. To breathe is intensely beautiful, a thousand springs all at once. She treads water and sucks in deep lungfuls, careless of the cold now—all that matters is unrestricted air.

Andromeda swims to the side. She deposits the key on the path, as far in as her arm will reach so as to not risk it falling back in, then hauls herself from the water.

At once she begins to shiver. Her flesh looks freshly plucked. She puts on her clothes quickly, secures the key in a pocket, and leaves the cistern. Her need now is to get warm.

Andromeda returns to her room. She finds that the bath has been filled, and wonders whether it is a coincidence or if her progress has been monitored. But Andromeda is too cold to care. She sinks into the tub, lies back with eyes closed, and allows the warmth to envelop her.

XXXII

THE DRESS THAT HAS BEEN laid out tonight is made of shiny aluminum discs, each an inch or so in diameter, linked together. The dress is lined, but for comfort rather than modesty: the fabric is sheer to the point of transparency. Again no underwear. She asks where her own clothes are, but in reply Leila just shakes her head and Andromeda is too exhausted to argue the point.

She sits at the dresser and submits to Leila's attentions. Today is bouffant day, and Andromeda emerges with Barbarella hair. When Leila leaves Andromeda removes her robe, puts on the dress, and stands before the mirror. No visions tonight, just the impossibility of modesty. The dress is micromini short, the gaps between discs wide, and no matter how carefully she arranges them any movement results in a random redistribution.

Andromeda sits at the desk and places on top of it the objects that she recovered during the treasure hunt: riding crop, flight attendant's badge, driver's license, photograph, and the three keys. The riding crop and badge together form an admission that Gidding made *Diotima*, but they are also vaguely threatening—a reminder that right now he exercises absolute power over her. She is held *cum manu*, in hand, at the mercy and whim of the male—Gidding may do whatever he wishes without consequence, he is saying, here on his sovereign isle. The driver's license goes a step further: he is admitting not just that he made *Diotima*, but also that he knew Margot was underage when doing so. And the photograph is a declaration that he knows where to find her now.

Andromeda puts them aside and slides the three keys in front of her. She tears a sheet of paper from her notebook and writes on it Isaiah 14:12. She places this with the three physical keys and spends a long time considering them. Each was supposed to unlock something. The first physical key was for the reliquary; the second for the pistol case. She has yet to discover what the third unlocks. The key that she found in the chapel, Isaiah 14:12, led her to the planet Venus and the driver's license inside.

Four keys, but Gidding said there were five.

She opens the National Trust pamphlet and places each key on the map where she found it. The only point on the pentagram without a key is the bell tower, and Andromeda suddenly realizes why the model had been returned to its original position: it is the alignment of the heavens that is the key.

The presence of the astrolabe is now explained: it is the tool needed to interpret that key.

She goes to the library, grabs the astrolabe, and returns to the bell tower. She finds the torches alight, as if it had been expected that she would return here. The model is Copernican—heliocentric—but the astrolabe is Ptolemaic—geocentric—and it takes Andromeda a moment to figure out that to get the right aspect she will need to sit directly beneath the planet earth. The next question is which way to face. She locates Scotland, which is facing directly away from the sun: it is midnight on Rothermore. She sits facing the same way, and after several minutes has the pieces roughly in place, except for Neptune and Uranus, presumably unknown in the time from which the astrolabe dates.

Andromeda studies the results. She does not know Margot's zodiacal sign, but she knows Margot's date of birth and so steps back from her own sign—Aires—to arrive at what must be Margot's. It is

Leo, and it is in the Twelfth House. The House is labeled *carcer*. Andromeda does not know what the word means.

She returns to the library and locates the Latin lexicon. She takes it to the reading table and looks up *carcer*. It means prison. Ah, she thinks, in*carcer*ate.

The abbey has no dungeon and Andromeda does not recall any location suitable for detention, but presumably the monks had a disciplinary system and so there might have been a room intended for such purposes, even if only from time to time. She unfolds the National Trust map, lays it flat on the table, and searches the descriptions for something appropriate. She comes to an abrupt stop at the top of the table, at the very first word.

It is the word *key*.

Andromeda realizes that it is not the *name* of the House that would be the clue; it is the *number*. She looks up the number twelve on the key. It is the sacristy.

THE SACRISTY IS A small room off the chapel, according to the pamphlet used for the storage of valuable sacramental objects, and therefore one of the few rooms in the abbey that was lockable—like a cell. This last convinces Andromeda that she has calculated correctly, but when she arrives in the sacristy she finds it empty. There are no sacramental objects, no furnishings, not even a window. Andromeda continues to look anyway, peering into the corners and pressing at the walls to locate a loose stone or some such, unable to believe that with so much deduction neatly falling into place she has come up empty-handed, but after a quarter-hour of fruitless searching she is forced to admit that she was wrong.

Andromeda studies the astrolabe once more, checking the sequence of zodiacal signs, making sure that she did not miscalculate. Her own sign is in the Eighth House, occupied by a single planet. She pauses when she recognizes that planet's alchemical symbol: it is Mercury. The House is labeled *mors*, a word that she does not need to look up.

Andromeda wonders if this is all that Gidding intended to convey: nothing more than a simple death threat.

She checks the number eight on the National Trust map. It is the Chapter House: not a house but—according to the accompanying explanation—an apartment set aside for abbey business; a large, well-proportioned room intended as the place where the abbot would receive important guests.

ANDROMEDA ENTERS THE Chapter House and sees at once that this is the room Gidding meant for her to find. On the far wall, projected onto a large screen, a video clip is playing. It runs in a continuous loop, like an installation at an art gallery, repeating itself every few minutes. The subject is Andromeda.

The video was taken in the main hall of the palazzo on Isola Bisi. It is a single continuous shot, apparently recording the final of the three acts that night. The camera begins at one end of the room, low, wide-angled. There are two files of people standing on either side of the chamber, forty or fifty in total, backlit by flames from the fireplaces. They are still dressed in ball gear, but many of the women have discarded some or all of their clothing, although everyone retains a mask. Andromeda identifies a number of them: the two female acrobats; all of the card players, with La Perla now wearing nothing but her mask, shoes, and pearls; the Nubian attendants; the auctioneer; her abductor; the woman who was auctioned immediately before her, still without having replaced her red dress; and the man she thinks of as the master of ceremonies, *Il Dottore della Peste*. One woman wears a Harlequin mask, perhaps the source of Andromeda's Arlecchino vision, but she can find no similar candidate for Scaramouche or a skeletal Pierrot.

Initially they all look at the camera, but as it tracks past them they turn and face the other way, toward the focus of the shot. There, at the far end of the room, Andromeda sits enthroned. She is chained. She has been painted silver; she gleams. Her back is straight and she stares ahead, wide-eyed but apparently unseeing. Her feet are splayed and her hands grip the arms, as if she fears falling. The throne is large, elaborately decorated, and situated on a raised platform so that Andromeda sits a little above the audience. The ends of the arms are carved as lion's heads, and gilded wings protrude from the sides. The back rises high above her, and embedded into it is an astrological clock face rendered in brilliant gold and lapis lazuli. Andromeda recognizes it, a replica of the Torre dell'Orologio in St. Mark's square, but this one is rotating rapidly counterclockwise with the heavens in frantic retrograde, as if to emphasize the unreality of what was taking place in the room.

The camera approaches. Andromeda is not entirely naked: she still wears the Tiffany collar, and to it has been added more jewelry: an ornate diamond-studded head dress, earrings, armbands, bracelets, breast pendants, and a large gemstone in her navel. In the middle of her forehead, painted in a darker silver almost graphite in color, as if having been etched there, is the sun-within-mercury symbol.

There is a soundtrack, a single continuous note like feedback from an electric guitar brought too close to the speaker, something that is barely audible to begin with but which increases to an almost painful intensity by the end of the scene, distortion on the point of breaking into white noise.

The camera slowly tracks forward, at the same time gradually rising and zooming. In the beginning it is difficult to make out Andromeda's expression, but as the camera approaches it becomes clear that whatever she sees is not the scene before her but some interior vision; she is in a trance.

The video is intercut with stills, suddenly there and then gone, so fast as to be all but subliminal. It takes Andromeda a moment to understand that they are shots of interstellar space, nebulae and supernovae in phantasmagorical shapes and colors, shots taken by the Hubble space telescope perhaps. Presumably they represent Gidding's gloss on what Andromeda must be seeing and, considering her visions of orbiting the earth that evening, are not entirely inaccurate.

The camera comes closer. Andromeda looks uncomfortable now, breathing fast, her ribs visible with each intake. Her expression is hard to decipher, part wonderment, part fear, part ecstasy. It is an expression that might make a viewer long to see the same thing. The camera comes to a halt above her, looking down, and although Andromeda is staring straight up into the lens she still shows no awareness of the camera's presence; her eyes are focused on infinity. She begins shaking, an unnaturally rapid and constricted motion, something a person would have difficulty doing consciously. Andromeda knows that it must have been the point at which the wave of liquid gold was about to cascade down.

The camera continues to zoom, going into extreme closeup before disappearing into the blackness of her pupil. The last thing before the scene ends is a brief reflection of the filmmaker in her eye. Gidding, sitting at the end of a mechanical boom—presumably some sort of hydraulic armature used to achieve the shot—looks out from behind the camera, his expression curious, as if this is something that he needed to see for himself, without intervening apparatus.

The video ends. A brief pause, and then it restarts.

She watches it again, several times.

Sun within mercury, she thinks, light within quicksilver—an echo of the catoptromancy from *Diotima*. It is a symbol of visions, she decides. Or perhaps it is a symbol of Gidding, the maker of visions.

Andromeda realizes that Gidding has recorded her own *katabasis*.

XXXIII

ANDROMEDA ARRIVES AT the top of the stairs. In the Griffin Room below Gidding is reading a book. He sees her and stands but keeps the volume in hand.

"I hope you enjoyed the treasure hunt."

"Very entertaining, thank you. The dip in the cistern was particularly refreshing."

"So you found the keys?"

"I did."

"And what they unlock?"

"All but the last."

"Then you know almost everything now."

"I know very little."

"But surely the meanings were clear?"

"That you made *Diotima*, yes. That you knew Margot Vaughn was underage at the time, and that you know where she is now, also yes. But I'm puzzled by the video in the Chapter House."

"That's simple," Gidding says. "That's what I want from you."

"Enchainment?"

"Transformation."

"Transformation?"

"Stasis is a myth. There is only metamorphosis, or decay."

Andromeda considers this elliptical response and wonders if quicksilver—ever shape shifting—is meant to signify not vision but transformation. Probably that is why the last key had been placed at the bottom of a cistern: it had necessitated diving into the water: a cleansing act; a symbolic baptism; a purification for what is to come, as in *Diotima*. Purification as a prelude to transformation then, but transformation into what?

"I still don't understand what you want from me."

He walks to the base of the staircase and holds up the book. "There's a poem I would like you to read."

"By whom?"

"Can't you guess?"

She looks again at the book, and recognizes the blue cover.

"Ezra Pound."

"Yes."

"I should have realized that the Pound came from you. Another American exile, like you. Someone else who belongs nowhere, like you."

"Pound was insane."

"The similarities amaze me."

Gidding laughs. "Well, he had red hair and you can't accuse me of that."

Andromeda begins her descent of the stairs.

"So it was you who was following me on San Michele?"

"You dropped the book."

A response, she understands, that does not precisely answer the question.

"Was it just meant to scare me, or was that a failed abduction attempt?"

"Neither."

"Then what?"

"Preparation."

"For what?"

"For what was to come. For now. For this moment." She reaches the bottom of the stairs, and Gidding offers her the book. "Page twenty-six."

He goes to the sideboard and begins mixing cocktails. Andromeda examines the volume. It is the same copy she had in Venice. There is some dirt on the cover, perhaps from when she dropped it, four days and a lifetime ago.

She opens it to page twenty-six. There is a short poem titled 'The Garden.'

"Should I read it out loud?"

"Please."

She recites the poem:

Like a skein of loose silk blown against a wall
She walks by the railing of a path in Kensington Gardens
And she is dying piece-meal
of a sort of emotional anemia.

And round about there is a rabble
Of the filthy, sturdy, unkillable infants of the very poor
They shall inherit the earth.

In her is the end of breeding.
Her boredom is exquisite and excessive.

She would like someone to speak to her,
And is almost afraid that I
will commit that indiscretion.

Gidding finishes mixing and pours the cocktails.

"A beautiful poem, don't you think?"

"The *unkillable infants of the very poor*?"

"And honest, too. No wonder they broke him." He joins her with the drinks. "I like the compression of ideas in the poem. Just twelve lines, but he's revealed her completely, and himself, too. I would sell my soul to wield such compact power on film."

"So you're Faust, and that's why you wanted me to read it."

"No."

"Then why?"

"Because tonight I'm going to tell you how I met Margot Vaughn."

THE FIRST COURSE is again soup, this time made from turnips into which Leila has mixed wild herbs and mushrooms plucked from the crannies and crevices of Rothermore. Andromeda feels unnaturally alert, as on that first night at the abbey. She imagines that she can taste each ingredient separately—the peppery tang of the dandelions, the truffle-like pungency of the mushrooms. It is as if her sensory powers have been heightened, allowing her to separate what would normally have been muddled. Her vision, too: it has become unnaturally precise and accumulative—despite the low candlelight she can easily read the label on the bottle of wine standing on the sideboard thirty feet away, even the minuscule *mis en bouteille au château* at the bottom, and at the other end of the table she can make out a tiny shaving nick on Gidding's left jaw, perhaps the result of a straight-edge razor like the one in Faust's drawer. She wonders if her newfound powers are the result of the brisk climate or just an aftereffect of opium.

"I was in Miami scouting locations for my next film," Gidding says. "More than scouting—I hadn't written a script yet. I knew that I wanted to make something tropical and steamy: lush saturated colors, dense shadows. I had the technique in mind, but no story. So I went to live in Miami to get inspiration and write a script. But after a while I realized that I just wanted to do what had already been done before. I wanted to be Volker Schlöndorff or Brian de Palma." He puts down his soup spoon, as if the recollection had taken away his appetite. "It is the worst crime in art: to copy someone else."

"Like publishing rehashes of the latest bestseller."

"Same in Hollywood—it's all remakes. Even the nominally original films are really just remakes under different guises, which is why I never let those people near me. But after two weeks in Miami I woke up one morning and realized that I was doing the same thing. I immediately scrapped the project. I decided that I would go back to Paris. I wondered if I was losing it—the ability to be original, I mean, the ability to create. I was in a bad mood. I went down Ocean Drive to one of the outdoor cafes for breakfast. South Beach still had an edge then, but already the mob was moving in and you could tell that it would soon be ruined. They were out in droves that morning. On the way I walked past one of them, an overweight and underdressed heifer, ugly tattoos on ugly flesh, her shorts in danger of being swallowed whole by her rear end. She was walking past glass storefronts and took the opportunity to admire her reflection as she waddled along, puffing her stringy hair and obviously pleased by what she saw, self-absorbed and apparently blind."

Kalki enters the room and clears the soup bowls. Gidding stands and refills their glasses while the main course is brought to the table, dark meat Kalki identifies as a hare that had fortuitously hopped past while he was hunting the partridge. He leaves, and Gidding resumes the story.

"That morning I kept walking past the place where I usually had breakfast in case the heifer was headed there too. Instead I found a cafe down the other end of the Drive, hopefully beyond bovine range. I was shown to a table by a gum-chewing vacancy. There weren't many people there, but that day everyone seemed ugly to me. I decided to bury myself in the paper.

"A menu was brought to the table but I didn't look up. Then coffee, but again I didn't look up. Eventually I accepted that I was going to have to order, so I put the paper aside and looked at the menu. The waitress came to the table, and I looked at her for the first time. The waitress was Margot Vaughn.

"My initial reaction was relief, I think. I ordered, but when she left I was no longer interested in the paper. I didn't exactly watch her but I was aware of her. She had some other tables. She moved gracefully between them, taking orders, bringing food, efficient but not hurried, pleasant but not friendly. I don't know how but I could tell that she lived in a private world of her own, a mental cocoon almost. And I could also tell that she was exceptional."

Andromeda nods, remembering having had the same impression when first seeing Margot's photograph in Renzitti's office.

"It's difficult to describe what came next, but a minute after seeing Margot for the first time I knew that I was going to make *Diotima*. Ideas were billowing forth like a ship under full sail. The script was already in my head. The locations, the costumes, the lighting—everything. I started scribbling notes on the napkin. They fell on top of one another, coming faster than I could write them down. I was careful to conserve space but then a fresh pile of napkins silently appeared at my elbow: Margot had noticed the problem and brought more. I continued to write, and by the time breakfast was finished I had a stack of napkins as high as my coffee cup, filled with notes.

"Margot came to collect the check. I had already been considering possibilities for the lead actress, but then I suddenly realized that the obvious candidate was standing right in front of me. I introduced myself. I told her that I was a movie director and I would like to make a movie with her in it. She showed no reaction, not even suspicion, which is what I would have expected. I put my wallet on the tray with the tab. I told her that my driver's license and credit cards and so on were all in there, so that she could at least establish that I was who I claimed to be. I told her that I would be sitting on a bench across the street in Lummus Park at four o'clock that afternoon. If she was interested she could return my wallet to me then, bring some people she trusts with her, and listen to the proposal. If not, just leave my wallet with the hostess and I'll come by and collect it later.

"She made no reply. I left. At exactly four o'clock that afternoon Margot came walking down the path and sat down next to me. She was alone. She was wearing different clothing but simple, nothing special, and no makeup. She handed me my wallet. I asked her why she hadn't brought someone with her. She said that what she chose to do or not to do with her life was entirely her own business, and no one else's. I thought that was a good answer. I told her that I wanted to make a movie based on the ancient Dionysian rites as depicted on the walls of Pompeii. *Oh, in the Villa dei Misteri*, she said—*Yes, that's a good idea.* I was astonished. It turned out that she had been there not long before and was fascinated by those same frescoes. I made it clear that the film would necessarily be sexual. She shrugged her shoulders and said *Of course, how else could it be done?* In short, she agreed.

"I told her that the next step was for her to get representation, then when she had an agent the contractual side of it could be sorted out and we would begin organizing production. For the first time she was hesitant. She asked me why we needed a contract, and I explained that for a start it would cover her compensation, which we hadn't discussed. She asked me flatly how much I was offering. I plucked a figure out of the air; I hadn't considered it myself. She said nothing in response, just held out her hand. I took it and we shook. *Now we have a contract*, she said.

"I spent the next few weeks furiously preparing, writing the script, getting a casting agent to fill the roles as they took form, hiring a crew, renting the château. Margot and I met on most days. We went through the scenes as they were written. Sometimes she had suggestions: the Concorde was her idea, including the suggestion that we surreptitiously film the scene in the boarding lounge's bathroom, and just risk it. It was an exciting time: things were coming together fast, far more quickly than is usual in movie production, and that lent an edginess to the process that I hoped to capture on film.

"Eight weeks after having met her, we began filming. The scenes were shot pretty much in the order that they appear in the movie. I had long been wanting to get greater realism into my films, and the way we worked helped with that. We filmed the journey as it was taking place and without the artificiality of formal movie production: the bathroom scene at the beginning was shot by a single camerawoman in there with Margot. She wore an earpiece and I was outside in the boarding lounge, ready to warn them if someone headed in, but no one did—the plane ended up being nearly empty, and there were no other women on the flight. I filmed Margot coming out and boarding the plane with a minicam concealed in a carry-on: I pretended to be rummaging through it and searching for something, but actually I was looking at the viewfinder and trying to track Margot. It turned out well: the graininess of eight-millimeter worked, and because I was shooting from so low it made Margot look all leg: imposing and transformed, as I wanted her to appear. The three of us took the flight—we had to because it was the only way to get into the boarding lounge.

"So it continued. We were already halfway through shooting in the château when the casting agent sent me the Section 2257 compliance documents. It reminded me that I needed the same from Margot. I asked her for her driver's license but she said that she didn't have one. Even then it didn't occur to me why she didn't have one; I assumed that she simply didn't drive. The primary cast and crew were living in the château. After shooting that day I asked her to go upstairs and bring me her passport. The office had a photocopy machine. It wasn't until the photocopy came out that I thought to actually check the date. At first I assumed that I was getting the calculation wrong, since anyone working in an establishment that served alcohol would have to be at least eighteen—I didn't then know that the cafe where she'd been a waitress had no liquor license. And I thought Margot was too tall to be fifteen. More than that: she had a confidence about her, a quiet self-assuredness that you don't see in teenagers. But then I did the calculation more carefully.

"I took Margot for a walk around the grounds. Yes, she admitted matter-of-factly, she was fifteen years old. In Miami, she had already told me that she lived with her parents. Until then I'd assumed that the reason she never introduced us was that she didn't much care for them, and was pleased for an excuse and the means to move out. Now I realized that she had run away from home to make the movie. It hadn't occurred to her that this was a problem. Margot considered herself to be an adult, and of course she knew nothing about Section 2257 compliance. Even when I described the purpose behind it she still thought there shouldn't be an issue, since she didn't engage in any actual sex. I explained that it didn't matter: the film we were making was unreleasable. To her the solution was simple: fake ID. I told her that a fake ID was fine for getting a drink in a bar, but using one in this case would constitute a felony. I considered recutting, turning the thing into an R-rated release, but if it was released in any form then the nature of the production would become public, and anyway cutting to that level would have emasculated the film—I'd rather not release it at all. In short, that day I discovered that I was making a movie that could be never seen."

"But I've seen it."

"Yes," Gidding says. "In the end, I opted for the felony."

XXXIV

IN THE CRYPT, GIDDING threads a new reel into the projector. Andromeda settles herself against the dead abbot. She has difficulty finding a position where the dress's discs are not digging into her.

"No opium tonight?"

"Something more prosaic, at least around here."

"What?"

"Whiskey." He goes to a cabinet on top of which a decanter and ice bucket sit ready. He puts cubes into a pair of double Old Fashioned glasses, adds whiskey and a shot of soda from a siphon. "Mrs. Campbell would be appalled at us drinking it diluted, but I think that whiskey and soda were made for each other." He joins Andromeda and hands her a glass. "Single malt from Islay," he says. "Tastes like a peat bog."

She accepts the glass. The whiskey smells of earth and smoke.

"Here's to peat bogs."

IN TONIGHT'S REEL Mephistopheles continues her recruitment of Faust. She throws him a party to meet the future dead. It is a swinging

'Sixties-style affair to which she wears the disc dress. It takes place in a large Factory-like loft decorated in aluminum foil and helium balloons. A band plays psychedelic rock. Go-go dancers gyrate on small platforms. Shifting abstract images are projected onto the walls. The guitarist looks like Jimi Hendrix, even to an inverted right-handed Stratocaster, and he plays with a ripping overdriven snarl that might have pleased Jimi himself.

The performance fascinates Faust. When the song is finished Jimi joins them.

"Blackamoor, such extraordinary sounds are barely to be believed. Hast thou made a pact with the Devil?"

"Voodoo, baby," Jimi says with a nod.

"Methinks thine instrument must harness lightning."

"No, man. I'm the lightning."

"How hast thou becomest lightning?"

"Hey, I just kissed the sky." Jimi laughs and moves on.

Faust turns to Mephistopheles. "Could I also kiss lightning from the sky?"

"With a Marshall stack and sufficient practice."

"Remarkable."

A camera flash momentarily blinds him; Faust has had his picture taken. The photographer is Andy Warhol. He lowers the camera and approaches.

"Ah…," Warhol says, "…nice clothes."

"Thank you, sir." Faust looks at Warhol's shock of white hair. "I observe that thou hast encountered Satan, evidently an alarming experience."

"Ah…"

"And this device, it contains lightning too?"

"Ah, it's a Polaroid."

"What does it do?"

"It takes pictures."

"Andy is an artist," Mephistopheles explains.

The photograph slides from the camera, and Warhol wordlessly hands it to Faust.

"What be this?"

"I guess you have to…like…peel it."

Faust peels off the cover and then watches in increasing astonishment as the paper beneath, initially blank, resolves into an image of himself before his eyes.

"What incredible magic! Sir, thou art indeed the greatest of artists."

"Well, ah…you can keep it," Warhol says. "But please don't leave without giving me the number of your tailor."

He moves on. An agitated Brigitte Bardot soon replaces him.

"*Monsieur*, you are a doctor, yes?"

"Fourfold, madam: Philosophy, Law, Physik and Divinity."

"*Bien*, you must help me. I think that I have twisted my ankle." She hustles him over to a sofa and puts a shapely leg into his lap. Faust undoes the strap of her stiletto and removes it.

"Such footwear will inevitably cause injury, madam. This back part is too narrow and too high."

Bardot pouts in response. He carefully palpates her ankle.

"A little swelling and a slight contusion. It will mend itself, but keep weight from it, and do not wear such shoes in future. I will remove the other."

"Men are always taking my clothes off."

Faust removes the other shoe. "The tissues that connect the tibia and fibula to the *calcaneum* will not tolerate such strange footwear."

"The *calcaneum*?"

"This part, madam."

"Ah, *le talon*. The heel, no?"

"Yes, but in Latin it is the *calcaneum*."

"*Calcaneum*. I like that word much better. Please, *monsieur le medecin*, tell me the Latin names for my other parts."

"Other parts?"

"Work your way up from the *calcaneum*."

She reclines and sips champagne as he proceeds. Faust negotiates his way through knee, thigh, and hip, but hesitates as he approaches the *pectus*.

"Truly, madam, thou art the work of the Devil."

Bardot considers this while sucking on a pinkie. “My first husband claimed that God created me,” she says, “but now that I think about it, you’re probably right.”

By the time the party is over Faust has made up his mind: for a guaranteed twenty-four years of Mephistopheles’ service, with access to all knowledge—past, present, and future—he will consign the rights to his soul.

BACK AT THE ABBEY, Faust tests his new powers.

“Show me Eden,” he demands, “before the Fall.”

“There was no Fall, but if you wish to see an Eden then an Eden I will show you.”

Mephistopheles leads him to the cloister, and Faust is astonished to find it now occupied by a dome housing a tropical rainforest. Other creatures have been added to the snake with which Andromeda is already familiar: brightly colored toucans and parrots, leaping monkeys and lemurs, a sleek black panther. Faust stands where Andromeda stood yesterday, staring at it in wonderment.

“To think that all this was lost,” he says.

“Not lost. Just not yet found.”

“Found by whom?”

“By man.”

“Which man?”

“The Portuguese in their caravels; the Spanish in their galleons. By explorers and adventurers. By many men, Faust.”

“And God allows this?”

“God doesn’t have anything to do with it. There is no God.”

“Thou art compelled to say such things, demon. Thy master demands it.”

"The only thing that I am compelled to speak is the truth, Faustus. I am not allowed to lie to you."

"Hast thou a tail?"

"I have many forms."

"Speak to me of Purgatory."

"It is a place that people make for themselves."

"How so?"

"By stupidity. Purgatory is a state in which the stupid are too stupefied to realize that they are stupid. They are thus trapped within their own stupidity. It becomes an invisible barrier through which they can never penetrate."

"Are they punished?"

"Relentlessly. Television, for a start."

"What is television?"

"Something to keep the dull too preoccupied to realize that they are already functionally dead."

"May one ascend from Purgatory?"

"Life is without limit, Faustus."

"What does one see in Ascension?"

"Endless depth."

"Is it beautiful?"

"Profoundly."

"Is there music?"

"Silence."

"Why did God not save all men?"

"There is no God."

"Yet thou hast just told Faust of Heaven."

"No, I have just told you of the heavens."

"An answer worthy of a Scholastic, Mephistopheles. Truly, thou art the Saint Thomas Aquinas of the Underworld. Show me then these 'heavens' that thou speakest of."

MEPHISTOPHELES LEADS Faust to the bell tower. He is delighted by the model and spends a long time examining it. Mephistopheles demonstrates the mechanism, and soon the planets are in motion. Faust looks at it in wonder.

"What be this?" he asks.

"An orrery."

"And the motions of the cosmos are thus?"

"Heliocentric ellipses, doctor. It's more complicated than that, but let's just leave it at heliocentric ellipses for now."

"A mistake," he says.

"How so?"

"Too many planets."

"Actually too few, if Pluto still counts."

"Nevertheless a mistake. The sun cannot be at the center."

"Yet it is."

"The earth is at the center. God created it thus."

"There is no God."

"Then who created the cosmos, demon? Or is it all just an incredible accident?"

"In a sense it is—just energy taking various forms, of which one is matter."

"So it is an accident? Ha! That is the worst explanation I have ever heard."

"Yet you replace this accident with the word 'God' and count that a better explanation?"

"Belief in God is the path to Heaven."

"Belief in God is a form of Purgatory."

XXXV

ANDROMEDA AWAKENS ON THE bed of mercury. Her dreams have been wild, fragmented, chaotic, erotic, and they have exhausted her. She needs sleep to recover from her sleep, but it is already noon.

There is a tray with rolls and a flask of coffee on the table—Leila must have lost patience keeping a warm breakfast downstairs for her today. Again there is a note from Gidding, less formal than the first:

> *I asked Leila not to disturb you: you had an exhausting day yesterday, and it was a late night last night.*
>
> *I regret that I am again occupied today. The abbey is yours; please make free use of it. You might choose to explore the island.*
>
> *See you at cocktails,*
> *Gidding*

Andromeda opens the shutters. The wind is still high. The sky is filled with racing clouds, but the rain has at last stopped. She watches as far below the waves swell monstrously during their slow inbound roll and then crash against the rocks, sending up spectacular plumes of spray. There is no possibility of a boat.

No new outfit has been laid out for her today but the riding habit has been returned, freshly laundered and with boots brightly polished. Andromeda ignores the rolls and drinks a cup of coffee while getting dressed. She puts the fifth key in her pocket.

ANDROMEDA SEES NO sign of Kalki or Leila when she goes downstairs. The torches are aflame and the fireplace in the Griffin Room is lit, but otherwise everything else is still. Andromeda goes through the hall to the main door. It is unlocked, and for the first time since her arrival Andromeda steps outside the abbey.

The fresh air feels like freedom, but she knows that it is an illusion. It is not the abbey that is her prison, it is the island. Andromeda begins a circumnavigation of the building. For a while she is able to follow a path, but soon it begins to descend toward the sea and so she is forced to scramble over gorse-covered ground and rough bare rock to continue.

Progress is slow. Andromeda takes frequent breaks. The abbey might technically be a ruin, but the walls intended to withstand Norse raiders seem as formidable as the day they were built. She comes to a copse on the far western side, a group of surprisingly large trees, oaks and elms gathered together in one of the few patches of earth sufficient for them to take root. She enters into the cool dark shade. Then Andromeda realizes that she is not alone.

A wild boar is staring at her, fifty feet away, apparently having been disturbed while rummaging. Two tusks protrude from its jaw, a male. The animal is no more than three feet high but is at least double Andromeda's weight, a solid lump of compact muscle as unstoppable as a freight train. They stare at each other for a long contemplative moment. Then the boar steps forward.

The animal suddenly rears backward as if struck by some invisible club, followed a fraction of a second later by the crack of a gunshot.

Andromeda turns. Kalki is a hundred feet behind her, still with the rifle at this shoulder.

Andromeda has never heard a real gunshot before—much louder than they are in the movies, a hard sharp thwack that she can well believe would cause an already fractured rock ledge to finally give way.

Kalki lowers the rifle and approaches.

Andromeda turns back to the animal. She can see the wound in its shoulder. It has fallen but is not yet dead, eyes wide open, legs twitching, its labored breathing the only sound breaking the silence. Kalki arrives by her side. The rifle is now slung. There is a knife in his hand. Over his shoulder is a length of rope.

"Tonight's dinner," he says.

He goes to the boar and slits the animal's throat. While it dies he throws the rope over a branch, ties one end around the animal's hind legs, and then pulls on the other, hauling the carcass aloft. He ties off the line, takes the knife, and with a single slash opens the viscera, allowing the contents to flood out onto the ground.

He looks around at Andromeda, who has remained frozen in place since she first encountered the boar.

"This might take some time," he says.

Andromeda just nods, not trusting herself to speak, and Kalki quietly resumes his butchering. She turns and walks away, heading back to the abbey.

XXXVI

THE BATH HAS BEEN FILLED but Andromeda sees no other sign of Leila tonight and assumes that she must have her hands full preparing the wild boar. She bathes leisurely while reading the Pound. The *Cantos* are as convoluted as Andromeda remembers from college. She flips back to page twenty-six and rereads 'The Garden,' regretting that the syllabus had not found room for such shorter, more concentrated works.

The dress that has been left out for her tonight is made of gold lace and is no more modest than the others, but this one is still in its original box—presumably a costume that never made it into the movie. On the dresser next to the jewelry case Andromeda finds an envelope with her name on it. The note inside reads:

> *If you bring the fifth key with you this evening, I'll show you what it's for.*

There is no place in the dress to put a key. Andromeda opens the jewelry box and picks out a simple bracelet. She threads it through the key and then attaches it to her wrist. She puts her hair up loosely with a single clip. Minimal makeup—Leila had concealed her scar, but this evening Andromeda will be seen plainly for who she is.

She puts on her shoes and, as the last step before sliding into the dress, ties two ribbons taut around her thigh, and uses them to secure the straight-edge razor.

ANDROMEDA ARRIVES AT the top of the stairs. Below in the Griffin Room Gidding is standing by the fireplace and talking on a phone. He sees Andromeda and ends the call.

"I take it that the satellite dish has been repaired."

"No."

"I thought you said there was a problem with the antenna."

"A convenient fiction."

"So you told a story."

"Filmmakers are storytellers."

Gidding moves to the sideboard where an ice bucket and two champagne flutes are waiting. He takes the bottle from the bucket and begins removing the capsule. Andromeda descends the stairs.

"I wonder how many other stories you've told me, or are intending to."

"As for the past: very few, only where necessary, and none of any consequence. As for the future: there will be no more stories—from now on only the truth, raw and unadorned." He adds an exclamation point with the pop of the cork.

"Will that truth include what became of Margot?"

"I've got better truths than that to tell."

He meets Andromeda at the bottom of the stairs and offers her a glass of champagne. He holds his own aloft, and they drink to the toast not made.

"Are we celebrating?"

"At the completion of every film I always host a formal wrap dinner. It's a good way to end things."

"And this is an ending?"

"Yes. Tomorrow you will be gone. In fact, that's what I was doing on the phone: arranging to have you picked up in the morning."

"What time?"

"Ten o'clock."

Tonight there is a slender aluminum case sitting on the table in front of the sofa.

"Is that what the fifth key is for?"

"No, it's already unlocked. Why don't you look inside?"

Andromeda sits on the sofa and puts down her glass. The object before her is wide and shallow, broader than a standard briefcase. The sides are corrugated for strength, the locks solid and recessed—it is a case designed for transporting something of value. She unlatches the lid and opens it. Inside is a drawing, matted but without glass, sitting amid black foam that has been cut to precisely accommodate the frame. The drawing depicts a woman, naked and prone, looking back over her shoulder at the artist. The eyes are strangely delineated, almost mask-like, and even before inspecting the signature she knows who must have drawn it.

"Picasso," she says.

Gidding sits beside her, admiring a drawing that he must already have known well.

"The subject is Marie Laurencin. She was an artist in her own right and at the time this was done, around 1907, she was the mistress of the poet Apollinaire. Picasso was then relatively unknown but he had recently been introduced into the circle of Gertrude Stein, which is likely where he met Marie. At the time he was contemplating or perhaps already painting *Les Demoiselles d'Avignon*, and so was on the cusp of changing the art world forever. Picasso's own mistress at the time—Fernande Olivier—was the model for one of the *demoiselles*. I think we can assume from this drawing that Marie was another."

"How did you acquire it?"

"Margot saw it offered in a Christie's catalog. She thought it symbolized the duality aspect of the Diotima character: woman as a creator herself, but also an inspiration for creativity in others. I took a train to London for the auction and bought it shortly after we finished filming."

"I can understand why you keep it so well protected."

"So you think it has worth?"

"It must be very valuable."

"That's not what I meant, as I think you know. Look at it again. A few haphazard lines of lead pencil on a piece of not very good quality paper. The line is nothing special; any competent art school student could do as well. So I will ask you a second time, does it have worth?"

Andromeda looks again at the drawing. The paper has yellowed at the edges—Gidding is right: not very good quality paper, but probably all that Picasso could then afford. He is right about the control of line, too: it is indiscriminate, almost awkward. But the drawing has a quiet authority, and the eyes—as penetrating as on the famous portrait of Stein herself—form a powerful focus.

"Yes," she says. "I think it has a great deal of worth."

Gidding puts down his glass, takes the drawing, walks to the fire, and tosses it into the flames. He returns to the sofa and resumes his seat.

"A copy, of course, although I do own the original. It's in my Paris apartment, and the insurers do not allow me to remove it from there without their written approval. So I think we've established that if the drawing has any worth, then that worth is not intrinsic: it does not reside in the object itself. Now I will ask you a third time, does it have any worth?"

Andromeda sips her champagne while contemplating a response. "Yes," she says. "The worth is no more in the physical paper than the worth of your movies is in the physical celluloid. It's not the object, it's what's behind it."

"And tell me, what is this strange Platonic something lurking in the shadows behind the paper, mysteriously imbuing worth like a Higgs boson imbuing mass?"

He is goading her because he wants a serious answer, and she tries to give him one. "The idea, I suppose. But it's not entirely distinct from the object. I mean the idea can exist, but until it's executed it has no substance."

"So art is giving substance to ideas?"

"Yes."

"Not a bad definition. But what is it that makes a Picasso a Picasso?"

"I suppose it's the relationship between idea and execution."

"What about it?"

"Originality."

"Damien Hirst put a shark into a tank of formaldehyde and called it art. Certainly original. Also exceedingly dull—the sort of stuff Hughes characterized as *the tedious spectacle of ineptitude*."

"Okay, scratch originality."

"No, don't scratch it. Originality is a necessary condition, just not sufficient."

She thinks again. "Well, there has to be a rightness to it. It doesn't have to be grand or noble—a Fragonard is art."

"What makes rightness?"

"It's a kind of truthfulness, I suppose. An honesty between the idea and the execution. I saw a Jeff Koons painting recently, just a bracelet on a piece of shiny foil. The idea behind it was basically vacancy, but it was vacancy beautifully expressed—a fine work of art, I think. The execution got through to the idea, the connection was almost pure."

Gidding says nothing for a long time, considering her response. He stands and walks to the sideboard where he retrieves the bottle from the ice bucket. He returns and refills their glasses. Andromeda watches him, a more serious man tonight, a man approaching some form of extremis.

"What do you think?" she asks.

"I think that good art expands the artist—he somehow learns from his own creation. I think that's a very curious phenomenon, and I frankly don't understand it. More than that I can't say."

"Are you going to tell me where I can find Margot?"

"Yes."

"When?"

"Before you go. But first I have to show you the final reel of *Faust*."

"Will it end tragically?"

"All tragedies end tragically."

"Then tragedies annoy me. What's the point? Why bother if the outcome is inevitable?"

"Any other ending would make it a fairy tale."

"Really? There's only tragedy or happily-ever-after?"

"For anything worthwhile, yes—everything else is just filler. Which reminds me, if we don't dine soon the boar will be ruined, and that really would be a tragedy."

XXXVII

THE FIRST COURSE IS once again soup, this time made from the boiled bones of the wild boar, followed by a second course of the flesh itself, pungent and primitive, served with its marrow and a green that Andromeda cannot identify. Gidding seems disinclined to talk and, for the first time since arriving on Rothermore, Andromeda feels the need to carry the conversation.

"When I was growing up we would always eat like this. Not wild boar, but meat with vegetables. Or chicken or fish. And we always had wine with dinner. I used to be jealous of the other kids whose parents brought home pizzas, and who got to drink Coca-Cola. Sodas weren't allowed in our house."

"What happened to your parents?" Andromeda notices his use of the past tense; she wonders if this is a simple slipup, or whether by now Gidding can no longer be bothered pretending that he does not already know everything about her.

"They died when I was a sophomore in college."

"And so you were left on your own?"

"I was already on my own, and by then I suppose I was eating as much junk food as anyone else. But now I find that I long again for real food. Not necessarily the food of my childhood, but food with flavor that is not a chemical additive. A good meal to me is a ripe tomato, a fresh mozzarella, some fine oil and vinegar, and a crusty baguette with a glass of rough red."

"*A loaf of bread, a jug of wine, and thou*?"

"Don't expect me to start singing."

Kalki leans in to remove her plate, silver nose gleaming.

"What was the side dish?" Andromeda asks.

"Thistles, Miss. Leila collected them this morning."

"I haven't seen her today. I hope that she's well."

"She was gathering in the morning and has been cooking all afternoon. She wanted to make sure that the dinner was special."

"Please tell her that it is."

Kalki agrees to do so and leaves the room. Gidding sits back and stares into his wine, brooding. The only sound is the flicker of flame in the fireplace. Andromeda breaks the silence.

"I think that you're wondering what to do with me," she says.

"I think you're right."

"I think you're contemplating killing me."

"Possibly."

"An accident, perhaps? Slipping and falling into the sea?"

"Something easy enough to engineer, I would think."

"And hard to disprove."

"Very."

"There's no boat arranged for tomorrow morning, is there?"

Gidding leaves a long pause before answering.

"No."

The frankness of the response startles her.

"If you're wondering whether or not to make an appeal to me then I can tell you right now that it would be a waste of time. If I have the opportunity I'm going to write my article, whether or not you tell me where Margot is."

"I never doubted it."

"And so this particular ending is to be a tragic one."

"So it would seem." Gidding stands and picks up his glass. "But I haven't shown you the final reel yet."

THE FINAL REEL COMPRISES just three scenes. It begins the morning after Faust's recruitment, his first full day of possibility unlimited by anything save time. He sits on the sofa in the Griffin Room, arms spread along the back cushion, legs casually crossed, a posture of self-satisfied repose. Mephistopheles stands before him.

"So now thou art mine for the next twenty-four years, Mephistopheles."

"Yes."

"Thou wilt obey my commands?"

"I am thy servant."

"Thou wilt fetch for me?"

"I am thy dog."

"Thou wilt perform for me?"

"I am thy fool."

"Thou wilt procure for me?"

"I am thy pander."

"Unquestioningly?"

"Servants do not question their masters."

"I thought thy master was Lucifer."

"To serve you is to serve him."

"Faustus dost much like thou this way, demon."

"To please Faustus is my only pleasure."

Faust claps his hands together in delight. "Excellent. Now, where shall we begin?" He scratches his chin, considering the matter. "Faust finds that he is thirsty."

I small silver tray appears in Mephistopheles hand. Upon it is a glass of orange juice. She steps forward and offers it to Faust.

"What is this?"

"Orange juice."

"What is *orange*?"

"A fruit from Persia."

"Faust does not drink fruit." He slaps away the tray, and the glass smashes on the floor. "When Faust is thirsty, demon, thou wilt bring him ale, and nothing else."

A tankard of beer appears on the table. He picks it up and takes a deep draft.

"That's better." He wipes his mouth with the back of his hand. "And now food."

Plates appear on the table, next to the beer. Faust leans forward and frowns.

"What dost thou call this?"

"What Faustus asked for."

"Is there mutton?"

"No."

"Beef?"

"No. These are different foods, Faustus. These are not meats."

"Dost thou take me for a peasant? Get rid of this. Bring me a leg of mutton, and a haunch of beef."

The plates disappear, replaced by wooden boards bearing large pieces of roast meat. Faust disjoints a bone and begins eating. Mephistopheles watches him in silence. After a while Faust realizes that she is staring at him, and momentarily stops chewing.

"Well?"

"Does Faust no longer wish to know the wonders of the world?"

"Yes, demon, I would like to know the wonders of the world. One wonder in particular."

"Name it."

"Show me Helen."

"Helen who?"

"Helen of Troy."

"The wonder Faust wishes to see is Helen of Troy?"

"Indeed it is, demon. I have a mind to pass my own judgment upon this face that launched a thousand ships."

Helen of Troy enters from the hall. She wears classical clothing. Her hair is up, secured with a silver fillet. She crosses the room, apparently oblivious of the other two, then climbs the stairs and disappears.

"Too skinny," Faust says when she is gone. "I prefer my wenches with more meat on the bone. Bring me one, and see that she is bawdy."

A wench appears by his side, naked and slightly drunk, fat breasts jiggling as she laughs.

"A pair, I say."

A second appears on his other side, similar to the first. Faust seems much pleased with them.

"Perhaps Faust would like to see Troy itself."

"An excellent idea, Mephistopheles. Show me Troy."

"We shall thence anon."

"Dost thou not hear me, demon? I did not tell thee to *take* me there. I told thee to *show* me."

"How am I to show you without taking you?"

"By using the magic mirror. Bring it here, and while I dine have the quicksilver reveal to me the towers of Ilium all aflame."

The quicksilver mirror appears before Faust. He sits back and stares at the images with his beer. The bawds eat and drink loudly. After a while he realizes that Mephistopheles is still in attendance, and he turns away from the mirror, annoyed at the distraction.

"Well?"

"*Panem et circenses*?"

"What's wrong with bread and circuses?"

"Is this to be your future, Faustus?"

"My future is Perdition, thanks to thou. Why should Faustus look to the future?"

"Do not concern yourself with death, Faustus. You are alive, so live."

"I am denied Heaven, demon, so I am resolved that from now on I shall make my own heaven on earth within these walls."

"You intend to remain here?"

"A former abbey, alas the nearest I am destined to attain to God."

"You will not travel?"

"No."

"But you will study?"

"Certainly."

"Then I shall bring you books."

"Just one. A Bible, and be sure that it is lavishly illuminated, for I wish the comfort of seeing pictured that to which I can no longer aspire."

A large Bible appears in Mephistopheles' hands, and Andromeda recognizes it as the one she found during the treasure hunt. Mephistopheles puts it on the table before resuming the conversation.

"You said that you wanted to see farther than other men, Faustus, to know the true causes of things. But now you wish only to close your eyes."

He throws the tankard at her. "Do not vex me, demon."

"I merely warn you, Faustus. A man who has ceased becoming has ceased to be."

"I tire of thy sight, Mephistopheles. I tire of thy voice. I tire of thy boney frame."

"But I am at your service."

"Then hear me, servant. From now on you will see to it that my tankard is always full and that my larder is always supplied. I will have bawds aplenty. And I wish thee to delight me with images in the quicksilver: great battles by preference, and on Sundays gladiatorial games, now that the comforts of the sacrament are denied me. Other than that, you are dismissed. Let me not see thou unless I call." Faust returns his attention to the mirror, but Mephistopheles remains unmoved.

"Was not the agreement with thy master that thou wouldst obey me, demon?"

"Yes."

"Then why art thou still here?"

THE PENULTIMATE SCENE COMES AT the conclusion of the twenty-four years. Faust sits despondent in the Griffin Room. The remains of a feast lie about him. He drinks the dregs from a goblet. A plump bawd sits by him, mechanically stroking his shoulder with the back of her hand. Other half-naked women lie scattered about the room. The years have taken their toll on Faust: his hair is stringy and his jowls droop; he is bloated and sluggish and dull.

Mephistopheles enters. She wears a business suit and carries a sleek aluminum case that Andromeda immediately recognizes: it is the case that held the Picasso. Unlike Faust, Mephistopheles has not aged. She sets the case on the table, opens the top, and withdraws not a drawing but the document consigning Faust's soul. She puts on a pair of glasses in fashionable frames to read it. Faust stares at her with a snarl.

"So thou hast appeared unbidden, demon. No doubt thou art come to collect thy debt."

"No."

"No?"

"No. Your soul was lost long ago, Faust. There is nothing for me to collect."

"Thou speakest in riddles, demon."

"It's really quite simple. You have no value. You are of no further interest to us."

Faust is still bleary but brightens at the prospect of an unexpected reprieve.

"I may keep my soul?"

"You have no soul."

"Will I still die?"

"Yes, within the hour."

"Am I going to Hell?"

"This is your Hell, Faustus."

"What dost thou mean?"

Mephistopheles takes off her glasses and looks directly at Faust.

"Twenty-four years ago you were a man in his prime. I came to you offering the greatest of gifts: the gift of knowledge. All you had to do was agree to use it wisely. You thirsted to know, you said, and you agreed. But then when I showed you the possibilities all you did was balk. Now you are old and beyond new things. You are guilty of the supreme crime, Faust: to have lived your life badly."

"All I ever saw were the results of thine own conjuring, demon. Thou never taught me the spells."

"There are no spells. Everything I showed you was discovered by humankind, or developed by humankind, or invented by humankind. The future is indeed full of fabulous wonders: miraculous cures will be effected by the simple swallowing of a pill; people will travel as if hitched to a hundred horses; to fly through the air will be commonplace. But all of these will result from the application of human reason. Magic is just another superstition, Faustus, functionally indistinguishable from belief in God, or Santa Claus, or the Easter Bunny."

"I believe. I have faith."

"Then your mind is diseased."

Faust stands and brushes away the bawd. "I must pray for forgiveness." He makes his way unsteadily out of the room.

IN THE FINAL SCENE Mephistopheles finds Faust in the chapel, as dark as a Caravaggio. He is on his knees before the altar, rapidly mumbling prayers. Mephistopheles walks slowly down the nave. The camera tracks her from the side. She removes her jacket and allows it to fall to the floor. She begins unbuttoning her shirt. Her heels echo on the flagstones.

Faust turns and sees her disrobing. "Thou wilt not tempt me from salvation, demon." He resumes his prayers.

She peels off her shirt and removes the hairclip. The shirt floats rather than falls, as airy as a wisp. Her hair tumbles to her shoulders. She unzips her skirt and steps out of it with no interruption to her pace. She comes to the prostrate form of Faust and walks up onto his back without pause. Her stiletto heels dig into him. His only reaction is to pray more loudly.

Mephistopheles leaps up onto the crucifix mounted on the wall. She lands heavily and the wind seems momentarily knocked out of her. Her hands lock behind Christ's head, her legs splay either side of the cross, the soles of her shoes hard against the wall. She extends a long tongue and licks the figure's face. She gyrates her hips against the statue. A sheen of sweat breaks out on her body. She arches her back and closes her eyes.

Faust stares up, no longer praying.

Mephistopheles pants and gasps and emits an extended cry that reverberates through the chapel. She throws her head back. Her glistening body glows with reflected torchlight. For a brief pause the only movement is that of her breathing, chest expanding and contracting rapidly as she takes in air, but then from beneath her body a gelatinous globule gradually emerges. It takes Andromeda a moment to realize that it is mercury. The quicksilver elongates, fat at the base and extending upward in a long tapering concave curve, soon a foot, then several feet, eventually a body length below Mephistopheles. The camera remains unmoved, a neutral and objective observer, filmmaking that is slow and formal and rigorous, offering no commentary no matter how bizarre the subject matter.

But then everything changes: the globule bursts apart, seemingly having blown through its surface tension, and suddenly there is an explosion of mercury, as if gushing from everywhere. The eruption physically jars the camera. Quicksilver sprays onto the lens. The camera falls to the floor but it continues to film, capturing the tidal wave, a mercury tsunami. Now there are multiple cameras and multiple angles, some normal speed and some slow motion, all recording a monstrous turbulent chaos of flowing quicksilver.

Eventually the flood abates. The floor is left covered in a mercury sea, slowly undulating. Faust stares open-mouthed, dumbstruck.

A bell begins to toll midnight.

Mephistopheles drops like a ninja onto the altar. She lands in a crouch, facing Faust, replicating the posture of her first appearance in the film. Her flesh gleams. One of her knees is scraped from the encounter with the wall, and a thin stream of blood trickles down.

"The gift you were granted was life itself, Faustus, but you spurned it for having lost a worthless promissory note on an imaginary hereafter," she says. "Now, it is too late."

The last bell tolls. Faust clutches at his chest.

Mephistopheles sits and assumes a relaxed posture, one foot upon the altar with an arm resting on the knee, the other leg dangling over the side. She opens the reliquary. It contains cigarettes made of brightly colored papers in various shades. She takes a pink one and lights it from an altar candle, then casually smokes with an expression of mild curiosity while watching Faust die.

At last his agonies cease. He stares up amid a pool of quicksilver, open-mouthed, open-eyed, and still.

Mephistopheles takes her time finishing the cigarette and stubs it out using the ciborium, intended for Eucharistic wafers, as an ashtray. She stands and steps around Faust's body, then walks back down the mercury-drenched nave. Her stride is long and fluid. The camera tracks back with her, but at a slower pace so that Mephistopheles gradually approaches and then walks past, out of frame. The shot freezes on all that remains: the cross, the altar, and the fallen form of Faust.

The scene smash cuts to black and loud music blasts forth. A pause, and then the closing credits begin to roll. Gidding allows the reel to continue, for which Andromeda is grateful, allowing her to collect her thoughts. She is sure that what she has just witnessed is a work of the highest order, but it will take her time to absorb it. All she knows at the moment is that it is a tragedy shorn of all sentiment and all pity, tragedy cut to the bone.

She completely understands now why Gidding had to use real props, and shoot in a real location.

The reel ends, and the tail of the film flaps on the projector. Gidding switches it off. Andromeda breaks the silence.

"How did you get the mercury to behave like that?"

"We used a transparent balloon, made from the same stuff as weather balloons. In the upper atmosphere they expand to many times their original size, so it's a suitable material for what I wanted to achieve. The feed line for the mercury was concealed in the cross."

"And the eruption?"

"We had a reservoir of the stuff, forty gallons, mounted overhead, which we simply released. There were another two hundred gallons in a stainless-steel container with a dozen high-pressure braided-metal hoses and a pneumatic compressor. The difficult part was the timing: everything had to go off at the same instant."

Gidding would have no way of knowing, but the scene had echoed the golden wave of her LSD-fueled *katabasis*. That vision had felt like a premonition, and seeing it realized on film, even in quicksilver rather than gold, had shaken her.

"How did Soline manage that leap?"

"A trampoline. She suggested it. I was willing to shoot her jumping off the cross and falling backward into the soft foam we use for stunts—the film would be reversed in the movie to make it appear as if she leaped up onto the cross. But Soline said that if we got one of those small trampolines she would give the real thing a try—apparently she was a gymnast in school. It was dangerous but she was game. She ran down the nave in those high heels, jumped onto the trampoline, and then sprung right up onto the cross, fifteen feet above the floor. We nailed it in the first shot.

"Is that how she scraped her knee?"

"Yes. Before we did it I told her I was concerned that any injury would be visible in the rest of the scene. She said *And so it should be. I've just had bruising sex with a supposed god, have I not?*"

"It's going to upset the religious right."

"I hope so."

"There'll be cinemas across the Bible Belt that will refuse to show it."

"For sure, but I'm not going to cut it. When art adjusts itself to the sensibilities of the audience it ceases to be art and becomes merely craft. In Hollywood, they changed a movie about a Chinese invasion of America to be a North Korean invasion of America, so as not to upset Beijing. Forget for a moment the absurdity of the idea that North Korea, starving and bankrupt, could mount an invasion of the U.S. The people who made that movie are not men, they are eunuchs. And not just eunuchs, but self-emasculated eunuchs."

"I don't think anyone will ever accuse you of that."

XXXVIII

ANDROMEDA AND GIDDING return to the Griffin Room, filled with flickering light from the fireplace and torches—in Rothermore, flame is never far away. Kalki serves coffee. Gidding mixes Scotches and soda. He gives one to Andromeda then takes his own and stands by the fire. Andromeda sits on the sofa. She waits for Kalki to leave before speaking.

"You told me there would be no more lies, but at dinner you admitted that there is no boat tomorrow."

"Nor is there. The sea is still too high."

"But earlier you said that you were arranging a boat on the phone."

"No, I said that I was arranging *transport*."

"Transport?"

"A helicopter will be here tomorrow morning to pick you up."

Andromeda sits back and sips her whiskey, wondering if this is just another clever lie.

"Has the time come for you to tell me where I can find Margot?"

"No, the time has come for something else."

"The time for what?"

"The time to show you what the fifth key is for."

Gidding walks over and sits by her. He puts his glass down on the table and then gently removes Andromeda's from her grip, placing it next to his own. He takes Andromeda's left hand and twists it to reveal the bracelet's latch but instead of immediately opening it to retrieve the key he stares, like someone having turned over a stone to be surprised by what lies beneath.

"Look how different we are," he says.

Andromeda looks. His arm is not much longer than her own but is greater in girth. His skin has the reddish-brown weathered hue of a man who spends a lot of time outdoors, sharply contrasting with her own, pale to the point of translucency and revealing the complex blue canal work of veins beneath. She has long hands for a woman but her fingers are narrow and tapering, too brittle for real work. Compared to hers Gidding's are potent and blunt, with the power to crush. Her flesh feels alien to her now, as if she had never really noticed it before; the skin seems artificially pallid, the wrist ridiculously thin—she wonders that her hand has never snapped off.

Gidding unlatches the bracelet and looks at it a moment before raising his eyes to Andromeda. He reaches out with his free hand and rests his fingers on her neck. Andromeda closes her eyes. He slowly draws her toward him, and she can feel slight pressure from the pad of his thumb under her jaw pushing upward, whether to ease access to her lips to be kissed or to her neck to be strangled she does not know.

She is neither kissed nor strangled. Instead, she hears the snap of a lock.

Andromeda opens her eyes. Gidding holds up the titanium collar in front of her, open. The key is in the lock, still with her bracelet attached.

"But I've been shown the key," she says. "It's nothing like that one."

"No, you were shown *a* key," Gidding says. "But the key that Renzitti showed you was not the key to this collar."

"You know Renzitti?"

"I do."

"How?"

"Professionally. I engaged him."

"You mean that *you* are the anonymous client?"

"Yes."

"That's impossible."

"Not at all."

"Why would you want me to find Margot? Why would you want me to reveal something that threatens to ruin you?"

"I want you to find Margot because it is your role to find her."

"I don't understand."

Gidding stands and walks to the cabinet next to the sideboard. He opens the mirrored doors.

"Come and see."

Andromeda joins him. Inside the cabinet is a camera, a movie camera mounted on a small motorized frame. There is a film cartridge in the back. A little red light on its face is blinking.

"It's on?"

"Yes."

Gidding holds out his arm, the collar still in hand. The camera moves slightly, pointing toward it. Gidding moves the collar in a sweep across his body and the camera pans with it. Next he moves the collar up and down, more rapidly. Again the camera tracks it.

"There's a transponder embedded in the collar," he explains. "The tracking frame sends out RF pulses—that is, radiofrequency pulses—thousands of times a second, and listens for responses from the transponder. That gives it range and direction. Wherever this collar is, the tracking frame will follow. The camera's inbuilt autofocus and light sensors take care of the rest. The mirrors are one-way. The servo mechanisms are professional motion-picture grade, which means that they are fast, smooth, and absolutely noiseless. In filmmaking there can be no noise because it might get picked up in the audio, but it also means that a camera hidden like this one will not give itself away."

"Who controls it?"

"No one—once the thing is set up it's completely autonomous. It will run whenever it detects a response from the collar, and continue until the film runs out. The fact that the film might run out is why I always add these. He picks up a small wooden box from the sideboard. The box is inlaid with marquetry.

"See this?" He points to a piece of marquetry on the side, just an eighth of an inch wide, but a little different from the rest. "This is a camera lens, much like the camera lens in your cell phone, but better quality." He opens the lid and pulls away the lining, revealing a small rectangle of metal embedded underneath. He pries it loose and shows it to her in the palm of his hand.

"A digital motion-activated movie camera. No bigger than a thumb drive—remarkable what they can achieve in miniaturization these days. The power supply is just a simple hearing aid battery. The video is stored in flash memory. I don't normally film in digital—I use celluloid whenever I can—but sometimes there is no choice. I also use them for backup, like this one. There are four or five of them in this room now, still recording."

Andromeda stares at the object in his hand in disbelief.

"You've been filming me?"

"Yes."

"And this arrangement with the cameras is left over from *Faust*?"

"No. They were set up specifically for you."

"But you couldn't have known that I would come to Rothermore."

"You were always going to come to Rothermore. I must admit that I was surprised when you showed up in Burrenhead on your own, although in retrospect I shouldn't have been. I expected you to return to New York and contact Renzitti. When you did so he would have reported that you had received an invitation to come to the island and interview me."

Andromeda takes the collar from Gidding and stands directly in front of the camera. She moves the collar from side to side, as if to check that Gidding's demonstration had not been a trick. The camera follows, although not precisely.

"It hesitates," she says.

"There are tracking algorithms. If it followed every fractional movement of the transponder then the film would be jittery and unwatchable. Instead, it remains steady while the transponder stays in frame, but follows if the transponder is about to move out of frame. It calculates angular velocities, panning earlier if the transponder is moving faster, later if it's slower, to avoid any jerkiness. In combination with the camera's own internal electronic stabilization it keeps everything nice and smooth, as good as if shot by a professional cameraman."

Andromeda stands closer to the camera, reducing the field of vision. She moves the collar slowly across her body. At first the camera remains unmoved, but then as her arm stretches to the side it silently and unerringly follows. She whips the collar back and this time the camera reacts instantaneously. Even just a few feet away, it would keep up with any speed a human being was capable of.

She turns from the camera to Gidding.

"How long have you been filming me?"

"Since the beginning. If you recall, in the office where you first met Renzitti one wall was mirrored. On the other side of that mirror was a thirty-five-millimeter Panavision camera. You were filmed there, and you have been filmed ever since. Miami, L.A., Paris, Venice—everywhere. That's why we had to make all the travel arrangements, so that we could get equipment in place, setting up as much as possible ahead of time. It's also the reason for the hard deadline. I need to be in Cannes for the premiere of *Faust*, so the filming had to be completed beforehand."

Andromeda looks again at the collar, then back at the camera. She turns to face Gidding directly.

"Why?"

"You've already answered that question."

"What do you mean?"

"Earlier this evening, you said that for art to be worthwhile there must be an honesty between the idea and the execution."

"You call this honest?"

"What could be more honest than a movie in which the actress is unaware that she is acting?"

"What movie?"

"That's what it's all been for: a movie. I am making a movie, and you are the lead actress."

"How can this be a movie?"

"Simple. The story will be the truth: a journalist accepts an assignment to find out what became of a girl who ran away from home ten years ago. Movies often tout themselves as being based on true events, but my movie will not be *based* on true events, it will *be* true events. The journalist discovers that the girl ran away from home in order to appear in a strange film. But that's not a story, it's the truth. The journalist is threatened and thwarted and even abducted, but overcomes all obstacles. That's not a story either, it's the truth. She tracks down the filmmaker and confronts him. All truth."

A long silence follows. Andromeda stares again at the collar in her hand.

"I don't know what to say."

"Don't say anything for now. We have to begin the trial."

"What trial?"

"Mine. I will plead my case, and you will render your verdict. Let's go to the courtroom."

XXXIX

THE COURTROOM TURNS OUT to be the crypt. When they enter Gidding gestures toward the tomb.

"The judicial bench."

Andromeda sits back against the dead abbot. Gidding goes to a table and leans against it, facing her, legs crossed at the ankle.

"My case is this," Gidding says. "The overriding paradigm of modern art is the attempt to break through form and get at the underlying truth. Monet broke the strictures of representation, and so Impressionism was born. Picasso broke up images, and so cubism was born. Matisse broke the rules of color, and so Fauvism was born. Joyce and Woolf and Faulkner broke up narrative, and so stream-of-consciousness was born. Miles Davis and John Coltrane broke up conventional key and conventional technique, giving birth to that great flowering of mid-century American jazz. So it goes, from Cezanne to the Sex Pistols. In every case, it's an attempt to get past form and reach the underlying fundamentals. The idea, you called it, and when the execution got through to the idea you said that the connection was pure.

"But the trouble with filmmaking is that the entire enterprise is sullied with obvious artifice. It's impossible to get that pure connection because the actors are always aware that they are acting. They have a script, they occupy sets, they are surrounded by crew, and the cameras are always there. So my idea was straightforward enough: no script, no sets, no crew, and no cameras. Of course it really was scripted, very carefully in fact, but the lead actress was unaware of the existence of the script—for her the story is reality. For sets, I took the world. No crew, at least no visible crew. And no awareness of the cameras, because technology has advanced to a state where for the first time it is realistic for them to remain concealed. People underestimate the role of technology in art: think how painting blossomed in the Sixteenth Century following the development of oil-based pigments, or music in the Twentieth Century after the invention of the electric guitar. So I took advantage of the new technology. What I wanted was absolute truth: filmmaking in its purest form, art without artifice. And now, I will show you the evidence."

Gidding picks up a film canister.

"The reason that I've been unavailable for the last two days is because I have been furiously working on this." He taps the canister. "It's a trailer, of sorts. I rushed to get it ready in time, and the results are not as polished as I would like, but it should be sufficient to give you the flavor of the film."

He moves to the projector and threads the reel.

The screen lights up, firstly bright white, then it is filled with Andromeda's face. She is staring directly at the camera, which then slowly zooms out to reveal the sofa upon which she sits, and an expanse of beige wall behind: it is the conference room in Renzitti's office. A voiceover announces, *A writer*. Then the screen shows Renzitti reaching down from his armchair and retrieving the envelope from his document case. *A commission*, continues the disembodied voice. There is a close-up of Margot's photo as Andromeda withdraws it from the envelope—they must have had a camera concealed in the ceiling—and Renzitti's voice: "Your assignment would be to find out what became of her." *A commission with unusual conditions*. Andromeda opening the Tiffany's box. A brief shot of the collar inside, then Andromeda looking up at the lawyer. "Am I expected to accept this?" Then Renzitti's reply: "No, you are expected to wear it."

Until now there has been no music, but suddenly a driving beat begins, loud and heavy. Andromeda recognizes it: the music that she had imagined she heard after diving into the cistern yesterday. Gidding must have been playing it at the same time, and the proximity of the cistern to the crypt had allowed her to hear it echo through the rock while underwater.

The screen goes frantic with images, none lasting more than a few seconds, barely long enough for comprehension, piling on top of one another in frenetic confusion. The first is from the Pelican Hotel lobby, Andromeda staring into the camera with chin up and thumb hooked under the collar as she had posed for Clare, still unused to this new thing stuck around her neck. A reinforcement shot, Andromeda realizes, driving home the point from the previous scene. But it is soon replaced by the next and then the next, brief glimpses in no particular order: Andromeda on the terrace of the Bauer sipping prosecco; Trilby Top approaching her on Miami Beach; a short *Bullitt*-like chase scene apparently shot from a camera mounted on the pursuing car's wheel arch, showing the back of the Pantera fishtailing under power and in the foreground the little hybrid's suspension bouncing wildly as it struggles to keep up; Andromeda on the table in the anatomatoria with *Il Dottore* standing above her, scalpel at the ready; in the car headed for Miami Beach, shot from the sky—Andromeda recalls the helicopter that had briefly tracked her along the causeway that day; Andromeda being shown into the Hispano-Suiza atop the barge; Andromeda diving into the cistern and swimming down to find the key, shot from underwater—she understands now why it had been so brightly lit; Trilby Top walking toward the camera with the building in Paris aflame behind him; Andromeda on Cherry's deck with Pixela and Plasticina entwined behind her; at the grave of Ezra Pound, shrouded in fog while reading from the book of poetry; with the Ferrari in front of the château, a long telephoto shot from a camera that must have been concealed in the trees; in the tent at the Venice ball, arrayed on the rug and unaware that she is about to be abducted; on the balcony of the Ritz, filmed from the place Vendôme; a shot overlaid with a target graticule, showing her standing still and facing the wild boar—the animal rears backward just before it ends, and the accompanying jerkiness from the recoil reveals that the scene was shot through a genuine boresight camera; at the sidewalk table in Miami with the wild-haired man reaching out with the DVD; emerging from the mist on Rothermore, the unseen camera approaching—the film Gidding had shot when she first arrived, her face a mixture of expectation and fear. The two final scenes are intercut in time with the music: the first showing Andromeda lying on the bed of mercury, shot from above, hair and limbs splayed as she stares up, the camera spinning as it slowly zooms in as if spiraling earthward; the second is the scene Andromeda saw in the Chapter House, closing in on her enthroned in the Dogandili palazzo. The combination is effective, both seeming to approach the viewer at the same rate, building expectation of a collision to come. As the shot dissolves into the blackness of her pupil the music ends with a crashing E-major chord that continues to reverberate while the screen transforms into a black-and-white still: it is the first photograph that Clare took of Andromeda, capturing her unrehearsed reaction, a hand reaching unconsciously toward her face—an effective shot in this context, inviting the viewer to wonder at the cause of her evident anxiety. Then, fading in across the screen in slashing red letters, two words appear: *Andromeda Graphika.*

The reel ends. Gidding turns off the projector.

A long silence follows, which Andromeda eventually breaks.

"Do you have any idea what a selfish, shameless, reckless, wanton indulgence this is?"

"I think so."

"It's voyeurism."

"All art is voyeurism—how can you see if you will not look?"

"And you want my judgment?"

"Yes, I do."

"My judgment is that you are not exactly insane, but that you have gone beyond common understanding, and you are never coming back."

"No doubt true, but you've mistaken my meaning. The final judgment you will make is not on filmmaker; it is on the film."

"What judgment?"

"The imperial one: life or death." He walks over to the computers, lined up like soldiers, sufficiently spaced to ensure that they have enough air to keep cool. "Right now, the entire digital content of the film, primary and backup, is contained on these servers." He gestures toward the series of metal canisters stacked nearby. "The raw film I normally store separately because celluloid is so flammable, but tonight I've brought it all in here, too."

He leans by one of the servers and pulls out something hidden behind. It takes Andromeda a moment to realize that the object is a sledgehammer.

"As you say, an incredible indulgence. Now you must deliver your judgment. At your word I will not just erase the video—I will physically destroy the servers and their discs so that there will never be any possibility of recovery. Same for the film. I'll simply throw it into the fire. There are no secret copies or hidden backups—nothing like that. Everything will be destroyed, utterly." He looks from the servers to Andromeda. "So this is where you decide. What will it be? Thumbs up or thumbs down?"

Andromeda responds without hesitation "Destroy it," she says. "Destroy it all."

She can tell that Gidding did not expect such a fast response, or perhaps not that response at all, but he pauses only briefly and manages to disguise his disappointment.

"So be it."

He lifts the sledgehammer and with a wide swing brings it down hard on the nearest server. The plastic casing splinters and the frame collapses. There are no sparks but the wreckage gives off an odor of electrical burning. He gives it two more solid swings and then moves to the next server, again raising the sledgehammer overhead

"Stop," Andromeda says.

Gidding stops. Andromeda gets to her feet and strides to the gate. She turns before leaving.

"Go ahead and make your movie," she says, "but don't ever speak to me again."

XL

GIDDING DOES NOT APPEAR AT breakfast the next morning. Andromeda ignores the chafing dishes and pours coffee instead. Leila makes cooking gestures, offering to fix her something else, but Andromeda tells her that she has no appetite and only came down to ensure that she was in good time for the helicopter.

Leila leaves the room and returns a few minutes later, but she is no longer Leila. Now, she is Margot Vaughn.

Margot stands mutely before Andromeda, allowing her to absorb the transformation.

Andromeda puts down her coffee and says, “I think I’m going to be sick.” She stands and walks quickly through the hall and outside into the open air. The cold hits her. She feels weak, barely able to stand. She walks down to the cliffside, trying to put distance between herself and the abbey, but then realizes that the last place she should be now is at the edge of a precipice. She retreats to an outcrop of rock and finds a place to sit and recover.

She would like to either vomit or cry, but finds that she can do neither.

After a while Margot quietly joins her, taking a seat on a rock slightly apart, saying nothing. It is Andromeda who eventually breaks the silence.

"Do you speak?"

"Yes."

"Why did you play mute? You never spoke in *Diotima*, so it's not as if I would have recognized your voice."

"How would someone supposedly from the Middle East have acquired an American accent?"

"You could have disguised it."

"Even so, you might have asked me about myself, and I would have had to make up stories. I'm no good at such things. You would have become suspicious."

"I doubt it. The makeup changed you completely."

"It was actually a mask, made of formed latex, the sort of stuff they use in movies. A series of identical masks, to be precise. I took it off each evening and had to put a new one on in the morning before you got up. I'm glad to be finally rid of them; they made my skin ache."

Another silence follows, again broken by Andromeda.

"I dreamed about you the other night."

"It wasn't a dream."

Andromeda looks at Margot directly. "It was real?"

Margot nods. "You were given a drug cocktail to make you susceptible. The first night's really hit you, I think."

"The first night's?"

"There was one every night, in the soup to disguise the flavor."

"What was in this drug cocktail?"

"I don't know all the ingredients offhand, but strange to say there was testosterone—apparently it encourages impulsiveness; it's the reason men are stupid. Also, there were three hundred grams of Mescaline in your port on the first night. That's why Gidding put opium into the hookah; its only purpose was to make you attribute any strangeness to having taken a few puffs."

"What's Mescaline?"

"A psychedelic hallucinogen. You know Huxley's *The Doors of Perception*?—Mescaline was the key that opened those doors. The aim was for you to awaken in a trance-like state. The dream had been suggested to you in Venice, along with various other things."

"Suggested to me?"

"You were hypnotized that night in the anatomatoria. The final edit will show you splayed on the quicksilver staring up at the camera, and then I will fade into the shot. It's supposed to represent you dreaming of me."

"Then what?"

"We just embraced—art might have no limits but I do. In his hands he can make that suggest whatever he wants to anyway. Tell me if you want it left out: he will if you ask."

Andromeda looks away and says nothing. She can feel Margot's eyes on her.

"I'm glad you changed your mind," Margot says. "About destroying the film, I mean."

"There won't be a film."

"Why not?"

"When I get back home I'm going to complete what I undertook to do: I'm going write about you."

"That's what he wants."

"Then what he wants is professional suicide. The article will include the fact that Gidding made a pornographic film with an underage girl. His career will be over."

"It's true that he shot *Diotima*, but there's more to 'making a film' than just rolling the cameras. It has to be commercially released and distributed: it's a business enterprise."

"I've seen the final product."

"No, what you saw was a DVD specifically cut for you. The legalese at the beginning was added to make it appear as if it had been commercially released, and of course Cherry Falco agreed to play the part of the disappointed distributor, but the truth is that until that DVD there were only two copies of *Diotima* in existence: one in Gidding's possession and one in mine. It was never released, never distributed. In strictly legal terms, *Diotima* is therefore just a private affair between consenting adults."

"The age of consent is sixteen."

"Not in France. In France, the age of consent is fifteen."

Andromeda says nothing for a long time. She feels off-balance, unable to distinguish the ephemeral from the real. This is the opposite of good art, she thinks—good art provides clarity, but all she can see now is fog.

"How did he convince you to do it?"

"To make *Diotima*?"

"Yes."

"It is I who had to convince him," Margot says. "Did he tell you about when we met that first day, on the bench in Lummus Park?"

"He said that he presented the idea and that you agreed."

"Well, that's true, as far as it goes. But there's so much more to it than that. It was the day that changed my life. When he proposed making the film I asked him, 'Why me?' I expected the sort of declaration that I'm sure you're used to: something along the lines of 'I knew from the moment I first saw you that you were' *et cetera, et cetera*. Or, worse still, 'because you're so beautiful,' as if the random arrangement of facial features constitutes a basis for decision-making. If Gidding had said something like that I would have handed him his wallet and walked away, but instead he thought about it for a long time before responding, as if it had just been an instinctive impulse at the time and now he needed to understand the nature of that impulse for himself. I liked the fact that he took the time to get the answer right.

"In the end, he said, 'It's because you are trapped, and at some level I think you know that you are trapped but you don't understand the nature of the trap, let alone how to escape it, and it's frustrating you.' I asked him if he knew the nature of the trap, and he said that yes, he did. He asked me if I remembered the line from the old Kurt Cobain song: *I wish I was like you, easily amused*. He said that was my trap, that I was not easily amused—that what life had to offer, or at least what I had seen of what life had to offer, was inadequate. He said that the point of the initiation depicted on the walls of Pompeii was to move beyond the trivial—beyond the stuff of the easily amused—and advance to something more fundamental and meaningful. Since I would be doing it for real it would hardly be acting, he said—a concept that he has taken to its ultimate form with you, I think."

"And so you became a work of art," Andromeda says.

"We both are now. We're a pair of sculptures, you and I, metaphysical sculptures. Perhaps he'll place us somewhere prominent in the garden."

Andromeda smiles, despite her anger.

"It didn't bother you that it would be pornographic?"

"I made it clear that I wouldn't agree to be in the film unless it was. Gidding was considering making it R-rated—right against the limits of an R-rating, but nevertheless R -rated. I said that the walls of Pompeii were pornographic, and therefore any realization of those walls in a film that was not also pornographic was necessarily a lie. It was the first important thing that I had ever said in my life—I had already begun to change."

Andromeda's nausea has retreated. She looks squarely at Margot. Her face is more or less unchanged from when she was fifteen. There is a piece of latex caught in her hair. Andromeda finds herself still liking this woman who as a girl she had instinctively liked when first seeing her photograph in Renzitti's office.

"Margot, I have something unpleasant to tell you. Your mother is very ill."

"I know. We've been in contact."

"But not with your father?"

"No."

"May I ask why?" Now it is Margot who looks away.

"He wants me dead."

"He wanted you dead?"

"No, he wants me dead. Present tense."

"You mean that he wants to kill you?"

Margot laughs. "I doubt that he would have the grit for such a thing. No, what I mean is that he wants me declared dead."

"What do you mean?"

"I guess that I should explain what happened before I left home. My father runs a hedge fund. Unfortunately, he's not very good at it. *The trend is your friend*, he would always declare, as if a single glib phrase could be the secret of clever investing. Sure enough, he would buy into every trend, usually just as it was ending. The returns sagged. His investors started making redemptions, and once that begins it's the death knell for an investment manager. So he recapitalized by taking on new clients, clients with plenty of money but limited investment options."

"Limited investment options?"

"Drug money. Miami is overflowing in it."

"How did you find out?"

"When legitimate investors are unhappy with their returns they withdraw from the fund. When drug lords are unhappy with their returns they take a more direct approach. One of them paid a personal visit to the house, unannounced. They met in my father's study, but the conversation was loud enough to be overheard."

"Why do you think he wants you dead?"

"For my mother's money. She's quite wealthy, and she was smart enough to keep her money out of my father's hands. Unlike him, she invested wisely—the two Koons alone would fetch several million—enough to help bail my father out of his troubles. A person who has been missing without a trace for ten years can be declared legally dead, even without actual evidence of death. If that happens my father would expect to inherit the entire estate. He has already begun the legal proceedings, behind my mother's back. And anyway, he's not my real father."

"I've seen a copy of your birth certificate."

"Which is a lie. My mother told me. My purported father has no idea."

Andromeda now realizes how it is that Margot could have been so much taller than her parents, but she doubts the assertion that her father has no idea—Nathan Vaughn had not used the phrase 'my daughter' because, subconsciously or not, he did not believe it.

"Who's your real father?"

"Someone in France. A doctor."

"Have you met him?"

"No, nor do I care to. Blood ties mean little to me. I'm more interested in people for who they are than for whom they're related to. Gidding is the person I feel most closely related to."

"You've been with him since *Diotima*?"

"Well—yes, but not in the sense I think you mean." Margot smiles, whether at Andromeda's assumption or some past remembrance she cannot tell. "One day during the filming of *Diotima* the crew were talking. They liked the château and wondered how much such a place would cost. 'More than we'll ever make,' one of them said, 'unless we get a really hot stock tip.' He called over to Gidding, 'Hey, Boss, got any really hot stock tips?' 'You're asking the wrong guy,' Gidding said, 'I don't own any stock at all.' We continued shooting and finished the scene.

"Afterward, while they were setting up for the next take, I went with Gidding for a walk in the garden. I asked him if it was true that he didn't own any stock, and he said that it was. I asked him if he had any investment accounts. He didn't know what an investment account was. It turned out that he kept all of his money in a single bank savings account, the same one he'd had since he was a child. I asked him how much was in it but he didn't know—he never read the statements. I asked him to guess. He thought several million, but he wasn't sure.

"I was astonished by his financial childishness. I explained that, apart from anything else, by keeping all that money in a single account with a single financial institution he was incurring huge counterparty risk, way beyond the FDIC insurance limits. He had no idea what I was talking about. I told him that the rates he would be receiving would be money-market at best, well below what a properly diversified investment portfolio should return. He wasn't familiar with the term money-market and didn't understand diversification, so I had to explain the differences between fixed income and equities and commodities and cash; how credit spreads work; why the shape of the yield curve is important; the monetization of precious metals; how to hedge foreign exchange exposure. You have to picture what this would have looked like to an outside viewer. I was still undressed—putting anything on between scenes might leave crease marks, which would hold up shooting until they disappeared—and so it was basically a naked fifteen-year-old girl giving an Investment 101 class to a grown man while taking a walk in the garden—Giorgione meets Harvard Business School.

"When I'd finished he was chastened to the point of understanding that he was financially irresponsible, but he was more confused than when I'd started. 'What should I do?' he asked. I told him that he needed professional guidance, and that once people got into the multi-millions that would often mean hedge funds. He'd heard of hedge funds but I could tell that he wanted no part of them. I realized that expecting him to choose wisely between investment managers would be like expecting a minnow to choose wisely between sharks.

"I made him an offer. I said that after we finished filming I would agree to be his financial advisor for one year, until his affairs were in order and during which time he could get comfortable with the basics. I explained that hedge funds usually charge two percent of capital to cover administrative costs, and twenty percent of profit as a performance incentive. I said that I would only charge ten basis points—that is, a tenth of a percent—since my administrative costs would be so much lower, and just ten percent on the upside. I don't think I've ever seen a man so relieved. He agreed, but with an unusual condition: I had to go back to school and earn my *Baccalauréat.* I explained that although I had basic French from my mother I didn't speak it well enough to be suddenly plunged into a *lycée* and expected to pass such a rigorous exam. He relented on the *Bac*; instead, I would have to go to an American school in Paris and graduate from there.

"After filming was finished we returned to Paris. I got in contact with the investment banks and began opening accounts. I intended for everything to be under Gidding's signature, but he was going down to Venice to finish editing *Diotima* and insisted that they had to be under my signature as well. At first I called before making new investments, giving him the reasoning and pointing out the risks, but in the end he asked me to stop—it was interrupting his work. In short, I soon became more than just a financial advisor; I was an investment manager. This was a lot of extra work. I made it a point to carefully account for every penny, and I sent him detailed monthly reports, whether he wanted them or not. Perhaps this was a reaction to my father's weakness. I did pretty well. The truth is that markets are not rational—often just the opposite—and so to make money is not that difficult: all you have to do is keep your head and be patient, no matter what happens. The Picasso is an example. The art market was still depressed from the dot-com bubble having burst—everyone was selling, an obvious time to buy. I researched the auction catalogs and suggested some items as a means of diversification. Gidding chose the drawing, which turned out to be an excellent investment—right now it is securing a loan many times the original purchase price, a loan that is helping to finance *Faust*.

"Meanwhile, I went to school. My classmates were the children of American diplomats or business executives whose work had brought them to Paris. By then I had long ago left home and was supporting myself as an investment manager after having made a pornographic art film: I had absolutely nothing in common with them. To me, they all seemed flaccid and formless; I could barely tell them apart. Their heads were always buried in screens, living out their lives by proxy in video games or television shows. I wanted to get an evening job but not speaking fluent French was a handicap. I ended up working somewhere fluency wasn't required: I became a dancer at the Crazy Horse."

Andromeda laughs and Margot smiles in response.

"I actually enjoyed it," she says, "and I don't think I've ever been so fit. I was only in the chorus line, and so I could limit my hours. Once I'd learned the routines I would fill out the calendar with my availability and if they had a requirement they would let me know. I thought of it like any other after-school activity—basically, a more honest form of cheerleading. I usually did the early shift right after school and would be out in time for a quick meal at the corner bistro while finishing my homework, followed by a good night's sleep after all that exercise. You would think that my grades would have suffered but just the opposite happened: dancing at the Crazy Horse got me straight As.

"Meanwhile, Gidding made *Madison Square Garden*, and after its success he went from being affluent to genuinely wealthy. It made no difference to his lifestyle—he lived in exactly the same way, whether rich or broke—but it meant that handling the investments was now a full-time job. By then I had graduated; in fact, I was the valedictorian. How horrified those doting parents would have been to learn that their little dears had taken classes with someone who worked at the Crazy Horse. I told Gidding—he had been living back home to make *MSG* but returned for my graduation; he laughed and asked me not to quit until he'd seen one of the shows. He came, he saw, I quit.

"We had dinner afterward at Le Grand Véfour. He said he wanted to make a movie about it, but I told him I had a new interest: market theory. By now I spoke French well enough and so college in France wasn't out of the question, but the thought of having to endure four more years in the company of the same sort of people I'd just gone to school with was depressing. I already had a theory I wanted to develop—that the free-market is not the empirically based rewarder of enterprise that it is usually depicted to be but instead a chaos of irrationality operating within a tightly bounded space: a Feyerabendian tumult within a Foucaultian constellation of power relations. I wanted to define those limits mathematically, then use fractal analysis of price movement to fill it out.

"Gidding said, 'Margot, you are unfitted by mind and temperament for the academic world. Your mind is too advanced, your temperament too uncollegial—as you say, a bachelor's degree would be a waste of four years.' But it's what I want to do, I told him. Then do it, he said, and ignore the conventions. Conventions are for people who have neither the time nor inclination to think. For such people, conventions are a boon; for you, they are a straightjacket. You can write a paper or a book without going to college. Franklin never went to college, nor did Lincoln. Einstein developed the Theory of Relativity while working as a patent clerk. Formal academia is just a factory, he said, an assembly line in which units of humanity move slowly along, gradually acquiring parts: papers, post-docs, professorships, and so on. Skip it, he said, and do what you really want to do. If your work is good then recognition will follow.

"It was the best advice I ever received. I've had two papers published, the latest in the *Journal of Political Economy*, which is a major publication in the field. They've been cited dozens of times, a sign that the work has had an impact. I actually did go to college and still do: one of the great institutions of Paris is the Collège de France, where the lectures are free and open to the public. It's just across the Jardin du Luxembourg from where I live so I often sit in, but of course there's no degree. That doesn't matter to me: I don't want to be certified; I want to learn. In the end, Gidding was right: do what you want, and if the results are worthwhile then recognition will follow. His own career is an illustration of that." Margot sits back, her arms straight out behind her, looking up at the first patch of blue to have appeared in days. "And so that's what has become of me: I'm a full-time investment manager, part-time market theoretician, and occasional co-conspirator with Gidding in an enterprise that I don't blame you for finding unforgivable, but which I would not have agreed to unless I believed in it."

They sit in silence as Andromeda absorbs all that Margot has told her. She has imagined many outcomes for Margot, but nothing like this. Her reverie is interrupted by a distant sound that soon resolves itself into the hard thump of a helicopter rotor.

"Your ride is coming," Margot says. She turns to Andromeda. "I should tell you that Gidding left it up to me as to whether or not I would reveal myself. That's one of the reasons I played the maid: I wanted to be able to get close and see who you really were before deciding." She takes a folded envelope from the pocket of her uniform and hands it to Andromeda. "All of my contact details are in here. No doubt you will have more questions—please feel free to ask whatever you want. I wish you good luck with the article. I look forward to reading it."

They stand and face each other awkwardly.

"Guess I'll see you in the movies," Andromeda says, and they both burst into laughter.

The helicopter is at the island now but still circling, as if uncertain about landing and getting its skids muddy. It is a small craft, just two seats inside a plastic bubble at the end of a lattice-work boom, and the engine looks no bigger than a lawn-mower's. It twists one way and the other, then finally settles into a hover and slowly descends to the grass.

Andromeda and Margot walk over and come to a halt at the edge of the rotor wash. They turn and face each other. The helicopter is too loud for them to talk without shouting; they embrace instead. With her lips next to Andromeda's ear, Margot says, "He would have done it, you know. He would have destroyed *Andromeda Graphika* entirely. Think about what that means."

Andromeda ducks under the rotor and slips into the helicopter. It immediately takes off and turns toward the coast. Soon Rothermore is just a distant speck on a wind-swept sea. She thinks about Gidding's offer to destroy the film, but the only meaning she can see is that he is as reckless with himself as he is with everyone else.

XLI

ANDROMEDA ASSUMED that they would land in Burrenhead, but instead the helicopter flies straight past. She turns to the pilot and points toward the town.

"My car's down there," she shouts, hoping to be heard above the engine noise, but the pilot shakes his head. He taps his earphones and then points to a second pair stowed beside her seat.

She puts them on, adjusts the boom mike, and locates the talk key on the cord.

"My car's in that town we just flew over," she repeats.

The pilot keys his mike.

"Silver Range Rover?"

"Yes."

"It was brought over to Dunraven this morning."

"Dunraven?"

"That's where we're headed."

"Where's Dunraven?"

"Not far. We'll be there in twenty minutes." He keys off the mike and returns his attention to flying, discouraging further conversation.

Andromeda studies the instruments. The compass reads 270: they are heading west. The airspeed indicator shows ninety knots, so twenty minutes would cover around thirty nautical miles. She cannot recall if nautical miles are shorter or longer than statute miles, but the knowledge will help her relocate the site of her latest abduction, should she ever need to. Visibility is good—the last of the clouds have blown away to the east, and the sky is a clear blue so pale that everything seems to have been washed from it, even the color. Andromeda studies the terrain below, searching for visual markers that might guide her later, but by now they have left the narrow coastal plain and entered Highland country, a rugged landscape of rough hills covered in gorse and heather, unrelieved by any sign of civilization.

Eventually a cultivated area comes into view, something that at first Andromeda mistakes for a farm, but which soon resolves into the formal gardens of a large country estate. Dunraven is not a town, she realizes, but a Highland manor.

The pilot lands on the broad front lawn. He does so quickly, without the exploratory circling at Rothermore—he is familiar with this place. He keys the microphone.

"They're expecting you," he says. "Don't forget to duck."

Andromeda disembarks and trots in a crouch out from under the blades. Behind her she can hear the helicopter take off again. In front of her the lawn stretches away for another fifty yards, then beyond is a gravel forecourt and eventually the house itself, a large Palladian structure built of honey-colored stone. She approaches.

The front door remains closed, although whoever is inside cannot have failed to hear the arrival of the helicopter. There are two vehicles parked on the forecourt: a large black limousine whose winged-*B* radiator badge identifies it as a Bentley, and behind it her own Range Rover, gleaming in the sunlight—someone has washed the vehicle since it was brought from Burrenhead.

She comes to the steps, and above her the front door opens. A woman emerges. Andromeda recognizes her, the woman who was auctioned ahead of her in Venice, but now instead of a red dress she wears an outfit made from brocaded black silk, cut in a deep V revealing the curvature of her breasts and between them a ruby-studded pendant hanging on a silver chain. The woman's eyes follow Andromeda's to the necklace.

"Do you recognize it?"

"No."

"I wore it to your initiation."

"Initiation?"

"You were initiated."

"Into what?"

The woman does not answer, instead stepping back and opening her hand in a gesture of invitation. Andromeda climbs the steps and enters the house.

She would have expected the interior of a Highland manor to be all wood paneling and hunting trophies, but the space she enters lacks ornamentation: it is a marble-floored expanse devoid of furniture. On the far side is a broad staircase that sweeps aloft.

The woman leads her up to the next floor and into a large bedroom.

"Am I expected to stay here?" she asks.

"No, you'll be wanting to get to Edinburgh before dark."

"Then why a bedroom?"

"To change."

"Into what?"

In response, the woman opens the wardrobe door. There is a single item hanging inside, a simple white dress of gossamer-thin fabric. On the floor beneath sit a pair of sandals.

"I'm not putting that on," Andromeda states flatly. She crosses her arms to signal that the matter is closed, but the other woman smiles in response.

"I'm afraid that you've misunderstood. The fact is that the man you are about to meet has many enemies, including several governments. This is simply a dignified way of ensuring that there's no wire concealed either on you or in your clothing."

"And if I refuse?"

"The keys to your car are in the ignition. The tank is full and your luggage is in the back. You are free to leave anytime; no one will stop you."

Andromeda makes no reply.

"Perhaps you'd be more comfortable if I were wearing less than you." The woman reaches a hand behind her back. She undoes the zip, shakes the dress from her shoulders, and allows it to fall to the floor. The woman is naked beneath, and Andromeda realizes that she had prepared for this eventuality. Her body is more rounded than Andromeda's. There is a mark on her hip, the same brand as on the acrobats. The woman senses her recognition.

"It was I who painted the same thing on you," she says. She steps out of her dress and up close to Andromeda. She places a finger on her brow. "Here."

In her high heels she is as tall as Andromeda. The woman's breasts are close enough to brush against her. She pauses a moment, inviting inspection, before returning to the wardrobe and taking the hanger from the rail. She holds out her arm in offer.

"Now or never, I think."

The story comes first, Andromeda supposes. She steps forward and accepts the dress.

ANDROMEDA ASSUMES that she will be taken somewhere dark, Dunraven's equivalent of the crypt or, worse, the anatomatoria, but instead she is led into a space filled with light. It is a conservatory, a half-dome of glass framed in metal and extending from the manor's south wing. There is a multitude of plants, seemingly all in flower.

They come to a halt in the center of the space. Her guide departs, leaving Andromeda alone with the room's remaining occupant, whom she recognizes: it is the same man who at the ball in Venice joined her on the terrace, offering her a Black Russian cigarette and telling her about their host. He sits at a small table bearing a tray with a tea service. He is reading a book, and it is not until the other woman is gone that he looks up at Andromeda. The light is behind him, best for reading, but it means that the sun shines full upon her. He studies her in silence, and she is conscious of the thinness of the fabric.

"Does it bother you to wear something so revealing?" he asks, apparently having read her mind.

"A little late to be asking my opinion on the matter."

"I have a theory that I will share with you." He closes the book. "I believe that the degree to which society permits the female body to be revealed is a direct measure of a civilization's advancement. One can hardly picture ancient Athens without the caryatids of the Parthenon or Praxiteles' cool marble nudes: freedom of the female form seems always to accompany freedom for the human mind. This was again true in the Italian Renaissance and then again in the French Enlightenment, and I think that it is also true today. The most barbaric governments bundle their women up. In Tehran, a woman who appeared in public without a headscarf would be in serious trouble, but in Saint Tropez she could shed her bikini top without a second thought." The beach reference makes Andromeda wonder if he received a briefing from Trilby Top. He takes off his glasses, as if to see her more clearly. "Excepting orchids, the most beautiful thing in creation is woman. By contrast, we men are ridiculous things, little more than monkeys—it's hard to believe that we are of the same species. In backward societies, that beauty is feared. In advanced societies, it is embraced as the gift that it is."

Andromeda realizes how the plants could all be in flower; the variety is an illusion: they are all orchids.

"What was in the cigarette you gave me that night?"

"Just tobacco."

"Am I being filmed?"

"No."

"Who are you?"

"I am he about whom I told you."

She considers the reply. "Do you mean that you are Jasper Slade?"

"I am."

"And so that night in Venice you were warning me about yourself in the third person."

"Yes."

"Why?"

"I wanted to see you for myself."

"Inspecting the cattle?"

"Hardly."

"But you do brand your cult members, don't you, Mr. Slade?"

"Ah, yes—Heather is fond of showing off. No, Miss Chamberlain, the brand has nothing to do with me. Gidding intended for the symbol to be inscribed—just with theatrical makeup, you understand—on those women who were to appear sufficiently disrobed for it to be visible during the ceremony, but then some of them decided to get the real thing instead. They had a glassmaker over on Murano create the iron, and then made a party of the actual branding. A local anesthetic was applied beforehand, of course, so there was no discomfort. Souvenirs, I suppose, like sailors getting tattoos."

"Is it Gidding's symbol?"

"No, it is yours."

"Mine?"

"Gidding created it for you. Heather refers to it as her *Stigmata Andromeda*. Gidding says that it represents ungraspable light, which he claims is why he had to film you. He says that it is a quality he has never seen before, and expects never to see again."

This revelation momentarily silences her. Gidding is in love with her, she realizes. Or, more accurately, he is in love with his own image of her; a modern-day Pygmalion working in celluloid rather than stone. That was what Margot had meant by her comment *think what that means* before Andromeda boarded the helicopter.

"Heather said that in Venice I was initiated."

"I suppose that you were. We don't normally make such a fuss; that was just for Gidding's movie. In our cult, as you call it, one really initiates oneself."

"You're surely not going to pretend that any of this was voluntary?"

"I think that you're confusing two different things. Gidding's activities are entirely his own affair."

"But I was abducted at your ball."

"Certainly. He asked if he could film there, and I consented. Such of my guests who chose to also joined in the theater."

"I hope that I was entertaining for them."

The comment just makes him smile. "Ah, madam, I regret that I am of an age when a woman can no longer goad me, even one such as yourself."

"Why have I been brought here?"

"Would you care for tea?"

"No."

The old man takes a cup from the tray anyway. He pours tea ceremoniously, placing a strainer carefully on the rim and half filling it from a silver teapot, battered but well-polished, and then topping it with hot water. He takes milk from a dainty pitcher and uses tongs to add a single sugar cube from the matching bowl.

"Come, let us both sit." He gestures with an open palm toward a second chair, but Andromeda ignores the invitation.

"Are you going to tell me why I was brought here?"

"Because of your acuity, madam."

"Acuity?"

"And other qualities. Intelligence, honesty, courage."

"How flattering—you don't abduct the dishonest or the dull."

"I don't abduct anyone. As I told you, Gidding's activities are entirely his own affair." He shakes his head. "I do wish you'd sit down. I have poor eyesight and, as I will probably never see you again, I would like to look at you more closely now."

The request is so straightforward that Andromeda relents and takes a seat. He studies her in silence for a long moment with a gaze that penetrates not her clothing but her eyes. At last he nods slightly, as if having satisfied himself over something, then takes the second cup from the tray. Slade repeats the tea-pouring ceremony, pushes the cup to her side, and places the milk and sugar beside it. He takes the last remaining item from the tray, a plate of finger sandwiches from which the crusts have been cut.

"Cucumber sandwiches," he says. "I find that wherever one is it's best to eat regionally, although perhaps these are rather more English than Scottish, and I do draw the line at haggis." He places the tray between them and looks at her directly. "Tell me, that article you wrote titled 'Incident at Manoukaram'—in the larger scheme, did it make any difference?"

"No."

"Why do you say that?"

"The women were killed."

"Yes, the women were killed. But I think you are wrong when you say that it makes no difference. And that is why you were brought here today, so that I may tell you that."

"A letter would have sufficed."

"Certain things must be done face-to-face." He takes a sandwich and slowly consumes it, facing not Andromeda but the orchids. Andromeda sips her tea and matches his silence.

He finishes the sandwich and turns to Andromeda. "Read any good books lately?"

"Are you serious?"

"Perfectly."

"Then no, not really."

"What was the last piece of music you enjoyed listening to? Genuinely enjoyed, I mean."

Andromeda considers the question. "*Bitches Brew*," she says. "Miles Davis—Gidding had it on Faust's turntable."

"Faust has a turntable?"

"His Faust does."

"Then I look forward to seeing the film. Gidding thinks that movie-making is the only surviving art form, but that it too is dying. When a young and apparently intelligent woman confesses that she has not read any good books lately, or that the last piece of music she enjoyed listening to was half a century old, then I am inclined to agree with him."

"Just inclined?"

"Old men have been lamenting the decay of society since Cato the Elder. It is a trap that I try to avoid."

"I believe that you are in danger of coming to the point."

Slade laughs. "Indeed, madam, I am. In truth I do perceive a certain creeping decline: a subversion of the collective consciousness from rationality to banality; an erosion of that clear-eyed critical mass necessary for democracies to function. Not to mention a rise of religious fervor that I find frankly incredible, whether in Kentucky or Karachi—a sort of self-incendiary mass stupidity: humans as intellectual lemmings."

Andromeda realizes that she is hungry and takes a sandwich. The cucumber is crisp and smells of summer, despite the season. She wonders if there is a corner of the conservatory set aside for vegetables.

"I think that you want something from me," she says between mouthfuls, "but I still don't know what it is."

"Then I will ask you plainly, madam. Are you Elect?"

"Elect?"

"Yes, are you Elect?"

"Elected by whom?"

"By nobody. By hazard. By a lucky roll of the genetic dice, perhaps."

"I'm afraid that I don't know what you're talking about."

He picks up the book he had been reading. "The protagonist in this novel is asked the same question, and he gives much the same answer that you just gave me. In his case the response may have been justified; in your case it is not, as I think we both know."

He offers her the book. She takes it and examines the cover.

"*The Magus*," she reads. "John Fowles."

"The meaning of 'Elect' is never explained, and after that initial inquiry it is not brought up again. One can therefore put any interpretation on it that one pleases. I choose to interpret it as meaning those people who, for one reason or another, do certain things well. I named my little group the Elect from that episode."

"My little group?"

"Miss Chamberlain, I do not pretend to understand what it is that separates the extraordinary from the ordinary—I will leave such stuff to biologists and behaviorists—I know only that, for whatever reason, some people are Elect. All that I do is to gather some of them in an informal association."

"For what purpose?"

"Global domination." But the assertion is delivered with a smile. "I merely mean to encourage. There are tremendous pressures to conform, subtle and otherwise. Conforming means acceptance of the status quo, however absurd or ridiculous. Hence stupidity survives, in fact thrives, as even the most casual perusal of a newspaper demonstrates. I assume that when the Founding Fathers gathered—surely the greatest gathering of the Elect in human history—and decided to establish a new and enlightened republic they must have imagined that under the profound freedoms they were bringing forth such stupidities would naturally wither and die. They were of course not religious men; just the opposite. How horrified they would be to see the role of religion today. Not just religion; I mean all tribalisms under whatever guise, of which religion is just an instance. Most people do not reject stupidity—the truth is they grasp at it."

"What role does Gidding play in your Elect?"

"None. There are no roles. There is but one gathering a year, the ball that I host in Venice. An appropriate venue: Venice has always been a city of unusual tolerance, and historically it has defied those various powers who have tried to impose their ideologies upon it: the popes, the emperors, the Inquisitors, the Ottomans, the fascists. Many people come into the city during Carnival, which allows my gathering to go unremarked among the general influx, and of course the purpose of a masked ball is anonymity. Had they been unmasked that night you would perhaps have recognized some of the faces there."

"And that's where you initiate new recruits?"

"I invite people who have come to my attention in one way or another. Most of them accept—curiosity is a common quality in the Elect, I find. During the evening I will have a quiet conversation with them, something like the conversation we are having now."

"And Gidding?"

"Gidding is different. I knew his father. I've never had this conversation with him, as it obviously wasn't necessary: he is fully aware of his own gifts, and already has a healthy contempt for the established order."

"So exactly what is it that you are trying to achieve?"

"The preservation of thought in an increasingly thoughtless world."

"Nothing else?"

"Nothing else."

"And what do you want from me?"

"For you to be strong. For you to keep your courage. For you not to be undone by what surrounds you."

"You think that I'm weak?"

"No, but I do fear that you might choose to retire from the fray. There is another book, written around the same time as the one in your hand: *Atlas Shrugged*. In it, Ayn Rand imagines a world in which those I term the Elect essentially go on strike. They retreat in every sense, hiding out in a valley in the Colorado Rockies. Society at large collapses; theirs thrives. It is a myth, as are all utopias, and I warn you against what will be a very real temptation in your life: the temptation to just say *Enough!* and do battle no more. This is the nub of the problem at present: the Elect have essentially given up, retreating not into the Rockies but into themselves, declining to engage in a society they find increasingly absurd. But this very act of withdrawal creates a vacuum, and into this vacuum pour the third-rate. This is what is happening today: the leadership of society—cultural, commercial, political—has been taken over by those unfit for the task. Hence, decline." He pauses, regaining his breath before continuing. "There, we have just had a discussion of ideas informed by two novels, but both of them are over half a century old." He sits back, and she can tell that the meeting has exhausted him. "I am the opposite of John Galt," he says. "I call not for the Elect to leave the world but instead to remain part of it. And so to answer your question, what I ask of you is quite simple: for you to remain true to yourself, madam, valiant and steadfast."

"That's it?"

"That's it. Please keep the book. On the inside of the back cover you will find that there is a telephone number. That number will be answered at any time, day or night. Should you ever be in trouble, call that number."

"Is it your number?"

"No, it is the number to an organization that I have established, an organization that will outlive me."

"And what does this organization do?"

"It evaluates the situation at hand, and then in order to resolve the problem will provide an appropriate mix of Warren Zevon's three fundamental elements."

"Warren Zevon's three fundamental elements?"

"Lawyers, guns and money."

Andromeda smiles, recalling the song.

"You are destined to do battle," Slade continues, "think of it as the cavalry."

Andromeda opens the book's back cover. There is a telephone number under the dustcover flap, the numbers shaky and uncertain, and she guesses that Slade must have written them himself. She looks back up at the source of this strange offer.

"Thank you."

"Very likely you will never need it, but it's there if you do." He waves with the back of his hand in a dismissive gesture. "Now go forth, Andromeda Chamberlain. Go forth and write!"

XLII

ANDROMEDA LEANS ON the rail and lifts her sunglasses. She gazes out over the sweep of the Côte d'Azur and the Alpes Maritimes beyond, still snow-capped despite the season. She is the first one up this morning and has the deck to herself.

It is a year since *The Tragical History of Doctor Faustus* won the Palme d'Or at Cannes. Now, Gidding is trying to repeat with *Andromeda Graphika*. Other directors have won the award twice, but none has ever done it two years in succession. According to yesterday's edition of *Nice-Matin*, Ladbrokes of London is making him a five-to-two favorite, despite the fact that neither the bookmaker nor anyone else besides Gidding has ever seen the film.

All that will change with the premiere tonight.

Gidding's reluctance to reveal any detail has only excited interest in the movie. He admitted early on that it was made entirely without the main character being aware of the filming—a technique that has since been dubbed *contre méthode*, the annihilation of histrionic technique. The press has made much of him having discovered another new actress, just as he did with Soline Djahidra, despite the fact that someone who is not acting cannot by definition be an actress. Andromeda has politely declined all interview requests, and the one press release—part of the package the movie's publicity people issued at the beginning of Cannes—made clear that *Andromeda Graphika* was her first and last movie, and that she had no further comment to make, now or in the future.

Technically, the press release is a lie. In fulfillment of her impromptu auto rental agreement Andromeda has also appeared in *Aquamarine Dream*, an adult film shot last spring on the island of St. Barts. In it she is seen wandering through a villa's jasmine- and bougainvillea-shrouded garden wearing mirrored sunglasses, a platinum blond wig, shoes whose high heels had kept sinking into the lawn, and a body-hugging mesh sheath the late afternoon sun had little difficulty in penetrating. She comes to the pool. She peels off the sheath, allowing it to fall to her ankles, and then steps out to apply body oil. She never enters the pool, instead wandering around it, still in high heels. The scene ends with her by the edge of the terrace overlooking the sea far below. The camera slowly pans up her body, her normally pale skin cast by the combination of honeyed oil and slanting sunlight into a vibrant glow, almost metallic. The camera comes to a halt on her face, smooth copper with the scar invisible under makeup. The sun is reflected in her sunglasses, a pulsating orb about to fall into the sea. As photography it was first-rate—the ending shot would have been suitable for a spread in Vogue—but as pornography Andromeda thinks that it is probably the most boring seven minutes and twenty-six seconds in history.

Andromeda unexpectedly found that she enjoyed making it, and decides that she must have an exhibitionistic streak. She names her new alter ego Rose de Seitas, the credit she appeared under in the movie.

The legitimate press have given up on Gidding but the paparazzi never let go, and so he chartered the two-hundred-foot motor yacht *Merak* rather than have his party run the phalanx of photographers haunting the hotels along la Croisette. They change anchorage each evening, making it harder for the press to catch up, although one enterprising paparazzo had hired a helicopter and buzzed the yacht until the captain contacted the authorities and had him ordered to lay off.

Gidding has not yet appeared on board; he has remained ashore to see to the preparations for tonight's premiere. He has not spoken to nor communicated in any other way with Andromeda since Rothermore—all the film-related work and even the invitation to join the rest of the cast on the yacht came through the publicity firm handling the film's promotion. A single exception had occurred a month after Andromeda's return to New York, when an anonymous parcel wrapped in brown paper had arrived through the mail. Inside was the blue-bound volume of Ezra Pound. There was no accompanying note, but at page twenty-six she found a silver bookmark. On it were engraved the words *To Andromeda, without tragedy.*

ANDROMEDA HEARS footsteps on the deck behind her.

"Great body," Cherry declares by way of greeting.

Andromeda laughs; he says the same thing every morning. She has to admit that he is in a position to judge, as she is wearing nothing but sunglasses and the bikini bottoms she put on for her morning swim.

On the first day onboard she, Margot, and Clare had been sunning by the pool, all three prone with their backstraps undone, and in Andromeda's case sleeping off the effects of the red-eye from JFK. Margot had stood to get some water without securing her top and the men, who had been in discussion around a table further along the deck, had broken into spontaneous applause. This woke up Andromeda in time to witness Clare flip onto her back and make a show of covering herself in suntan oil, again to appreciative comments from the men. Andromeda had realized that to do nothing now would be to let the team down, and so she sat up and strapped on her high-heeled sandals, made a leggy circumnavigation of the pool as she had in *Aquamarine Dream*, then took them off again before diving in.

Ever since, by unspoken agreement, the three girls sunbathed topless—their way of celebrating this time, Andromeda supposes, but a spell that would have been broken were it to be articulated.

Cherry saunters over to the long table where among the fruits and juices and pastries laid out for breakfast there is a cocktail glass and an insulated flask—the staff have learned by now that Cherry prefers to take his morning fruit in the form of a Daiquiri. He pours the drink, adds a little umbrella that the cheeky stewardess left for him, and joins Andromeda by the stern rail.

"So today's the big day," he says.

"You'll look good in a tux."

"I just hope I didn't overshadow you too much in our scene."

"My guess is that I'll be practically invisible."

"Olivier and Leigh." He raises his glass in salute and takes a long drink. "Say, I heard a funny story last night, after you'd gone to bed."

"What was that?"

"Apparently Gidding offered to destroy the whole thing if you wanted him to. At first you told him to go ahead, and by the time you changed your mind he'd smashed a twenty-five-thousand-dollar server to smithereens."

"We women can be so whimsical, can't we?"

"What made you relent?"

"The library at Alexandria."

"What?"

"An ancient library that was destroyed by their version of the jihadists, or whoever the freaks of the day were. It's hard to create—creation requires time and thought and effort—but it's easy to destroy—destruction requires nothing but stupidity. I didn't want to be a destroyer."

Cherry looks at her for a long time in silence, and for once she has the sense that it is something other than her physique he is evaluating.

"Well, I'm glad you changed your mind," he says, turning back out to sea. "I'd hate to think of a posterity deprived of my scene."

Andromeda laughs. She is dry enough to dress now. Cherry watches her walk to where she left her bag and put on a shirt for breakfast.

"Let me know if you change your mind about the Pantera," he says.

The others gradually come on deck. Firstly Margot, always one of the earlier risers, sun-drenched and gauzy with light. She starts the day by checking the Far-Eastern markets, apologizing that her job is not one that can be turned off.

Jason Phillips arrives next, a man Andromeda still thinks of as Trilby Top, an accomplished actor from New York who they had been concerned Andromeda might recognize from his many theater roles in that city, including a much-lauded Othello at Shakespeare in the Park. Jean-Benoit Lasance is next, who turns out to be not a thief but a French actor with a non-metallic nose, then Ernesto Rovera, *Il Dottore della Peste* in Venice, someone she has finally managed to convince no longer needs to apologize.

Last is Clare, coming lazy-eyed and long-legged onto the deck half an hour after the others, apparently exhausted despite having just risen, completely naked and equally uncaring.

"Sunglasses," she says, to no one in particular. The young crewman who has stood transfixed since her arrival immediately takes off his own and offers them to her. When she makes no move to accept them it becomes apparent that her eyes are shut. The crewman hesitatingly presses the sunglasses into her hand. She fumbles them on like a blind woman and mutters, "Coffee." The crewman quickly fetches her a cup. She accepts it with a smile and says, "Sweet boy," before retiring to a chaise at the stern to complete her return to full consciousness. An all-around bravura entrance, Andromeda thinks, something that crewman will relate with fond remembrance for years to come. Of the three women on board, she decides that it is Clare who is the real actress.

The captain comes down from the bridge.

"Good morning, everybody. I hope that you all slept well." He turns to Cherry, who has been acting as Gidding's unofficial deputy in their host's absence, but continues in a voice loud enough to be heard by the entire deck. "We've just received a message from the Carlton. Mr. Gidding will be checking out at fifteen hundred and joining us then. My intention is to sail in close by the harbor so that the boat picking him up won't have far to transit. During that time we'll be clearly visible from the shore." He glances in Clare's direction to make sure that she is listening. "Fifteen hundred is three P.M."

Clare does not turn but raises a lazy hand in acknowledgment.

Cherry asks the captain about the plans for the evening.

"The premiere is scheduled for six o'clock. We'll cruise offshore until five, then come back in close and land everybody via the launch. There will be limousines waiting, plus a police escort. Meanwhile, we'll make our anchorage. I understand there is a cocktail reception following the movie, and when that's over you'll be picked up and brought back on board. Dinner will be served on deck, and there'll be fireworks over the harbor."

ANDROMEDA IS IN HER CABIN that afternoon when at three o'clock she feels the changing throb of the *Merak*'s engines as they briefly go astern, taking off way so that the boat ferrying Gidding from shore can safely come alongside. She hears the rattle of the ladder being recovered, followed by distant voices, male: the captain and Gidding conferring, but the intervening bulkheads make the conversation impossible to decipher. Then she hears Cherry joining in, followed by Margot and Clare, the conversation brighter now and punctuated by laughter. Andromeda ignores it, and continues laying out her clothes for the evening.

AT FIVE O'CLOCK there is a knock at her door. Andromeda answers. It is a steward.

"Good evening, ma'am. The captain is requesting everyone on deck in five minutes to go ashore. Will that be convenient?"

"Yes, I'll be there."

Andromeda closes the door. She has been ready for some time and has spent the last quarter-hour standing in the middle of the cabin, unwilling to sit for fear of crushing her evening gown. Periodic excursions to the mirror have revealed nothing going out of place in the interim. She makes one last check, sighs in resignation, and leaves the cabin.

GIDDING HAS CHANGED in the year since she last saw him. Not exactly aged—physically he looks the same—but he seems less intense, and perhaps a little wiser. Or maybe it is simply an inner confidence, she thinks: the demeanor of a filmmaker who, having already won a Palme d'Or, has nothing further to prove. He stares smilingly at her but without saying anything, and Andromeda realizes that he must still feel bound by her last words to him.

"You may speak to me," she says. "I wouldn't have come otherwise."

"I find now that I'm at a loss for words."

"I'm sure you'll think of something."

"I enjoyed the article. You write well. Sparingly."

"In a sense I'm still writing it. It is to become a book."

"Can I film it?"

"You already did."

"How does it end?"

"I haven't got to that part yet."

"Perhaps you'll end it here," he says.

"On the deck of the *Merak*?"

"Not so tragic."

"But hardly an ever after."

"There are no ever afters. Just an endless ongoing flux."

"You've given it some thought then?"

"I've thought of nothing else for the last year."

Andromeda realizes that they are now alone; the others have retreated to the far end of the deck, politely out of earshot. Her cheeks redden, but Gidding does not seem to care. She looks back at him.

"Shouldn't it end after they announce the winner, with you triumphant on stage, holding the Palme d'Or aloft in victory?"

"No, that would be a mistake."

"How so?"

"That's no ending. It would just be an incident along the way, like a rock in a river. The rock doesn't matter. It's the river that counts, and it flows endlessly forward, on and ever onward, indifferent as to what's carried along with it, or what gets left behind."

"But that means I can never finish the book."

"True."

"Then what shall I do?"

Gidding is about to reply but the captain, who after shepherding the rest of the party down into the launch has been standing anxiously at the rail and frequently checking his watch, now approaches.

"I'm sorry to interrupt, sir, but if we're to get you there on time we really must go ashore now."

"Yes, of course." The captain retreats to the ladder. Gidding turns and offers his arm to Andromeda. "It's traditional at these things for the leading lady to accompany the director."

"I hope that later you'll remember to tell me what it was you were about to say."

Andromeda takes his arm and they—

Typographical Note

The fleuron used for section demarcation throughout (& for convenience shown again here, enlarged) is taken from the final page of The History of the Damnable Life and Deserved Death of Doctor John Faustus, *a 1592 English translation of the German* Historia von D. Johann Faustus, *a collection of Faustian tales often referred to as the* Faustbuch, *and so the translation is usually called the* English Faustbook. *It is believed to have served as a source for Marlowe's famous play.*

The English Faustbook *was printed by Thomas Orwin 'to be solde by Edward White, dwelling at the little North door of Paules, at the figne of the Gun.'*

More famous than Orwin is his wife. Thomas was the third and last of Joan Orwin's husbands, all three of whom were printers. This is not the strange coincidence that it appears: printing rights—to both equipment and texts—were then controlled by the Stationers' Company, and if the widow of a printer married outside of it she forfeited these rights. After Thomas's death in 1593, the thrice-widowed Joan continued to operate the company herself until her son took it over in 1597, printing 67 or 68 titles under her own name.